MY PORTION FOREVER

Karen Roth

For Evelyn, my mother

With grateful acknowledgement to

The Christian Writers Group of Greater San Antonio

and the

William K. Jensen Literary Agency

Chapter One

Cedar Rapids
April 15, 1938

Sana Toledo hurried down the steep wooden stairs to the grocery store below. Just before she stepped out of the shadow of the stairway into the dim yellow light, she paused to button the cuffs of her blouse and smooth stray tendrils of dark hair back from her forehead. It was six o'clock in the morning, and she was late. She tucked one last curl into her thick French braid, smoothed down her straight gray skirt, and walked into the little store with its morning smells of rich coffee, dill pickles and fresh bread.

"Good morning, *Sitto*," she said to her aunt, who sat behind the counter with a cigar box full of coins. Mary Tabcharani wore an old dress and a frown when she was at work. Sana respectfully called her by the traditional Lebanese title for a grandmother, instead of the casual *Aunt Mary* that other sixteen-year-old American girls would say.

Her aunt didn't look up. "Put on your headscarf before you set out the bread."

Sana pulled her white-and-blue embroidered scarf from its hook and touched the crucifix on the wall before she began her morning chores. Her family was Christian by faith and Arabic by culture, but her aunt and uncle had worked out their own set of traditions after moving to America. Touching the crucifix first thing in the morning was one of them. Making Sana modestly cover her hair when she worked in the store was another. Elderly Mary did not need to wear a scarf herself anymore, because she was past the age of attracting men, but Sana, with her dark-lashed eyes and finely featured face, was another matter.

Sana tied the scarf over her hair and began arranging bread and pastries on the battered table that stood in the middle of the store. Workmen on their way to the factories stopped in for Lebanese fiftayah rolls stuffed with cheese and flavored with cumin and coriander, or for buttery fruit-filled Czech kolaches. The men who walked through the dark morning streets with lunch pails in hand might come from different nations, but they were all hungry in the morning.

"You're late," Abraham Tabcharani said from his place at the front door.

She flicked a glance at her gray-haired uncle. He stood with a cigarette in one hand and a cup of black coffee in the other, ready to greet the customers who could pay and drive away those who could not. Pinch-faced women and children slipped through the stores during the day, searching for something to eat, and it was easier for Abraham to run them off at the door than to let them in and listen to them plead for food. Mary threw out some scraps when they closed at night, and that was all a store owner could do for the poor and stay in business.

"You stayed up too late," he said. "Look what happens."

"Sorry, Uncle." Saying anything else now would cause trouble, but she added, "I'm getting the highest marks in algebra."

He frowned. "Only for your dead father's sake do I tolerate a girl your age still going to school," he began, and continued in a lecture Sana knew by heart. "Only because you are ruined and no one will marry you, and because of my respect for my beloved brother's wish for you to be educated, God keep his soul, do I allow you to run around town like..."

Mary rolled her eyes. "Shut up, Abe. She's almost done anyway. And you"—she glared at Sana—"be quiet. If you're so smart then use the sense God gave you. If you ever, God willing, get married, your husband's going to get tired of you talking like that."

Sana hid a grin, but the flicker of fun slipped away as she floured her hands and rolled out more dough. She would graduate from high school in five weeks, and then she would work in the store all day, every day, for the rest of her life, unless she could find a husband, which was not likely because the entire Lebanese community knew that she was ruined.

Footsteps thumped up the wooden stairs in front and the first customers of the morning pushed through the screen door. Men in stained shirts and trousers greeted Abraham and moved on to the bread table. Sana retreated to the back of the room and stayed busy washing potatoes until her aunt called her over to wrap up half a dozen kolaches.

"Good morning, beautiful." The big yellow-haired factory worker looked her up and down with his frank blue eyes. "Speak English yet?"

Sana glanced at Abraham. Her uncle could speak in a tone exactly calculated to discourage a customer but not insult him to the point where he wouldn't return to the store.

"My niece," he said in that tone now, and then flourished his cigarette to end the conversation. Since the customer was not Lebanese and would not be interested in marrying her, there was no point in saying any more. The man took the hint and left.

"You should marry off that girl," another customer said to her uncle, in Arabic. Her uncle did not know how well Sana spoke that language, and she had gained many precious bits of information by pretending not to understand certain comments. "She's trouble. Every man who looks at her has one thing on his mind." He used a word that made Sana flinch and turn her face away.

"No," Abraham replied. "We will keep her here. After my brother died she was sent to live with those godless cousins of mine, and they forced her, even though she was a child. Now she's ruined. No decent man would take her as a wife. Not the Lebanese, not the Czechs. She can stay here and work for us in the store, since we have no children of our own."

"Abraham, old friend." The man was gray-haired like her

7

uncle, a regular visitor to the store. "That's no good for a young woman, not to be married. She's tall and skinny but there's still men that would take her. Old men aren't so choosy."

Sana flinched again and glanced at the brass clock on the counter beside Mary's cigar box. There was still another hour until she could leave for school. *Oh God above, why do You keep me alive? For more of this torture? Oh, just let me die today.*

When the clock finally reached seven-thirty Sana hung up her headscarf and left for school. In spite of her prayer to die, nothing happened, so she went to class as usual. The girls at school ignored her because she was a dark-haired foreign girl who knew about men, and the boys sometimes harassed her, trailing her in the hallway or pressing up against her in a crowd, for exactly the same reason. Sana kept a haughty look about herself to distance them all.

Ahead of her, two pony-tailed girls sang a song from the radio and danced a few steps down the hall. Tall boys grinned and called out compliments. Sana stole glances at the young men who would marry soon and the girls who could talk to them so freely. They all sounded happy, as if they had just eaten breakfast at a kitchen table with their parents.

If her parents were alive, she would still be living in a pink stucco house in Constantine with a cook, a gardener, and three maids. She would be attending convent school during the day and playing piano or reading at night in the plush red-and-gold front parlor. She would still be looking forward to a comfortable life with a wealthy husband.

On one evening when she was twelve, the after-dinner talk had turned to her future, and her mother had promised to find her a husband.

"Don't worry, *cherie.* I'll find you a wonderful man," her mother had said. "I'll find a man who's educated and can afford a good home. I don't want to spend the holidays with a son-in-law who's an idiot and a cheapskate."

"That's right," her father had said. "I'll inspect all the applicants before you even see them. I'll make sure they have all their teeth and lots of money in the bank. That's all women care about, right?"

"Daddy!" Sana had protested. "I want a handsome husband who drives a car like you do." They all laughed, and she had gone to bed that night dreaming of what her life would be like as a woman in her own house with her own life. But the next day while she was at school her parents took a drive in the high mountain passes, collided into a truck, and did not come back alive.

Now, four years later, her last days of freedom were flying past. Even the push through crowded school halls seemed like heaven compared to the life back at the store. Sana lingered after her last class, doing chores for her teacher and putting off the dreaded moment when she would have to return home. She sorted homework papers and sharpened pencils while afternoon sunlight poured through the classroom's open windows and glowed on the polished wood desks.

"You can clean the blackboard now. Are you going to water my plants today?" Zula Hruska, the senior math teacher and Sana's favorite person in the world, looked up from a stack of homework and smiled at her. "Here's your test back."

Sana walked over and picked up a paper. A large red A crowned the page.

Mrs. Hruska frowned. "Now what's the matter? A pretty girl with all your life in front of you, and you haven't smiled once today. Did you fill out those citizenship papers like I told you to?"

Sana dropped her gaze.

"Don't sulk at me," the teacher said. "Come over here and tell me what's wrong."

Sana dropped into a chair next to her, still holding the rag she used to clean the board. "I can't fill them out yet. I've only been here four years and I have to be here for five."

"Oh. Well, time will take care of that, right? So that's not really a problem. What else is wrong?"

Sana felt tears brimming up. "Oh... I hate to bother you, Mrs.

Hruska." She folded and refolded the rag she was holding into a tiny square.

"Just tell me, honey," her teacher said.

"Oh... I'm... sad that school's going to be over," Sana said, and the tears spilled over. She wiped her eyes and swallowed. "I'll miss you so much."

Mrs. Hruska reached out to put an arm around her. The friendly touch brought a rush of tears and Sana put her head down on the older woman's shoulder and sobbed. Her teacher knew the story about her parents and let her cry for a while before patting her back and offering a hankie.

"All right. Here, let's see about all this. You can come and visit me any time you want after school is over. Now, what's the matter with you? Are you just down in the dumps today, or is something wrong?"

"I won't be able to go anywhere anymore," Sana choked out. "My uncle will make me stay at the store all the time. And no one will marry me, so I'm going to be there *forever*." The thought of dusting cans and sweeping the floor every day for the rest of her life made her bury her face in the handkerchief. "I miss my mother," she whispered when she could speak again. "I miss my mother so much."

Zula Hruska was wiping at her own eyes now. "I'm so sorry, dear. I'm so sorry about your parents. But why on earth do you think that nobody will marry you? You're a bright attractive girl. The boys must be nuts about you."

Sana shook her head and started crying again. This woman must be the last person on earth who didn't know about her. "My uncles... when I lived in their house in Constantine... they..." she choked out. She could not bring herself to say the actual words. "That's why my aunts over there sent me away." She gazed at the floor, hoping she wouldn't have to say any more to make her teacher understand. "And my uncle tells everybody."

"Ohhh. Oh. I see." Mrs. Hruska's arm tightened around Sana's shoulders. "Hmm."

"Besides, my nose is too long. I'm too tall. I just want to die."

"No you don't. You're smart. If you don't get married right now then you ought to do something for a while until you meet the right man."

Sana shook her head but her teacher went on. "Don't think this hasn't happened before. Someday someone's going to fall in love with you. Until then you ought to do something. You could be a teacher or a nurse. Make a little money of your own. Why, when Marie Curie was your age..." Mrs. Hruska launched into a story about how the famous scientist had moved away from her home town, attended a university, met the love of her life, and went on to discover radium and develop the world's first X-ray machine.

Sana dried her tears as she listened and decided that she had said too much about her past.

"That's fine about Marie Curie, Mrs. Hruska, but my aunt and uncle would never let me." She made a little movement, asking to be released. Her teacher studied her face, then let her go.

"Well, I just want you to think about it," she said. "You never know these days where life will take you."

"Thank you very much for trying to help me," Sana said. "You are so kind to me, ma'am."

"You darling thing." Mrs. Hruska gave her one more hug. "You have such a sweet little foreign accent. I should think that every boy who meets you just falls right in love. Don't worry, honey. Just give it time and it'll all work out."

"Maybe, ma'am." Sana forced a smile. "Thank you again."

After cleaning the blackboard she left to walk home, and she could not stay gloomy as she walked in the bright spring afternoon light. New-leafed trees and tender flowers were opening in the warmth, and a woman tending rose bushes in her front yard smiled at Sana as she passed. Violets had come and gone already, but irises and wild roses were blooming, and as she crossed a street she caught sight of a brilliant purple lilac tree in full flower down an alley. She impulsively turned toward it, picking her way across the rutted mud to breathe the sweet scent.

She was almost to the tree when footsteps sounded behind

her. A hand gripped her shoulder. "Whatcha doing here?"

The tone made her skin crawl even before she turned and saw three boys standing between her and the street.

"Don't touch me," she snapped, shrugging off the hand. Her voice cracked and the nearest boy caught her arm, pulling her back. She recognized him from school. He wore a ragged cap, an uneven fuzz of reddish beard, and a grin.

They won't do anything. They're just picking on me. They're trying to scare me. Her heart pounded as she jerked away again. The other boys came closer, grinning.

"I said get away from me," she said in her haughtiest voice. The grins got bigger. She was stiff with fear. If people saw her in a back alley with a group of boys, that would be bad enough, but if the boys started touching her...

"Looking for someone?" The first boy grabbed both her arms. "Come here often?" He jerked her forward, pulling her up against himself. Sana panicked when she felt his hand slip behind her waist.

"Stop it! Get away from me!" she cried out. "Let me go!" She shoved and wrestled, but he kept her pinned against him. The other boys were laughing.

Rage flamed inside her. *Not again. Not again. I will die before I suffer that again.* Sana lunged forward, biting at the leering face. Her teeth sank into the flesh of a lip and she bit down hard. She felt his hot saliva against her mouth, and then the rusty taste of blood. She clamped down harder.

People were shouting. The boy was pulling back. Sana wrenched away from him and backed off down the alley, glaring at him and wiping blood off her lips with the back of her hand.

A new person was standing there, yelling something she could not understand. Her attackers looked embarrassed. The boy with the bloody lip hung his head.

The new person switched to English. "Yeah, go tell your mommies about how you beat up a girl. Go on, you..." He switched back into the other language and yelled again, pointing toward the street. The boys fled.

Sana backed up a few more paces when he swung around toward her. She recognized him now. He was a tall Czech boy from school.

"You all right?" he asked.

Sana nodded. Now that her moment of rage was gone, she was shaking.

"Bit him, huh?"

Sana felt sick at the memory of the boy's mouth on her own. She couldn't speak.

"You okay? You know me? I'm in your math class." He walked closer to her, and Sana felt her heart thump up into her throat, but her legs were shaking and she could not move. He came close enough for her to catch a scent like grass and wind from his jacket. His eyes were blue, a bit of blond stubble showed on his cheek, and a thin white scar ran down the left side of his face from temple to jaw.

"It's okay," he said as if he was soothing a pet dog. "Which way do you go home?" He took her elbow.

Sana would have stepped away from the invading touch but her legs were still trembling and she was afraid that she might fall. She let him walk her to the end of the alley before she felt steady enough to take her arm away.

"Thank you," she said, and then, trying to pull her world back into order, offered him her hand. "I'm Sana Toledo. My uncle is Abraham Tabcharani."

He shook her hand until she withdrew it. "Joe Vesely. That's Tabcharani's Grocery?"

"Yes." Her heart was still pounding and she put her hand to her chest, trying to calm the painful thumps.

"Here." The boy took her arm again. "You're still upset."

Sana sprang away and started to weep. Her heart hammered even harder and she turned her face from him.

"Sorry," he said. "I didn't mean to scare you."

She shook her head, still weeping. "Thank you," she forced out. "I want to go home now." A sob rose in her throat but she swallowed it down and straightened up. "By myself."

"Wait," he said. "Someone should go with you."

"No," she whispered, blinking back a surge of tears that burst from a whole new place inside her aching chest. "Sorry," she added as she turned away.

Joe Vesely stared at the dark-haired girl until she turned a corner. He finally shook his head and walked the other way, down the street toward his own home, his palm still tingling from her touch. *I'm Sana Toledo.* She was so pretty. How was it that he had never really noticed her before? Dark, brilliant eyes under finely arched brows... the curve of her cheek, the heartbeat in the hollow of her throat, her skin the color of palest honey... her eyes had filled with tears and she had seemed to fold up into herself like a flower at night when he reached for her arm the second time. The girl must have been scared to death. He would have liked to walk her home and listen to her talk in that clear cool accent that sounded like rich English people talking. He would see her again tomorrow in math class, though. Maybe he would talk to her then.

He jumped the three steps up the porch, opened the front door and smelled onions frying. He saw his grandmother standing at the stove in the kitchen before his legs were trapped and he crashed to the hard wood floor. Someone climbed on his back and pinned him down.

"Ow!" Joe rolled to his feet, grabbed his attacker by the ankles, held him upside down and shook him.

"Put me down!" Stephen hollered, trying to kick free. There was not much furniture in the front room – only a threadbare couch and two rocking chairs – but the room was small and the boys managed to hit every piece as they scuffled across it. Joe dragged the smaller boy clear across the floor by his heels before giving him his wish and dropping him with a thump.

"Try that on Johnny, you brat." Joe's other cousin would be home from school soon. Stephen stuck out his tongue and went back to crouch by the door.

Joe walked into the kitchen. "*Dobrý den, Bubi.* What's to eat?"

Josefina Vesely stirred the onions in her frying pan and frowned. *"Bouktha,"* she groused at him. "You raise the dead with all your noise."

Joe grinned and leaned down to kiss his grandmother's wrinkled cheek. *"Prominte."* He looked around the kitchen for a plate of food.

"Sedět," she said. "Here." Josefina handed him a plate with a peanut-butter sandwich and leftover fried potatoes. Joe gave her another kiss before he sat down to eat. She shook her head and waved him away before turning back to the onions.

"Is Uncle John up yet?" he asked between bites.

"I'm up now." His uncle walked in and sat down, yawning. "A herd of elephants came through the house and woke me up."

"Sorry," Joe said through a mouthful of potatoes. "Tough shift last night?" He looked his uncle over. John Mark worked nights at a factory and pastored a church during the day. His uncle started to say something, yawned instead, and watched Joe wolf down food.

"You know," John Mark finally said, "we're going to eat supper in half an hour."

Joe forked up another mouthful. "And I am so happy about that Hey, listen to this." He told the story about the girl in the alley. "I would've walked her home," he finished up, "but she started crying and said no and left. How do you figure that?"

"Abe Tabcharani's girl?" John Mark asked. "Tall and skinny?"

"Yeah."

"Huh." John Mark thought for a moment. "And you ran 'em off? One against three?"

"Ah, they were just dumb kids. I yelled and they ran away." Joe pushed a last crumb of bread around on his plate. "I didn't really do anything. That girl bit the kid pretty good."

John Mark laughed, and as he did Joe noticed the little lines around his eyes and mouth, etched in shadow by the slanting afternoon sun.

"You gotta quit working so hard," Joe said. "Make the factory give you a desk job. Look at you, all worn out. You've even got gray hair now. Look. Right here." He leaned over and tousled John Mark's graying brown hair, still unruly from sleep.

His uncle kept on laughing. "I wouldn't have gray hair if you boys didn't eat me out of house and home. I gotta hang onto this job." He turned serious. "Listen. Don't tell anyone about that girl in the alley."

John Mark had his own unique reasons for saying things. "How come?" Joe asked.

"It'd be bad for her. Get her talked about."

Joe looked at his uncle for a while. "What do you know about her?"

John Mark shrugged. "Her parents died, she came over here, now she lives with a couple of people who don't like kids. The Czechs don't talk to her because she's Lebanese and for some reason the Lebanese won't have anything to do with her either." He leaned back in his chair. "What do you think happened?"

That put things in a different light. Joe stared at his uncle and thought about the girl's shy manner and elegant voice.

"'Treat the elder women as mothers, and the younger as sisters, in all purity,'" John Mark quoted. "First Timothy, five-one. That girl doesn't want people talking about her and neither do I. She's had a hard life." He looked at Joe. "Just like you."

Sana lay wide awake in bed early the next morning, thinking about the handsome boy in the alley. *Joe Vesely. I'm in your math class.* Would he speak to her again? He was so kind. And good-looking. Why had she never noticed him before? He was taller than she was. He was perfect. She snuggled deeper under her blanket and pictured him asking her to marry him.

That thought made her jump out of bed and dress with extra care. She pulled her long dark curls into a womanly twist instead of her usual schoolgirl braid and checked her face in the mirror. Her nose seemed longer than ever. She tingled with a delicious mix of fear and delight as she set out the bakery and watched the brass clock tick its way to seven-thirty.

At school she wore out her eyes watching the hallways for

him. It would be too forward of her to speak first, but she would smile when she saw him. Then he would probably speak to her. She was half afraid that she might not see him, and half afraid that she would. What if he didn't want to talk to her because she wasn't Czech? But what if he did want to talk to her? What would she say? The hours passed in exquisite agony.

She went to math class early and waited, watching the door out of the corner of her eye. He walked in and glanced at her. She managed a smile, but he did not smile back right away. He looked at her thoughtfully instead.

"Sana, please come here a minute," Mrs. Hruska called, and Sana groaned inside. Her teacher gave her a stack of homework to hand out but she kept her eyes down when she handed Joe his paper. She didn't want to look at him when everyone could see her face.

She watched him out of the corner of her eye all during class. When the bell rang he looked over at her. She managed another smile, but a group of students clustered in front of her desk just then, and he ended up leaving the room instead of talking to her. Sana trailed hopefully out the classroom door, thinking he might be waiting there, but he was already down the hall.

"Sana! I have something for you, dear. Come look at this." Sana sighed. There were only five weeks of school left. Twenty-five days of math class. And she had just wasted one of them without finding a way to talk to the man she intended to marry.

"Yes, Mrs. Hruska?"

"Look what I brought for you." The teacher handed her a piece of paper. Sana had to read it twice before she realized what it was.

"Thank you, ma'am, but I don't have any money for teachers' school. Nursing school either." She studied the information again and shook her head. "My uncle would not allow it." *And I might get married instead*, she almost said, but stopped herself. After all, nothing had happened yet.

"Well, teachers' school costs some money. But nursing school doesn't. Look, they take high school graduates, and your room and board is free because you work in the hospital while you learn. And look here. Once you graduate, you make sixteen cents an hour. See, if you can just get yourself to the school, you could do it."

Sana looked at the paper again, surprised that nurses made so much. Maybe her aunt and uncle would like the idea of her working outside the store and bringing in some money. She folded the paper and tucked it away.

"Thank you. I'll ask my aunt. Oh, Mrs. Hruska, I have a question for you. Do families come to graduation?" Sana asked her teacher first about one student's family, then another's, and finally about Joe's.

"What about Joe Vesely? Does he have a family?"

Mrs. Hruska looked at her. Sana looked down.

"Well," her teacher said, "from what I understand, something happened to his mother, so his aunt and uncle took him in. I don't know the whole story but I know the uncle. John Mark Starosta, the minister." She liked to talk and she kept going now that she had started. "I had Joe's cousin Anton in my class two years ago, a very nice boy. Went on to college. I have his little brother Johnny in my sophomore class right now." She shook her head. "I hope he comes along and makes something out of himself someday."

"Are they really brothers?" Sana asked.

Her teacher shot her another look. Sana realized what a ridiculous question she had just asked, and dropped her eyes again.

"They're cousins but they act like brothers so that's what I call them." She winked at Sana. "Joe's on the baseball team and his uncle wants him to get a scholarship so he can go to college and be an engineer. Anything else you'd like to know about him?" She laughed when Sana blushed. "I saw him watching you in class today. He had his eye on you."

Sana felt her face flush. "Really?"

"Um-hm. But don't forget what I told you about going to school." Mrs. Hruska shook her finger. "These times are bad. Getting worse every day. A girl in your situation ought to use her head and find a way to make some money. I'd like to see you have a good life, after what you've been through."

"Yes, ma'am. Thank you." A sudden lump rose in Sana's throat. "You're my favorite teacher."

"Now, don't start that or we'll both be crying." Zula Hruska shook her finger again. "Go on and think about what I said."

In the store that evening, after her uncle had locked the door and gone upstairs, Sana swept the floor and cleaned fingerprints off the glass canister jars while her aunt counted up the day's profits. Abraham and Mary maintained a look of shabbiness to seem poor and save money, but at the end of the day Mary always tucked away more coins than she had started with. Counting money put her in a good mood and she smiled at Sana.

"Did you do those return bottles, *binta*?" she asked from her spot behind the counter.

"Yes, aunt," Sana replied. Returned bottles had to be cleaned and sorted for the soft drink salesman.

"Good girl," Mary said. The soft clink of coins under her fingers filled the quiet room.

Sana took a breath. "*Sitto*?"

"Yes?" Mary looked up when Sana did not reply right away. "What?"

"*Sitto*, my teacher told me today that if I went to nursing school, I could make sixteen cents an hour after I graduated." Sana kept her eyes on the canister she was cleaning, polishing the clean glass over and over as she spoke. "She told me that it doesn't cost anything because the students work in the hospital while they learn. She said that I should think about it so I could make some money. Would you like that?"

The clinking sound stopped and Sana looked up. Mary was glaring at her. Sana looked back down.

"In the name of all that is holy!" Mary slapped the counter so hard the coins jumped. "This is what happens when girls go to school. A nurse! *A nurse!*" She stood up and came around the counter with a ferocious step. Sana moved back.

19

"It is not... not... *decent*. After all we have done for you! To think of shaming us like that! A *nurse*! Do you know what nurses do? They *touch* men's... men's..." She sputtered for a while and finally shouted, "No decent woman knows about those things. Shameless whore! Touching all kinds of... filthy things! Who would come to the store, if we had a nurse here?" She was six inches away from Sana's face now. "Abraham will not have such a thing happen and neither will I! You will ruin us!"

Sana took a deep breath and mastered her voice. "Sorry, *Sitto*. Please don't worry. I'm sorry. I thought I should tell you. I promise I won't talk about it anymore."

Mary muttered something in Arabic and turned back to her money. Sana picked up her rag and polished the same clean jar again, feeling cold shock grow into a great empty numbness that spread clear through her soul. *I won't get out. I'll never get out. I'm going to be here for the rest of my life.*

"Never speak of it again," Mary said. "It would break your uncle's heart. After all he's done for you."

Sana did not look up, but she cleared her throat and said, "Yes, *Sitto*." She moved on to the next jar.

"Go to church tomorrow morning before school and pray for God to keep you from such sinful thoughts."

Sana kept her eyes on the jar. "Yes, *Sitto*," she said again.

She walked to the old stone church before school the next day. The cool air inside smelled of incense and candle wax, and Sana pulled her scarf over her head as she slipped into a pew on the women's side, kneeling and crossing herself. Other people knelt or sat around her, waiting for the service to begin. Dust motes danced in the shafts of light pouring through the narrow stained-glass windows. Sana bowed her head and folded her hands.

What's going to happen to me? The chants of prayer began, but her thoughts drifted to Joe Vesely. He would never marry someone like her. Aside from being ruined, he and she were too different. His family wouldn't want her, and hers wouldn't want him. But he was the only boy she liked. If she couldn't get married to someone, then what? Work in the store for the rest of her life?

Go to nursing school?

Dear God, if you will make Joe Vesely fall in love with me, I will... go to church every day. That was a little strong. *I will go to church three times a week.*

What if nothing happened? Sana had smuggled a secret treasure out of Constantine — a few pieces of her mother's gold jewelry and ten gold coins that her father had given her for her birthday, all sewn into a thick wool chemise that she had worn every day under her clothes while traveling. No one knew she had it. But if she just ran away and used the money to live on, then she would use it up and there would be no way to replace it. She would be out on the streets begging for food.

I'm too tall. I'm ruined. I'm so lonely. I wish my mother was here. She put her forehead down on her folded hands and closed her eyes. *I just want to die.*

But she cheered up later that day when Joe walked in to math class and said hello just as if they were old friends. When class finished the teacher was busy at her desk and did not ask Sana to stay.

Joe stood just outside the door, fiddling with his books, looking even taller and more handsome than he had before. Sana stopped to greet him but couldn't think of what to say. *I love you.*

"Hi," Joe said, and cleared his throat. "Everything okay?"

Sana nodded. "Yes, thank you," she said, and immediately wished she hadn't. It sounded like she was talking about the scene in the alley. But wasn't that what he meant? She hastily opened her mouth again. He started to speak at the same time.

"Oh, excuse me," she stammered, and "What?" he asked, then grinned and said, "Ladies first."

She cast about for something to say. "I saw you got an A," she finally got out. "On your test." Standing so close to him, she looked at his eyes and then, suddenly shy, looked at his forearms instead. They were muscled and tanned, with a sheen of golden hair. "Do you like algebra?" *Stupid, stupid, stupid.*

"Better than English. Hey, I was thinking about coming over

21

to your uncle's store sometime." He looked at her and glanced away.

Not the store! "That would be nice."

"Joe." A blonde girl in a pretty blue dress walked up to them. "You coming over tonight? Oh, hello," she said to Sana. Her lips shone with a hint of lipstick and the dress made her eyes look very blue. Sana looked at Joe.

"Ah, this is Rose Prazsky," he said. "Rose, this is Sana Toledo."

"Hi," Rose said.

"It's very nice to meet you," Sana automatically replied, her heart sinking.

The blonde girl turned back to Joe. "Dad said for you to come over after supper for cards and don't be late." She put a hand on her hip and tilted her chin. "Like you were last time."

"Ah, tell him I'll be right over." Joe looked back and forth between them.

Sana drew in her breath. She could not compete with this. "I hope you have a good evening," she said to Joe, and looked at Rose. "Very nice to meet you," she said again, and immediately felt like an idiot for repeating herself. She smiled with all the self-control she had learned from four years of life with Abraham and Mary. "Excuse me." She turned around and walked back into the classroom.

For once, her teacher didn't want to talk. Sana sorted papers and cleaned chalk dust from desks and counters, hardly aware of what her hands were doing.

How long had they known each other? *Dad said for you to come over.* How could she have been so foolish, to think that he didn't have a girl already? *Don't be late like you were last time.* They must be practically engaged, for her to be so familiar with him. And she was Czech.

He said he was going to come over to the store. He must want to see me. She took heart at the thought. *What if he comes to visit and brings her with him?* Her little flicker of hope faded away.

As she walked down the hall a flash of color caught her eye. A new poster hung alongside the usual recruiting announcements. Instead of men in uniforms, it featured an angelic young woman in a white uniform, gazing bravely out at the world.

"Enter a proud profession! Join the Army Nurse Corps at your local Army Recruitment Center TODAY!"

Sana stared at the confident nurse, remembering Mary's words. *Do you know what nurses do? No decent woman knows about those things.*

There was no man, no family, in that picture. Only the nurse. *Whatever she does I could do. Sick people wouldn't care if I'm tall. Besides, I'm already ruined.*

Spring days glided by. Sana caught Joe looking at her once in a while, and if he said hello she spoke politely back. He walked to school in the mornings with a younger boy, probably his cousin. Some days he walked home with Rose. Other days he practiced with the baseball team after school, and she lingered to furtively watch him field balls and run around bases.

One night she asked her uncle if he would like to go to a high school ball game, but Abraham gave her a hard look and said "No" so sharply that she did not ask her second question, which was whether she and her aunt could go with him.

The next morning Abraham steered one of his friends outside the store. They stood there for a long time on the little cracked sidewalk, smoking and talking in Arabic, and Sana thought nothing of it until she saw them both take a long look inside, right at her. She ducked behind a rack of canned goods and edged up to the side of the screen door where she could hear them but not be seen.

"Wait until her schooling is over," her uncle was saying. "I'll tell her then."

"She can still work for you," the other man said. "I will allow that. Until, God willing, there are children."

Shocked, Sana glanced at her aunt. Mary was making change at the counter. Sana leaned forward until she could peer around the door and see the man who was talking. His back was turned to her, but she could see his hair. It was gray.

She moved away from the door and back to the bread table, angling around it to see the man's face. Her eyes widened. He looked as old as her uncle. He looked in at her again and she glanced away, but not before she had seen his eyes. There was a look in them that she had learned to avoid, when she was twelve years old.

She glanced at the clock. Ten more minutes before she could leave for school. The men were tossing their cigarettes into the street and turning to come inside. Sana quickly stepped over to her aunt.

"*Sitto*, I have to go upstairs before I leave today," she whispered. "It's, ah, you know, that time." Her voice trembled. Mary nodded and Sana stamped noisily up the stairs, then stole quietly back down them and escaped through the back door to school.

Joe stayed late at school on the last day before graduation. High school had turned out to be more fun than he thought it would, and he hung around in the hallway a little longer than he usually did. Students milled around, yelling louder than usual, because tomorrow they would leave for the last time and never come back.

"Ves!" A herd of senior boys thundered past and a hand smacked him on the back. "Coming over tonight?"

"Yeah," Joe yelled back. "See ya." The herd lumbered on down the hallway.

Sana Toledo walked past, holding a stack of books with one hand and tucking stray curls behind her ear with the other. She wore a plain white blouse and a slim gray skirt, and she still looked classier than any other girl. Maybe it was the way she walked, or the way she did her hair. Joe took a few long strides forward and caught up with her. If he didn't speak to her today he might not get ever another chance.

He stole a sideways look. Her eyes were down and her head was tipped a little toward her shoulder as she worked the strand of hair back into place. She hadn't even noticed him yet. Even though her expression was composed he could see her sadness, partly because of a certain tragic set to her lips and partly because of a feeling that he knew from his own lonely years. John Mark's words came back to him. *She's pretty but the Czechs don't talk to her because she's Lebanese and for some reason the Lebanese won't have anything to do with her either. She's had a hard life. Just like you.*

"Hey," he said, and touched her arm. She jumped like a spooked cat and almost lost the books. He grinned at her and she grinned back. Two dimples played in her cheeks and he was so close to her that he could see the long dark tangle of her eyelashes and the soft smooth hairs along the inside corners of her brows. His stomach flipped, then melted.

"Tomorrow's the last day, huh?"

"Yes," she said, and smiled again. The world around him vanished except for her dimples.

You're so pretty, he almost said. "I'm gonna miss high school. Some parts, anyway."

She nodded. "Me too," she said. "I love school."

I knew she'd say that, Joe thought. *She's just like me.* "So, ah, what are you going to do now?" he asked.

"Oh... work at the store," she said. The tragic look was back on her face and the dimples were gone.

Her family's kind of different. Maybe I shouldn't have said that. Joe hesitated. "I'm going to look for work but I might go to college instead. I got a baseball scholarship and my uncle says I shouldn't waste it. There's no jobs now anyway."

She was looking at him intently now. Joe's hopes rose. "So I'll probably go to college next fall. But I'll come home on weekends. Uh..." She stopped walking and looked straight at him. Her lips were smooth and full, rose-colored and beautifully shaped. *Can I see you this summer?* The words stopped in his throat before he could say them.

She said, "My father went to college. In London. Your family must be very proud of you," and the clear cool sound of her voice with its lilting accent went right through him and made his backbone tingle. He took a breath and pushed on.

25

"London. Wow." She looked happier now, not so sad anymore. Maybe all she needed was someone to talk to her.

"So, you'll be working at the store this summer?" he asked. "I might come by. You know, say hello." Fascinated, he watched her eyelashes flicker down, then up, before she replied.

"That would be very nice. Please do," she said, as if she were inviting him to dinner. *Everything she says sounds so special when she says it.* Her dimples played again. *I must be grinning like an idiot, for her to smile at me like that.*

"You're there, ah, all the time?" *That was dumb.*

"All my life." She made a sudden sound of distress and drew her brows together. The tragic look was back. "My uncle..." she began. Her voice trailed off.

"Oh, my family is coming to graduation tomorrow," Joe said. "Maybe you could, ah, meet them. I could, you know, introduce you. Is your family coming?"

She was looking away now. "Perhaps." She looked back at him, which made his insides melt again, and gave him her hand, a gesture that might seem strange from any other girl but seemed perfectly natural coming from her. "Please do come by and say hello. I look forward to it." Joe ended up shaking her hand, and then she turned and walked away. He stared after her, watching her go. *She's so beautiful when she walks away like that.*

He watched her until she turned the corner. Someone jumped out at him from a side hallway and shoved him hard against the wall. "I saw you talking to that skinny foreign girl," Johnny said, and shoved him again. "How come you're hanging around *her*? I'm telling Rose."

Joe shrugged. "Tell her." He grabbed Johnny's cap off his head and smacked him with it, to get even for the shove. "Maybe she'll start running around after you instead."

"I don't get why Rose likes you anyway," Johnny said. "Especially now you've got this funny-looking other girl."

Joe smacked him with the cap again. Johnny grabbed it back. "You going straight home?"

"I guess."

"Mrs. Prazsky baked today," Johnny said. Rose's mother's kolaches were high on their list of favorite things. "Rose told me to tell you to come over." He pursed up his lips and made kissing noises. "She wants to marry you."

Joe snorted. "You think I'm going to live with Karel?" Rose's father was famous for his size and strength when he was sober, and for his thunderous temper when he was not. "You take her."

They headed out the doors toward the Prazskys' house, but as he walked Joe glanced down the streets, looking for a dark-haired girl.

The next day Sana woke before sunrise and lay staring up at the eaves of her tiny room. It was only a kind of attic space, not a real bedroom, but her aunt had whitewashed the rough plank walls and found a little bed that would fit. She had given Sana a goose down quilt, warm enough to keep her cozy even in the winter, when snow blew in through the slits of the roof's eaves and frosted the top of the fabric. When the nights turned hot during the summer, she slept on top of the quilt to stay cool. Now the morning air was only a little chilly, fresh with the smell of spring.

School is over. Everything will change after today. The morning light changed from gray to gold and the day began rushing forward. *Dear God, what am I going to do?* What if it was the will of God to marry that old man? *Please, please, please, don't make me do that. I want to marry Joe Vesely, and if you just help me this one time, I swear I'll never ask you for anything else ever again for the rest of my life.*

She waited in bed a long time, hoping for a miracle. But nothing happened, so she dressed and went downstairs as usual.

Mary smiled when she walked into the store. "We have a guest for dinner. Fix *tabouleh* and *hummus* when you get home and make sure the kitchen's clean. I'll cook the *kibbee* and the *roz* myself."

Panic surged in Sana's heart. "But *Sitto*, tonight is graduation," she said cautiously.

27

Her aunt shook her head. "School is over now. You are a woman and you should act like one." She smiled at Sana again. "You've had a hard life. Time to settle down in your own home."

"Yes, niece," her uncle said from his place by the door. "No more of this running around town after today."

Sana kept her head down as she worked. Bakery, tobacco tins, new spring onions, round white eggs in wooden holders... the room seemed to tilt and her own hands looked strange to her, as if she were touching things that were under water. *I have to get away. I have to get away.*

"Sana?" Her aunt's voice pierced the turmoil in her head. "Do you hear me?"

"What did you say?" Sana asked.

Her aunt studied her. "Go upstairs and lay down," she said. "You don't look good."

Sana looked past her aunt, out to the street where cars and trolleys trundled along filled with people making their way in the world. "Yes, *Sitto*." She walked over and embraced first her aunt, then her uncle, before she left. They looked a little surprised.

Once up in her room, she pulled her old travel bag from under the bed and stuffed her extra clothes into it. She stripped off her blouse and put on the woolen chemise with its hidden treasure, then took it off again and ripped out one of the gold pieces to put in her coin purse. Her hands were trembling. She put the chemise back on and buttoned her blouse over it. She could wear her jacket over everything, although it would make her hot. What else? Her immigration papers. Those went into her bag, along with her little sewing kit and the inlaid brush and comb she had brought from Algeria. She looked around. That was all.

No, there was one more thing. She pulled a thin leather folder out from under her pillow. Her photos of her family, her father and mother and home, would be her treasure now. On impulse, she opened it. Her parents' happy smiles looked up at her.

Mommy and Daddy, I'm going to be part of a proud profession, and I promise you right now that I will only marry a man that you would approve of. I love you and I beg a blessing from you now. Sana kissed the photo and held it to her heart for a minute, then placed it back in the leather holder and tucked it deep into her bag. She knelt down and buried her face in the feather quilt.

Then she raised her head, shouldered her bag, and slipped silently down the stairs.

After the graduation ceremony ended Joe Vesely searched the through the groups of people crowding the auditorium. Families were starting to leave.

"She's here somewhere," he said to his aunt and uncle. "Just wait a little longer." They nodded and kept on talking.

He found Zula Hruska surrounded by students saying goodbye, and he lingered beside her until they left.

"Well, dear, congratulations. Your family must be so proud of you," Mrs. Hruska said with her brisk smile. "Good luck in college now. Keep your head on straight." She shook his hand and patted him on the back.

"Thanks, Mrs. Hruska. Did you see Sana Toledo?"

She paused. "No."

"Do you know where she is?"

She studied him. "Can you keep a secret?"

Joe stared at her,

"Just between you and me, she left town. She told me so this morning when she came to pick up her diploma." Mrs. Hruska nodded. "Now, don't let that get around."

"You mean she left? Just up and left? Why didn't you stop her?"

"There's worse things for a girl than to go out and make a little money." She nodded meaningfully at him. "Lots worse."

"Mrs. Hruska." Joe bit off the words. "I want to find her. Where'd she go?"

"I can't tell you that."

"I swear I won't tell anybody."

"I promised her I wouldn't." "Please." "She said she didn't want anyone to know." Mrs. Hruska patted his back. "Sorry."

Afterwards Joe walked with his family to the Prazsky's house, because Rose's brother Rudy had also graduated and the families were celebrating together. The house was so small that they held the party outdoors. His uncle made a funny speech and Joe shook hands with what seemed like the entire neighborhood. Finally he slipped off to the tiny kitchen and found Johnny there with Wence, Rose's older married brother, eating cake and washing it down with cold water from the pump. Wence had crammed his massive six-foot-five-inch body into a rickety kitchen chair, and he held his one-year-old son in the crook of his muscled arm, feeding him frosting.

"So you're going to college now." Wence said. "Gonna miss the all the fun around here."

Joe cut himself a slice of cake and crammed half of it into his mouth so he didn't have to answer. He motioned for the water jar and took a slug.

"I signed up for the National Guard," Wence said while Joe chewed and swallowed. "They pay good," he went on when Joe looked surprised. "You oughta join too and then we could go to training together. They take college students." He reached out a calloused finger, swiped frosting from Joe's cake, and smiled at his baby boy. "Here you go," he crooned. "And-a one, and-a two..." he waved the frosting-coated finger in front of the baby's delighted face and then popped it into the little open mouth.

"What's Rachel going to do?" Joe asked after swallowing. Wence and his wife lived down the street in a rooming house.

"It's only one weekend a month." Wence reached for more frosting and Joe pulled his cake out of reach. "We're gonna save up for a house." He dipped up frosting from the cake pan instead and waved his finger in loops like an airplane. "Bombs away! Coming in for a landing! Right on target!" The baby shrieked with joy.

"We're leaving now," John Mark called in over the commotion.

"Later, Uncle John," Joe called back. "See you at the house." He watched Wence dip up more frosting. If the one girl he liked

30

didn't think enough of him to tell him she was leaving town, he might as well go see the world.

"Where do you join up?" he asked.

Back at home that night, Joe sat in the kitchen and stared out the window. Josefina came in and looked at him.

"Too much cake," she scolded. "Have some tea."

"I'm fine," he said. "Thanks anyway."

His uncle drifted in, opened the ice box and took out a quart jar full of beer. "Karel sent this home with me. Want to split it?"

Joe got up to fetch two glasses. Josefina sniffed and hobbled out of the kitchen. "Sorry, *Bubi*," he called after her. She waved her hand without turning around.

Joe and John Mark looked at each other and shrugged, then shared out the beer and sipped silently for a while, listening to the radio playing in the other room.

"What's new?" John Mark finally asked.

Joe swirled his beer. "I think I'll sign up for the National Guard."

John Mark nodded. "I would if I was your age." He set down his mug and stretched. "Did you ever find that girl you wanted us to meet?"

Joe shook his head. "Zula Hruska said she left town. I bet she ran away."

"What? Tabcharani's girl?"

"Yeah."

"What'd she do that for?"

"I have no idea. I guess she didn't want to stay here." Joe kicked the leg of the table.

His uncle took another sip. "What's she like?"

Joe considered that. "Well, really pretty." John Mark did not look impressed.

"Smart, too," Joe offered.

"Rose is smart and pretty," John Mark said. "I don't see you all steamed up about her."

"Rose is spoiled rotten; besides, it'd be like kissing my sister."

His uncle grinned. "What would be like kissing your sister?"

Joe groaned. John Mark laughed.

"Maybe Mrs. Hruska's wrong," Joe said after a while. "Maybe she didn't really leave. I'm going over to that store tomorrow and finding out. Maybe her uncle knows where she went."

John Mark laughed again. "You kidding? You go ask Tabcharani where his girl is, he'll knock your teeth out."

Joe slapped the table. "What am I supposed to do, just sit around? Why didn't she tell me she was leaving?" The words came out a little louder than he intended. He took a sip of beer, trying to cool down. "I'm just worried about her, is all." He chewed on the inside of his cheek. "Maybe she ran off with someone else."

"Come on," John Mark said. "You hardly know this girl."

Joe raised his hand, trying to find words, and then dropped it again. "I just wanted you to meet her." *I love her*, he wanted to add, but that would sound ridiculous, since she had just left town without telling him.

His uncle stared into his beer glass.

"What do you think?" Joe finally asked him.

After a while John Mark said, "There must be a reason why she left. People do things for reasons." He swirled his beer again and looked up. "Don't give up yet. You never know."

Chapter Two

Des Moines

Dear Sitto and Uncle Abraham,

I am very sorry that I have caused you so much trouble. You must be very angry with me and I hope that sometime in the future I can repay you for all your help, as I know my father would want me to do. After I start working I will send you some money. Thank you for the many kindnesses you have done for me and I pray you will forgive me someday.

Your niece,
Sana Tabcharani

Sana sealed up her letter and put on the stamp. She was free. She was hundreds of miles away from the grocery store, enrolled at nursing school, and now she was free as the sky-blue jaybirds cackling in the trees outside, at least until tomorrow when training started.

"Ma'am, can you please tell me where I can mail this letter?" she asked the secretary behind the big wooden desk. "And where do I go now?"

"I'll mail it for you, dearie. Room number fourteen, student nurse dorm, over there."

Sana picked up her bag and stepped out of the dark cool office into the warm afternoon outside. The dorm was a two-story red brick building surrounded by oak trees abloom with bright green leaves. She walked along a crumbling concrete sidewalk, carrying her bag and admiring the stately oaks and the green grass glowing in the sunlight. The breeze was warm and gentle. This would be a fine place to live, a lovely new home for her. She liked nursing school already.

The front door of the dorm sagged on its hinges and creaked a little when she opened it. The walls inside were peeling layers of faded gray paint, but the linoleum floor was brightly waxed and she could hear a radio playing somewhere. Sana walked down the echoing hall, glancing at the numbers of the rooms on either side and trying to keep her heels from clacking too loudly on the floor. Number fourteen was at the end of the hall. She opened the door to a narrow little room furnished with two bunk beds, a chest with four drawers, a rack for hanging clothes, and a window. It looked like heaven. She flung her bag on a top bunk and went over to open the window and lean on the sill, admiring the view.

Someone else's heels clacked along the hall. A young woman dressed in a stylish navy blue suit dragged a heavy trunk through the door and let it fall flat on the floor behind her. She wore white gloves, red patent-leather heels, and a chic red hat.

"I'm Margie Browne," she announced, taking off a glove and offering her hand. Her glossy brown hair was cut in a bob and her fingernails were polished the same bright red as her hat and shoes. "Brown with an "e" on the end."

Sana shook hands. "I'm Sana Toledo."

"Pleased to meet you." Margie looked around the room. "Is that your stuff on that bunk?"

"Yes."

Margie gave an appraising glance at Sana. "You don't look eighteen."

Sana stiffened. "I graduated." She had shown her diploma to the secretary at the registration office and the woman had not asked any questions.

Margie grinned. "I'm seventeen," she said. "I just told them that I was eighteen and they let me in."

Sana relaxed a little. "How nice to meet you."

Margie flung a red patent-leather handbag on top of the other bunk and started rummaging through bureau drawers. "The woman at the office said there'd be sheets and towels for us. Did you see any?"

Sana was preparing to explain that she had only just arrived when more footsteps echoed through the hallway and two girls carrying suitcases walked in, both of them blue-eyed and buxom, with springy blonde braids pinned across their heads.

"Hello! Hello! We're your new roommates!" The first girl enthusiastically shook Margie's hand and moved on to Sana. "Hello!" she said again, and laid her hand across the pillowy expanse of her lace-trimmed blouse. "I'm Barbara Janacek and this is my sister Mary."

They got into a pleasant tangle of introductions. When they sorted themselves out Sana and Margie had the two top bunks, and Barbara and Mary were slinging their suitcases onto the bottom ones. Barbara found sheets and towels and passed them around while Margie hung a little mirror over the bureau. Sana scrambled up on top of her bunk and watched as the other three pulled armloads of belongings out of their bags and tried to stuff them into the drawers or hang them on the rack. Soon the floor was covered with a spectacular jumble of clothes. Sana folded up her own skirts and blouses and set them in neat piles along the side of her mattress next to the wall to keep them out of the mess below.

Margie gave up first. "Look, we get our uniforms tomorrow and we're going to have to redo everything anyway. Let's just leave it for now." She sat down on Mary's bed and lit up a cigarette.

Mary's eyes widened. "You smoke?"

Margie rolled her eyes. "Where are you from?"

"Moline."

"Wow." Margie blew a plume of smoke. "Good thing you got out of there."

Barbara laughed, her broad expanse of lace jiggling up and down. "My brothers are so jealous they wouldn't even say goodbye. They're still getting up at four in the morning for milking."

"You... mean... cows?" Margie held out her cigarette at an elaborate angle in order not to drop ashes on the bed.

"Mom and Dad have a dairy farm," Mary said. "Holsteins."

"Good Lord."

Sana spoke up. "How come you left?"

"Because it's like jail, only harder." Barbara's open smile beamed clear across her face. "I don't care how bad people say nursing is, it can't be worse than milking cows and scooping poop twice a day."

Margie crossed one elegantly stockinged leg over the other. "Well, I'm from Chicago. My mom was an Army nurse and that's what I'm going to be." She flicked cigarette ash on the floor. "I'm going to marry an officer. No farm for me."

"Does everybody have to wear those kind of stockings here?" Mary asked.

Margie raised an eyebrow. "Do I hear the sound of someone falling off a turnip truck?"

Mary blushed. Sana felt sorry for her and changed the subject. "I heard Army nurses make eighty-eight dollars a month and get to be lieutenants."

"Second lieutenant," Margie said.

"What's the difference?"

"First lieutenant's higher. Nobody salutes you anyway but you get a raise." She shrugged. "My mom was a first lieutenant."

Sana flopped down on her stomach and propped her chin in her hands. "Someone else told me nursing's not, ah, decent."

They all looked Margie, who grinned. "Well, you'll see everything the first day." The other girls looked uncomfortable and Margie relented. "It's not so bad. My mom liked working with men. She says they treated her like an angel. "

"What's your dad think about her doing all that?" Mary asked.

"Well." Margie took a deep drag. "Well, she doesn't have that problem."

"Goodness sakes! Did your dad die?" Barbara asked.

"Nope. Ran off and left her before I was born." She blew out a hard line of smoke. "I figured the only way for me to find a decent guy is to move out of town and start over."

Sana blinked at such an audacious display of openness. Margie took another drag and tossed her head.

"Gee." Mary sounded awestruck, either by the story or by Margie's boldness in telling it. "You look like a high-class girl."

Margie smiled and smoothed her skirt over her knees. "That's the plan."

Barbara craned her head out from her bunk to look up. "Sana? Come on, sit down here by me," she said, patting the mattress. Sana was glad of the invitation and slid down to perch on the edge of the lower bed. Barbara fluffed a pillow and curled up companionably. "Your accent is so pretty. Where are you from?"

Sana laced her fingers together. "Cedar Rapids."

Margie laughed. "Oh, please."

"Come on, tell us where you're really from," Barbara coaxed. "You sound French. Are you from France?"

Sana took a deep breath. "Well, no. I'm from Algeria. People speak French there."

The other girls made little sounds of awe. "Where's that?"

"North Africa. Across the Mediterranean from Spain."

"Holy cow," Margie said. "How'd you get way over here?" Sana hesitated. "I came over to live with my aunt and uncle and help them with their grocery store."

"What about your parents?" Mary asked.

Sana weighed again how much to say. "Oh, well, my parents aren't here because they, ah, they died. When I was twelve. That's why I left." The edge of the sickening memory, always sharper when she told it again, made her stomach clench up.

Barbara reached over and hugged her. "I'm so sorry."

"Me too," Mary said.

"How come you want to be a nurse?" Margie asked.

Three friendly faces waited, open and interested, wanting to hear her story. The rigid grip in her middle eased away and Sana looked conspiratorially around the circle. They all drew in a little closer. "My uncle was going to make me marry this horrid old man so I ran away."

The sisters gasped. Margie choked on her inhale. "You have got to be kidding," she coughed out. "I didn't think things like that happened in America."

37

"You poor thing! How awful!" Barbara exclaimed. She put her arm around Sana's shoulder again. "Don't you worry, we won't tell anyone you're here. They'll never find you."

"You came here all by yourself? Weren't you scared?" Mary asked.

"I came across the Atlantic by myself," Sana pointed out.

"You're so brave," Barbara marveled.

"Pretty, too," Mary offered.

"Yeah. I love your eyelashes. Don't you have a boyfriend?" Margie asked.

"Oh, there was this one boy, and I thought maybe..." Sana shrugged and let the sentence trail off.

"It happened to me like that." Margie nodded, sharing the misery. "The guys always want to marry a blonde."

Sana thought of Rose. "I think you're right."

"I'm blonde and nobody wants to marry me," Mary said.

"Oh, honey, don't lose any sleep over that. We'll be right in the middle of hundreds of men next week," Barbara said. "Don't worry about it." She turned back to Sana. "You are so... so... stylish. Everything you say sounds romantic. Say something in French for me."

"Je suis trés heureuse de vous encontrer."

All the girls exclaimed in admiration.

Sana smiled. *"A'quelle heure dînons?"* "What's that mean?" they chorused. She laughed. "'When do we eat?'"

"When *do* we eat?" Mary asked.

Margie jumped up. "I'm starving. Come on, let's find a diner. Or a bar."

"I don't know about that," Barbara said. "I've never gone into a bar without my Dad."

Sana's stomach rumbled loudly. "Can we get dinner in a bar?"

Margie picked up her hat and settled it at a flirtatious angle on her shiny hair. "Sweetie pie, we can get all kinds of interesting things in a bar. Do you dance?" She looked around at three blank faces and arched her brow again. "Ladies. Time to learn."

The next morning Sana stood in a hospital ward, fighting a hangover and trying not to throw up from the reek in the bedpan she was holding. She finally set it down and vomited into an empty emesis basin. The young woman next to her dropped the urinal she was holding and headed for the door of the ward, walking faster and faster until she was almost running as she left.

Barbara Janacek sailed past with a bedpan in each hand as if she had been doing this kind of work all her life. Sana fought down another heave and covered her own bedpan with a towel as she had just been taught.

"Sorry, miss." The whisper made her look around. Her patient, a haggard-faced man with the yellowish skin of liver disease, was looking at her. "Sorry."

She swallowed down the taste of bile. "Don't feel bad. It's just my first day." The man closed his eyes. He was so weak that he couldn't lift his head.

Sana tucked the sheet and blanket around his shoulders. "I'll be back later," she said, and he opened his eyes. "When it's time for baths." He hastily shut them again.

By the end of the day, over half the new students had deserted the nursing program. The others collapsed into the ragged chairs in the nurses' break room, resting their feet before walking back to the dorm.

Margie lit up. "What'd those other girls think they were going to do? Stand around looking like Florence Nightingale? They acted like they'd never been in a hospital before."

Sana unlaced her shoes. "I've never been in a hospital before."

"I thought I was going to die when we gave those baths," said another girl. "My mom would be turning in her grave if she knew. I never saw men's parts before."

"Me either," Sana said. In the last twenty-four hours, between her night in a bar and her day of ward duty, she had just learned more about men than she ever dreamed she'd know.

"I grew up on a farm," Barbara said cheerfully. "Seen all kinds of parts."

"I'd rather change a bedpan than marry one," Sana said.

"Not me," Margie said. "I'm going to find a really great guy and marry him. An officer. I always like them the best." She blew a stream of smoke.

"Something to do with the pension?" Sana asked. Everybody laughed.

"Don't tell me you'd turn down money." Margie took off her cap and ran her fingers through her hair. "Anybody want to go out tonight?"

Barbara groaned. "Are you serious?" She waggled her shoes. "My dogs're barking."

Sana sat back and propped her own feet up on the table. "I'll go with you."

Margie nodded. "Atta girl."

Chapter Three

England
October 12, 1942

Second lieutenant Joe Vesely gripped his rifle, shook sleet out of his eyes, and jumped off the side of a platform into a mud pit twenty feet below. The hard shock of landing turned into a muddy scramble to get out of the way of men jumping down right behind him.

"Get your fat arse moving or your kids're gonna grow up speaking German!" yelled the drill instructor. "Lieutenant, get your men up that hill! Bayonets fixed! Kill Krauts on top! Now!"

Joe grabbed the arm of one of his men who had fallen face down in the mud and pushed him toward dry ground. "Get going!" He dragged out another floundering soldier and sent him after the first. "Up the hill! Bayonets fixed! Kill Germans at the top!" Nobody asked why German soldiers would be on a hill in Scotland in the middle of a winter storm, helping them train for war. They saved their breath for the run up the ice-glazed hill instead.

Sure enough, German soldiers met them at the top. Rifle shots exploded and Joe ran bayonet-first for the nearest enemy, but a blow to his ribs knocked him off his feet and sent him tumbling backwards. He hit the ground hard on his left hand and scrambled to his feet, ears ringing from gunfire and eyes smarting from smoke. Soldiers were struggling all around him and someone cried out. The Germans backed off and stopped shooting.

Men picked themselves up off the ground. Enemy soldiers

took off their helmets and turned back into British commandos dressed in German uniforms. Joe pressed a hand against his side to see if he had broken any ribs. His wrist hurt worse than his side. He looked around, counting his men. Most of them were either on the ground or had been pushed back down the hill. Only one had broken through the German line.

"Man got hit, sir." Bill Sedlak, one of his two sergeants, came up to him. "They were using live ammunition and he got hit in the leg. Uh, I think we need a medic." Bill's helmet was crusted with ice and a purplish bruise was spreading over one side of his face.

Still holding his side, Joe crossed over to where commandos clustered around a man on the ground. The soldier was grimacing and holding his calf. Blood soaked his pant leg down to the top of his boot, and he looked up at Joe. His lips were turning blue.

"Lieutenant, your job is to get your sections to the next station," a commando yelled at him. Bullet-and-bayonet drill was scheduled at the field down the other side of the hill.

"Fall in!" Joe called the platoon to order and headed off at a fast march.

"Did you know they were going to do that?" Sedlak panted. "Live ammo?"

"Uh-uh," Joe gasped back. His side throbbed with every step and he could feel his left wrist swelling. He could see the next drill station clearly now and he recognized the battalion commander standing there, watching his platoon. "Move it, Rangers!" he yelled. "Darby's watching!"

After bullet-and-bayonet was over, they marched back to barracks and, finally, mess hall. The line for mess was shorter than it had been three months ago because so many men had given up on the training and gone back into the regular Army. Joe picked up a tin plate heaped with beans and mutton and sat down at a long plank table.

"Geez, Robichaux, use a fork," Sedlak said. Alafair Robichaux, the only man who had fought past the commandos at the top of the hill, was scooping beans straight from the plate into his mouth with his fingers. "I don't care if you eat meat with your fingers but I draw the line at beans." Robichaux ducked his face and picked up his fork. "

El Darbo's up to something." Manny Garcia, Joe's other sergeant, jerked his head towards the commander.

Joe glanced around. Darby had personally led the bullet-and-bayonet practice, jumping in when someone botched the drill. Now he was walking through the mess hall, bantering with the men as he passed through the tables.

"I had fun out there today," he yelled above the noise. "So much fun I'm going to do it all over again tomorrow." He paused to let them groan. "I have an announcement. Twenty-five mile speed march tomorrow. We clocked ten miles in eighty-seven minutes last time and I expect you do the twenty-five in about three and a half hours. In fact, I'm going to be extra nice and give you pansies four hours because of those little hills you call mountains that you're going over. Officers, you will set the pace and make sure your men arrive on time."

Joe sighed. Garcia grinned at him and then winced when the movement hurt his swollen black eye.

"That's what college gets you," he whispered. "Sir." Joe had entered the Army straight from his junior year in college, which made him an officer, and now he had to tackle every new assignment first to prove it could actually be done.

"Then we'll do demolitions," Darby went on. "I like blowing things up even more than I like watching you guys play in the mud."

Joe looked up, wondering if he would be called to lead the demolitions exercise. He had taken classes in chemistry and combustion science, which made him one of the very few soldiers here with any practical knowledge of dynamite.

The colonel caught his glance. "Vesely the Moral Marvel likes to blow things up too. Marvel! Anyone in your platoon cussed yet today?"

The mess hall shouted with laughter. "No sir!" Joe yelled

over the racket. "Not that I heard, sir!"

"Moral Marvel,'" Sedlak said under his breath. "Sir."

"Marvelette," Joe hissed back. The nickname had bothered him at first. But after his platoon won some speed marches people stopped ribbing him so much about not cussing, and when he\ turned out to be the camp expert on TNT the hazing dropped off even more. Then, on a Sunday morning furlough, while he was walking into town to go to church, Darby himself had driven past, picked him up, and gone with him. After that his platoon started calling themselves the Marvelettes.

Now Darby held up a newspaper. "There's some news today that I want you all to hear." The hall fell silent.

"This month's horoscope," he read, "says to avoid high places and overbearing people. So how come all you guys are up here with me?" Everyone laughed, relieved that the announcement was not about more Nazi victories. "Also avoid unnecessary strain tomorrow. Finally, stay out of rainy weather." He lowered the paper and looked around. "Have these people ever been to England?" The mess hall roared.

"Now I have some real news. Next week we go back to the coast and practice amphibious landings under fire." He paused. "And then," he paused again, "we sail! We're the first ones out the gate, boys! We're the first strike! They called us first!"

Men whooped and shouted and then settled into a long rolling roar, pounding the tables and drumming their feet.

Darby held up a hand. "Don't ask me where we're going because..." he pointed at them.

"Loose lips sink ships!" they shouted back and roared again, drumming a thunderous roll.

"Get to bed early, because tomorrow we're going to march over high places and put up with overbearing people and strain ourselves in rainy weather so we can win this war! See you at oh-four-hundred! Good night!" Men shouted and drummed on the tables for a while longer before turning back to the task of chewing down tough mutton and British beans.

"*Madre de Dios*, take me someplace it doesn't rain," Garcia said between mouthfuls.

"Texas," Joe said. Garcia came from El Paso.

"Naw. I want to shoot something before I go back."

"Me too," said Fred Ratliff, a skinny nineteen-year-old corporal from Kansas City. "I want to shoot at stuff I'm supposed to hit."

They all made bleating sounds at him. A week ago Ratliff had been reprimanded for shooting something that turned out to be a neighboring farmer's sheep.

"I coulda swore that sheep was a Kraut." Ratliff leaned back and stretched. "That was one good shot for that distance. My dad would've been proud a' me. Like picking off coyotes in a wheat field."

"That sheep was big as a barn and you were right next to it," Elmer Taffington said through a mouthful of beans. He was a big farm boy, taller and heavier than Ratcliff, but not as accurate with his rifle, and that fact bothered him.

"I'm going to shoot the hair right off your skinny behind if you don't shut up about it," Joe said to Ratliff. The Army had to pay for the sheep and he was still smarting from the reprimand.

"Oh, Lieutenant, that sheep looked a lot like something else. It was a really long ways away, sir."

"Where you think we're going?" Taffington asked. "Italy?"

Joe looked around the table. Two months ago his men limped back to camp at the end of the day and fell asleep over half-eaten plates of food. Now they were muscled and calloused from war games, singing cadences as they strode back from the hills, still moving fast just because they were hungry and wanted to be first in line at mess.

He bared his teeth in a wicked smile. "Wherever it is, God help the other guys."

Miles away, further south along the coast of Great Britain, Sana selected a tattered playing card and laid it down on the little metal table, then shivered and pulled her old wool sweater higher around her neck. Sleet pattered on the roof above and clicked against the windows. She had been playing gin rummy for four hours.

Margie dragged hard on her cigarette, tapped the ash into an empty can, and frowned. "Don't you ever throw a little card?" She laid down one of her own. In spite of the damp weather she had kept up her manicure, and her pretty scarlet fingertips tapped impatiently on the table.

"That is a little card. You should see my hand," Sana said. She shivered deeper into her sweater. "Brrrrrr. Somebody poke up the stove."

"You can wear my robe if you want to," Barbara said from where she sat on her cot, cuddled under a pile of blankets. She wore a blue knitted stocking cap with a tassel on top that made her face look very round and her eyes very blue, and she was knitting an identical one of cherry-red for Sana.

"Thank you, Checky," Sana said absently, organizing her hand of cards. Barbara had corrected so many people about the pronunciation of her last name ("it's Jan-a-*check*, not Jan-a-*seck*") that Sana had affectionately embellished it to Checky, and the nickname had stuck.

The nurses had been given the best quarters in the training camp, which translated into a low brick building with cots, a table with four chairs, and an old-fashioned coal furnace for heat. They were trying to make their little supply of coal last as long as possible, because no one knew how long they would have to stay in England, or when they would get any more coal.

Adele Ross, who had come out of retirement to help in the war, set down a card and tapped it. "There's a little one for you."

Sana stole a glance at her. Adele's curly brown hair was streaked with gray, and she had a way about herself that made people stand up straighter when she looked at them. Her hands were strong and sinewy and her fingernails short and bare. Right now she was wearing a sensible gray coat buttoned over her Army uniform.

Adele's partner, Orene O'Brian, drew a card from the deck. Orene was a quiet little woman from someplace in Texas, and she had never played cards until her trip across the Atlantic, but now she briskly discarded and rapped the table sharply with her small freckled hand. Then she folded her arms across her skinny chest and tipped back in her chair, grinning. The other players sighed, spread out their cards and counted.

"How many does that make for you this week? Thirty-nine?" Adele asked.

Orene ducked her freckled face and shook her mop of auburn curls. "Forty-one, ma'am," she said in her twangy hill-country accent.

"You," declared Adele, "are amazing." Orene ducked her head again, smiling and flushing bright red clear down to her collar.

Margie laughed as she gathered up cards. "Good job, Red. You could clean out a roomful of bad-boy gin players any day."

The smile vanished from the freckled face. "I hate that name. That's a man's name. Don't ever call me that."

The other three looked up in surprise. Orene had barely said more than ten words at a time since they had all been together.

"Okay," Margie said cautiously.

"People call me Obie back home."

Margie started to laugh again but Sana frowned her down. "I like Obie better." Obie wore an ancient black raincoat, and her back-country combination of beat-up galoshes and thin dun-colored socks had drawn some condescending looks.

"I like it better too," Margie said generously, and held out the newly-shuffled deck. "Here, cut."

Sana shivered again. "Let's get the fire going before we play again."

Another group of women clustered around the furnace, styling their hair for the trip to the evening mess hall, which had become the high point of the day. Jo Ellen Jackson, who was from Savannah and particular about her looks, was trying to heat up her curling iron by holding it inside the furnace right over the little heap of coal.

"Sister, I'd be *so* obliged," she said. "It's not like anybody's going hog-wild with the coal today. I'm fixin' to turn into an ice cube."

Checky laughed. "You're fixing what?" Jo Ellen, who had been more or less cold since she got on the boat for England, ignored the question.

"We should wait until we get back from dinner," Adele said. "It'll just waste good coal if we put it on now."

"Just spread around what's in there and blow real hard on it," Obie offered. "Here." She pushed back her chair and went over to tend the stove.

Thunder rumbled over the tap and patter of sleet on the roof. Someone turned on a radio and a British broadcaster impassively recited the list of bad news from around the world. The German army, which already controlled Egypt, North Africa, most of Europe and half of Russia, was now attacking Stalingrad. The Russians were fighting bravely to defend their country. Stalin had kept the civilians of Stalingrad in the city instead of evacuating them, and women and children were working side by side with soldiers on the ramparts, fighting and dying rather than surrender. Unfortunately, the Russians were sustaining heavy losses. In the Pacific, the Japanese had taken Burma, Hong Kong, Singapore and New Guinea. American troops were resisting the Japanese. Unfortunately, they were sustaining heavy losses. In England, strict ration laws continued to be enforced. Meat, and sugar were rationed. Tea, and were rationed. Breakfast cereals, cheese, eggs, milk and canned fruit were rationed. British citizens could still eat fish and chips.

"That Hitler's taking over the whole world. Somebody needs to fish or cut bait pretty soon," Jo Ellen said.

"He needs killin'," Obie agreed.

No one had a reply for that. Sana took another card, sighed, and discarded. For a month they had done nothing but play cards, take walks in the endless rain, and page through old magazines. Every day the radio reported more Nazi victories.

"Be patient. We could get orders any day," Adele said, exactly as she had said last week. Margie drew and discarded with an elegant flick of her red-tipped finger.

Brakes squealed outside and a heavy motor rattled to a stop. Seconds later a knock shook the door. Someone opened it to a blast of rain and a half-frozen soldier.

"Mail," he called. Obie and Margie abandoned their cards and joined the general rush. Women gathered around the soldier, giving little cries of delight as their names were called. Sana and Adele stayed where they were.

"Go ahead, dear," Adele said. "I'll wait."

"I'll wait too," Sana said. The mail carrier never called her name.

Checky broke out of the crowd, smiling, and jumped back into her bed holding a handful of mail and a box. She tossed the box to Sana. "Here you go, Frenchie."

"It's your present," Sana protested, but she took the box and hefted it. "Feels like cookies."

"I hope they're molasses again," Checky said. Sana tore off wrappings and opened the lid. Sugar and nutmeg scented the air. They both reached for cookies and bit into the sweet flavor of home. The letter inside was wrapped in wax paper. Checky unfolded it and started reading while she chewed, and Sana watched her expression as she smiled over the handwritten pages.

"How's Mary?" Sana asked.

"Mom says she's finally getting over morning sickness." Checky started reading out loud. "'Mary looks so pretty now that she's over her morning sickness and she can hold something down. Orville wants a boy but Mary's carrying the baby pretty low so I think it's going to be a girl.'" She looked up. "A little girl! Wouldn't that be fun! I'll share her with you. I'll be Aunt Checky and you'll be Aunt Frenchie." Sana laughed and Checky went back to the letter. "'The pasteurizer broke down last week and your father was pretty low about that. Just one bad thing is all it takes to wipe out the savings. I thank my lucky stars that so far the cows are staying healthy. Corn prices are coming up and that's good for most people around here but not for us because we have to buy feed. Milk is selling good but your father is working way too hard on account of all the boys being gone to war now. Your father says he's always in the wrong business at the wrong time.'"

Sana murmured sympathy and reached for a second cookie as Checky on read about the apple harvest and the unusual birth of a late-season calf. "Oh, Mary says hi. 'Mary says to say hi to Frenchie. Now, you girls take care of yourselve and don't get too worn out with all your nursing work. Your father and I miss you and we want you and the boys to all come back home soon and in one piece. Love, Mom.'" She folded up the letter and sighed.

Sana sighed too, picturing a kind woman in a lamplit kitchen, sitting at a table writing a letter and hoping that her children would come back home soon. "That's so nice of Mary. Tell her I said hi and best wishes for the baby."

"You ought to come visit some time," Checky said. "Mom loves having people around." She winked. "More hands for milking."

"I wouldn't mind," Sana said, envisioning herself in that lamplit kitchen, washing dishes and talking with someone's mother at the end of a long day.

Another soldier staggered in with an ice-crusted crate. He let it bang down to the floor and saluted. "General delivery for the American nurses," he said. Everyone left the mail carrier and crowded around the man with the box.

"Thank you, hon," Jo Ellen said, stroking back her freshly curled hair and smiling sweetly.

The soldier swallowed and looked uneasy. He seemed to be waiting for something.

"Thank you," Jo Ellen said again, and pushed him aside to get to the box. The soldier looked confused and went back out.

Margie was already dragging clothes out of the crate. "Uniforms!" She held up what looked like a pair of olive-drab trousers, but turned out to be a one-piece coverall instead.

"Oh, isn't that wonderful," Checky said.

"Are you kidding?" Margie said. "I'm not wearing this."

Obie raised her eyebrow. "Olive green don't show blood."

"Are you kidding?" Jo Ellen asked. "That thing fell off the

ugly tree and hit every branch on the way down."

Checky laughed. "You crack me up." She measured a coverall across her bosom. "Is there a size 42?"

"That's a man's uniform," Adele said. "What else's in there?" Margie dug through more coveralls and found big wool socks underneath.

"Here's another box, miss." The soldier was back with another load. "I think there's shoes in here." He dropped it and heavy items thumped inside.

Sana had joined the group by now. She worked open the new crate and pulled out a pair of boots with thick soles and bulky shoelaces.

"This must be a mistake. These are all men's," she said in dismay.

The soldier coughed and held out a piece of paper.

"Let me see that," Adele said, glaring at the soldier as if doubting his ability to deliver boxes.

The man handed her the paper and saluted. "Ma'am," he said. Adele saluted in return and the soldier backed out the door.

"No mistake," Adele said after a minute. "We get men's uniforms because there are no women's uniforms for where we're going. There's supposed to be helmets, packs and mess kits." She leaned over and poked around deep inside the crate. "What else is in there?"

The soldier came back with a third box containing canvas shoulder bags and tin mess kits. A fourth turned out to be full of helmets.

"Everyone gets two musette bags, two blankets, two coveralls, five pairs of socks, one helmet and one pair of boots," Adele read out loud. "And one mess kit. We're supposed to pack our nursing whites but no rubber boots or raincoats."

Sana tried on a helmet. "Does this mean we're leaving pretty soon?"

Checky was inspecting a mess kit, opening and closing the hinged sides like a clamshell so that it folded out into two shallow halves. A matching tin knife and fork were tucked inside.

"Well, really, it's very nice," she said. "Just like a picnic. Just think, there's soldiers out there right now eating out of these and grateful to have them."

Margie was sorting the coveralls. "Medium... medium... medium." She looked at Sana and grinned. "Hey, you want this medium?" She tossed one to Sana, who held it up against her shoulders. Long olive-green pant legs trailed on the floor. Everybody laughed.

Adele looked up from the paper, disbelief written on her face. "This isn't any mistake. This is what they sent for us." She shook her head, then looked around at all the faces.

"We need to pack up. Each of you can take whatever you can fit into two of these bags." She looked at the coveralls again and shook her head. "Maybe we can hem them up."

Chapter Four

The Atlantic

Sana stared out a rain-streaked window, watching long lines of men slowly file into the battleships loading for war. Fog hung low in sky and curled over the water as trucks crept through the rain, delivering loads of crates to the gray boats crowding the docks. Thousands of soldiers still stood in the drizzle outside, waiting their turn to board. The nurses had been allowed to wait inside a warehouse.

"Coffee, dear?" A gray-haired little British woman in a Wren uniform was handing out peanut butter sandwiches and black coffee in paper cups.

"Thank you very much, ma'am." Sana was still unsure about whether or not to salute. The nurses had been finally been given a lecture about rank and military protocol, but the Wren just smiled at her and moved on. Saluting seemed unnecessary. Sana turned back to the window, took a sip of bitter coffee, and grimaced. Out in the rain, more Wrens in raincoats and rubber boots handed out coffee and sandwiches to soldiers.

"Don't those boats look awfully small?" Margie said. "I thought they'd be bigger. Look at all those poor men out there getting soaked to the skin."

"Girls! Get your bags!" Adele called. Sana scooped up her two canvas musette bags and slung them over her shoulders, staggering a little as their group hiked off through the warehouse. She had stuffed her bags full of uniforms, shoes, underwear, and all the little things she thought might come in handy wherever she was going. One bag held her sewing kit and blue satin cosmetics bag, and the other held her blankets and extra coverall. If some emergency forced her to keep only one bag, she planned to keep one with the sewing kit and trust the Army to provide everything else.

Checky came up, stomping her feet to settle her oversized boots. "I'm wearing two pairs of socks and these things are still too big," she said. A bit of pink-flowered fabric showed under the collar of her coverall. She and Sana were both wearing their pajamas underneath their uniforms, to keep warm and to make more room in the bags. "Do you have any room left? I'm trying to fit my purse in." She was carrying a black patent leather purse along with her bulging bags. A bright blue yarn tassel poked out from one of her pants pockets.

Sana looked doubtful. "I'll try."

"I'll take it," said Obie, walking behind them.

"Oh, thank you. Are you sure?"

"Yeah, I got lots of room." Sana and Checky turned around to look at Obie's bags. They were, indeed, half empty.

"Thank you so much," Checky said. "I'd hug you but then I'd clobber you with all this stuff I'm carrying."

"Did you ever decide about your necklace?" Sana asked her.

"I mailed it home to my mom. I'd just lose it somewhere if I took it. Hey, Mom sent me another letter, saying the Germans are bombing hospital units even if they have the Geneva red cross sign showing."

"The radio said that too," Obie said.

"So I wrote her back and said I would be careful and for her to be sure and get my insurance money if I don't come home." Checky laughed.

Margie, just ahead of them, turned around and walked backwards as she talked. "I wrote my mom and bet her a dollar that I'll be married by the time I come home."

Sana hitched her bags up on her shoulders and kept her eyes on the floor. There was no home waiting for her at the end of the war. She had written her aunt's name on her own insurance benefit form, trying to ignore the painful problem of having no one else to claim. But even the letter she had sent to Mary, telling her about the insurance, had not brought an answer. The old lonely feeling had come back after that, creeping over her heart like the gloomy gray fog outside. If she died in the war, her aunt and uncle would probably forget about her right after they cashed the check.

They walked through a door and straight into the weather. Whipping rain stung their faces and they all put up their hands against the wind.

"What idiot said to not bring raincoats?" Margie yelled. "Whew!"

"Over here," Adele called, signaling them towards a truck.

Sana pulled her bags tighter and yanked up the collar of her coverall as high as she could. "Come on, run for it," she called, and they broke into a jog and jostled into the nurses ahead of them.

"Move it!" Margie yelled. A male officer further up the line turned around and frowned.

"These people need to hurry," Checky shouted, rain streaming down her face. "Somebody tell them we're drowning back here."

"American women! Look at that!" Soldiers standing in line along the dock were gaping at them.

Sana swung around. That voice... her heart leaped at the sudden memory of fresh coffee and dill pickles, bakery and cigar smoke... she stared at the blue-eyed soldier looking straight at her. He was big and tall, like the Czechs in her uncle's store, and his voice was so familiar... But just then it was her turn to scramble up into the truck, and when she turned around to look for him again the line of soldiers had moved and she couldn't see him anymore.

"You know that guy?" Margie asked.

"He reminded me of someone." Sana craned out the back of the truck, ignoring the calls and whistles, looking for that face from home again.

"He's a cute medic. I bet we see him again." Margie winked. Sana rolled her eyes.

Checky, still holding her purse, slipped on the truck's wet

bumper and fell back to the muddy dock. All her bags tumbled down and the men in line guffawed.

"Shut up! That's a woman!" snapped another soldier. "Here, miss," he said, giving Checky a hand up.

"A woman!" "A woman!" "What's a woman doing here?" Men everywhere turned to look.

"We're the nurses!" Margie called, waving. Sana didn't look around. She was staring at the soldier. It was Joe Vesely.

Joe stared back at the dark-eyed woman in the truck. The thick soft tangle of her lashes, the beautiful eyes... it was the girl from the grocery store back home.

"Sana?" he called. His line of soldiers began to move away but he walked backwards, keeping her in sight.

"Joe? Joe?" Her truck was starting to move, too, and she leaned out to catch his answer.

"Yeah!" The truck roared forward and she waved at him as it turned and carried her out of sight. "Dang!"

Sedlak was laughing. "You beat all, Lieutenant. One American woman on this..." he started a curse and then cut it off when he caught Joe's warning glance, "...uh,
island... and you know her. Does she have a sister?"

"She's from my hometown," Joe said. "I can't believe it. I can't believe she's here." He shook his head in amazement. "Women going to the war."

"Nurses," Sedlak said, savoring the word. They both stared for a while at the place where the truck had turned.

The men slowly filed onto the boat and into their quarters, squeezing themselves and all their gear into narrow cots slung in stacks and rows. They waited for hours, swinging gently against each other as the boat rocked in the harbor, napping on and off until they felt the boat move out. When the room started to tilt and lurch they knew they were in the open sea, and after that men began to get sick. When the call finally came for mess, some of them got sick again.

Those who could walk and eat were allowed to go on deck afterwards. On the officers' deck Joe walked around, stretching the kinks out of his arms and legs, gazing across the gray-green waves or up at the misty sky. He passed a group wearing white armbands with red crosses and heard someone call his name.

"Ves!" Wence Prazsky was running toward him, looking taller and brawnier than ever in his bulky army jacket. "Hey!"

"Praz!" Joe slapped Wence on the back. "Where's my twenty, you crazy Czech?" Wence had borrowed twenty dollars on the day they were called up and they hadn't seen each other since.

"I can't believe it! Can't believe it!" Wence pounded Joe's back with his oversize fist. They stopped beating each other long enough to exchange stories.

"Three thousand miles away from home and here you are." Wence shook his head. "I thought you'd be in some safe little state-side post drinking beer."

"Naw, I joined the Rangers. What's this?" Joe slapped Wence's armband. "Dr. Praz?"

"I got medic training because I can carry a man by myself and I don't mind changing dirty diapers. I felt about as dumb as a two-headed donkey in there with all those medical types."

"I did training for explosives, demolitions stuff."

"You can cover my butt in the field then. I'll make sure your ugly behind gets covered up if you ever get hit and land in a hospital bed."

"Don't you get weapons?"

"Naw. We get this little booklet in German and if krauts shoot at us we're supposed to read the Geneva conventions to 'em."

"We all got these little medical kits," Joe said. "Morphine, bandages, everything. The only thing I don't have is a nurse. Did you see those nurses? One of them's the girl from Tabcharani's grocery store."

"Skinny foreign girl? Yeah, I saw her." Wence hawked and spat over the side, taking care to aim away from the wind. "I can't believe they're sending women. First they'll get in the way, and then they'll hurt themselves on something, and then everything will get all..."

"If you see her again before I do, tell her I said hi."

Wence grinned.

"You'll probably see her at the hospital or something."

"Good thing for you I'm a married man," Wence looked around. "This is a pretty big operation, huh?" Hundreds of warships dotted the Atlantic, all heading south.

"Over a hundred thousand men," Joe said. "The 34th Infantry is practically all from Iowa, is what I heard."

"You know where we're going?"

"Nope." Joe eyed the cloudy sky. "South."

"I tried to sign up for the Rangers but they wouldn't take me because I'm married," Wence said. "What do you guys do that's so dangerous?"

"Scouting, raids, blowing things up, stuff like that. Hey, you get any letters? What's everybody doing back home?"

"Dad's an Air Raid Warden. Keeping Iowa safe from the Nazis." Wence grinned. "He goes around at night checking for blackouts, knocking on doors, raising cain any time he sees a light in a window."

Joe laughed, picturing Wence's bearlike father arguing with someone's wife about her curtains.

"And the nuns sold war bonds to buy a jeep for the 34th. They got so much money they bought twelve."

"Wow. That's pretty good."

"You haven't heard the best part," Wence went on. "The real killer's my little sister. You will never, ever guess what Rose's doing." He paused, enjoying the drama. "Second shift at the packing plant."

"Naw," Joe protested. "Things can't be that bad."

"Oh, yes they are. Mom says she goes to work in overalls every day, just like a man. She even tried to talk Rachel into going with her." Joe whistled and Wence rocked back on his heels, shaking his head. "I went nuts when I got that letter. They must've heard me clear back home because Rachel wrote and said not to worry, she's doing some kind of Red Cross work at the church instead and she's not going to do any war work at the factory. You hear from Uncle John?"

"He's okay. Still at the factory." Joe frowned. "Johnny signed up."

"What'd he do, lie about his age?"

"He's nineteen." Joe shrugged. "I hope he stays out of trouble. What about Anton and Rudy?"

"Rudy's in the Pacific. Anton's supposed to be doing something in England, like working on a newspaper or attending some school or something like that. Uncle Vincent thinks he's a spy."

"You're kidding."

"Nope. You know what else? So many guys went to war that the college closed down and there's no baseball this year."

Announcements blasted out above them, concluding with news of a prayer service on B deck for all who wanted to attend.

Wence made a face at him. "You going to go pray?"

Joe scoffed back. "I bet you pray before you go back home."

Wence brightened. "Another twenty?"

They slapped each other's backs and drifted on. Joe joined the group on the B deck, where everyone was standing around with their hands stuffed in pockets and chins tucked down against the wind. He saw Garcia and Taffington standing at the edge of the crowd, miserable in the blowing spray, and he walked over to stand with them. Robichaux showed up.

The chaplain read a psalm and called a prayer through the whipping wind. "Oh God of all mankind, whose command even the wind and oceans obey, we look to You now. Our lives are in your hands." Men nodded. "Protect us from the dangers of the sea and the dangers of the enemy. Strengthen us in the day of battle. Give us courage to do what must be done. Watch over us, keep us safe, and draw us together in one united will to serve you and fight against the evil that threatens us."

"Amen," they chorused. Garcia and Robichaux crossed themselves.

"Remember Psalm 91, the soldier's psalm. The Lord is your refuge and your fortress, your God in whom you trust. Surely he shall deliver us from the snare, and we will not be afraid of the terror by night, nor for the arrow that flies by day; for he shall give his angels charge over us, to keep us in all our ways.'"

"Amen," they all said again.

Joe shoved his hands deeper in his pockets and felt his uncle's latest letter crinkle under his fingers. *I hate this war*, John Mark had written, *but it's a war we have got to win. Stand strong because we need soldiers who can keep their heads on straight and be good leaders over there. No matter where you go or what happens, remember that the Lord is there too, and no matter how bad things get He will be walking through the fire right along with you. Be strong in that. I pray for you and your men every day. Your Aunt Kate sends her love and these oatmeal cookies.*

He stood there for a while after the service ended, thinking about the letter and staring out at the hazy points of light from other ships around them. He was going to war. Would he ever see this ocean again? A stinging blast of salty rain buffeted over the deck and he turned to go, bumping into someone who looked too slight to be a soldier.

"Hi," Sana Toledo said.

She was so close that he could smell the fragrance of her skin. "Hi." He held out his hand and took hers. Her fingers were wet and freezing cold.

"You don't have a coat?" he asked. She was wearing a helmet and clutching an Army-issue blanket around her shoulders. He pulled the blanket up higher around her neck and guided her to the shelter of a bulwark. "What are you doing here?"

She laughed and the two dimples flashed, just as he remembered. "I came on deck so I wouldn't get seasick. What are you doing here?"

"I'm a Ranger. Second lieutenant."

"Me too." Her smile was a little reserved this time. "Nice to see you again, Lieutenant Vesely."

He shook his head, moving his hand in a little deprecating gesture. "No, no..." They grinned at each other. "Come on, it's Joe."

"Sorry I had to leave so fast..." she began, and at the same time as he said "Hey, how come you left town so fast?" They both laughed.

"So how come you left?" Joe asked. "Without telling..." He wanted to say "me," but he settled for "anybody?"

She looked away. Her fine-boned face looked more elegant than he remembered, even when framed by the harsh olive drab of her uniform. "Oh, my uncle wanted to marry me off to marry one of his horrid old friends and I didn't want to, so I ran away." Her voice still held that sweet cool trace of accent. She lifted her chin with a hint of defiance. "Now I'm a nurse and I can do whatever I want."

Her life had come to this? Huddling in a wet blanket on a boat in the freezing Atlantic? Joe raised an eyebrow. "You want to live in an Army camp and get shot at?"

She laughed. "I'm a nurse. I don't think that's what I'll be doing."

He shook his head, disapproving. She should have told him about her trouble. He would have taken care of her. "You shouldn't be here. This is no place for a woman."

"And I'm happy to see you again too."

Joe blinked, suddenly warm in spite of the blowing spray. "I didn't mean... I'm happy to see you but..."

"Don't try to get out of it now." Dimples flashed again and her eyes sparkled. She looked so fascinating that Joe forgot what he was going to say.

"I am really happy to see you," she said. "Joe."

The sound of her voice saying his name shot a pleasant little thrill through him. Her nose was so lovely, even if it was a little red from the wind right now. She looked much too delicate to be going into battle and he wanted to put his arm around her, shield her from things that might harm her.

There were too many people around to do anything like that. "Be careful," was all he could think of to say.

"I will. You too."

"All below. All below," the loudspeaker announced. "All

below deck." Soldiers passed by, not noticing them in the gloom.

"Are you married?" Sana asked. Joe looked at her, surprised. He held up his left hand to show that he didn't wear a ring.

"Some married men don't wear rings," she said.

"I would if I was." Somehow he knew that she was not married either. "You're not married."

It had not been a question. She looked embarrassed.

"All below. All below deck."

They stepped out of their little shelter into the line of soldiers heading back below. Joe thought of another question, but he couldn't just ask her if she was in love with anyone else, not right now in the middle of a crowd. Sana walked with her face tucked down into her collar, as if she did not want to be noticed. He touched her arm when they neared the stair where he would have to turn, and she looked up at him and nodded before they parted ways.

"You found him at the prayer meeting?" Margie asked. Six nurses were trying to sleep in a cabin meant for two navy officers. Four were in makeshift berths, two crowded together on the deck, and so far no one was sleeping. "What'd he say? Is he married?"

"No," Sana said from her place on the bunk above.

"You knew him from before?" another nurse asked.

"Uh-huh."

Margie chuckled. "I've been kissing all these frogs for years, waiting for my prince to show up, and now here comes Frenchie with this dreamboat. I saw him. Trust me, girls, I saw him."

"Don't be silly," Sana said, but she was glad the darkness hid her face.

"If there's another prayer meeting tomorrow I'm going with you. I'm going to pray to that a good-looking officer falls in love with me."

The hatch opened and yellow light spilled into the cabin. Adele, who was now officially their head nurse, looked in.

"Did you find out?" all the nurses asked at the same time.

"Arzew."

"Where's that?"

"North Africa," Adele said, and "Algeria!" Sana said at the same time. "That's where I'm from, that's my country! Oh my goodness!" She sat up and banged her head. "Ow!"

"Don't get excited," Adele rapped out, "because there's still forty-eight hours until we land and there's a lot to do. Tomorrow we meet with the whole surgical unit at oh-seven-hundred. Breakfast at oh-six-hundred. So get some sleep." She began to close the door.

"Wait! What else do you know?" Margie called.

Adele paused and then came back in. "The fleet's splitting up to attack in three different places along the coast. The soldiers go in about three in the morning and then the medical units." She paused again. "I guess we just go in with the men."

"How come we're going to Africa?" Checky sounded puzzled.

"They say it's where the Axis forces are the weakest. There's mostly Italians and the colonel said they don't fight very well, so our boys are going to land in the middle of the night and try to take the coastal forts before anybody knows what's happening."

"There's French people in Algeria," Sana declared. "They'll help us. The French are Allies."

Adele frowned. "No, they said not to count on that. They say no one knows for sure which way the French'll go. There was something that happened, something about how the British blew up some French battleships to keep them out of German hands, so now the French are mad at the British, and they say they're mad at the Americans too, because we're on the British side. So the French might fight against us." She leaned farther into the room. "They said FDR's going on the radio, asking the French to support us."

"Huh," Obie said. "That's different."

"I'm still not exactly sure where we're going," Checky said.

"I'm excited," Margie announced. "I'll never get to sleep tonight."

Adele laughed. "Enjoy your beds while you have them. See you tomorrow, dears." She closed the door.

"What's Algeria like?" came a question in the darkness.

"It's warm," Sana said, picturing her beautiful stucco home nestled in the hills of Constantine. "It's beautiful. My mother grew roses there. And the food's wonderful and the sun shines all the time." *And I met Joe Vesely again today.* If he fell in love with her, why, then that changed everything, because someone cared if she lived or died. It was as good as having a home. And he was so incredibly handsome, even more than she remembered. She rolled over in the darkness and hugged herself for joy.

More men showed up at the next prayer service. More women did too. "There he is," Margie whispered to Checky. "Didn't I tell you?"

Checky poked her in the side. "Stop it. It's a prayer meeting."

Sana stood a pace away from them, lost in the beauty of the evening sky. The sea was calm, the sunset glowed on the horizon, and a few stars winked in the deep blue eastern sky. The chaplain began a hymn and men's deep voices rang out fine and strong over the sparkling water.

Checky wiped her eyes and blew her nose. "I can't stand the thought of them getting all shot up and dying." Sana blinked back her own tears and flung her arm around Checky's shoulders.

After the service Joe looked around for her, and Sana felt a shiver run down her back when his eyes met hers. He walked straight over to the little group of nurses, his platoon trailing behind him.

"Hi," he said. All the men looked at her.

"Hi," she replied. His smile flashed in the sunlight.

Margie poked her in the ribs. "Ah, everyone, this is Margie Browne and this is Checky Janacek..." Sana made hasty introductions. "We went to nursing school together. Is this your... unit?"

Joe pointed to men and called out names. Up close, the soldiers looked less like men and more like boys, grinning and saying hello. Sana met Joe's eyes as people bumped and shouted around them. The two of them pushed over to the ship's rail and leaned against it side by side, looking out together over the sea.

Joe laughed and Sana glanced at him. "Hi," he said again. Men jostled past on the narrow deck, crowding them together. The muscle of his upper arm felt like iron. They held on to the rail to keep their place and she looked down at his hands. An old scar puckered the side of his left hand, as if he had been burned there long ago. She wondered what had happened to him.

"How is your family?" she asked instead, conscious of the people all around.

"They're fine." He was looking at the sunset and did not seem bothered by the crowd. "Isn't that something?"

Sana looked toward the west. The rose and amber splendor of the sky, along with the feeling of Joe's arm tight against her own, brought back the tears she had blinked away while the men were the singing. "Oh, yes. Yes, it is. It's so beautiful. I hope..." she could not think of words to say.

Joe looked at her, then back out to sea. The golden light made his eyes look very blue. "I want to see this through," he said after a while. "I'm going to go out there and keep my head on straight and take care of my guys and see the whole thing through and then go home." He looked back to her. "And start my family."

Sana swallowed hard.

"I'm going to... ah..." Joe's voice trailed off.

"Going to what?" she said after a while.

Joe stared at the last sheen of sunset. "You believe in God?"

"Huh?"

"You believe in God?" He looked at her, then back at the horizon.

Sana took longer to answer this time. "Yes."

He took a deep breath, as if he had been holding it. "Me too." He moved his hand on the rail so that it covered hers. She could feel his calloused palm, warm against the cold, and she leaned in closer to him, wondering what he was going to say.

"I'm thinking pretty hard about this." He paused and she stole a quick glance. He was looking down at their hands on the railing. "It's not going to be any cakewalk when we get there. The

Germans have better equipment than we do. They're dug in and they fight hard."

It was Sana's turn to stare down at the rail. Rumors had been whispered, that they could not possibly win this war. She could feel Joe looking at her, waiting for a response. She finally nodded, not meeting his eyes.

"But if the Lord's with us then we can win." She looked up, relieved. "I figure I can be one of the guys that goes back." He looked at her again, with an open boyish smile that Sana loved immediately. "So I'm going to pray every day that I get through this and go back home. You want to do it with me?"

Sana blinked. She had not thought about praying since she left Cedar Rapids.

"You pray? By yourself?"

The boyish smile disappeared. "Yeah."

"You mean you go to church and you don't drink or anything?"

Joe let go of her hand. "I like a beer once in a while." His voice sounded defensive.

Sana stared down at the darkening water rushing along the boat, the traces of foam and waves disappearing in the ocean beyond. She could never flirt with this man, could not toy with this precious heart. *He's too good. He's way too good for me. He wouldn't want to be with me if he knew what my uncles did.* But she had dreamed of him for so long, of his blue eyes and his sweet decency, and here he was, practically in her arms.

"Well, do you dance?" she finally asked.

He leaned his forearms on the rail and looked up at her, his eyes crinkling at the corners with laughter. The grin was back. "Yes, I dance. I'll dance you right off your feet. Anything else you want to know about me?"

She could not help smiling. His face lit up again.

"I'll ask when I'm ready." In spite of herself she arched a teasing brow and added, "Later."

"When's later?"

"Later." She felt her smile growing.

"So, ah, what do you think about the prayer idea?"

His gaze was intense. The world hung silent, waiting for her reply.

"All right," she said. "I will."

Chapter Five

North Africa

Black waves slapped the side of the little craft. Joe gripped his rifle in one hand and a four-foot metal pipe packed with explosives in the other, staring into the darkness ahead, straining to catch sight of the approaching shore. Sweat gathered under his arms and trickled down his back.

Ratliff nudged his arm. "There," he whispered, pointing to a darker mass ahead. They could hear surf breaking on the shore. "I get to shoot at stuff now, right, sir?"

Joe grinned. "Yeah." Their objective was to capture a battery high above the harbor, a strategic fort armed with massive guns that could shoot five miles out to sea. Then more troops would land and join them, and they would all advance into Arzew while the rest of the force came ashore in safety.

The landing craft's keel scraped across sand and they bumped to a stop. The ramp splashed down and men charged out through the water onto the beach and took the hills at a run. When they came closer to the fort they found barbed wire looping through darkness and they slowed down, pulling out cutters and working their way through the wire as quietly as they could. Joe directed his soldiers into position and glanced back down the hill. He could not see their mortars yet.

"*Qui va là?*"

He froze. A sentry wearing a French field helmet stood outlined against the sky, not fifteen feet away.

"*Qui est-ce?*" some Ranger called back, buying time as two soldiers circled behind the man. They jumped the sentry and took him down before he could call a warning, but a sudden blast of machine gun fire from the battery walls tore up the ground in front of them.

"Come on!" Joe bolted for the fort. Machine gun fire spurted in the darkness and dirt popped around his feet. A mortar blasted out from behind them, the shot arcing over their heads towards the fort, but it landed too far to the right to do any damage.

He spun around, sucked in a huge breath and yelled, "Come back left and pour it on!" The next volley whistled over and exploded squarely inside the fort.

The machine gun stopped. Joe leaped for the wall and scrambled over the parapet, dropping down right in front of a French soldier standing guard with a rifle loose in his hands. Joe had slung his own rifle over his shoulder for the climb up the hill, but he swung his heavy metal pipe full force at the guard's ribs and the man went down just as more Rangers opened fire at the fort's main entrance. Yellow lights blinked on and sluggish moan of a siren spiraled up into a screaming wail.

Now men were running everywhere. Another mortar shell hit a building and smoke furled across the sky. Joe saw Robichaux drop down from the wall, followed by Sedlack and then Ratliff. The big guns would be on the other side of the fort, pointing out to sea. He took off running in what he hoped was the right direction, threading his way through a smoky maze of trucks and piles of ordnance. People were shouting and guns were firing but he kept running and did not look back.

The blocky concrete base of a harbor gun appeared out of the smoke right in front of him. He signaled the platoon to fan out along the line of armaments. Everyone jumped to pack the long barrels full of explosives, with Sedlak covering them from one side and Garcia from the other. But in the dusty confusion no one seemed to notice them, so at his signal they unhurriedly lit their fuses with careful precision. Then they all bolted for cover. Joe flung himself down behind a little cinderblock shed and felt someone hit the ground next to him. He looked over and met Garcia's eyes. They stuck their fingers in their ears and put their heads back down.

An orange-white blast split the night and the ground bucked in a great rolling shock beneath him. Hot air roared overhead in a whirling rush. The explosions rolled on and on and Joe began to wonder if he had overestimated the amount of explosives needed to destroy the guns. The whole cliff, fort and all, seemed to be blowing up, and if it did then he had just ruined his chance to live through the war. After what seemed like a long time while the earth stopped shaking. He opened his eyes.

Garcia was still flat in the dirt, arms over his helmet. Joe poked him in the ribs.

Other helmeted heads were rising from the ground, faces peering out to see what damage had been done. Someone started to cheer and they jumped up to look at the line of guns, now tangled wreckage strewn along the cliff.

"Wow! Wow!" Taffington was babbling with excitement, jumping up and down. Sedlak stood with both fists high in the air, howling wordless triumph into the smoke. Garcia grabbed Joe's hand and gave him a handshake that almost shook his arm off. *"Bueno. Bueno."*

Joe grinned, savoring the metallic stink of molten steel. His first real demolition mission had just gone off without a hitch. "Yeah." He gripped Garcia's hand and shook it back. "Good."

After they finished cheering they joined the rest of the force. No one had anything worse than scrapes and bruises, and they were now in full control of the fort. The defenders had barricaded themselves into a bomb shelter, so the Rangers surrounded it and called on them to surrender. When no one replied Robichaux tossed a grenade down the vent. Coughing men soon walked out with their hands in the air. The battery commander came last, still dressed in pajamas, along with a disheveled woman wrapped in a blanket. Everyone had a good laugh at the sight.

A bloom of mortar fire lit up the western sky and the laughter stopped. Somewhere else, another fort was putting up a better fight. Joe called his sections to order. His next objective was to secure an oil refinery that would be useful for the invasion, if they could take it before it was sabotaged by the French, or the Italians or Germans or whoever was out there fighting back. Another flash of light bloomed, to the east this time, and another thunderous explosion shook the ground. The battle for North Africa was on.

Boom. Sana could hear the roar of heavy guns as she stood on deck with Adele in the cold gray dawn, watching soldiers climb over the side of the ship and jump into things that looked like little rafts. Another *boom* rumbled over the water, growling low like thunder, and then another one.

Whenever a boat full of soldiers headed for shore, the men turned and waved until they disappeared into the smoke screen drifting across the water. A thick mist hid everything else from sight, glazing the ship with moisture and beading their hair with tiny droplets. Sana licked her lips and tasted salt.

The sounds of guns rolled on. "I can't believe they're fighting us," Sana said. "Why would the French fight Americans? I thought they were on our side."

"Maybe they're Germans," Adele said. "They said the Germans would fight hard." A thin crackle of rifle fire chattered over the growling guns. "Something must have gone wrong."

"All nurses report to B-deck," rang the loudspeakers. It was time to leave the boat. Sana's heart raced and her palms sweated as she picked up her packs and followed Adele down the narrow steps to the deck below. Seamen moved along the line of nurses, adjusting their gear and giving advice.

"Keep the straps on your pack and your helmet loose, ma'am, and untie your boots. If you fall in the water instead of the boat, kick everything off right away, otherwise it'll pull you down and drown you," an earnest young sailor told her, and moved on down the line to the next group. "Keep your straps loose, ma'am..."

Sana loosened her twenty-five pound pack and let it ease down her back. All their musette bags with their special belongings were stowed somewhere in the ship's hold. Now they carried packs stuffed with medical supplies and C-rations instead.

She looked over the rail at the foamy gray-green waves below, wondering how cold the water was. The metal rail felt icy under her hand.

The soldiers in line before them were climbing one by one over the edge and down the side of the boat. Sana leaned out to see how they jumped into the landing craft. As each man reached the bottom rung he paused for a moment, judging the waves, then leaped over the water as the craft rose to the top of an eight-foot swell. Then the landing craft fell away down the side of the wave again and the next man stepped into position.

"Miss Adele?" Jo Ellen's voice was strained and her teeth were chattering. Sana turned around and looked. Her face looked like the color of bleached linen and her lips were turning blue.

"Yes?"

"Miss Adele, I don't swim."

Adele patted her arm. "I don't think you'll have to, dear." Jo Ellen swallowed hard and clenched her jaw. "You just stay here by Obie," Adele said. "She's been out on the water before."

"Oh, ma'am, I don't swim neither," Obie said, her brown eyes wide. "I just went on a rowboat one time."

"Well." Adele sounded strained. "It's very natural, completely natural, that we all feel scared under these circumstances. Just stay calm. Here, I know what I'll do." She rearranged them in the line. "Obie and Jo Ellen, I want one of you on each side of me. Marge and Sana, you go first. Everyone watch Marge and Sana."

The line took a sudden move forward and a sailor tugged at Sana's arm, pulling her up to the edge of the rail. She would be next. She looked down at the tossing white foam and quickly looked away. Margie, Jo Ellen, Adele and Obie were all watching her with the same kind of intense concentration they used when assisting in a particularly difficult surgery. Sana made a face and Obie grinned.

Margie shook out a cigarette and tried to light up. The wind was damp and her hands were shaking, and after five attempts she ran out of matches. She flung the empty matchbook and the rest of her pack right over the rail.

"If I fall in, tell somebody I can't swim," she whispered to Sana.

Sana gripped her arm. "If you fall in I'll jump in with you."

Margie looked astonished. "You swim?"

"They say you'll float if you move your hands and feet."

"Why did I throw away my smokes?" Margie lamented. "Right when I need them?"

Two seaman led Sana to the side and helped her over. She put a foot on the outside ladder, then the other, straining to keep her loosened boots on her feet as she scrabbled for the rungs. Step by step she went down, gripping the wet rails so hard that her knuckles turned white and her hands cramped, fixing her gaze at each rung as she passed it in order not to look down and lose her nerve. When she finally reached the bottom rung she looked over her shoulder for the little boat. There it was, tossing on the waves, much too far away.

"Come on! We'll catch you!" Soldiers in the landing craft were holding out their arms, motioning her to jump. "On three! One, two..." Sana threw herself toward them and hands caught her as she came down. Margie tumbled in next to her. More hands hustled them along to the other side of the boat and they both looked back at the troopship and waved goodbye, just like everyone else was doing.

An acrid drift of smoke screen surrounded them, cutting off their view. *Boom.* The guns sounded closer now. Nobody spoke as they bobbed along.

I didn't pray yet today, Sana realized with a start. She had told Joe that she would pray every day. *Of all the times to forget.* She mulled over her childhood prayers, working through the time-worn phrases, but the gunfire kept distracting her and she finally put her face in her hands and begged God to just get her to shore without drowning or being shot.

"You okay?"

Sana looked up. Margie and a young soldier were watching her. "I was praying."

Margie gave half a smile. "That's g--"

"Get down!" someone yelled. Sana and Margie ducked. "Exit the craft when" — the words were lost in a watery crash as the boat slammed to a stop and a ramp splashed down into the green waves. "Move out! Move out!" Men jumped off the ramp into water that came up to their necks.

Sana froze. Her feet would not move. Two soldiers grabbed her and dragged her along with them as they jumped. Icy water slapped her face and broke over her helmet. She went under and came back up, coughing and floundering, but the men pulled her through the surf until her feet touched ground. *Boom. Boom.* Now the ground shook when the guns thundered. A patter of rifle fire crackled and sand spurted up in front of her.

Margie grabbed her hand and pulled her into a stumbling run. Someone was shouting but the roar around them swallowed up the words. Get *under cover.* Her loose wet boots slid around on her feet as she lurched through the sand. A pile of lumber on the beach turned out to be an abandoned pier and the two women dove beneath it.

For a long time the wood frame rattled above them when the guns sounded, but after a while there was no more rifle chatter or spurting sand. Sana finally sat up and looked around. Troops were still arriving from out of the mist, wading ashore and running past them. She huddled against Margie, shivering from nerves and cold.

Finally soldiers fanned out over the beach and the big guns quieted down. A group of people in damp olive drab coveralls walked past their pier. One of them was shorter than the rest, with a busty figure and wet blonde curls straggling out beneath a helmet.

"Checky, is that you?" Sana called.

"Frenchie!" A bright round face looked around. "Hey, girl, how'd you get all wet?" Sana struggled out from under the pile of wood and into Checky's warm hug. Margie rolled out after her.

"Look, everybody, this is Sana Toledo and Margie Browne," Checky called out.

"Toledo? Like Toledo Ohio?" a man asked with a smile. Sana

recognized him from the boat, but her face felt too cold and stiff to smile back. He held out a hand to help Margie get up. "You girls okay?"

"Margie Browne," Margie said, shaking his hand. "Browne with an 'e'. Are you a doctor?"

"Nice to meet you," the man said. "Uh, yes. John Schmidt. Uh, major."

"Pleased to meet you, Major Schmidt." Margie's smile looked very fetching.

"What on earth happened to your hair?" Sana asked Checky. "Didn't you have braids this morning?"

"I cut it."

"Just now?"

"I didn't have anything to do on that little boat, so I decided to cut it."

"I helped her," Schmidt said.

"Well, I was scared to death the whole time." Margie sounded a little miffed. "I wouldn't think somebody would do something like that during a landing." Sana suddenly felt warm enough to smile.

They tied up their watery bootlaces, pulled on their packs, and walked down the beach to a tumbledown building under a grove of palm trees, where the rest of their unit stood around comparing stories. Adele, soaking wet from boots to helmet, stood at the door with a clipboard and checked off names.

"All you girls go inside," she said. "There's good water so fill your canteens. Eat something before we go."

Inside, soldiers were clearing garbage and bloody clothes off a grimy floor. Jo Ellen was sitting perched on her helmet, combing her hair into a little flip. Obie squatted beside her, tearing into a can of rations. Sana sat down and Obie held out the can in silent invitation.

"Jeet?"

"Huh?"

Obie nodded at the half-eaten can of hash. "Jeet yet?"

Sana shook her head. "Uh, no, thank you."

75

"Just try a bitty bit." Sana finally took a taste from the tip of Obie's mess-kit fork. The food felt greasy in her mouth and as soon as she swallowed it upset her stomach. She wrinkled up her nose in disgust and Obie gave her a reproving look.

"It's better'n what my folks got back home."

Sana wondered what the folks back home could possibly be eating. "I'm still a little seasick." Obie shrugged and finished the rest of the can by herself.

When night fell they all lay down in their damp clothes and tried to sleep, but flashes of artillery fire lit up the room like lightening and *booms* still shook the ground. When the call finally came to head out for their first assignments, Sana felt more relieved than anything else. Adele packed everyone's pockets with extra syringes and morphine.

"Lord knows what you'll find out there. Maybe this will help those poor boys. Be strong and God be with you," she said as they filed out the door.

Sana and Checky squeezed into the back seat of a jeep. Soldiers holding machine guns crowded in with them. As they tore off into the dark with the rest of the convoy, the driver yelled over the roar, "They're still fighting in town so everybody stay quiet 'til we get to the aid station."

Sana and Checky exchanged amused glances. Another person sitting with them leaned over, peering at their faces in the dark. "Hi there, Checky. Who's this?"

Sana recognized the doctor from the beach. "Hi, Dr. Schmidt."

"Oh, I remember you. Toledo Ohio, the one from France." A flash of artillery fire lit the sky and a boom followed.

The man sitting in front next to the driver turned around and held out his hand. "Bob Beaufort." The jeep lurched over a pothole. "Chest surgeon. I'm from Nashville."

"Nice to meet you, Dr. Nashville," Sana said, holding on to her seat with one hand and shaking hands with the other. "I mean, Dr. Beaufort."

"Frenchie and me went to nursing school together," Checky said. "In Iowa. This's the first time I ever met southern people.

You guys talk so funny."

Beaufort flashed a smile and winked. "Honey, let me tell you about the south. That's where the men are real men and women are real happy about it."

Checky blinked. Sana leaned forward. "Does anybody know what's going on?"

"Shhh," one of the gunners called. They were driving between buildings now.

"I doubt it," Schmidt said.

The jeep pulled up to a chain-link gate and the driver muttered a password to the guards. Inside the fence, soldiers helped the nurses out and took their packs. The night was so black that Sana could not see their faces.

"Over here." Someone took Sana's arm and led her forward in the dark. She stumbled over rocks. Somewhere in front of her a door rasped open and then she was pushed through the overlapping folds of a blackout curtain. She heard a moan.

Her guide turned on a flashlight. Wounded men were everywhere, rows and rows of them lying across the floor of a cavernous room, more than could be seen in the flashlight's dim circle. Blood seeped through dirty uniforms and pooled out from under dark red bandages that had been saturated hours before. Some men were unconscious; others groaned or clenched their jaws in pain. A voice in the back of the room pleaded for a drink of water.

More people crowded in. A voice started giving orders. "There's a room up those stairs with a table and a light bulb. Doctors, go set up for surgery. Nurses, triage for severity of wounds, need for surgery, and chance of survival. Surgery cases go over here and then into OR one at a time. One medic goes with each nurse to do whatever she says to do. Complete blackout as you work. No lights except flashlights. There's snipers outside."

"I'll take your pack, ma'am." The medic assigned to her was already covered with blood. He held his flashlight for her and they moved to the nearest soldier, a young man with red hair and freckles. He was half conscious, but one forearm was gone and blood crusted the bandage around it. An empty syrette was clipped to his shirt and one black M was scrawled on his forehead to record a shot of morphine. The next soldier had a broken jaw and a slash wound gaping open along his thigh.

"Don't you close the wounds?" Sana asked her medic.

"No, ma'am. We just sprinkle sulfa and give morphine and bandage them up. And strap 'em on a litter."

The man after that had a chest wound oozing bloody froth. The one after that was dead. Sana took pulses and checked under bandages, sending the most urgent cases to surgery. Her medic gave morphine shots and marked M's on foreheads with a grease pencil.

A dark-haired, good-looking boy stirred under her hands as she took his pulse. "Who... are... you?" The floor beneath his head was dark with blood and when he opened his eyes the pupils were large and uneven.

"We're the nurses. You're going to be all right now," Sana soothed. There was no M on the soldier's forehead and she patted over the his pockets, looking for the little medical pack with the single-dose syrette inside. A red-soaked dressing was wrapped around his middle and when she moved it, loops of intestine slid across his belly to the floor.

"So... thirsty..."

"Is somebody taking water around?" she asked the medic.

"There isn't any more water, ma'am. It got cut off."

Sana licked her lips and pulled out her canteen. The medic moved around to prop up the boy's head and together they managed to give him a drink.

"I gave out all my water already," the medic apologized. "I can't stand to hear them ask for a drink like that. Does this one go to OR?"

She wiped her hands on her pants and knelt there for a moment, looking around at the bobbing circles of flashlight, the bodies covering the floor.

"No," she said at last. "Just morphine."

Oh, God. Oh, God, help these poor men.

"Ma'am?" She looked at the medic. He was crying. She patted him on the back and silently handed him her canteen. He gave it back to her untouched and put his hand under her elbow to help her up.

They worked on men until they ran out of morphine. Sana sent her medic to find more, then sat down to rest. The room was still inky black except for bobbing flashlights and bloody bodies illuminated by the circles of light. How long had she been here? A flashlight shone close by, lighting up a new line of wounded men lying across the floor.

"Sana, I want you to go up to surgery." Adele's voice came from the same direction as the flashlight. "Up these stairs." The light pointed to a stairway. "Where's those supplies that're supposed to be coming? All these doctors and only one scalpel up there, for heaven's sake. Who's in charge around here?"

Adele moved off and Sana pulled out her flashlight and climbed the stairs. At the top she found Obie standing in a little room, flashlight propped between her jaw and shoulder, rinsing a surgical clamp with a thin trickle of alcohol. The rusty sink in front of her had no tap or handles on it.

"Where do I go?"

"Over there," Obie said with a nod toward a door. "They got a blanket hung over the window for blackout so open the door slow."

Sana cautiously opened the door. A light bulb hung from the ceiling and two blankets covered part of a wall. People clustered around a table in the middle of the room.

"Here. Nurse, hold this here," someone said to her. Sana moved to hold the patient's jaw open and an ether mask in place. Beaumont from Nashville, his coverall still sandy from the beach, was using a pair of surgical scissors to pull out a shard of metal lodged deep in the patient's groin. The nurse who had been holding the ether mask stepped back, shaking her hands as if they were numb.

"Get me that other clamp again," the doctor said, going deep into the bloody tissue for another fragment. "And I need sutures."

A medic hurried out and when he opened the door a rush of air stirred the hanging blankets.

The light bulb exploded and the room turned black. Shots rang off the walls. People yelled and Sana tried to duck while still holding the patient's jaw open and ether mask in place.

"Hey!" a voice shouted. The curtain stirred again, letting a slice of light into the room. Someone was yelling out the window. "Hey you! Cut that out!"

"Get him down!" People blundered into each other. Things whizzed through the room and smacked the wall. "Doggone you, get down!"

They heard a new kind of explosion outside. "Got him!" came a yell.

Everybody relaxed. Flashlights turned on and Beaumont went back to work.

"Where are those sutures?" he asked.

"Right here, sir," someone said.

"What took you so long?

"I had a good line on that sniper so I shot him, sir." Everyone murmured appreciation.

"Who's got the ether? Is that still you over there, Ohio? Know anything about anesthesia?"

"No, Dr. Beaumont," Sana said.

"No you're not Ohio or no you don't know anything about anesthesia?"

"I'm Toledo and I haven't done anesthesia for two years."

"That's good as an outhouse breeze around here, sweetheart. I like for pretty girls to call me Nash." Sana made a face at him in the dark as he tied off the last suture and moved back from the table. Medics stepped in to remove the patient. "Ever seen anything like this before?"

"No, sir."

"Me either." The next casualty was laid on the table and the team's dentist helped Sana place the ether mask. Everyone trained their flashlights on the body to find the wound. The chest was purple with bruising and a ragged gash packed with blood-soaked rags ran the entire length of the soldier's leg.

"We're out of sutures again," someone said.

"Use hair," the dentist said. "Who's got long hair?"

They all looked at Sana.

"Ohio, pull out some hair. Somebody else hold the ether."

The dentist took the mask and Sana disentangled her heavy braid. She jerked out hairs and found a shallow tray to soak them in alcohol. There were no sterile dressings, only a pile of bloody bandages under the table.

The door creaked open and they all stopped what they were doing until it closed again without disturbing the blackout. Adele spoke into the silence. "There's no more sutures. The ships aren't unloaded yet. We're setting up a water station. I've got the medics looking through the men's pockets for extra morphine and I've got soldiers looking through all the buildings for anything we can use. So far they found some navy blue uniform capes and red sashes. We're using capes for blankets. Do you want the sashes?"

The dentist made a strangled noise halfway between irritation and disbelief. "Who is supposed to be in charge around here?"

"Just bring everything," Nash said. "We need sutures, Adele."

"Yes sir." Adele took a breath as if to say something else, then left the room instead. Sana jerked out more hair and then went back to take over the ether mask.

They used the hairs until Adele came back with a spool of thread. Sana's hands grew numb from the strain of holding the mask in place, and she traded off with the dentist throughout the night as bodies were carried in and out and the heap of bloody rags on the floor grew higher.

Finally no one put another patient on the table. They all wiped their hands on their uniforms and stumbled down the stairway, bumping along the walls in their fatigue. Outside the air was fresh and dawn was glowing. Someone handed Sana a tin cup of lukewarm coffee. She sipped at it and rubbed her gummy eyes, then saw her hands, still covered with sticky blood. She rubbed them on her pants again and looked around. Large dark shapes slowly turned into trucks and buildings in the morning light.

Adele walked over, carrying two dark capes. "I saved these for you." Her face looked haggard and specks of blood smeared the pink flowered edge of pajama showing under the collar of her coverall, but she smiled at Sana. "You did good last night." She tucked a cape around Sana's shoulders and handed her the other one. "Another medical unit just got in, so you can go get some sleep now." She pointed to another building. "There's a room for the nurses in there."

"Where are we?" Sana asked through a yawn.

"Arzew."

"I mean, what is this place?"

"It's the French hospital. Go get some rest, honey. There's rations in there for you." A medic came out of the hospital and dumped an armload of dirty bandages on the ground. Adele frowned. "Those bandages need washed right away because I don't know when we'll get any more. And there's four hundred men, the ones who lived anyway, who're going to wake up hungry... Colonel!" Adele started walking toward a group of officers. "Go on and get some sleep," she called over her shoulder. "If we get more wounded I'll wake you up."

Sana looked around. The hospital behind her was quiet. No nurses were in sight. She walked across to the building Adele had pointed out and found a room filled with people sleeping on the floor. She pulled one cape around her waist, draped the other around her shoulders, and fell asleep as soon as she lay down.

Chapter Six

Arzew

Obnoxious honking tugged Sana out of a deep well of slumber. She pulled a cape over her head and twisted around, trying to get comfortable on the concrete floor, but first the sand and grit against her cheek bothered her, and then she realized that her capes smelled like manure. They kept sliding apart, letting the cold air seep in around her middle. Someone outside was shouting orders. Finally she gave up and opened her scratchy eyes.

Women in dark blue capes were sleeping all around her. Sana stretched, ran her tongue around her sticky teeth, and wondered where her toothbrush was. Then she wondered where a toilet was. She got up, pulled on a cape, and walked outside into the gray light of a cloudy day.

A soldier was spreading wet bandages over a clothesline. "Holy cow! A woman!"

"Can you please tell me where the latrines are?"

"Uh, over there... well, maybe not over there... I don't know where a woman would go... I mean, go..."

"All right," Sana said. She wandered back inside the building and followed a smell to a lavatory down the hall. The walls were foul and the toilets inside stopped up with waste, but at least it was private. A tarnished mirror hung over a sink. She peered at her dirty face and started to run her hands over her hair, then stopped when she saw dry blood packed underneath her fingernails. She tried to wash her hands, but when she turned the taps no water came out of the rusty faucet. She pulled her cape closer and went back outside.

The soldier seemed to have recovered from the shock of seeing a woman. He nodded at her as he pulled another dripping cloth from the pile and wrung water out of it.

"Did you wash all those?" Sana asked.

"Yes ma'am." He yawned. "All night."

"Is there anything to drink?"

He pointed to a group of people standing by the hospital door. "There's coffee."

"Thank you." Sana trailed over. The coffee was black and thin, but at least it was hot. She sat down on an empty crate and warmed her hands around the cup.

A thin cold breeze was blowing. Soldiers tended a barrel of water set over a fire, making instant coffee with their rations. A few dipped out water with their helmets for a makeshift wash and shave, working up lather with scraps of soap and taking turns peeking into a little mirror.

People everywhere were washing bandages. Another group was opening little individual cans of rations, dumping them into pots over the fires, and then spooning warmed hash back out onto white china plates. More soldiers carried the filled plates into the hospital. Sana watched them for a while, wondering where the china plates came from. Her stomach growled.

The smells of coffee and hash, the sight of unhurt men working together, all blended into a sense of normal life. A thin streak of sunlight broke through the clouds, brightening the air and gilding the red tile roofs. The sky suddenly blazed blue and gold. Sana closed her eyes and turned her face up to the warmth.

Her thoughts strayed to Joe and his intense blue eyes, the way he had held her gaze and said *I'm going to pray like I've never prayed before.* She had said that she would pray too. *Dear God.* What to say? *Thank you for this coffee.*

He had said that he wanted to go back home and have a family, but after the butchery she had seen last night it seemed unlikely that either of them would get through this war unhurt, especially Joe, since he would be at the front for most of it.

Nevertheless, she had promised him. *Dear God, please take care of Joe, wherever he is. I pray that I can stay awake and do my job today. Amen.*

"Hey." Checky stood in front of her, smiling in the sunlight, her helmet on her head and another one in her hand. "Here's your helmet. You left it in surgery. Look, I found these bars of French soap! Let's go wash up."

They washed their hands and faces and then ate some hash, which tasted better than it had the day before. After that they headed back to the hospital and found Adele outside the door, arguing with a supply sergeant.

"There's no more plates," the sergeant was saying, his arms crossed and his chest stuck out. "We gotta wait and get back what we already gave out before we can feed anybody else."

"All these wounded boys hoping for something to eat and you're telling me they have to wait because you can't use those dishes I saw right over there in that building?" Adele was furious. "You're going to make them wait? Did you eat today, sergeant?"

The sergeant dug in his feet and leaned forward. "Ma'am, those dishes belong to the officers' mess and they are not for enlisted men. If they get broke it comes out of my pay." He rocked back and crossed his arms again.

Adele stared at him. "I am a lieutenant. I am ordering you to get those dishes out right now and put food on every single one of them. I'll pay for them myself if they get broke."

The sergeant turned red and saluted. "Yessir!" He shot her one more furious glare. "I mean ma'am!" He spun on his heel and stalked off.

Adele glowered after him. She turned around and soldiers jumped to get out of her path. Even Sana and Checky stood up straighter when they saw her expression. "Go in and get started," she ordered. "We took in four hundred and seventy wounded last night and there's no beds, no sheets, no plasma, no clean bandages, and we're running out of morphine. The least we can do is feed them." She shook her head. "Those supplies better get here soon or by God I swear I'm going to get them off that boat myself."

***

Deep inside the little desert town of Arzew, Joe crouched behind a mound of rocks and shrub while he studied the rickety barn in front of him. Boards had been knocked out at intervals along its side, creating a perfect hideout to shoot from but not be seen. Garcia had seen a flash of gunfire spurt from one of those gaps.

Joe signaled Robichaux, who already had three grenades hanging loose on his belt and was ready to make a move. Robichaux flashed back a toothy grin. Joe glanced at Ratliff and Taffington. They nodded. Robichaux ran forward, lobbed a grenade and jumped behind a stone water trough. The blast sent bricks and boards sailing overhead and as debris rained down he lobbed his second grenade. Half the barn collapsed and two men in French uniforms stumbled out. Rifles started firing right as Robichaux lobbed his third grenade and a whole troop of men burst out, bayonets fixed and rifles firing, running to break through the surrounding circle of Rangers.

Everything exploded into charging bodies and guns firing. Joe fought through bodies and gunfire until a blow whacked him hard against the trough. Another blow knocked him to the ground and a bullet pinged off the trough above him.

His ears were ringing. He couldn't breathe. The ground tipped crazily beneath him and dirt clouded his eyes. Joe scrabbled with hands and feet, trying to get up, and then something knocked him over again. Pain stabbed his arm and he squinted up into a hairy face not twelve inches away from his.

The eyes in the face bulged out at him and the mouth opened in a shriek. Joe yelled back and frantically scrambled away. There were boots in front of him now, Army boots. Another pair of feet stood next to the boots but there was something was strange about them. Joe blinked dirt out of his eyes and looked again.

86

They were not feet. They were hooves.

He looked up. A black and white goat stood there, bleating at him. Garcia was standing next to the goat, holding out a hand to help him up. "It's okay, *teniente* Vesely. *Cabra, entiende*, okay?

Somebody somewhere was laughing. "Look at all that goat crap."

Joe sat up, trembling, and pushed himself to his feet. Something sticky was all over his nose and mouth. He wiped at his face and his hand came away covered with dirt and blood.

"*Madre.*" Garcia grabbed at Joe's left arm. "Lieutenant, you better sit down."

A flash of agony seared straight up through his shoulder. Garcia was still trying to make him sit down. Joe shook his head, wiped more blood off his face and pointed east. "Take the patrol to the right, over that way. Keep going. I'll catch up." Garcia was arguing. A sudden crackle of rifle fire made them both duck behind the trough and the agony flashed through his arm again, clear up to his head this time, and the world turned dark for a moment.

He shook his head to clear it and gripped at his left arm. Blood felt warm and sticky between his fingers.

"Sir, put your head like this." Garcia made him tip his head back. "Hold your nose." Joe gasped for breath when Garcia pulled his hand away to see the damage to his arm. Four of his soldiers had already been hit, one of them with a thigh blown out by shrapnel. The wounded men had been left behind at a reconnaissance point for the medics to pick up.

"Go," Joe said when he could talk again. His voice sounded funny. "Take the patrol and keep on working east until you meet up to Sedlak's patrol like we said." They had been in continuous action since the capture of Fort du Nord the night before, capturing the refinery and then flushing soldiers out of the port's warehouses. Now they were working their way through Arzew, checking one dusty building after another, finding little groups of soldiers holding out even though the walkie-talkie had reported the city's surrender hours ago.

Garcia was talking. "Yes sir. I will. Keep your head back or you're going to bleed all over yourself. We gotta get you some help."

"No. You have to go now. Don't stop for this," Joe said, speaking as firmly as he could. "Johnson can put a bandage on it and then we'll catch up." Duffer Johnson was the private who carried extra bandages and sulfa for wounds.

"Yes sir. Johnson!" Garcia shouted orders and then looked anxiously back at him.

"Go on," Joe said. "I'll see you at the recon." Garcia nodded and the patrol headed toward the next group of buildings.

Johnson gave him a bandage to hold against his bleeding nose and led him back to the main road. Army trucks and jeeps were already driving along it, ferrying supplies. "Here, sir. Sit down. Let me look under your helmet real quick."

"What for?"

"You got a big ol' dent there." Johnson gently lifted his helmet, peeked underneath and then set it back on his head. "Doesn't look like you got hurt though. Jeez, your nose's bleeding like a stuck pig." Joe kept his head tipped back while Johnson sprinkled sulfa over his arm and tied on a bandage. Blood immediately soaked through.

"Dang." Johnson put his hand over the bloody part of the bandage and pressed hard.

Joe thought he should get up and start walking, but his legs were heavy and his eyelids wanted to close. Johnson pulled out a canteen and shook it, but it was already empty, so he rummaged through his pack and offered Joe a ration bar.

"Maybe you oughta eat something."

Joe managed a grin. The bars were so tough that eating one took thirty minutes of concentrated chewing. "I can't even breathe." He could feel his eyelids closing again.

Johnson jumped up and waved his arms. A truck stopped and two medics got out.

"It's not that bad," Joe protested as they walked over to him. "We're going to go catch up with the patrol."

"I don't think so," said a familiar voice. Joe blinked. The hulking medic in the blood-crusted uniform was Wence Prasky. "How'd you get all covered with poop?"

Joe scowled. "Where's my twenty?"

"Get in," Wence said. "No twenty for you until you get inside."

Joe protested again when he saw the crowd of wounded soldiers inside the vehicle, but Wence squeezed him in anyway. Johnson waved and the truck lurched forward. Someone whimpered at the jolt.

"Let me get a compress on that." Wence deftly snipped off Johnson's bandage and frowned when he saw the wound. "If you don't bleed to death you'll live." He tied off the compress. "Does it hurt?"

"Not too bad."

"Then hold this." He handed Joe a bottle of plasma. "Up high if you can." The needle on the end of the bottle's rubber tubing was inserted into the arm of a soldier stretched out flat on the floor. The soldier's legs were masses of bloody tissue with shards of white bone sticking out. They were strapped together with a rifle for a splint. Joe looked away, feeling queasy.

"How you doing, Praz?" he heard himself say. His lips felt numb.

"Okay." Wence moved to the next soldier. "We must of pulled in about five hundred wounded last night. Guys all shot up every which way. *Sacramente* holy God, what a mess." His new patient was clutching a thigh wound and shaking so hard that his teeth chattered.

Wence set his big hands on the man's shoulders and calmed him down. "There. Easy now. We'll be at the hospital pretty soon." He pressed a surrette against the soldier's upper arm. "That pain's gonna all go away in about ten minutes. Then I'll tuck you in to sleep right here by me. Now, why couldn't you have been born a beautiful woman?" The soldier grinned.

Joe's arm hurt more every time the truck jolted. "How come so many?" he asked, more to distract himself than anything else.

"You guys did good at Fort du Nord but the guys at Oran got caught. The Germans got tipped off after the first assault and tore up them up the minute they hit the beach." Wence rubbed sweat off his forehead and left a fresh streak of blood on it. "One stinking run-down hospital, no water, no plasma, no lights. They had an OR with no water or lights. Wounded coming in all night long."

Joe looked out the back of the truck. Goats were scrabbling for weeds between the dusty buildings. Skinny barefoot boys looked back at him with curious eyes.

"There's a hospital here?"

Wence spat. "You could call it a hospital. I wouldn't put a dog in there. Junk all over the floors, toilets don't work, broken glass all over the place. Oh, I saw that nurse you like, that foreign-looker."

Joe felt better at the thought of nurses being so close by. If women were at the hospital, surely that meant the town was safe. "Did you tell her I said hi?"

Wence shook his head. "Too busy."

"Is it close?"

"Not too far."

The smell of blood thickened in the air and the truck lurched sideways. Joe fought down a wave of nausea and looked around. Bleeding men were packed close all around him. "I don't want to be a pain in the butt but I think I'm gonna be sick."

Wence looked over at him, took away the bottle of plasma, pulled off his helmet and handed it to Joe. Another lurch of the truck made Joe retch into it, helplessly spewing out bile from his griping belly. His whole body throbbed with pain.

Finally he stopped, gasping and gagging from the smell of his own vomit. Wence took the helmet from him and flung the contents out the back of the truck, then took out his canteen, poured a little water into the helmet and swirled it around. He tossed out the second dirty mess, grinned, and clapped the helmet back on his head. Joe thought he would be sick again at the sight

"Aw, geez, sorry..." he said, embarrassed.

"Nah, don't worry about it." Wence pushed him gently backwards until he could lean against something, and then he fell asleep.

He woke up when he heard people outside shouting. The ambulance slowed, bounced, and made one final lurch. A stroke of pain sliced straight through his head. He tried to cry out but his dry tongue was stuck to the roof of his mouth.

"Here we go, soldier. Up you come." Hands were at pulling him and the pain seared again, up and down his arm this time. He wanted to tell the hands to stop, but they made him stand up and walk.

"Wait," he croaked, trying to open his eyes. The light made them hurt and he closed them again. "Wait."

"Right over here, soldier." The hands kept him walking. "This one's ambulatin'," someone said. "Put him over there."

"Drink," Joe whispered. The hands helped him sit down and then he felt a canteen press against his lips. He gulped greedily at the water, panicking when it spilled around his mouth and down his chest, worried that there would be no more.

"Easy. Easy. Slow down." The canteen was taken away and Joe heard a little whimper from somewhere. "Don't worry, there's plenty more." The hands were soothing now, adjusting his arm and helmet so he could lean back. Something pricked his arm and his hand began to feel cold.

"Here." A full canteen nudged his good hand. "Now, stay put."

He was allowed to be still. Joe kept his eyes closed and raised the canteen, trying to sip slowly, but he could not stop himself from drinking until the water was gone. After a while his head felt better and he opened his eyes.

He was sitting up, propped against a wall. A needle was taped into his good arm, with a rubber tube trailing from it to an amber-colored plasma bottle set high on a crate next to him. Other bandaged and bloody soldiers lay on litters or sat along the wall beside him, all connected to rubber tubes and amber bottles like he was.

Joe looked down at his left arm. The bandage was dark and stiff with blood, but he wiggled his fingers, and then, with a great effort, lifted his forearm. Everything still worked. He heaved a sigh and looked around.

Soldiers and medics hustled back and forth, opening crates, shaking out blankets and setting up cots. Someone started hammering and the sound made his head hurt, but he kept on watching as the room slowly turned into something that looked like a hospital ward. Medics began to carry away the men on the litters.

Two pairs of dirty boots stopped in front of him. He looked up and his eyes opened wide. One of the people looking down at him was Wence, and the other was Sana Toledo.

She hunkered down to check his pulse and temperature, her bare fingers touching his skin with a butterfly lightness that raised goosebumps along his arms. She took off his helmet and passed her hand over his head. He stared at her smooth brows and feathery lashes, the lovely curve of her cheek so close to his.

"What'dya think?" Wence asked. Joe looked over, wondering what he was talking about, and then realized that the question was directed not to himself but to Sana.

"Another bottle of plasma. Joe? Can you see my fingers? How many?" She was holding up two fingers.

"I can see you," Joe said. "You have beautiful fingers."

Her dimples flashed. Wence snorted. "Knock out this blockhead. He needs morphine, right? The double dose for nincompoops?" He raised his voice. "I'm on special morphine duty around here. I personally protect the nurses by knocking out all you overheated G.I.s the minute you come off the truck."

A few men grinned. Joe felt a needle stab his right arm. He glared at Wence. "Shut up."

A soldier chuckled. Wence made loud wet kissing noises as he finished the injection. Joe sat, fuming, both arms trapped.

Sana stayed with him after Wence moved on. She and Joe looked at each other, then away, then back again at the same time. Joe grinned and Sana flushed. She shook her head and busily tended to him, replacing the empty bottle of plasma with a full one and cutting off his tattered left sleeve. She untied his bandage and checked the wound, brushing the skin of his upper arm and the side of his chest, and the intensity of mingled pain and pleasure made him twitch beneath her hands. She finished her examination by flexing his fingers, and when she touched the old burn scar on his left palm she looked up at him with a question in her eyes. Joe said nothing, conscious of the other men close by.

"Does it hurt?" she asked. "The morphine should help." Her voice still sounded cool and elegant, even though she was dressed in a man's green uniform and soaked with layers of drying blood.

"Looking at you helps." His tongue felt thick.

She smiled and leaned in closer, making little adjustments to his bandage. "I prayed for you this morning," she whispered.

She loved him. She understood him. She was like him and she was the best person he had ever met. Joe tried to lift his good right arm, in order to take her hand, and she saw the little movement and clasped his cold fingers in her warm ones.

"I think I prayed more since I got off the boat than I ever did my whole life." The words came out a little slurred and he wanted to laugh at the funny sound of his own voice. "An' look what happened. Here I am." He frowned at all the blood on her coverall. Even her ears were spattered with it. "All dirty. You okay?"

"I'm fine." She smiled again. He loved her smile. "They say we'll have cots to sleep on tonight, so we've got all the comforts. There's regular food now, too. Spam. You can have some when you wake up."

All of a sudden Joe thought of his platoon still doggedly fighting their way through the town, going from one danger into another, fighting without him. "When can I get up?"

She shook her head. "Not yet. I need to go now. I'm on duty."

"Wait." Joe tightened his fingers on hers. Her face was blurring. There was no time to waste. "I love you."

"I love you too." A tear ran down her face. "I always loved you."

He tried to raise his other hand to wipe her cheek, but his arm got tangled up in rubber tubing instead and the plasma bottle tipped off the crate. She reached across him to catch it and her smooth neck brushed his scratchy jaw. She smelled like some kind of flowery soap, and even though he was floating off the scent of her nearness stirred him.

"I can't wait to marry you," he said, and then he went to sleep.

When he woke up it was dark. It felt so good to lay still. After a while he realized there was a blanket over him, and when he finally opened his eyes there was a little bit of light, just enough to see that he was surrounded by other sleeping men. He was in some kind of bed. He closed his eyes again, unutterably tired.

Someone near him was snoring and another man grunted and mumbled in a dream. Further away, someone started sobbing and the sound made him shiver. A brilliant white light flashed, followed by a sickening *boom*. The sobs turned into a scream and Joe jerked upright, a shot of pain stabbing through his arm and shoulder.

"It's okay, guys," a young woman's voice called. "That's not their guns. They're our guns. You're safe." A nurse was walking through the rows of cots. "It's a nice clear night and the whole U.S. Army is out there protecting us. Hey, do you guys know this song? "Oh, we ain't got a barrel of money, maybe we're ragged and funny, but we'll travel along, singin' a song, side by side...'" Her voice had a plaintive, back-country twang that sounded endearingly homey against the rumbling gunfire.

Joe relaxed again. If there was a woman here, and she could sing so calmly, then they must be safe. The next *boom* did not sound as frightening and he drifted off to sleep, listening to her song.

A hand shook Sana's shoulder. "Hey. Frenchie. Wake up. Rise and shine." Obie's voice paused and Sana heard her yawn. "I took care of your Ranger all night. Him and all his friends. You can have him back now."

Sana stretched luxuriously. Supplies had finally come in, and the nurses' canvas bags had arrived along with cots, regular food and real coffee. Soldiers had scrubbed down their sleeping quarters and built them a latrine. She sat up, pushed hair back from her face, and pulled on her boots. She could get a plate of breakfast and a helmetful of hot water for her morning wash before she started ward duty.

Her Ranger. "Is he doing all right?" she asked, with a delicious sense of ownership.

"Slept like a baby all night long. It was pretty quiet, except for the artillery. We sterilized every single instrument for morning rounds."

"Thank you."

"And it was a lot of work so don't use them up too fast." Obie yawned again, kicked off her boots, and fell backwards on her cot. "Goodnight."

Sana found Adele at the hospital door, holding a clipboard in one hand and tugging at her curly gray-brown hair with the other. "Oh, Sana, here you are. I'm assigning you to O'Neal with debridement in that ward where your Ranger is." She grinned.

"Yes, ma'am."

"You've got five special cases. Check them first. Medics are to shave and toilet every patient. Everybody gets a bath and pajamas today. Get a tray ready for debridement and make sure the used bandages get washed right away."

"Yes, ma'am."

"Oh. Wait a minute." Adele fished some cigarette packs out of her pocket. "Here."

"You're an old softie," Sana told her. Adele waved her clipboard in dismissal and Sana headed off to her ward, smiling all along the way at the thought of her special Ranger waiting there.

She looked for Joe the second she stepped inside the tent. There he was, sound asleep on a cot. She longed to sit by him, stroke his hair and wake him up, but she contented herself with tucking his blanket around his bare shoulders before she went to check her specials.

Of the five, two were still unconscious. One was groggily blinking at the canvas tent above him, and the other two were playing gin. They dropped their cards when she walked up and one of them whistled.

"Did I die and go to heaven?" he asked. Sana could see that one of his legs was gone, but his voice sounded strong.

"Nope," she told him. "You're alive and well. Looking pretty good yourself, soldier." He winked and she laughed, happy to share the joy she felt toward the world.

The second soldier looked younger and sicker, with bandages over one eye and half his face. He was naked under the sheet and Sana tucked it firmly around his dirty chest before she took his wrist.

"We'll give you a bath today," she told him. The boy blushed clear to his ears. "And a shave, too. You'll feel better when you get cleaned up."

"I feel better already," he said. "Uh, do you have a smoke?"

She gave him two of Adele's cigarettes and then went back to Joe, who was still sleeping. She could not resist smoothing back his hair this time, and his eyelids creased and he moved a little beneath her touch. She traced her finger along the thin white scar that ran down through his stubble of beard, then took his hand to check his pulse. It was full and even. She placed his hand back under the blanket and brushed the bare skin of his side. It was smooth and warm.

He stirred again and a tender pang shot through her heart. She breathed in his warm scent. She loved his straight nose, the firm line of his lips, his eyebrows that drew down level over his eyes when he was serious. If they both lived through the war, they would get married and she would have him all her own like this forever. She would sleep in his arms every night. The sweet pang stirred her heart again.

"Hello, hon." O'Neal, the dentist who had shown her how to hold the ether mask, came in with a cup of coffee and looked around. "Ready for me?"

"Hello, sir." Sana stood up. "Everything's ready. Will you please take a look at these five specials before we start?"

O'Neal joked for a while with the two men playing cards, then began his rounds. His main purpose that day was debridement, the painful task of scraping away decaying tissue from the ragged, half-scabbed wounds. Men winced and gasped under his scalpel, gripping the sides of their cots and clenching their jaws through the procedure. Sana ordered the medics to give morphine well ahead of time to the soldiers with extensive wounds, hoping to dull the pain.

O'Neal cut and swabbed his way steadily down the row. He kept his coffee cup with him, sending a medic for refills between patients. Sana helped him with the difficult cuts and kept him stocked with supplies.

Cut, swab. Cut, swab. O'Neal was using up linens as if he were in a fully-serviced hospital back in the States. Sana tightened her lips as she watched him toss one after another, only slightly smudged with pus and blood.

After he used twenty-one bandages on a single man, she whispered, "Dr. O'Neal, we have to wash all the dirty bandages before we go to sleep tonight."

He handed his empty coffee cup to a nearby medic. "I know."

"Maybe we shouldn't use so many."

He frowned at her. "It's more important to be careful with these wounds." He bent over the next patient. Sana counted as he swabbed and tossed. Nineteen for one patient. Seventeen for the next. Twenty-five for the one after that. She pulled him aside when they came to the end of the row.

"Dr. O'Neal, we're running low on bandages."

He sniffed. "I'm not going to lower my standards of practice just because a few more linens have to be washed."

"That's not what I talking about, sir, I'm just saying that..."

"If you had attended medical school, as I have, you would know about the danger of sepsis and the importance of using only sterile materials." His voice was loud enough to make the men look around. She caught sight of Joe, wide awake now and watching the argument. The surgeon raised his voice another notch. "That's much more important than orderlies staying up late to wash a few bandages. You can't be afraid of a little work around here, nurse."

Sana stared at him. "Sir, I know about sepsis. We're just not in a situation where we can afford not to think about—"

"Ask these brave soldiers if they care if they care about how many bandages I use." O'Neal flung out his arm in a theatrical gesture. "I think you ought to be a little more concerned about keeping them alive and a little less concerned about laundry."

The men all looked at her. Sana stood her ground and raised an eyebrow at O'Neal. This doctor might be rude, and he might be embarrassing her in front of the whole ward, but he was not nearly as frightening as her uncle Abraham, or any of her other uncles either. Besides, he was wrong. "Sir, we are all very much concerned with the men's lives. That's not my point. I am talking about the work of the whole ward here."

The patients looked back at O'Neal. His neck flushed a dull red. "I will be talking to your senior officer about this insubordinate attitude of yours. I'll be talking to Colonel Kelsey himself."

Sana looked him right in the eye. "Yes, sir. He should know about this."

They glared at each other and then turned to the next patient. The medics went back to their work, clattering basins and bedpans in the silent tent. Sana gritted her teeth and focused on the next patient. Sixteen bandages. Twenty.

Joe was getting his sponge bath just as they came to his cot. The medic hastily pulled his wash basin out of the doctor's way and Joe jerked up his sheet, anchoring it to his middle with his good hand. Sana smiled at him. A flush rose along his cheekbones.

"Hello, doc," he said, keeping his eyes on the surgeon.

"Feeling pretty good this morning, huh, soldier? Is it just the arm here, nurse?" O'Neal asked.

"Yes, sir. Just the arm. A bullet wound."

"Looks pretty good," the doctor murmured, examining the

wound. It was already closing, with healthy scab tissue forming under a neat row of black sutures. "A little more rest, soldier, and I think you'll be all right."

"How long before I get back to my company, sir?"

O'Neal shook his head. "Just get some rest. You'll be here a while." He threw a cold stare at Sana. "With these pretty nurses."

Sana looked at Joe, anticipating a smile.

He would not look at her. "Yes, sir."

The doctor finished and the medic stepped forward to continue the bath, crowding her away from the cot. Sana looked back as she followed O'Neal, and caught Joe's intense blue stare aimed straight at her. He was frowning. At *her*? Was he taking the doctor's side against her? How could he do that after saying that he loved her last night? Maybe he had just been silly from loss of blood. Maybe he said things like that to every woman. She was a fool to think that a man like him would want to actually marry her.

Maybe he didn't like women who argued with men. Sana clenched her teeth to hold back a hot flush of tears. If that was how he really was, then it was over. She could not possibly love a man who could be so petty. A fresh pain twisted in her heart at the thought of losing him and being all alone in the world again.

She set up the next patient for O'Neal, mechanically smiling at the nervous man who could see the scalpel coming. Maybe someday she would find another guy. But no one else would ever be the same as Joe Vesely. Even if she could not marry him she would probably just go on loving him forever, until the lonely day she died.

O'Neal bent over the wound, an ugly laceration of the chest and arm, and the man jumped beneath her hands as the doctor began his work. Sana gently blotted beads of perspiration from the patient's forehead and then swiped sweat off her own with the back of her hand. This pain of love hurt even more than living in a town where everyone knew she was ruined. The sight of the scalpel scraping dead flesh off the raw half-healed wound made her sick, and she clenched her teeth as she steadied her hand on the clamp, helping O'Neal tear the away the bad flesh from the good.

"Wence," she called.

"Yes, ma'am?"

"Please give the fellas their morphine in plenty of time before we get to them."

"Sure thing, ma'am." The tall medic patted her back as he passed her and then raised his voice. "Listen up, everybody. I got something special for everybody here as has been shot at. Hey, soldier, you been shot at? I got something here for you. Hold still."

"I can't believe he would say something like that." Sana jumped up off her cot and paced around the nurses' quarters, which was starting to look like their dorm back at nursing school. Someone had hung a cracked mirror in an ornate gilt frame on the wall, and Obie had rigged a clothesline for hanging wet underwear. "After all we went through. I'm going to say something to somebody about this."

Checky had dumped her bags onto her cot and was sitting in the middle of all her belongings, washing her socks in her helmet. She wrung out a pair and handed them to Sana. "Would you hang these up for me? Did you tell Adele?"

"No. She's so busy." Sana spread the socks on the line, sat down on her cot and then stood up again, fuming at the world. "I'll tell someone. How do you find Colonel Kelsey?"

"Don't do that. You're still too mad." Checky started washing her feet with the water left over from the socks. "You'll blow it all up and then you'll sound stupider than O'Neal does. Just tell Adele. Why be so upset? Everyone knows you're right. I bet the medics love you now."

Sana flopped back down. "You should have seen Joe's face." She felt the heart-pang again. "I don't think he loves me anymore."

Checky chuckled. "Sure he does. He's nuts about you. Wence'll set him straight. Those poor medics haven't caught hardly a wink of sleep for three days and I know for a fact that the doctors slept on beds last night. That guy from Nashville told me so at breakfast."

Sana rolled over and eyed her friend. "How come he said that to you? I thought he was married."

"Oh, he's just being friendly. He's so sweet."

Sana raised a brow.

"Yes, he is married, and anyway he's too old. Do you have any foot powder?"

"*They* never think they're too old." Sana looked under her cot. Her little tin of foot powder sat right next to her blue satin bag. She tossed it over. "Well, I'm going to go tell Adele about what O'Neal said."

Checky dried her feet, powdered them, pulled on two pairs of mismatched socks and laced up her boots as tightly as she could. She stood up, ready for her shift. "I feel sorry for him already."

"All the nurses are like that. Every one of 'em." Wence was sitting on a crate of plasma cans, eating hash out of his mess kit and talking to Joe. "I wouldn't marry a nurse. Oh, they're angels in here. Angels." He waved his fork. "In here they walk on water as far as I'm concerned. But they'd be too bossy at home." He took another bite and chewed reflectively. "I think all women get like that if they work. Like Rosie. My own little sister won't be fit to live with by the time the war's over. Don't marry her either."

"I'm not going to. Joe kept moving his arm, trying to get comfortable. " Arguing with an officer in front of the men is bad for morale."

"It's good for *my* morale," Wence pointed out. "Maybe she wasn't, you know, that nice about it but she's dead right. I hope she gets that hell-raiser chief nurse on that guy's back." I been up three nights straight." He stopped chewing, pulled something out of his mouth that looked like a bone, and inspected it. "Doing your dang laundry."

"How come it takes you so long?"

"I got a fifty-five gallon drum and a gasoline fire, that's why."

Wence forked up the last bite of hash and mopped his plate with a cracker. "So you're having a fight with your girl already? Rachel and I went a whole week after our wedding before we had our first one."

"What'd you fight about?" Joe asked, avoiding the question.

"I forget. She went to bed and slammed the door." Wence grinned at the memory. "So I went to sleep on the couch." His grin got broader. "I didn't stay there all night, though. That girl loves me." He sat back and stretched. "Man, I wish you'd hurry up and get better and whip all those Krauts so we can go back home."

"Me too." Joe lay back and looked at the canvas tent above him. "I don't know if she's my girl anyway."

Wence snorted. "Officers. You are all as dumb as dirt. You drool like a goony puppy every time you see her. Go kiss and make up."

"Do you think you'll see her again pretty soon?"

Wence got up. "Yeah." He grinned again. "I'll tell her you said hi."

Joe woke up the next morning to the smell of coffee and the sound of plates clinking. A different doctor and nurse were making rounds. He counted the bandages the doctor used, since he had nothing better to do, and noticed that he didn't use nearly as many as O'Neal. Maybe Sana had been right. He still had not seen her since the day before.

"Hello there, you big beautiful thing. You're that cute Ranger from Sana Toledo's home town, aren't you?" A buxom nurse with curly blonde hair smiled as she took his wrist.

Joe grinned back and then immediately felt disloyal to Sana. He tried to straighten out his face into a serious expression.

The nurse smiled again and stuck a thermometer in his mouth. "Keep your mouth shut. I only flirt with guys when I take temperatures. That way you can't talk back." She twitched down the blanket to look at his arm, uncovering his bare chest. "Oh, my goodness. That Sana is one lucky girl."

Joe felt his face grow warm and he grinned again to cover his embarrassment. The nurse checked his wound, replaced the blanket and gently washed his face and hands. Joe closed his eyes, delighting in the touch of a woman's hands and the feel of warm soapy water on his skin. After she finished he was so relaxed that he drifted back into a doze.

Loud voices woke him up. Two officers were walking between the rows of cots, talking to the men who were awake, and one of the officers was his company commander.

Joe tried to come to attention while lying down. "Sir!"

"At ease, Vesely, for God's sake. How you doing there, son?"

"I think I'm doing pretty good, sir. They say I'll be back pretty soon."

"Well, you got yourself a Purple Heart." Darby sat down on the plasma crate. "Once you get back on your feet, I've got a job I think you can help me with. Feel up to a little light duty while your arm heals?"

"Sir?"

"I just got appointed mayor of this town and I need your help."

"You're the mayor? Sir?"

"And everything's in a holy mess. First they tell us to blow the place to pieces and now they tell us to put it back together again. I need to get the water running and the electricity back on."

"Yes sir. What about my platoon, sir?"

"They're fine. You can go back when we leave here. A couple weeks, maybe."

"Whatever I can do, sir."

"Good, because I need guys for MP duty, check the whorehouses, stuff like that." He laughed at Joe's expression.

"As long as you don't write home about it, sir."

"Deal." Darby rose. "We're quartered in the town center. Nice work on blowing up those big guns, soldier."

"Yes, sir." Joe blinked. It seemed like weeks since the landing. "Thank you, sir."

After the officers left Joe scratched at his bandage and turned over on the narrow cot. The blankets that had been so blissfully comfortable yesterday felt harsh and scratchy now. He wanted to get up, and what he really wanted to do was go find Sana and figure out if she was really going to be his girl or not. But he couldn't go running around camp dressed only in his underwear and a sling.

Dear God. Would you please make her come back here? Joe looked around the ward, at all the men stretched out in cots still attached to plasma bottles, some of them bandaged up to their eyes and not moving. *And help these guys get better... and take care of my guys...* he closed his eyes and went over his men one by one, picturing each face for a moment. Then Sana, then Wence, and then the whole war in general, to make sure he covered everything. *Please help me do what I have to do over here. And please get me through this war and go home and have my family.* He thought about his uncle's house back in Cedar Rapids, where people were probably right now sitting around the kitchen table, eating home-cooked meals and drinking beer. *And look after Uncle John and Aunt Kate.* Then he remembered that Johnny had enlisted. *And keep that dang kid out of trouble. Send him someplace where he won't get shot at.*

A clatter of dishes woke him out of a dream in which he and Sana were living in a little white-painted house, eating pork chops and mashed potatoes covered with gravy. The tent was dark now, lit only by a dim yellow light bulb hanging by the door. Joe sat up and tried to stretch without moving his left arm. The wound had settled down to a dull ache and did not hurt too badly.

Something new was on the floor by his cot. It turned out to be his rucksack, with a scrawled note pinned on top.

"Dear Lt, glad to here you are OK. We heard El Darbo wants you for desk duty. Lucky guy. Don't stab yerself with a pencil. The Marvellettes."

Joe rummaged through the pack with his good hand. Three ration bars, mess kit, empty canteen... his little hand towel... can opener, razor, scrap of soap. At the very bottom was his packet of letters and his uncle's worn leather pocket Bible, on loan to him for the war. He held it for a moment, fingering the thin paper pages, although it was too dark to read.

A large shadow coming toward him through the darkness turned out to be Wence, holding out a plate of Spam and hash. Joe reached for it and Wence pulled it back with a flourish. "Naw, you don't want this."

"I'll eat it anyway." Joe grabbed again but Wence only laughed and moved on. Another shape holding plates walked up. This one had a slender waist and long hair caught back in a braid.

Joe gawked. He made room on his cot and she sat down as casually as if they had been eating dinner together for years. Light glowed along the skin of her cheek and the soft long tangle of her lashes.

"I was watching for you all day," he whispered, trying not to call attention to the fact that a nurse was sitting on his bed.

She made a little breathy huff. "You were not," she whispered back. "You slept all day. I saw you." The dimples flashed.

"I dreamed about you," Joe said through a mouthful of Spam.

She took a delicate bite of hash. He could see that she looked weary. Dark circles showed under her eyes. "Did that doctor get you in trouble?"

"No." She flashed him a cool look and lifted her chin. "*He* got in trouble."

He grinned and she did too. They leaned a little closer together. "I might have to leave tomorrow," Joe whispered. "Darby came by. He wants me to help get the electricity going, things like that."

"Your sergeant told me, when he came to see you. Did you see your pack?" Joe nodded, busily chewing.

She took another dainty forkful. "I wish you didn't have to leave so soon."

Joe put down his empty plate. "You're so beautiful when you eat."

She almost choked, laughing. Joe took her plate and held it for her until she settled down.

"I thought maybe you were mad at me," she whispered. "About what that doctor said."

Joe reached out with his good hand and felt her fingers entwine with his.

"I wouldn't ever be mad at you."

She dimpled and shook her head. "You never know. It might happen."

He held her gaze, serious in spite of her teasing glance. "I want you to be careful," he whispered. "Promise me you'll stay safe."

Her dark eyes rested on him. "What about you?"

"I'll make it. We'll make it. I just want you to be careful. You still praying?"

She nodded.

"Me too. It's going to work."

She looked away, uncertain.

"Trust me. We'll do this right and it'll work." He could see that she still did not understand. "Did you ever pray for something and at first it didn't look like it would happen and then later on it did? It's going to work like that."

She looked off somewhere past his shoulder, then focused on him again. "I prayed not to get married to that old man. And I prayed for you to be safe."

Joe pulled her hand up tight against his chest. What would it feel like give her a real kiss? A corpsman hustled down the middle of the tent with a clanging armful of bedpans and someone else was walking around filling canteens.

"I want to give you something," he whispered. He groped in his pack for the little Bible. "It's my Uncle John's."

She shook her head.

"Take it," he whispered.

"I can't. It's your family's."

"My Uncle John would want you to have it. He knows who you are." He grinned. "I can't wait to tell him I met you again."

"They know about me?" Anxiety edged her voice.

He took her hand and made her look at him. She had been without a family for a long time, just like he had been. "Uncle John and Aunt Kate took me in when my mom died. I was a brat the whole first year. They'll love you."

She looked relieved. "I remember that boy you walked to school with."

"Well, Johnny." He made a face. "Can't have everything." She smiled at that. He put the little book firmly into her hand and pressed her fingers around it. "So now you have to stay safe so you can give it back to Uncle John. You're family now."

Her lashes glistened. "Thank you," she whispered. Their fingers twined together and tears spilled down her cheeks. "Oh, I love you."

Joe's heart wrenched with tenderness. He put his good arm around her shoulders, gathering her sweet softness close to him.

I love you. She leaned against him and he turned her face to his, seeking a kiss whether or not anyone saw. They clung together, wrapped in the tender darkness, until Wence came for their empty plates. Then there was time for one more kiss before she slipped away.

Chapter Seven

Algeria

"Okay, Bennie, hold it there." Sana stepped back and scrutinized the effect of a handmade tinfoil star on the top of an Algerian fir tree. "Up a little higher." The little red-haired medic stood tiptoe on a chair, straining to place the star just where she wanted it. They were decorating the hospital's deserted triage room for Christmas, and someone had brought in a twelve-foot tree to get the holiday spirit started. Even standing on a stool, Bennie's skinny arms could just barely reach the top. Sana smiled at the sight of him trying so hard, but she wished she had Wence Prazsky to help her instead. Bennie was a nice guy but he couldn't match Wence's long arms and creative style.

Now that the battle for Arzew was over, the troops had traveled east to Tunisia. Wence and most of the medics had gone too, leaving only a skeleton staff behind to care for the wounded still in the hospital. December rain had turned the dusty roads into deep gluey mud and the sky had been gloomy for a solid week. The nurses kept the lights turned on all day, trying to make the dreary wards look cheerful for Christmas, and the golden glow lit up the dark green tree and shone against the rainy windows.

"Hey, Big Red, stay there a minute," Obie called after Bennie managed to hook the star onto the top of the tree. "This chain's almost ready." She was sitting with a group of bandaged men at a long table covered with scraps of paper and they were all cutting out tin foil shapes and paper ornaments with the happy enthusiasm of a kindergarten class. Obie had passionately wanted to string a popcorn chain for the tree, but since no popcorn could be found anywhere in Arzew, she had talked the men into making a twelve-foot-long paper chain instead. The mess hall had made cookies and an empty plate with a scattering of crumbs sat on the table, half-covered with bits of paper.

"Wow!" Checky walked in, clasping a big bundle of red and white fabric against her pillowy bosom. She pulled off her helmet and ruffled her blonde hair. "The tree's terrific. Where'd you get the star?" She put down her bundle and sniffed. "You got cookies?"

Bennie pulled three cookies out of his chest pocket. "I saved some for you."

"You're such a sweetie." Checky gave him a generous squeeze and he blushed.

"X-ray gave us tin foil for the stars and that guy in the wheelchair painted all these decorations," Sana said. "Starting to look Christmasy around here, huh?"

"Look at this." Checky held up something red and white that turned out to be shaped like a stocking.

Sana inspected the stocking. "Where'd you get these?"

"The Red Cross person gave me a bunch of red fabric and then I cut up a sheet." Checky grinned. "Then I made everybody in my ward help me sew them. Aren't these just the cutest things you ever saw?"

Sana held up another one and laughed. "Look at those big stitches."

"They had fun." Checky sorted through the stockings, smoothing and patting them into shape. "I told the boys we're making fudge and now they're all acting like five-year-olds."

"That supply officer brought over another hundred pounds of sugar today," Sana said. "And more peanuts and cocoa. When I asked him where he got it he just winked and told me I didn't want to know."

"We can put the candy in the stockings. What else?" Checky considered her own question. "Maybe we could write letters. Like Christmas cards. And then when the men come in we can hand them each a stocking with candy and a Christmas card."

"Five hundred letters?" That seemed like a lot of handwriting. "Let's just make more fudge." Sana turned back to the bright red bougainvillea blossoms that she was stringing along the windows and doors. "Would you cut off these stems for me?"

They snipped away at the brilliant mass of scarlet blooms lying on the table. The little medic and two chaplains trundled an operating table into the room and flung a white sheet over it. Another medic nailed a cardboard cross on the wall behind.

"What's that for?" Checky asked, pausing to clean clumps of green leaves from her surgical scissors.

"They're going to have midnight mass and sing Christmas carols, then have cookies and hot chocolate."

"I've never been to a midnight mass. Are they going to let us heathens come too?"

"Are you kidding?" Sana laughed. "The rabbi's leading the choir." An unexpected thought struck her. "You aren't Jewish, are you?"

"Oh, no. My family's old-time religion."

Sana remembered the old stone church, the smell of incense and the beautiful solemn songs rising up through candlelight during midnight mass. "I used to go, back in Iowa. With my aunt and uncle."

Checky warmed to the subject. "I grew up going to this little country church where there were only eight families in the whole congregation and the preacher baptized people in the in the river."

"You're kidding. Did you get baptized?"

"Oh, sure. But I had mine indoors in a water trough, because it was in January and the river was frozen over."

That was an odd concept. "Did you feel different afterwards?" Sana asked.

"Hah! I was too busy doing chores to think about it."

Sana pictured a neat little clapboard farm house, with an entire family clomping out over a snowy barnyard to milk cows early in the morning. "You must have had so much fun."

"I wouldn't exactly call it fun. I guess we had moments." Checky's face lit up in an impish grin. "About the most fun we had was jumping off the barn rafters into the hay. We weren't supposed to, because you if you landed wrong you could break something. One of my brothers broke the same leg twice that way, once when he was ten and then when he was thirteen. My Dad whupped him for it both times." She laughed at the memory.

Sana laughed too. "That's pretty mean."

"Daddy had to do something. He was a real numbskull." She cleared away a pile of leaves and organized her flowers so they all faced the same direction. "When we go back you just have to come visit for a while. Mom and Dad would be so happy." The mischievous smile lit up again. "First they feed you a big meal, then they give you a bucket and point you toward the barn."

"I wouldn't mind," Sana said, delighted. "I'd love it."

Checky looked up with her frank china-blue gaze. "Didn't you say you were born in Algeria? Do you still have family here somewhere?"

The cheerful warmth drained straight out of the day. Sana felt her face go pale with the shock of the question and she bent over her pile of bougainvillea, trying to snip off leaves with shaky fingers while she pulled herself back together. She hadn't thought about Constantine since the night before they landed. She hadn't thought about her Algerian family, her aunts and uncles and cousins, for even longer. Where was Constantine, anyway? Was it close to Arzew? Was anyone she knew still alive there? What if they were alive but they were siding with the Germans? What if her uncles came to the camp and said she had to come back and live with them again?

She would never, ever let them find her. If they came to take her then she would hide in the surgery tent or under Adele's bed. Then she would jump into a truck and drive away as fast as she could back, back to the troopships if she had to, and swim right out to them where she'd be safe.

"I don't think so," she managed to say, acting as if she was concentrating on the bougainvillea.

"Oh." Checky sounded distracted. "There. These are all done now. You know, that cardboard cross looks so plain. Maybe we can decorate it."

Two rain-soaked soldiers carrying crates walked into the room and stared at the tree. "Well, shut ma mouth. Y'all are fixin' t' have a real Christmas!" one of them drawled happily. "Can Ah come?"

"Sure," everybody said.

"We got a special delivery he-ah," the other soldier announced in a Boston brogue. "For somebody named Brownie. Got any idear who that is?"

Sana and Checky exchanged glances. "Right this way," Sana said, and led them up the stairs to the empty operating room.

"Special delivery for Brownie," Sana called out. The combination of Margie's last name and shiny brown hair had made the nickname inevitable.

Margie was making fudge on top of the sterilizer. She allowed each soldier a swipe and then shooed them out before rummaging through the crates. "More sugar and more peanuts. This is perfect," she said. "Now we can make peanut brittle."

"I know how to make taffy." Sana reached out for her own fingerful of chocolate. "There's going to be so much candy we'll probably all get sick." She took second lick, then a third and a forth. "Who's getting this stuff for us? The colonel?"

Margie was busy counting pounds of sugar. "You're going to get sick right now, eating like that."

Sana took fifth swipe. Margie looked especially glamorous today, with her hair curled and bright new polish on her nails that matched her lipstick.

"Or maybe it's the supply officer," Sana went on, watching her expression. "The sergeant with the glasses. You know who I mean?"

"Oh, Mike?"

Sana leaned over to get a better view of Margie's face. "You mean Duncan?"

Margie kept her head down. "You're making me lose count."

"Mike Duncan. What a nice name. How long has this been going on?"

Margie gave up and sat back, her brown eyes sparkling. She hugged herself and smiled. "He's such a great guy."

Sana raised a skeptical eyebrow."

"I don't mean like that. Really, lots of times we just sit and talk."

"You fell in love with a non-com?" Sana went back to swiping fudge.

"I really think this's the one."

Sana shook her head and quoted an old skip-rope song. "'Margie-Pargie, puddin' and pie, kiss the boys and make them cry.'"

"Uh-uh. Not this time. I've never, ever met such a wonderful man. He does all kinds of thoughtful little things for me."

"Oh, Brownie, slow down. Bring him over so we can check him out." Margie's last boyfriend had persuaded her to take all the money out of her savings account and then had disappeared with the cash.

"Wait 'til you meet him. He's a total dream, writes home to his mom and dad every week. He shows me all his letters and he wrote all these wonderful things to them about me. He wants them to meet me when we go back." She swiped at her eyes with the back of her hand and left a streak of fudge across her cheek. "Don't tell anyone yet, but he asked me to marry him."

Sana flung her arms around Margie. "My gosh! Oh, my gosh!"

They both began to cry. "I finally found a really, really good guy and he loves me." Margie groped for a towel. "I'm so happy." She gulped and sniffed, mascara running down her cheeks. "I wouldn't care if he was just a plain old buck private."

Sana hugged her again and then clapped her hands with a flourish. "Hey! Can he get us long johns? And socks? Big steaks?"

Margie looked demure. "Oh, I couldn't possibly ask him to do things like that."

"I'm so happy for you," Sana said. She thought of Joe, probably far away somewhere getting shot at by Germans, and

113

felt a twinge of envy. Margie's soldier was right here with here at the hospital unit. He would probably make it through the war alive, and they would go home together and get married. She wondered where her own soldier was, and what his chances were.

Hundreds of miles further east, a line of soldiers walked through the dim gray dawn along a dry gulch bottom, moving steadily over the rocks and gravel towards the canyon's rim above. The rise of the hill grew steeper when they left the narrow bottom and they had to angle up the slope, leaning far forward under their packs to stay balanced against the dirt and rocks sliding beneath their boots. When they were almost at the top the grade became so steep that they climbed with their hands and kept their gazes fixed on the rim above them and away from the desert floor below. A cold sharp wind was blowing but as long as they kept moving, they stayed warm.

Joe crept the last few feet toward a clump of shrub that would provide some cover when he crested the top. Just before he reached it he paused, took a firmer grip on the rocks and looked back down. Men clung along the hill below, so dusted with dirt that they blended into the dun-colored ground. Three soldiers who had been wounded were not climbing with them but had taken cover in the gorge below, and at first Joe could not locate them. But they must have been watching for him to turn and look, because one of them raised his rifle slightly, attracting Joe's attention and letting him know they would cover any retreat.

Joe looked at the sky, then his watch. The platoon was due back at the reconnaissance point in an hour. They had hiked far into the desert to raid a German outpost, a mission designed to draw attention away from the columns of U.S. tanks moving east. Joe's platoon had hiked in at night and located the camp, moving in silent as a snake on a rock, and shelled it precisely as planned. But the Germans had not taken their pounding without a fight and just as Joe was pulling back out of range, Sedlak had been shot dead right in front of him, his whole back and chest exploding in a blast of random gunfire. Joe had jerked Sedlak's dog tags off his neck and maintained the retreat, but even now, clinging to the side of a cliff in broad daylight, he could not shake the feeling that Bill Sedlak was still alive back there, broken-hearted at being left behind.

He glanced back down at the climbers scattered along the cliff below. Their eyes were on him, watching for his signal. Each one was in a good position and he paused so they could rest before the final push over the top. The platoon had slowed its usual mile-covering stride on the return hike, partly because they were supporting the wounded men and partly because they were tired. They had taken only ration bars and canteens of water for the twenty-four-hour march and everyone was low on both. They going to be late, and now they would be even later because he had taken them on a detour. There would be hell to pay when they got back. Joe tucked his chin down against the wind and hoped that the inevitable chewing-out would at least warm him up.

He had taken the detour because he heard tanks clanking. At first he thought it must be the Allied columns moving east as planned, but then they heard the rumble of heavy fire and saw an amber glow light up the sky. No one was supposed to be engaging the enemy here. He had decided that the need for information outweighed the precious minutes they would lose. But the sounds had been farther away than he thought and now they were far off course. The clanking sounds had faded and black pillars of smoke were rising just beyond this canyon rim.

He gathered himself for the scramble up the last few feet to the top and peered into the dun-colored *wadi* below. A long line of burned-out tanks stretched across the valley to the next distant rise, each one still pouring out boiling plumes of smoke. Joe pulled up his binoculars. Twenty... thirty... over fifty U.S. tanks, turned into smoking ruins.

Garcia moved up beside him and groaned.

Joe continued his visual sweep and felt his stomach turn. Black-charred bodies with faces burnt off hung halfway out of tank turrets. Others lay dead on the ground. A distant rhythmic clanking still sounded faintly in the morning air.

"Oh, no. No, no, no..." Garcia pounded his fist on the ground and cursed in Spanish. Joe let him rant on and get it out while he decided what to do. He studied the line and direction of the tanks, the positions of the lifeless bodies. The nausea in the pit of his stomach settled and changed into something numb instead.

"Shut up," he finally ordered his sergeant. "How's the radio?" The desert's undulating hills had cut off their signal twenty hours ago.

"Still out."

"Bring it up here and try again." Joe turned his binoculars back to the blackened forms below. One of the bodies was moving an arm.

He ordered Garcia to take half the platoon south along the valley, to search for men who might still be alive and for any sight of the enemy. He positioned Ratliff and Taffington to stay on the ridge as lookouts and then signaled the remaining section to follow him to the north.

Every tank was a twisted wreck of hot metal with burnt bodies inside. The smell of charred flesh gagged them as they checked one tank after another, looking for survivors. They finally found one man still living. Joe knelt beside him and Johnson held up his head so they could give him a drink of water.

"What happened, buddy?" Joe asked after the man had swallowed a few mouthfuls.

The soldier's eyes wandered about. "What?" The word barely made it past his blistered lips. The skin of his face and chest was raw with burns.

Joe raised his canteen to the soldier's lips again. After a swallow he took it away. "What happened? How many were there?"

The man's eyes focused on him. "Tanks," he whispered.

"How many?"

"Just bounced off. Bounced off."

"What are you talking about?"

"Shells bounced off. Practice rounds."

"What?"

"All we had were practice rounds." The man was babbling now. "That's all we had. All we had to fight with. They gave us practice rounds to fight with." His eyes started wandering again. "We couldn't even reach them. When we got in range we fired but the shells just bounced off their tanks. Every time they shot one of our tanks blew up and every time we shot the shells bounced off." He moved restlessly in Johnson's arms. "They gave us practice rounds." He moved again and suddenly focused on Joe. "I don't know how many. They were better than us." He tried to lick his lips and Joe gave him another drink.

Another soldier came up and silently offered a curette.

Joe sat back on his heels. If they gave the soldier morphine now, he would not be able to walk. If they left him here, he would die. If they tried to take him back, they might miss their rendezvous entirely, and then the news of the German tanks would not get back to headquarters for another twelve or maybe even twenty-four hours. He was uncomfortably certain of what his commander would say if that happened. Darby had made it clear that wounded men who could not keep up on a march had to be left behind.

He looked at Johnson. "You got a signal yet?"

Johnson shook his head.

He turned back to the burned soldier. "Buddy, do you think you can walk?"

"Yeah."

Oh, God. Joe put down his head. *I don't want to leave him here to die.* He looked up. The men were watching him.

"Let's get you up." They hauled the man to his feet and pulled his arms over their shoulders. The burned soldier took a step and groaned, then another. Garcia's section came back into view, moving swiftly up the valley. No extra men were with them.

"Form two groups," Joe ordered as soon as they arrived. "I'll take the radio and go fast. You take the wounded and go slow. We need a signal and a medic."

Three days after Christmas, the entire mobile hospital unit

moved east to join the troops. Sana stood with the other nurses outside the Arzew hospital's front door, sipping thin coffee and trying to stay warm. The Christmas tree was still up and the decorations still in place, but everything else had changed. The rain was gone and the sky was a clear ice blue, with a cold dry wind whipping out of it that chapped her lips and cheeks. Wool field jackets had finally been delivered and everyone had layered on as many clothes as they could wear, but the morning was so cold that the mud puddles were iced over, and some of the nurses jumped up and down to stay warm while they waited. The British Army had provided a caravan of lorries for their transportation and an officer was making announcements.

"You are going into danger," he said in a courtly English accent, as politely and precisely as if he was inviting them to dinner. "You are going past the Atlas Mountains into the eastern Maghrib plain, where troops are spread out over a rather large area." He frowned at them for emphasis. "Unfortunately the Germans have considerable air power and you will almost certainly be attacked at some point before you arrive at the site of your new hospital. Keep your helmets on at all times as you travel. Each one of you must be vigilant. If you see or hear a plane, signal the truck drivers. If the trucks stop then you must immediately disembark and take cover at least fifty feet away from the road."

All the nurses nodded. "Maintain strict blackout conditions at night." They nodded again. "The caravan will stop every two hours. You will get a half hour for lunch at noon. No other stops will be allowed." He looked meaningfully at the women.

"Yes, sir," they chorused.

A smile warmed his reserved expression. "Well, shall we get going, then? Cheerio, my dears, and God be with you."

Engines roared to life and people started lining up to get into the trucks. "We better go hit the ladies' room one more time while we still have one," Obie whispered to Sana, and the two of them made a quick run to the nurses' latrine before squeezing into the back of a crowded truck. The trip, they had been told, would take two days. One by one the trucks lurched forward into line, rolling slowly out of Arzew and into the shining desert.

The road soon dwindled into a rocky track and then faded into a trace across the plain. The women jounced along, unable to nap because of the bumps and unable to see out because of the truck's canvas cover. Time crawled by. When the convoy finally stopped exactly two hours after leaving, they jumped out in relief and looked around.

Dirt and sand stretched flat to the horizon in every direction. They milled around and stood first on one foot, then on the other. Farther down the road soldiers lined up side by side in a long row, their backsides to the nurses. There was not a single tree, not even a big rock, to go behind.

"Any ideas?" Adele asked.

Margie screwed up her face. "Maybe we could go behind the truck."

"With these coveralls?" Adele looked at the lashings holding the canvas cover on the truck. "We could take this off and do something with it."

"Hold up some blankets," Checky said. "That's how we did on the farm." Four blankets were instantly pulled out and held up in a square.

"Just like the hog pen back home," Obie said when she came out.

Horns started honking and they scrambled back into the trucks. The day was warming up and Adele had figured out how to raise the sides of the canvas covers, so they could look out as they traveled. The line of trucks passed bomb craters and burnt-out parts of airplanes, silent reminders of the importance of this solitary road across the sand. Sometimes they saw the long black guns of antiaircraft artillery pointing out from holes dug along the side, and the soldiers inside whooped and whistled when they saw the women. The nurses waved back and blew kisses back.

The long convoy rumbled on. Mountains appeared, low and blue in the distance, and Sana stared at them for a long time, fascinated by the gleaming land, trying to pin down some gossamer wisp of memory that floated far back in her mind, too fragile to grasp and claim. But finally she tired of looking at the desert and decided to reorganize her belongings.

She folded all the socks and underwear that she had washed the night before and jammed hurriedly into her bag that morning. The Red Cross had given out soap and toothpaste for Christmas, and she tucked those treasures inside her satin bag, now fraying and looking more brown than blue. She rolled up her little hand towels, and then placed her personal stash of fudge and taffy, carefully wrapped in X-ray foil, on top of everything so it wouldn't get crushed. Finally she pulled out Joe's pocket Bible. She had tucked it deep into her bag on the night he gave it to her and hadn't looked at it since.

She examined it now in the light. It was supple and polished shiny from handling, the cover worn at the edges and imprinted with a delicate design of grapes and vines. It fit into her hand, old and pretty, like a piece of antique jewelry.

She opened and turned to the whisper-thin first page. *October 1921. For my dear husband John Mark Starosta on our first anniversary. Your loving wife, Kateřina.* Sana turned another page. *John Carl Starosta born August 1, 1922. Stephen Francis Starosta born November 5, 1928.*

She turned the pages, looking through the old-fashioned words. Some passages were marked with underlines, and others were stained with what looked like coffee spills. One paragraph was decorated with hearts and flowers drawn in a feminine hand. '*And the king loved Esther above all the women,*' Sana read, '*and she obtained grace and favour in his sight more than all the virgins; so that he set the royal crown upon her head, and made her queen instead of Vashti.*"

Sana marked the place with a scrap of fabric torn from her sleeve and moved on. Someone had drawn a strong black line under another verse. '*Delight thyself also in the Lord: and he shall give thee the desires of thine heart.*' Had Joe underlined those words? What was it he had wanted?

Her father had owned a Bible. He would sit with his coffee in the morning before breakfast, poring over the pages. She could remember looking at it. Some of the words had been printed in red ink. She flipped through the pages of Joe's Bible to the red-ink section. There were more underlines. *'The Spirit of the Lord is upon me, because he hath anointed me to preach the gospel to the poor; he hath sent me to heal the brokenhearted, to preach deliverance to the captives, and recovering of sight to the blind, to set at liberty them that are bruised, to preach the acceptable year of the Lord.'*

"Oh, a Bible!" Adele bumped against her as the truck jounced up and down. "Can I see it?" She browsed the pages, lingering over sections of text.

"Here's my favorite verse," she said. *"'Though I walk through the valley of the shadow of death, I will fear no evil; for thou art with me.'* Isn't that beautiful?"

"Yes," Sana said truthfully. The words seemed to lift off the page and take on a life of their own when Adele read them out loud.

"Here's another one. Listen to this. *'When thou passeth through the waters, I will be with thee; and through the rivers, they shall not overflow thee; when thou walkest through the fire, thou shalt not be burned.'* I love Isaiah."

"Have you read the whole thing?"

"Oh, yes. Many times, over the years." Adele turned more pages. "I lost mine on the ship. Can I borrow this once in a while?"

"Of course. I've never read it, to be honest with you."

"Oh, you should. Start in the gospels, back here. And I love the Psalms. Every time I read them, it's like something hits the nail right on the spot." Adele paged back to the front and studied the handwritten notes. "Is this your family?"

Sana blushed. "They're... a friend's family."

"Hmm." Adele looked at her. "Must be the handsome friend."

Sana looked down and smiled, remembering the feel of Joe's arm around her shoulders and the firm, tender touch of his lips. "Yes."

"He must really love you, honey. This is a special gift."

"Oh!" A massive jolt tossed everyone high in the air and they all came down hard on the wooden floor. Bags and belongings tumbled everywhere.

"Ouch! Dang! Ow, I bit my tongue!" Jo Ellen yelled.

After they sorted themselves out again, Adele put her arm around Sana and gave her a hug. "I'm glad you've got somebody special," she said, giving an extra squeeze for emphasis. "I'll pray for your young man."

"Do you pray every day?" Sana asked.

"All the time."

Sana tried to remember a time when she had noticed Adele praying. "What do you *say*?"

Adele considered the question. "I pray for God to take care of all these poor hurt boys. And for me to be strong, and for the war to be over soon." She gave Sana a meaningful glance. "Sometimes when I'm feeling really down I just count my blessings, like hot water and coffee, things like that."

"But what do you say?"

"Oh, one thing or another." Adele stared at the horizon. "Sometimes I just sing a hymn to myself, or I pray for all you girls."

"Does it help?"

Adele didn't answer at first, and when she did her voice was lower. "When we're losing men and everything's horrible, I pray for things to get better. And then something always does. I figure, well, I'm still here, you're still here, so that's something." She looked at Sana. "Maybe we haven't won the war yet, but we're moving east, so I guess that's something too."

Sana could not think of anything to say.

Adele looked away again. "When a boy comes in with his legs all shot off, or when a lot of them die even though we work so hard, sometimes I just can't find words. I just can't. I cry in my heart, cry to God all day long. Sometimes that's all I can do."

Sana laid her hand on Adele's.

"I tell you," Adele said with some of her usual fierceness, "there's a verse in Romans that says the spirit of God makes intercession for us when we can't find any words. So I figure I'm still praying even if I can't think of any words."

Everyone was listening now. "And then there's days when things don't seem so bad. I'll walk through the ward tents and say little prayers for the men, for them to feel good and cheered up no matter how bad off they are. Or I'll be walking through the mess hall and I'll just ask God to bless everybody there. Some days I pray for the food." All the nurses nodded.

"Then I'll pray for a whole bunch of medics come along and do all the chores so I can have a coffee break. I'll say, 'Dear God, would you please send me a bunch of big strong boys to do this work, so I can sit down and have a cup of coffee?'"

"I'll drink to that," Jo Ellen said.

Sana gave Adele a hug. "You're a great chief nurse. I don't know what we'd do without you."

"Honey, it's not me. It's the Lord." Adele stretched, easing her back. "I couldn't do this on my own steam, not as old as I am. I don't even know why we didn't get squashed like bugs the first day we landed here." She stuffed a blanket between her back and the side of the truck. "We could never have made it this far on our own power. The Germans have us outgunned, outmanned, and outsupplied. If I didn't think that God sent me here to do what I'm doing, I'd give up. I'd just go back home and try to live a few more happy years, until the Germans came and took everything over."

Sana made a little sound of protest.

"Either we win or the Lord takes me out." She handed back the Bible. "Keep—"

The truck slammed to a stop and they all slid into a pile. Brakes squealed as trucks skidded behind them.

"Out! Out! Now!" a driver yelled. "Get away from the road!"

The nurses started disentangling themselves.

"Is this your bag?"

"Oh, sorry, I didn't mean to..."

"Right now!" Adele yelled. "You hear that?" The sound of airplanes droned in the distance.

They poured out the back of the truck. Sana glanced up to see which direction the planes were coming from, but the sun shone right in her eyes, so she blinked and looked around for a tree or a rock for shelter. There was nothing but level sand clear to the horizon. She ran to a group of soldiers lying on the ground and flung herself face down by them. Checky landed right beside her and they both put their arms over their helmets.

The droning noise grew louder. Sana pressed her face into the dirt as hard as she could. Grains of sand crunched between her teeth and up her nose.

"Adele, you praying?" someone yelled.

One of the soldiers stirred beside her. "I think those're ours."

Checky raised her head. "Oh, good! That was scary."

"Get down!" someone else yelled. "He don't know a plane if it bit him in the backside! Stay down!"

The drone deepened into a roar with an edge of screaming engines rimming the sound. Shadows flitted across the ground and thunder blasted over them. Sana groveled in the sand.

And then the planes were gone.

She lifted her face out of the dirt and sucked in a deep breath of air. Checky was still laying face down on the ground next to her, with a soldier's arm wrapped tightly around her shoulders. He raised his head and looked around. It was Bennie, who had put the star on top of the Christmas tree.

Checky looked up and her helmet bumped his nose. "Red, you are such a sweetheart. That was so brave of you. Thank you." Red gazed soulfully back at her and didn't move his arm until she removed his hand and sat up.

"See, I told ya those planes was ours," a soldier said.

"Doggone them! Why'd they do that, then?" Checky brushed dirt off her face and hands. "As if we don't have enough to worry about."

"No they were not our planes. Those were Germans," someone else replied. "I looked. Musta been going somewhere else today."

"I don't care who they were. I got to lay on the ground beside a beautiful nurse," the first soldier said. "I hope they come back."

"You are just a bunch of silly boys," Checky scolded. "Only one thing on your minds all the time."

"Oh, yes, ma'am," the soldier said.

Everyone was sore by the time they stopped for lunch and most of them ate their rations standing up. Sana and Checky traded their cigarettes packages for gum, and Adele traded hers for an extra packet of instant coffee. The doctor from Nashville drifted over to their group and began a rambling conversation with Jo Ellen about being hungry for some good home-cooked wilted greens, and Sana arched a meaningful eyebrow at Obie when she saw him light Jo Ellen's cigarette for her. Obie grinned at the sight.

One of the lieutenant colonels walked up to Adele. "Listen, Ross, I have an idea. We're going to see more of those German planes as we go east. What if you girls make a big white cross out of sheets, to show that we're a medical unit, and put it on the ground next to the hospital?"

Adele considered that. "Well, sir, of course, if you think so. It'd have to be pretty big."

"That'll just look like a big old target to them," Obie said. "Sir," she added.

The officer stiffened. "The Germans respect the Geneva conventions," he said. "It can't do any harm and it might save some lives, young lady."

"It's a great idea. Anything to help out, sir," Jo Ellen said.

The officer beamed and nodded. "Now, that's the spirit. Fine work you women are doing here. I'll have someone send over sheets right now." He turned to walk away. Nash smiled at Jo Ellen.

"And needles and thread! Sir!" Adele called after him.

Obie was frowning. "Y'all are gonna holler like stuck pigs when you stab a finger going over them potholes."

"I'd rather stab my finger than get my head blown off," Jo Ellen said. "I declare, Obie." Nash nodded along beside her, a serious look on his face.

125

The trucks honked and they all climbed back in for two more hours of bumps. The sheets were delivered at the next rest stop and they sewed for the rest of the afternoon, poking needles through heavy cotton until their fingers got too sore to stitch any longer. They slept on the ground that night, woke early for a breakfast of more C-rations and stale canteen water, then loaded back into the trucks again.

They finally arrived at the new camp long after nightfall on the second day, stiff and tired of the travel. Soldiers helped them off the trucks and led them through the darkness to their tents.

Sana had been feeling achy around her middle during the last part of the drive, and the jump off the truck made her insides cramp up. She doubled over as she walked, tripped on a tent rope in the darkness, and would have fallen if her soldier had not grabbed her.

"Sorry," she said to her invisible guide.

"Pretty good blackout, huh, ma'am? Can't see a thing," a voice said proudly. "Oh, by the way, I'm Sergeant Schulte, but," the voice lowered conspiratorially, "you can call me Homer."

"Second Lieutenant Sana Toledo." She clenched her teeth through another cramp. "Pleased to meet you."

"Oh." A little silence followed.

"Where are we?" another nurse asked from out of the darkness.

"Constantine, ma'am. Here's your tent."

"Wait." Sana felt her middle churn again. "Where's the latrine?" Her eyes were adjusting to the night and she could see the shapes of tents outlined against the sky.

"Uh, over there." A rustle of fabric told her which way the soldier was pointing and she saw another dark shape outlined in the starlight. "Do you want me to take you?"

"I think I can get there by myself now. Thank you." Sana dropped her bag and headed off, half bent over, walking as quickly as she could over the frozen ground. She caught the whiff of a familiar reek and found the latrine with its wooden bench and round holes just in time.

Oh my Lord above, that was close. She sat there for a while in the darkness, trembling with relief.

A man blundered in and plunked down next to her.

"'Scuse me." The voice was unmistakably O'Neal's.

"Umm," Sana grunted in as low a voice as she could register. She fought down the urge to giggle. What would be funnier— sitting there pretending to be a man, or letting O'Neal know that he was sitting next to a woman? What had life come to? She clamped her teeth together in order not to make a sound and fled back to her tent, buttoning up her clothes and choking with laughter as she ran.

Chapter Eight

The Maghrib

More stomach cramps woke her early the next morning. She tried to ignore them and stay comfortably lost in dreamy sleep, but finally she pulled her blanket around her, stuck her feet into her boots, and trudged back to the latrine. She knocked before she entered and whistled all the time she was inside. When she came out, feeling better, a faint pink glow was lighting up the starry sky and glinting off the pine trees all around the camp. The luscious scent of baking bread wafted through the air, along with the distant clatters and bangs of a mess crew making breakfast.

Sana walked back slowly to her tent, looking at all the little signs of camp life that she hadn't seen the night before. Some of the tents had names posted on them like Hut Two and Fall Inn. A stake holding wooden signs shaped like arrows stood at the intersection of two main pathways, pointing directions to the mess hall and the hospital. Someone had nailed on a board with a hand-drawn arrow and the words "Brooklyn -- 4500 miles." Just below it someone else had added "Fargo -- 6000".

At her own tent, she raised a flap and looked inside. There were four cots, three sleeping women, and clothes all over everywhere. Somebody was snoring. Sana pulled her canteen and bag out of the shadowy jumble and took a seat on a rock outside.

She drank a swallow of water, then dampened her hand towel and soaped it up to wash her dusty face and neck. Her hair would have to do as it was for now. She took off her boots and socks, washed her feet, and turned her socks inside out before she put them back on so that they would feel cleaner. Then she settled her blanket around her shoulders and pulled out Joe's little Bible.

The Book of Psalms. Sana turned the thin pages, looking for something to read. A section marked with a coffee stain and blue-ink underlines caught her eye. *To the chief Musician, A Psalm of David. I waited patiently for the Lord; and he inclined unto me, and heard my cry. He brought me up also out of a horrible pit, out of the miry clay, and set my feet upon a rock, and established my goings. And he hath put a new song in my mouth...*

She looked out at the trees and mountains glowing in the golden dawn. The breakfast clankings rang out crisply through the morning air. *He hath put a new song in my mouth.* She could have been stuck in the grocery store for the rest of her life, working for Mary during the day and serving a horrible old man at night. She could have been hit by a bomb yesterday. But here she was, enjoying a glorious sunny morning. In the middle of a war, she had found the man she had fallen in love with years ago. And she was going to eat fresh bread for breakfast.

I'm happy, she marveled. *Even in the middle of the desert.* She remembered her promise. *Dear God, please take care of Joe, wherever he is right now. Please keep him safe until I see him again. I love him so much. Oh, God, please make this war be over soon. If you'll just end this war and bring Joe back to me, I swear I'll always be grateful and pray to you for the rest of my life.* After she married Joe they would undoubtedly go to church together. They would walk through the neighborhood on a sunny day, on a shade-dappled sidewalk under the big elm trees, her hand in the crook of his arm. They would walk up the steps to the church building and he would hold the door open for her to go in first. His family would be sitting in a pew and they would all look up and smile when they saw her. Sana sat on her rock and lost herself in daydreams as the last stars faded and the sky turned crystal blue.

The tent flap moved and Adele appeared. Her hair stuck out in gray-brown corkscrew curls all over her head and her pajama collar, brown from bloodstains and dust, showed underneath her jacket.

"It's over there," Sana pointed. "Keep your eyes open. The

men use it too."

Adele put on her helmet, turned up her pajama collar against the chilly morning air, and walked off. Stray curls stuck out from under the edge of her helmet and the pink underside of her collar made a curious sight at the top of her olive-green fatigues. Sana smiled when her chief nurse knocked briskly at the door of the latrine and flushed out a trio of soldiers. Then she tucked the Bible back into her bag, stood up to stretch again, and turned around.

She gasped. Rising up against the sky beyond the camp gleamed a walled city. The air was so clear that she could see tiled roofs and the delicate spirals of minarets, the dark green fronds of palm trees and masses of purple bougainvillea glowing on the walls.

She knew that city. It was Constantine. The line of the wall, even the smell of the morning desert air, was just as she remembered. Her old pink house was there somewhere, with red roses blooming in the garden. She thought of her elegant mother, greeting her at the door when she came home from school.

"Pretty, isn't it?" Adele was back.

"That's Constantine! That's where I'm from! That's where I grew up, right over there!" She scanned the distant line of buildings, straining to pick out some familiar outline.

Adele was saying something.

"What?"

"I said, maybe you can find a way to drive in for a visit. First we have to set up the hospital and then we have to dig trenches by four o'clock. If planes fly over they usually come through around sunset." Adele was already looking at her watch. "Mess is in five minutes."

Sana tore her gaze away from the gleaming mountain. "How'd you learn all that from one trip to the latrine?"

Adele went back into the tent. "It's all who you ask."

After a breakfast of hot bread and hash washed down with coffee, they unpacked the trucks. Soldiers built tents while the nurses and medics organized a logical progression of receiving tents, shock treatment areas, an operating room and recovery wards. After lunch they set up the sterilizer and instruments. Then they put Big Red in charge of organizing the laundry, went back to their tents and dug trenches. After that Adele had to go to another meeting but the rest of them had an hour left before dinner, so they started making themselves feel at home.

Checky built a table out of empty crates and hung up the gilt-edged mirror she found in the garbage at Arzew. Sana rinsed out some shallow ration cans to hold their helmets upside down for washing. They found a scrap of board, lettered the words "Ritz-Carlton" on it, and tied it to the outside of the tent. Then they pulled back the flaps and stretched out on their cots.

"Hey! Everybody! Look who's here!" Margie walked up carrying two empty number-ten cans. A plain-looking soldier wearing sergeant's stripes and horn-rimmed glasses came behind her, holding a little iron stove. Sana and Checky sat up.

"This is Mike Duncan," Margie announced. "Mike, this is Frenchie and Checky."

Mike set down the stove and wiped his hands on his pants. "Nice to meet you." He held out his hand and smiled, and suddenly the plain sergeant turned into a very attractive man. "I brought you guys a stove." He smiled the marvelous smile again.

Sana stood up and shook hands. Checky bounced over with her lively hug. Duncan blushed and stepped back to Margie's side. She slipped her arm around his waist and they looked at each other and smiled. Envy stabbed straight through Sana's heart.

"Mike's taking a stove to every nurses' tent. And these big cans. Now everybody can have their own hot water," Margie said. She put her other arm around Mike's waist and hugged him tighter.

Sana remembered her manners. "Thank you very much. I can't remember the last time I had my own hot water. I think it was before England."

"Brownie, you better watch out. All the nurses are going to fall in love with this guy," Checky said. "He's so cute."

Mike cleared his throat and adjusted his glasses with his free

131

hand. "Well, uh, we just think you're all angels, to come out here and do what you're doing for us." He smiled into Margie's eyes again. "There weren't enough stoves to go around for all the guys and I figured nobody'd complain if I gave 'em to the women."

"Isn't he great?" Margie asked. Sana and Checky murmured praise. Mike gave Margie's arm a pat, then gently set her aside in order to step forward and scrutinize the tent's setup. He shifted some of their cots around and placed the stove, carefully settling it on level ground. Then he went around their tent, checking the ropes.

"Just don't set anything on fire. Keep a can of sand right beside it in case things get out of hand," he said when he was satisfied with his job. "And don't use it during blackout."

"I'll go find some wood," Sana said.

"Oh, no, we wouldn't want the women doing that. My guys are out chopping wood for you right now." Mike grinned. "Want some cigarettes?" He reached into a pocket and pulled out a handful of packets.

"I'll take those," Checky said. "We give 'em to the patients."

"Can you get some more?" Sana asked.

"You bet." Mike winked and Margie smiled.

"This's great," Checky said. "Can you get us more hot cocoa?"

"He can do everything." Margie reclaimed her place by Mike's side, taking his arm again. Sana had to look away.

A plane droned in the distance and they all looked up.

"Don't worry," Mike said. "That's one of ours."

"How do you know?" Sana asked.

"You'll get so you can tell the difference."

The drone got louder. "Are you sure?"

"Pretty sure."

The sound faded away and they all relaxed. "How come everyone says they come at sunset?"

"They fly in from the horizon so it's harder to see them in the sun. Once in a while they'll come in the morning, from the east. If you hear a plane get any closer than that one, grab your helmet and jump in your trench." Mike did not seem worried about

German air raids. He and Margie were gazing at each other again. Checky looked at Sana and rolled her eyes.

They were sipping cocoa and heating water for their evening wash when Adele came back from her meeting. "Blackout starts early. That fire's got to go out right now." She looked around and frowned when she saw the helmets upside down on the crate table. "Put those helmets on your heads and don't take them off again," she ordered. "Even when you go to bed." She sat down on her cot and sighed. "Where'd you get that stove?"

Sana moved to douse the little fire. Checky crossed over and rubbed Adele's back. "Mike and Margie brought it over. Don't worry, Adele. We'll bring back hot water from mess to wash up."

Adele closed her eyes and let Checky work on her shoulders. "I'm going to start calling you Florence Nightingale. Just a little farther up, honey... there... oh, that feels good." She took a deep breath. "We better go now."

The mess tent was brand new and the cooks were serving roast beef, mashed potatoes with gravy, canned corn and fresh-baked bread with jelly on the side. The line was long but soldiers cheered when the nurses arrived and made room for them at the front. They had finished their first helpings and were into their seconds when the announcement came that ambulances were arriving and they all needed to report to the hospital. Sana grabbed an extra piece of bread and jelly and stuffed it in her mouth as she hurried out.

The first litters to unload carried burned bodies with rows of empty surrettes clipped to the scraps of uniform were still left on their skin. The nurses did what they could with plasma and morphine while the doctors debated treatment. They finally decided to send the burned men as fast as possible to a station hospital closer to the coast, so a fresh crew of drivers and medics loaded the silent bodies back into trucks and headed out again.

The rest of the ambulances were unloading now. Adele sent nurses to their stations, putting Sana in charge of triage. Sana organized rows and started teams of nurses and medics down each one. *Oh, God, show me what to do. Please show me...* They needed more water, plasma and bandages and she sent a corpsman running for supplies. *And please take care of those poor burned soldiers on the road.* She did not think any of them could live long enough to get back to the station hospital.

Where were all these casualties coming from? Were any of them Rangers? She scanned each new face brought through the door, half hoping that she would see Joe on one of the litters and half fearing that she come across him with all his skin burned off, or dead. Then the new group of wounded would be laid out on the ground and for a while she only thought about the problems right in front of her, until the next bodies came in.

Finally the long flood of casualties stopped. Sana left her position at the front of the tent and started working her way down a row of litters, keeping three medics busy right behind her as they followed her orders. As she worked she wiped men's faces and hands with a damp cloth and kept up a stream of cheerful talk.

"Here, let's clean you up a little bit," she told a soldier with a bloody stump where his arm had been. She wiped his face, gently cleaning crusted dirt from around his mouth and eyes. "Doesn't that feel good? Want a drink?"

The man blinked up at her. "How'd I end up with a good looking nurse like you?" he murmured thickly. "This war ain't so bad. You got whiskey?"

"This stuff's better." A medic injected morphine and gave him a drink of water. The man closed his eyes and sighed.

"Do you think I can go home now?" he asked, eyes still closed.

"Yes," she said as she washed his one remaining hand. "You can go home."

Most of the men lay quietly in their litters, waiting their turn for help. A few cried out or muttered to unseen listeners. One big man was delirious, flailing his arms and cursing, and Sana was struggling with him when a big medic came up and put his hands on the patient's shoulders, pinning him down for her.

"None of that, buddy. There's a woman here," Wence said.

The man turned his head back and forth, eyes wild, skin pale and damp. "It hurts," he gasped, trying to pull away as Sana injected a dose of morphine. "Stop it. Stop, please. It hurts." His face, chest and arms were blistered with burns and lacerated with shell fragments.

"You'll feel better pretty soon," Sana said. "Just rest now." The man grew quiet under her hands. "Here's a drink of water."

"Why so many burn wounds?" she whispered to Wence as he set in the plasma needle for her.

"Tanks," Wence whispered back. "German tanks shoot farther than ours." He rubbed his face. "Our guys can't even get in range before a Kraut tank hits 'em. Every time the Germans shoot, boom, one of our tanks catches on fire and burning guys jump out. Then I gotta go crawl over there and pull them back to the ambulance."

"Oh, no," Sana said in dismay.

Wence shook his head. His eyes were bloodshot and gummy. "They shoot right at me. Geneva conventions, my foot. I heard they took a whole hospital unit POW."

"No!"

"Yup." He settled the can of plasma on a crate and moved with Sana to the next litter. "This one's got shrapnel in the belly."

Sana took vital signs while Wence cut off dark red bandages from around the man's middle. "Did you see Joe?" she asked.

"Yeah." The soldier jumped and groped blindly in the air when he felt the stab of morphine. Wence caught his wavering hands and gently held them as Sana checked the gaping wound and sprinkled sulfa over it. "He does raids out in the desert, hit and run type stuff." The soldier relaxed and Wence began setting up the plasma. "He brought some wounded guys into the clearing station and went right back out again. He said to tell you hi."

"So he's not in a tank. That's good."

Wence glanced at her. "Right." He shook his head and looked away.

"What?" she asked.

"Naw, I don't want to say it." He hesitated. "We can't beat those tanks."

Sana stood up. "You're right. Don't say it. This one needs to go to OR right away."

They worked in silence on the next man, who had a head wound and a tattered leg held together by a few strands of ligament. His pulse was thin and his breathing shallow. They started lines of plasma into both arms and laid an extra blanket over him, hoping to pull him out of shock.

"This one's got a broken arm," Wence said as they came to the last litter. It was a relief to see something as simple as a broken bone, but the young soldier trembled and wept when they crouched over him.

Sana took his hand and stroked back his hair. "Hello there, fella." The soldier sobbed harder. Sana looked at Wence, who just shook his head. He readied a shot of morphine and she washed the boy's face and hands, hoping the gentle touch would quiet him down. He cried out at the prick of the needle. They talked to him and gave him sips of water until he fell asleep.

"We'll keep him sedated." Sana wrote out orders and pinned them to the front of his uniform. "What happened to him?"

"I don't know. We just picked him up along with everybody else. He pretty much cried all the way here." Wence's voice was hoarse.

Sana sat back on her heels and looked Wence over. His eyes were sunken and the front of his uniform was stiff with other men's blood. Even his hands and beard were grimed with it.

"Bed rest and a shot of morphine wouldn't hurt you either," Sana said.

"That's not the kind of shot I want," Wence said with a ghost of his old grin. He sat down on the floor and yawned.

"You big silly thing," Sana told him. "Go to bed."

Wence yawned again until it seemed like his jaw would crack, took off his helmet and absently scratched his head. He gazed inside the helmet for a moment.

"Hey. Look at this." He pulled a photo out of his helmet liner and held it over for her to see. A young woman held a curly-haired little boy and a laughing baby girl in her lap. "That's Rachel," Wence said. "And that's little Karl. Growing like a weed. And this one's Katerina. Baby Katy."

"What darling children! A boy and a girl! They're so sweet!" Wence smiled at her praise. "So that's the woman who keeps you on the straight and narrow?"

"That's the one." Wence kissed the photo and tucked it back into his helmet. "You know what? Anytime the guys sit around and pull out their pictures, Rachel's always the prettiest." He yawned even harder than before. "There's some more wounded outside. Ambulatories."

"I'll get one of the other guys to help me," Sana said. "You go on."

Wence nodded blearily and hauled himself up. Sana looked over the litters one more time, checking on the progress of the medics sending patients to surgery. Then she went outside.

A group of men stood silently together just outside the tent. The last rays of sunset glinted off strange-looking helmets and uniforms, and Sana realized with a start that they were not U.S. troops.

An Army sergeant stepped forward, his rifle ready. "These are prisoners of war, ma'am. Some of 'em are hurt and the captain said that they should get looked at before they get sent off."

Sana looked at the foreign soldiers. They looked warily back at her.

"Do they speak English?" she asked. "Or French? *Français? Parlez-vous français?*"

"They're Italians, ma'am. And a couple of Germans," the sergeant said.

"Have them go inside and sit down so I can look at them."

One of the prisoners bowed, his hand over his heart. "I speak English, *signorina*," he said. "It will be my honor to translate for you." He turned around and shouted orders. The men filed past her into the tent and sat down. The English-speaking prisoner bowed again.

"Thank you," Sana said. "Where'd you learn English?"

"I grew up in Jersey City." The man smiled, flashing beautiful white teeth. "I went home to Italy to visit *mi familia* and the government made me go into the army. I am honored to be captured, *signorina*. Thank you. You are beautiful and I love America."

"Well." Sana could not help smiling at such cheerfulness. "I'm happy for you."

The Italian soldier saluted and clicked his heels. The sergeant frowned and motioned with his rifle. "Knock that off and go sit down." The Italian went inside.

"Where'd you get them from?" Sana asked.

"The Italians just walked out and asked us to take 'em prisoner. There's two Germans in that group though. Watch out because they're still mad. I'll stay with you, ma'am."

She was settling a bandaged arm into a sling when she heard the drone of planes. The two Germans raised their heads alertly and looked around.

The sergeant jumped into action, pushing the prisoners to the ground and yelling at everyone to get under cover. He grabbed Sana and threw her under a supply table just as the droning sound turned into a roar. The roar turned into an eerie whistling scream that grew louder and louder until an explosion blasted right above them and rocked the ground below. The Germans cheered and the Italians booed. Sana closed her eyes and hid her face in her hands as another whistling shriek screamed above and a second explosion shook the ground, closer this time. A third explosion blew in the side of the tent and rained down a hail of debris.

The Germans cheered again and yelled out taunts in English. "You will lose, Yankees! You will lose this war! You will all d—" a thud and a grunt cut off the voice and the words turned into a sputtering cough.

The roaring faded away. Sana clenched her teeth to make them stop chattering and crawled out from under the table to check her litter patients. They were quiet, still sedated, plasma still flowing steadily into their veins. She brushed dirt and splinters from their faces and then went back to the prisoners sitting on the ground. One of the Germans was spitting blood and teeth. The English-speaking Italian looked up at her and winked. His knuckles were bloody.

"Don't make any more work for me," she said crisply to everyone in the area. "That's an order." She looked around. "This is a hospital and I'm in charge. *Compris?*"

They worked by flashlight after that. Finally the last surgery was finished. The doctors left and the medics began the long routine of sterilizing instruments and washing bandages. After more long hours in post op Sana and Checky headed out to their tent, but they got lost in the darkness of the blackout and had to ask two sentries for help. Another pair of soldiers volunteered to escort them back to nurses' quarters.

The night was cold and still. Icy ground crunched under their feet and a canopy of stars glittered overhead as the four of them walked among the quiet tents. Sana was looking at the moon and hoping that Joe was somewhere safe, looking up at the sky and thinking of her too, when she tripped over a frozen rut and fell to her knees.

"Here, let me help you," her escort said solicitously as he helped her to her feet. "Are you all right?"

"It's these big clodhopper boots I'm wearing," Sana said, and yawned.

"Sure is nice out tonight," the soldier went on. His hand lingered at her waist. She moved away.

"You're a sight for sore eyes," Checky's soldier said to her. "I think you're cuter than a little speckled puppy."

"You must be from the South," Checky said.

"Yes, ma'am. Gordo, Alabama. Y'all are the prettiest things I seen since leaving home."

"Good thing you can't actually see us. We're covered with blood."

"Oh, we don't care," both men assured her.

139

"I know a place where there's a real pretty view," Sana's escort said after a moment. You girls want to go take a look at it?"

"No," Sana said. "We just want to get back to the tent." She tripped again and the soldier put his arm back around her.

"Sure you don't want to go see that pretty view?"

What a jerk. Sana removed the arm and stepped away. "No."

They all walked in silence for a while, ice and gravel crunching under their boots.

The soldier from Alabama spoke up. "This is great, seeing women again. This is the most fun I had since I got here."

It was hard to stay irate after a comment like that. "Where did you land?" Checky finally asked.

"Oran. It's so nice to see an American woman again, ma'am. I'm homesick for women. The only woman I seen so far was when we went to this place where there were a whole bunch of --" he got cut off by a kick and a grunt from the other soldier.

"Anyway, we're here on R and R," he said, and everyone fell silent again.

Checky changed the subject. "You know, guys, I gotta say, this camp is great. We even have a little stove to make hot water right in our tent. We call it the Ritz-Carlton."

"If I had my own little keg of beer in my tent I'd call it heaven," the other soldier said. The path took a sharp turn in the darkness and Sana felt him take her arm again. She pulled it away just as the Ritz-Carlton sign loomed out of the darkness.

"Here's our tent. Good-bye," she said.

"Thank you for walking us home," Checky added.

"Oh, you're welcome. Just call on us, anytime you need anything. I'm Les and this is Bud." The soldiers shook hands, holding on as long as they possibly could.

"I'm Second Lieutenant Toledo," Sana said, "and this is Second Lieutenant Janacek."

"Oh," the two soldiers said together, crestfallen, and left without any more comments. Sana and Checky groped their way into the tent, brushed their teeth by the light of the moon, and crawled into their chilly cots.

"Here." Barbara handed Sana the red stocking cap she had finally finished knitting. "It's warmer if you sleep with this on.

"Thank you," Sana yawned. She fumbled with her helmet, stocking cap and blankets, trying to get everything settled into a cozy nest of warmth.

"Men," Checky said. "Can you believe those guys?"

Sana was already sinking into a deep well of sleep. "Um hmm," she murmured.

"Hey, did you see Joe?"

She was wide awake in an instant, heart pounding. "What? No! Did you?"

"No." Sana heard her yawn. "Just checking."

"Don't scare me like that. I practically had a heart attack, thinking something happened to him."

"Oh, dear. I'm so, so sorry. I'm about as sharp as..." another yawn, " ...Private Gordo back there. "

Sana laughed and snuggled deeper into her blanket. "Goodnight, Checkers."

"You too." A last yawn trailed off in the darkness.

A slender beam of moonlight shimmered through the tent's canvas flaps. Sana gazed at it and wondered where Joe was sleeping tonight. He was so special. He was so good. He was her sweetheart, her man, her hope of family after the war. Life without him now would be pointless. She felt her skin prickle at the thought of losing him. *Oh dear God, please keep him safe or I don't know what I'll do.* Did that count as a prayer? *I hope so.* Her eyes closed. *Wherever you are, Joe Vesely, I love you.*

The rumble and bump of trucks interrupted her dreams the next morning. A liquid trickling sound of water came next. A spoon clinked. Sana opened her eyes to see what was going on.

Two cans of water were steaming on top of the little stove. Checky was sound asleep with her blue yarn hat pulled down over her eyes. Margie was snoring. Adele was dressed and sitting on her cot, drinking coffee and reading Joe's little Bible. Sana yawned.

"Good morning," Adele said.

"What's all the noise?"

"Supplies and mail. There's hot water. Want a cup of hot chocolate?"

Sana snuggled back down. "How can you possibly know everything that's going on so early in the morning?"

Adele sipped her coffee. "It's not that early. I'm letting you girls sleep late." She went back to her reading.

Sana closed her eyes and cuddled deeper in her blankets, trying to drift back off to dreamland in a warm bed on a cold morning. But after so many early wake-up calls she could not get back to sleep, and she finally opened her eyes again and watched Adele read for a while.

"What're you reading?" she finally asked.

Adele glanced up. *"Ask, and it shall be given you; seek, and ye shall find; knock, and it shall be opened unto you."*

Sana curled up on her side and tucked the blanket a little closer around her shoulders. What kinds of things would Adele want? "Are you asking for something?"

"Oh... for the war to end, for all these wounded boys to get better, things like that."

"Do you ever ask for, maybe, to fall in love and get married?"

Adele mulled over the question. "Well, no, not anymore." She ran a hand thoughtfully through her graying hair. "I'm too old to put up with a husband."

Sana laughed. If Adele ever felt about someone the way she felt about Joe, that would change. "You're never too old to fall in love."

Adele shook her head. "I'm too bossy."

"Well..." Sana had to concede that. Adele laughed.

"But what if the right man came along and you fell in love?" Sana asked. "Wouldn't you want to get married then?"

"Oh, honey." A fleeting smile crossed her face. "I've been around that block already. This one guy was going to marry me..." her voice trailed off. Sana waited, thinking of all the things Adele might say, or might not ever say, about the life she had lived before.

The older woman recovered some of her usual briskness. "But then he decided to marry someone else instead. That's why I left home. I couldn't stand sitting around with nothing to do and everyone talking about me behind my back and saying I was all washed up." She looked around the little tent. "So here I am."

"That is just like me," Sana marveled. "My uncle was going to make me marry a horrid old man and work in the grocery store for the rest of my life, so I ran away. But I still want to fall in love and get married."

"Looks like you've already done the falling in love part."

Sana gazed dreamily into the little stove's fire. "He's a really good guy, a real straight-arrow type."

"That's good." Adele nodded approvingly.

"So, I'm turning over a new leaf. I'm going to live like he does."

Adele arched a brow.

"You know, pray, not cuss, things like that." She felt virtuous just saying it.

Adele smiled a little private smile.

"What?" Sana demanded.

"You have no idea what you're talking about."

Sana propped her chin on her hands and got comfortable. "What do you mean?"

"Those things don't change your life," Adele said.

"Then what does?"

"Meeting the Lord."

"You're not helping," Sana said. "I told Joe I'd pray every day. Why don't you just tell me what you say?"

"This isn't for the curious people. Only the serious ones." Adele sipped coffee and smiled to herself again. "Asking God to change your life isn't like asking some clerk for a pound of sugar. You have to really mean it."

"Doggone you, answer me."

"I'll pray with you," Adele said. "You'll figure it out. But you're putting the cart before the horse, trying to pray a certain way. Meeting the Lord is the key to everything."

143

"What do you mean?"

"John fourteen-six. *'I am the way, the truth, and the life: no man cometh unto the Father, but by me,'* Adele quoted.

"Is that in the red section?"

"Uh-huh. The gospels. Matthew, Mark, Luke, and John. It's in John."

The names brought back a poignant memory from long ago, of sitting at a table with her mother and father, eating bread with honey and living in blessed innocence. "I remember those names," Sana said. "My father used to read a Bible in the morning during breakfast."

Adele hesitated. "Whatever happened to your parents?"

The old familiar pain clenched up inside. "My parents died in a car accident when I was twelve," Sana finally said. "It was right here in Constantine. I think I can see my old house from the hospital."

"Where'd you go after they passed away?"

"Oh... I lived with my Constantine aunts and uncles for a while." After talking about God it felt odd to not share the whole truth about what had happened to her, and Sana decided to say a little more. "We didn't get along very well so they sent me to my American aunt and uncle."

That's amazing." Adele finished her coffee and set the mug down on the crate table. "You really should take a trip into town while we're here. Some of the rest-and-refits go in during the day to look around. I'll see if I can set it up for you."

"Thank you." Now that the chance of a visit was becoming reality, Sana wasn't so sure that she wanted to go anymore. She reached under her cot for the coveralls she had kicked off the night before. She pulled them on over the flannel pajamas that she had worn every day since leaving England, then located her pairs of socks and evaluated their levels of griminess, trying to find the least dirty ones to put on next to her skin.

"Do you think we'll ever get more socks?" she asked.

"I ordered long underwear, socks, Levine tubes, Wangensteen suction machines and IV stands. And I wrote my sister and asked her to send us more lipstick and fashion magazines." Sana gave her a questioning look and Adele shrugged. "The girls like them."

"Jo Ellen will love you."

Checky rolled over and pushed her blue cap back from her face. "What is all that racket?" she grumbled.

"Supplies and mail, so be grateful you're hearing it," Adele said. "Want some hot cocoa?"

"I have the worst headache," Checky groaned, and pulled her cap back down.

"You've still got a head. Don't complain."

Checky groaned again. Margie opened her eyes. "What time is it?"

Adele clapped the Bible shut. "Time to rise and shine. Now that you're all awake, here's what happened last night. The good news is no one got killed in the raid. The bad news is the mess tent got blown up."

"Our nice new mess tent. Wouldn't you know it," Margie said through a yawn.

"Out late again?" Adele asked, an edge of irony in her voice.

Margie stretched luxuriously and purred a little murmur of assent.

"When I find a man I want to marry, I'll ask him if he'll bring me breakfast in bed," Checky said from under her hat. "And that's how I'll know he's the one. Okay, I'll take some cocoa."

A little later on they headed over to mess anyway, hoping to find something for breakfast. All that was left of the tent was shattered wood and shreds of canvas scattered across a crater in the ground. Cooks were handing out ration packs and ladling oatmeal from a fifty-five gallon can.

"Here we are, eating out of a barrel again," Sana said.

"At least the tent got hit when there wasn't anyone in it," Margie pointed out.

"We need to lay out that big white cross by the hospital," Adele said. "Maybe that'll keep those planes away."

They washed down oatmeal with boiling hot coffee and then went back to get the cross, which was now fifty-four sheets large,

145

and spread it on the ground next to the hospital. Mike showed up with a jeep full of canned peaches for the ward breakfasts. Sana poked through the back seat to see what else he had and found a box of cigarettes hidden under a blanket.

"We need this too," she said, trying to haul out the box by herself.

"Oh, no." Mike blocked her move. "I got other plans for that."

"It's for the boys," Sana protested.

"Well, one carton, then."

"Two."

"Listen." Mike lowered his voice. "I'm going to trade these for maple syrup. Think about it, pancakes with syrup for breakfast."

Sana frowned. "Don't change the subject."

"Lieutenant Toledo Ohio, you have to trust me. Boy Scout honor, I'll get more smokes for your boys. Oh, here's for Checky." He dug into a pocket and pulled out packets of cocoa mix. Then he looked around and pulled out two candy bars. "For you."

"Well." Sana's resistance melted away. "Thank you."

Mike tucked the blanket back over the box, then gave Margie a hug and a smacking goodbye kiss. "Bye-bye, Brownie girl. Take care of yourself now." He jumped back in his jeep and drove away.

"Don't you just love him?" Margie sighed.

Another truck pulled up. "Special delivery," the driver said, puffing as he set down two crates with "HOSPITALS—NURSES" stenciled on the sides. "Did you girls order something?"

"Socks!" They pried off the lid. Inside were bulky packages of brown paper, and inside the brown paper were dozens of lipsticks. The nurses pawed through the crate, finding more lipsticks and then some bottles of cologne at the bottom. The second crate held dainty white handkerchiefs and cans of talcum powder. There was a silence after the last package was unwrapped.

"I bet that perfume smells really nice," said the soldier.

Adele waved her arms and kicked over a crate, scattering lipsticks and bottles. "Who is sending us this stuff? Don't they know men are dying out here? Our men? Their men? I asked for a Wangensteen!" She aimed another kick at a different crate and staggered back when it didn't budge. "Ow!"

The driver disappeared back into his truck. The nurses looked at each other.

Adele put her hands on her hips. "Doggone it."

"I hope you didn't break a toe," Margie said.

"I'm wearing three pairs of socks and I couldn't break a toe if I tried." Adele glared at the crates.

"Maybe we can trade the handkerchiefs for some socks," Checky said.

"Trade them to who? Company C?" Everyone laughed, and then a cloud of dust rose over the mountain road, signaling ambulances on the way.

Adele put Sana in surgery and Margie in triage this time, to keep up all the nurses' skills. She sent Checky to help O'Neal debride wounds in the ward tents, but another line of ambulances drove in before the first group finished unloading, so she pulled Checky from debridement and ordered soldiers to set up a second tent for triage as fast as they could. Checky sent Red to find extra help and he returned with all the chaplains and cooks he could find.

Nine surgeons worked in fast rotation in the operating tent. A steady stream of litter bearers flowed in and out, plopping bleeding men on the tables, then hauling them away afterwards and bringing in more. Medics kept the sterilizer busy but a moment came when Sana, assisting Schmidt, reached for a clamp and didn't find one. Schmidt stepped back and flung a bloody dressing to the floor.

"Can somebody around here please get me a clamp as fast as they're getting me patients?"

"Sorry, sir," she said awkwardly.

He passed a hand over his face. "Oh, it's not your fault." He raised his voice again. "Where's all these casualties coming from?"

No one knew. "I guess there's some big general out there

going right at it, sir," a litter bearer said as he passed.

Schmidt squinted against the sweat running down from beneath his helmet and turned to Sana so she could blot it for him. "Well, does anybody know who's winning? Does anybody know anything? Can't we ever get any news around here?" Sana blotted his face again and handed him a cup of water.

Jo Ellen stuck her head into the tent. "Hey, everybody, a British hospital unit just came in and they're setting up another OR. Adele's going to send half our wounded over there as soon as they're ready."

Sighs of relief sounded. All the doctors paused for a moment, blinking and grinning.

"Frenchie, you don't know how close you are to sewing up this guy by yourself," Schmidt said. "I have to go so bad I'm gargling."

"Did I ever tell you I went into the men's latrine by mistake one night and a guy came in and sat down right next to me?"

"Lucky guy. Was it me?"

"I'm not telling." Red appeared with a clamp and she slapped it into Schmidt's waiting palm. "Just be careful where you go at night."

"If I ever come into a john and sit down next to a good-looking woman and don't know it... " he sighed. "Don't tell me."

The rush dwindled away about an hour before sunset and they all headed to over to mess, blinking in the dazzling light. Supply trucks were still unloading and the camp had tripled in size since breakfast. Sana lagged behind and took off her helmet, ruffling her sweat-damp hair to let the dry breeze blow through, but an officer driving past in an open jeep frowned at her and tapped his helmet, so she put her own back on.

Straight ahead of her, Constantine gleamed in the evening sun. The air was so clear that she could see the little stucco buildings. Maybe she could see her house if she tried. It was big, painted pink, with a rose garden and a wrought-iron fence in front. It would be close to the convent school. If she could just locate that convent... the convent had a tall bell tower and she should be able to pick it out...

She tripped and a hand caught her arm. "Watch out, ma'am. Right here," Red's voice said. He turned her around and she saw a new mess tent right in front of her.

"Over here," Checky called. She waved Sana into line between herself and Obie. "You look awful. Have a drink," she said, handing her a canteen. Sana gulped tinny water and splashed some into her hand to wipe her face.

Obie poked Sana in the ribs and nodded toward a table inside the mess tent where Jo Ellen and Nash were cozily sitting together, a little apart from everyone else.

"Can you believe that skunk?" Obie asked. "Schmidt told me he's married."

Sana did not feel up to discussing anyone else's problems. "Maybe they're just eating."

Obie sniffed. "The man I marry better not two-time me like that."

"I wouldn't," Red said. Everyone looked at him. Someone coughed behind them. "Excuse me. May I introduce myself?"

The nurses turned around, Sana still mopping at her face. A man in a British uniform nodded to them. "Major Tennyson-Hayes," he said. And this is Major Dowling. And you'll be the American nurses, right?"

The two men were thin and tan, their khakis frayed at the edges from long wear. They politely shook hands, but Sana's fingers were still wet and the men rubbed their palms on their pants afterwards.

"Are you the British doctors?" Checky asked. "Are you stationed here now?"

"Yes to everything, miss. We drove in just today with the artillery," Tennyson-Hayes said. "And what a day it's been. How are you girls holding out? You didn't get hit in that raid last night, did you?"

"Not too badly," Sana said, her own trace of accent coming out a little more strongly in response to the sound of his voice. She

149

tried to smooth back her hair without taking off her helmet. "One side of a hospital tent got blown down."

"The mess tent bought the farm," Obie added.

Dowling looked confused. "Hope we don't get any more of that," he said. "Terrible thing, bombing a hospital. Disgusting."

"You're surgeons?" Sana asked.

"Yes. Actually, we're here to show you how to do blood transfusions."

"Really?" Checky's voice was sharp.

"Yes indeed." Dowling rocked up on the balls of his feet and clasped his hands behind his back. "A remarkable innovation. Not too tricky, either. A real lifesaver."

"Fresh blood makes a tremendous difference for the seriously wounded." Tennyson-Hayes was looking around as he spoke. "Saves a lot of lives. I'll talk some of these big Yanks into donating to the cause."

"How do you do it?" Sana asked.

"We sterilize empty bottles and find some fellows with big veins to drip blood into them. So we'll need lots of empty bottles and lots of good-natured healthy blokes." Dowling grinned and winked. "Our quarter-master gave us a lorrie full of bottled beer and if your fellows will drink it up, that should solve both problems nicely."

Ten soldiers in front of them turned around. "You got beer?"

"Beer and a gramophone and dance records," Downling said grandly. "Everyone who donates gets invited to the party." Everyone whooped and laughed until Red pointed at a cloud of dust rising from the eastern road. Schmidt and the other doctors started back to the hospital.

"You been working all day. Stay here and eat something," Obie said to Sana as the line moved forward. "I'll go."

"I'll go with her," Red added.

"May we come along?" Dowling asked. "Perhaps we'll find some good Type O's. We passed a company of your Rangers coming in this afternoon."

Chapter Nine

Sened Station

"Rommel's to the east." Darby's finger stabbed *Tunisia* on the map. "Von Arnim's to the west. Now, there are about ten times as many Italians and Germans in this area as there are Allied forces, but we are going to make them think that we have a much larger presence here than we actually do."

His officers, including Joe, leaned in a little closer. "Small groups go in under cover, at night, make a lot of commotion and then get away before anyone knows what's happening. We make simultaneous raids here, here and here." The targets were deep in German territory. All the officers, including Joe, crowded closer to the map. "The fourth target is this fort five miles north of the Sened train station. This fort is to be destroyed." He tapped the map again.

"What if we could take the train station, sir?" asked one of the soldiers.

Men sucked in deep breaths and looked at each other. Darby grinned. "No. Not yet. The Germans could bomb us back to the Atlantic if we did that. You have a different objective. Bring back as many prisoners as you can for questioning. We need to find out what's happening with the Axis troops moving into Tunisia. We're going to go in at nights and raid the forts, make a lot of noise, do a lot of damage, take prisoners and bring them back alive. Then we'll find out what the Germans are up to. And they'll have to start scattering their forces around to protect all these little desert outposts."

He went back to the map. "Now. Starting at sunset, trucks will drive you in to this French outpost, here. You'll get there just after midnight." The officers leaned over the table again. "Each group marches about nine or ten miles before sunrise. Take cover during the day, resume march at dark, attack when the moon sets at midnight. Each man takes one C-ration, a canteen of water, and a shelter half. The Sened group takes mortars also."

Joe studied the map. Each point of attack was about fifteen miles away from the French outpost and the terrain was mountainous, so the march would be more like a climb.

"After the raids all sections rendezvous back as fast as possible and we truck out. We will not wait for latecomers." Darby looked around. "As always, no waiting for any wounded. Any prisoner who can't keep up must be shot. Is that clear?"

"Yes, sir," came the murmurs.

"Have your men ready to go at sixteen hundred. We'll all meet back here day after tomorrow."

The next day Joe and his squadron were twelve miles deep in German territory, hiding out in their shelters under the cover of a shadowy ravine. Four men were crowded into each little tent and the day was getting long. Johnson was reading out loud from a British fashion magazine he had brought along.

"He reached out to her, running his hands across her soft, warm skin. She came into his arms. He gathered her into a long embrace, feeling something stir deep within him as he kissed her yielding lips."

The other soldiers leaned forward, listening. Johnson read on. "Raymond pressed her hard against his chest. 'Promise me you'll love me forever,' Marcia whispered huskily. He kissed her again. 'I swear I will,' he promised. 'Until the end of time.' Her warm body trembled against him, melting into his arms... Will Raymond and Marcia prove their love? Be sure to buy next month's issue for the final chapter of *Hearts On Fire*."

Everyone sighed. Sneaking a magazine along on the raid was technically against orders, but there was no point in making Johnson throw it away now. He had just read the fiction section to them for the second time.

"Man, I miss my girl," he said. "Jenny. Isn't that a beautiful name?"

"That makes five," Taffington said. He was counting how many times that day Johnson talked about his girlfriend.

"First thing I do when I get home is eat a great big steak and get married."

"Six. Geez, man."

"I added up all the pay I'll have when I get home and I figure we can go on a honeymoon and take in a Cubs game or something like that."

Taffington was sorting his bag. "That's a lucky seven times now. Hey, you guys, look at this." Everyone looked over. "I can use my empty rifle clip to hold my smokes. They fit perfect."

A faint drone sounded in the distance. Robichaux, oiling his M-1, stopped in mid-polish. Johnson wriggled around and stuck his head out of the little tent's opening, looking for the plane.

Garcia smacked his rear. "Get back in here, idiot."

"They can't see me under all this camouflage."

Joe rolled over, carefully lifted a tent flap, and peeked out. The platoon was camped along the bottom of a ravine, tucked among dry clumps of desert scrub. Sunlight gleamed in the crystalline-blue sky straight above, but the ravine lay in deep shadow, which helped hide them from any planes that might stray overhead. The drone faded away. He looked over the dusty canvas shelters where the other soldiers were waiting. Someone peeked out of another tent and they waved at each other.

Gravel rattled down the ravine. Joe froze in place, listening. More rock clattered. He reached back for his rifle and heard the men behind him reach for theirs.

A goat appeared. Another followed. Three bearded Bedouin in ragged cloaks came next, then a barefoot boy leading a loaded camel, and then more goats trailing behind. A skinny dog brought up the rear.

The men walked right up to the closest shelter and called a greeting. Joe rolled out of his tent and onto his feet, rifle ready.

The desert men smiled and raised their hands in soothing gestures.

"*Chocolat? Cigarettes?*" One of them held out two oranges.

"Oh, geez," Joe said. "Robichaux, keep 'em covered. We can't let them leave here now. Ratliff!" Soldiers rolled out from another tent. "Put these... people under guard. Over there," he ordered, gesturing.

The Bedouin argued back in French and offered more oranges. The boy came up and watched. Joe tried to make them understand what he wanted them to do. Finally he traded four candy bars and two cigarette packs for a dozen little oranges. The men expressed their thanks, then led their little caravan to the place where Joe was pointing and settled down. Ratliff set guards in watches. Finally everyone crawled back into their tents.

"You guys want to eat now?"

"Let's eat the M-units first," Johnson proposed. "Then eat dessert before we break camp. Save the candy for right before the raid."

They pulled out little cans of meat and beans and worked the lids open. Robichaux brought out his slender bottle of pepper sauce and passed it to Johnson, who handed it straight to Joe, who gave it to Taffy, who offered it to Garcia. Garcia doused his M-unit with hot sauce and gave the bottle back to Robichaux. Joe had traded his candy for an orange, and the fresh sweet scent of its juice filled the little tent when he peeled it. He shared out the sections.

Everybody chewed and swallowed for a while. "I got bullion. What'd you guys get to drink?" Johnson asked through a mouthful of beans.

"I got lemonade," Garcia said. "But I don't want bullion. You can trade me your crackers if you want lemonade."

Johnson pondered his options. Joe held up his packet of cigarettes and looked at Robichaux. Robichaux waved his can of apple dumpling and they tossed the items to each other.

"Naw," Johnson announced. "I'll keep the crackers. Who else has something to read?"

"I got a letter," Joe said.

The others exchanged grins.

"From my uncle."

They looked disappointed.

"He says the news is all about how good we're doing over here."

"What're they saying?" Taffy asked.

Joe pulled out his packet of letters. The other three settled down to listen. *"'Dear Joseph, We are all so proud of you. Every day we hear about the U.S. troops in North Africa and our nation is grateful that someone out there is finally giving those Germans a fight. We pray every day for God to protect you and your men from harm, and to strengthen you and comfort you in the midst of every trial. Remember that you are never alone. His angels stand guard all around you every day as you fight to keep our world free.'"*

"Does he really talk like that?" Garcia asked.

"He's a preacher," Joe reminded him. *"'Everyone is supporting you boys all the way. People are turning in everything they can that's rubber or metal for the war supplies. They give brass plumbing parts, old rubber tires, anything aluminum and tin. Your Aunt Kate even donated some of her old cast iron pots and pans. That old junk store on the Avenue is doing a land-office business, somebody always makes money off a war. I get a couple of extra gas ration tickets because I'm a minister, but I never did buy a car, so I trade my gas to Vincent for sugar, and then Kate bakes kolaches and babufka. There isn't any poppyseed at the store anymore so she makes some kind of filling out of apples instead.'"*

Garcia and Johnson sighed at the thought of fresh bakery. Even Robichaux looked sentimental.

"'Your Uncle Vincent's working evening shifts in the accounting department at the corn factory after he finishes his day job at the bank. You should see the all trucks and trains pulling in and out of that place. You can't hardly walk across the street for all the traffic. Karel's the chief Air Warden now and he's got the whole neighborhood toeing the line. We have to fix our blackout curtains as soon as the sun goes down or we get a knock on our door and a lecture about how everybody better be careful or the Nazis will be in our backyards tomorrow. I think he's enjoying

himself a little too much but nobody wants to be unpatriotic and say so."'

"Where do these people live?" asked Johnson.

"Iowa."

"How come they need blackouts clear over there?"

"Beats me. *'Your Aunt Kate is working at the Red Cross. She takes your grandma over there every day and they fix up socks and bandages and things like that for the troops. The meat packing plant needs so many workers for all the shifts that Karel finally let Ruzina start working there along with him and Rosie. I never thought I'd see the day he let his wife and daughter step inside a factory. You should see the three of them walking to work together. Ruzina and Rosie wear overalls and boots just like he does. They all carry lunch pails and Karel kind of marches them along."'*

Everyone laughed. Joe grinned at the thought of Karel marching his family past the line of shops on 16th Avenue and over the bridge to work.

'"Kate says the girls are getting a big kick out of working at the plant. Rosie says for you to say hi to Wence and that the packing plant is making lots of Spam for you and all your boys over there. She keeps telling me she's a foreman but Karel won't say for sure and I don't know if I should believe her."'

"Who's Rosie?" Garcia asked.

"You know Wence Prazsky? Big crazy Czech medic? His little sister."

"I hope to God she doesn't look like him."

"Naw. She's real cute." Joe considered Garcia. "She had her eye on me once, but Karel threatened to turn me into a girl if I got any ideas."

"*Hombre.*" Garcia shook his head. "Don't introduce me."

'"Johnny sent us a letter saying that he is in the Rangers now, just like you. He is going to a training camp in England and he says he won't have much time to write."'

"Got that right," Johnson said. Robichaux flashed a grin.

'"Rudy is in the Pacific and we hear from him once in a while. He wrote a letter asking Rosie to quit making so much Spam at the factory

and make more roast beef for the troops instead. Last we heard from Anton is that he's in London working at some newspaper. Vincent still thinks he's a you-know-what but we aren't supposed to say anything in case the Nazis have a spy over here or intercept the mail."'

"What's that mean?" Garcia asked.

Johnson rolled his eyes. "They think he's a spy."

"'I speak about you often, how you have gone into danger so we can be safe over here. I pray for you every day."' Joe cleared his throat. *"'You should read Psalm 91. They are calling it the Soldier's Psalm. 'I will say of the Lord, He is my refuge and my fortress: my God; in him will I trust. He shall cover thee with his feathers, and under his wings shalt thou trust; his truth shall be thy shield and buckler. Thou shalt not be afraid for the terror by night, nor for the arrow that flieth by day; nor for the pestilence that walketh in darkness; nor for the destruction that wasteth at noonday. A thousand shall fall at thy side, and ten thousand at thy right hand; but it shall not come nigh thee. For he shall give his angels charge over thee, to keep thee in all thy ways.' Well, son, that's all I've got room for. I hope you are safe wherever you are. Kate and Stephen send their love and so do I. Uncle John."'*

They fell silent for a while. The shadow outside had deepened as he read.

"Read that last part again," Taffy said.

"'A thousand shall fall at thy side, and ten thousand at thy right hand; but it shall not come nigh thee. For he shall give his angels charge over thee, to keep thee in all thy ways.'"

"Do you know the rest of it?"

"I'd look it up but I loaned my Bible to my girl." Just thinking of Sana eased the tension building in the back of all his thoughts. His girl was somewhere safe out there, bravely doing her part. He would not fail her. Joe carefully folded the letter and tucked it back inside his shirt.

The sunlight was fading. He gave the order to strike camp. A whisper of clinks and folding canvas filled the dark ravine as they packed up their shelters. They pulled wool caps over their helmets and blackened their hands and faces. Joe tried to think of Sana again, her mischievous smile and her sweet cool voice, but he could not. The only thing he could think of now was the raid.

Garcia walked around making sure that everyone's little bits of gear were taped down and would not rattle. Robichaux spent several minutes carefully organizing all his weapons about himself, sticking an extra pistol in his belt and strapping on two more knives than regulation called for. Ratliff joked about Johnson's fashion magazine and Johnson tried to tape Rat's mouth shut.

Joe released the Bedouin from their guard. The men stood up, the camel and goats surging to their feet along with them. The little group vanished into the dark, with the lanky dog throwing one last suspicious glance over its shoulder as it trotted away.

The sky had deepened to dark night now, lit only by the sparkling desert stars. In a few hours the moon would rise. Joe called the group close in around him.

"Before we make the last approach, fix bayonets. Move forward together in line. We charge on my signal. Mortars first. Then grenades, then rifles. When we get into the camp, you know what to do." He called out names, assigning procedures for taking prisoners.

"Our orders," he said at the end, "are to destroy this fort completely." They waited, silent, eyes fixed on him. "We are going to take it by surprise and stick to our plan and do the work until it's done."

A low murmur swept the group. "We came here to fight this battle, this one right here. No one else came here to do it. We are going into danger to keep our country safe and make sure we still have homes to go back to. Think about that when you go in. Remember how the Germans torched those tanks. Remember what Arzew looked like. That's what's coming for us, if we don't stop them now."

They kept to the low-lying folds of land, flitting quickly over the peaks of the hills and finally coming out on top of a ridge from which they saw a light twinkling on the plain ahead. They stole forward over the starlit ground until they were only about five hundred yards away. When the moon rose they saw the lines of triangular tents, gleaming silver in the light.

Joe signaled the mortar crews into position. "Bayonets," he whispered, and heard the little snicks of metal in the dark. "Fan out. Skirmish line." Robichaux hung his grenades on his belt, grinned his pointy-toothed smile, and crawled off into the dark.

Oh, Lord in heaven, be with us now. Joe crept out in front of the line and signaled backwards with a shaded flashlight. They all crawled forward, flat on their bellies. Three hundred yards. Two hundred. One. Sweat prickled his forehead and ran down his back. He could see motorbikes and vehicles parked among the tents now. The fort would have guards posted. They were probably looking through the darkness right at them now.

We have gone into danger so they can be safe back home. Brush crackled as a soldier made a clumsy move. He held his breath. *For he shall give his angels charge over thee, to keep thee in all thy ways.*

A little animal jumped and chattered. Some desert dog raised a howl and then a burst of blue tracer fire sparked out from the fort. Bullets whistled overhead. Joe flashed his signal backwards again and they kept on creeping forward. More blue fire exploded. Joe focused resolutely on the tents and not on the bullets spraying above him. *Whoever's shooting must be nervous. He's aiming too high.* Seventy-five yards. They crawled on beneath the fire. Fifty yards.

He flashed a different signal.

Gunfire erupted behind him. The blue tracers disappeared in a bloom of smoke. Joe jumped up and ran for the tents. He paused to lob a grenade and Robichaux ran past him, bellowing a wordless roar and firing pistols in both hands. Joe yelled names and signaled left and right. Men ran past him, circling the camp, shooting into the tents as the mortars boomed again.

Now he was in the tent rows, firing into the silvery canvas. Men were struggling out of the tents and shooting back. Others had their hands in the air. Joe kept shooting. It was not yet time to take prisoners. He caught a glimpse of Garcia's contorted face falling to the ground. A tent exploded in front of him and a man charged him from the side. Joe jerked his gun around and caught him on the bayonet with a thick deep stab. A fleeing soldier ahead of him turned back, pointing a gun. Joe yanked his rifle hard but it would not come free so he went for his pistol just as a shot glanced off the side of his helmet and the man shooting at him fell down. Taffington stood there instead, his own bloody bayonet in hand.

Most of the tents were down now, bloody heaps of canvas on the moonlit ground. Dark shapes of bodies lay among them. Fewer men were running away. Rangers were still shooting and the fleeing soldiers fell as they ran. Joe called the order to start taking prisoners.

The roar of a motor made him spin around. Three men without helmets were climbing into a jeep. Joe lobbed his second grenade at them. One of them threw it back. It landed right at his feet and he scooped it up and pitched it back again as fast as he could. The jeep exploded.

Someone was screaming. "Surrender! Surrender!" someone else was shouting back. Pistol in hand, Joe swung around. No one was running any more. He could see men on their knees, hands in the air. Ratliff's voice shouted nearby, ordering someone to lie down. Joe looked for his rifle, found it, and jerked it free.

"Robichaux! Check tents! That way!" Robichaux began the grim task of making sure that no one was left alive in the bloody tangles of canvas. "Johnson!" Joe called. No answer. "Garcia!" Still no call coming back.

"Colonel Darby, sir," someone gasped behind him. Joe swung around and nearly speared a corporal carrying a radio.

"Colonel Darby wants to know if we've reached our objective."

Joe scanned the field. Soldiers were going from tent to tent. Rifles and pistols barked in sporadic bursts. A man who had tried to start up a motorbike was being pulled off it and secured. The mortars had stopped firing.

"Tell him objective taken."

"Objective taken, sir," the corporal spoke into the radio. "He wants to know how many prisoners you have, sir," he asked a moment later.

Joe took a breath and looked again. Ratliff was standing guard over fourteen men lying on the ground with their hands clasped behind their necks.

"Sir." Garcia was at his elbow, nothing worse that a purple bruise on one cheekbone and a cut on his arm. "All tents checked. Uh... "

Something was wrong. "What else?" Joe asked.

"Johnson's hit bad. I don't think he's going to make it."

The radio crackled through a dead silence. "Sir?" the corporal asked again.

Joe swallowed hard. "Tell him fourteen prisoners."

"Fourteen," the corporal called.

"Great!" Darby's jubilant voice carried clear through the static. "Now get out of there!"

"Tell him 'yes sir,'" Joe told the corporal, and heard the tinny echo of his words across the air.

They counted seventy-five dead, all of them Axis troops. Most were Italian infantrymen, only a few German officers among them. Eighteen Rangers were wounded, two of them seriously, but they were all able to walk.

Garcia led Joe to Johnson. He was limp on the ground, another Ranger kneeling beside him trying to staunch blood welling up out of his belly. One side of Duff's face was blasted away. The moonlight was bright enough to show his remaining eye looking frantically about.

The other Ranger held up a curette, asking a silent question.

Joe knelt down and leaned into Johnson's line of sight. "Hey, Duff."

Johnson's eye focused on him. "Sir..." He struggled, moving his arms and legs, trying to sit up.

Joe took his hand. A great hurting pain groaned inside his chest. "Yeah, I'm here," he whispered back.

"I can walk," Johnson strained out. "No morphine, man."

The other soldiers looked at Joe.

"I can make it." A tear slid from the frantic eye.

"Duff." Joe stroked back his bloody hair.

He lay quietly for a while then, holding tightly to Joe's hand, the dark pool underneath him spreading over the moonlit ground.

"Hey." He was looking up at Joe again. "Listen. You gotta get back. I know. I'll stay here."

Joe gripped his hand, shaking his head, feeling the great pain rise up until he had to clench his teeth to hold it down.

"I'm gonna find a way to get you back," he said. "I'll come back for you."

"Don't be stupid," Duff said. "It's okay. Don't worry." Another tear ran down his cheek. "Just go...
oh..."

Joe felt his hand begin to relax.

"Listen..."

"Yeah?"

"Tell Jenny I love her."

Joe closed his eyes against his own hot tears. "I will."

"Tell my ma, too."

"I will. I promise."

Johnson gazed up at him. Joe took both his hands. "God bless you, Duff." They looked at each other. "You did good. You gave it everything you had. All you had. No one could do any better. God bless you, brother. I love you. I'll never forget you." They sat together for a while, there in the moonlight, and in the end they did not have to leave him, because Duffer Johnson left them first.

They finished up their work and headed back, climbing rocky cliffs in the dark and sliding down steep ravines as fast as they could go. Joe had lost his pack somewhere, and as they hustled over a level stretch of ground Taffington offered him a swallow from his own canteen.

Water in his clammy mouth was a treasure of liquid, exotic pleasure from some other world. He capped the canteen and handed it back. "Thanks. Thanks for last night too."

Taffington's big plain farmboy face lit up into a grin. "Oh, well, we don't want to lose you, sir. They might replace you with one of them awful salutin' officers."

Halfway through the march Joe realized they would not reach the trucks in time if they did not travel faster, so he divided the group and ordered Garcia to take the uninjured soldiers, the prisoners, and the radio as fast as he could to the reconnaissance point. He followed with the wounded and a few of the healthy men, nursing the group slowly over the hills. When they finally reached the recon the trucks had left already, but a scrap of paper stuck on a rock had "Tomorrow" penciled on one side and "Marvelettes" on the other. A pile of mismatched ration units and filled canteens lay under a tarp nearby.

They spent the day huddled under scanty shelters. Joe set lookouts and took the first watch, concerned about German retaliation. When his turn came to rest he stretched out on the hard dirt ground and fell deeply asleep. He woke up with a jerk, drenched with sweat, heart pounding from a dream where monster soldiers with bloody bayonets were slaughtering his men, tearing off their arms and legs and then eating them alive as they screamed.

After that he stayed awake and stared at the empty road. What had he done back there? Dead rock and sand stretched to the horizon in every direction. *He shall give his angels charge over thee.* He could not picture angels in this forsaken place. But he could not picture any other place, either. The entire world lay empty, under the burning sky.

They watched the road all day. Mirages shimmered in the distance, dark shapes that looked like trucks for a while and then disappeared. They tended the wounded with sulfa and makeshift bandages, morphine and sips of water. Around sunset, another shimmering line of trucks came into sight and did not disappear, but turned into real trucks instead. People helped them inside. Canteens of lemonade were passed around and Joe drank a whole one by himself before he tried to talk.

"Where're we going?" he finally croaked out.

"Rest and refit, you lucky dog," a driver said. "You're going to Constantine."

Chapter Ten

Constantine

"They're saying that medics aren't going to get combat pay because they don't fight." Mike Duncan took another sip of grapefruit juice spiked with something that smelled like rubbing alcohol. "You're supposed to turn in your combat badge, too."

"What about getting shot at every *sacramente* day? That doesn't count?" Wence demanded.

"That's no fair," Garcia said from where he sat next to Joe.

"You're right it's no fairt," Wence said. "I get shot at just like you guys and I ought to get combat pay."

Joe's squadron had been trucked into the Constantine camp, hustled through a shower tent, given clean uniforms, and sent to the mess hall. Now he and Garcia sat on the hospital's vacant operating table passing the time with Wence Prazsky and his hospital friends. Joe was waiting to see Sana, who was still on duty, and Garcia was waiting for a swig of grapefruit mixture.

The surgery tent was clean and empty. Margie and Wence had finished their shift, Checky and Red had arrived early to replace them, and for the moment no one had anything to do. Adele and Tennyson-Hayes strolled in for a visit and Duncan pulled up in a jeep full of cigarettes and canned grapefruit juice. After they unloaded, Duncan pulled out a bottle of something alcoholic and combined it with grapefruit juice, and now they were all having a discussion.

"If you get captured wearing that combat badge they're going to shoot you," Duncan pointed out. He sat on the ground, leaning back against a crate of plasma bottles, one arm draped around

Margie's shoulders. "Anyway, it's a hypothetical problem. Nobody's getting paid out here."

Garcia reached for the canteen of drink. "They'll shoot him anyway," he said between slugs. A medicinal smell spread through the room each time the canteen sloshed. "It don't make no difference."

"I think medics ought to get extra-special pay," Checky said. "And special medals. Think of all those poor boys who'd have died out there without them." Garcia offered her the canteen but she waved it away. "I'm on duty."

"Hey. The lieutenant here got a Silver Star and a battlefield commission for the Sened raid," Garcia announced. "First Lieutenant Vesely now. El Darbo pinned on the silver bar himself."

Everyone looked at Joe. He nodded but avoided their eyes. Pronouncing words was too much trouble. The only good thing in the world was the long gray oblivion of sleep. His men were napping in their tents right now, but Garcia had dragged him away from his bedroll and over to the half-deserted hospital.

"It's only thirty cents a day," Duncan was saying. "You won't miss it."

"You Yanks are spoiled rotten," Tennyson-Hayes put in. "You're overpaid in the first place and then you complain about it. Overpaid, oversexed, and over here."

"Hey!" Garcia's eyes were bright and a flush of red was showing along his jaw. "Y'all couldn't make it without allies like Texas and America."

"You'd be speaking German today, my boy, if the Brits hadn't been taking it on the chin all these years."

Adele raised her voice. "I'm going to look into this. I know clerks right now just sitting around back in Arzew who're collecting combat pay."

Garcia passed the canteen of grapefruit brew to Adele, ignoring Tennyson-Hayes's outstretched hand. "Ma'am?"

Adele took the canteen, grimaced at the fumes and passed it on to Wence. Wence took a sip and waved it at Joe.

Joe shook his head. The idea of drifting away in a drunken haze was inviting, but he could not stomach the poisonous smell.

I'd like a nice cold beer.

"Me too," said someone else, and he realized he had spoken the words out loud.

"I have beer," Tennyson-Hayes announced. "All I charge is a bottle of blood. Even exchange. Not a bad deal, considering where we are."

"Huh?"

"We stick a needle in your in your arm and you drip blood into a bottle until it's full. Then we give you a bottle of beer."

Wence put his arm around Adele. "So you're going to make sure I get my combat pay, Adele? Lieutenant Adele?" He kissed her cheek. "My favorite, dearest, darling, chief nurse Lieutenant Ross?"

She waved him away. "I'll see."

"She's got the look," little Red announced. "Watch out."

Garcia guffawed at Adele. "Who do you know? Omar Bradley?"

Adele crossed her arms and stared at him. "Private, she said, "you need to learn right now that there are some things I don't discuss with soldiers."

Garcia blinked. All the other men looked away. Checky and Margie giggled.

"She knows someone," Checky said. She was mixing up a canteen of plain grapefruit juice for the on-duty shift, adding water and powdered lemonade to soften the acid bite. "Red, honey, taste this for me and tell me if it needs more lemonade."

"Ah, do you Ranger fellows know there's a dance tonight?" Tennyson-Hayes said politely.

"How do you have a dance out here in the middle of nowhere?" Garcia asked.

"Superior British intelligence."

"We're all getting dressed up," Checky chimed in. "We're going to look and smell like real girls.

Duncan snuggled Margie closer and smiled his wonderful

smile. "You always look like a real girl to me," he said to her.

"You always smell good, too," Red added, looking earnestly at Checky.

"It's that box of perfume," Checky told him. "We use it when we don't have time to wash."

"It's really nice of you to do this, Major," Adele said. "Thank you."

"Our pleasure, ma'am. We're celebrating a very special circumstance. We haven't seen a single German plane fly over since the raids, so we're having all the Yanks over for tea and cake."

Wence smacked Joe. "Waddaya say, big lieut?"

"Huh?" "

Geez, what's wrong with you?" Wence complained. "You need a drink."

Garcia handed Joe the canteen again. The acrid whiff of liquor drifting from the open top brought back the smell of decomposing bodies and the sight of lifeless eyes. For an awful moment the eyes were looking at him.

His stomach knotted. "Naw."

"You don't talk, you don't drink, you just sit there?" Wence shook his head. "How do you keep the chicks away?"

Quick footsteps sounded outside. He knew who it was even before she rushed inside, helmet tucked under her arm, drying her hands on a towel and looking around. When she met his eyes her face lit up and a thrill of pleasure warmed his soul. Then she was in his arms. He kissed the top of her head, remembering joy.

Laughter roared. He pulled back just enough to look at her. "You cut your hair."

She dimpled. "Do you like it?"

The dark curls were thick and silky, just like her lashes. It looked strange for a moment, then pretty. "You look like a chrysanthemum."

The dimples disappeared. "Is that good or bad?"

The whoops roared out again. "The higher they rank, the dumber they get," Wence shouted.

"It's beautiful," Joe told her. Her eyes glowed. She was wearing perfume. He took a deep breath of it and suddenly realized that the sun was shining and he was hungry. He put his arm around her shoulders so she would not get away, and felt her arm slip around his waist in return.

People were still laughing. Wence was clowning with Garcia. "Hey, everybody, look, I'm in love with a beautiful nurse. C'mon, baby, give me a big smooch." Garcia tried to push him away and fell off the side of the table instead.

"Let's take a walk," Joe said to Sana. "I want to ask you something."

They picked their way through the huge moving mass of trucks and soldiers, bumping into each other with pleasurable little touches as they walked, not able to talk yet because people were still too close around. Dust billowed up from the roads, making them squint and sneeze, and Joe took Sana's elbow to steady her whenever the rocky ground seemed uneven or a truck past by just a little too closely. She leaned into his touch each time. They reached the edge of camp where the nurses were quartered and stopped by the last group of tents. Beyond the tents, a forest of pine trees covered the side of the mountain. Drying laundry flapped from ropes strung among the trees.

They found a place to sit in the shade. Sana took off her helmet and ran her fingers through her hair, loosening up her curls. Joe took off his own helmet, leaned back on his elbow, and looked up at her. He smiled as she brushed dirt from her overalls, glanced at him, and looked away.

"There's my tent," she said, pointing. "We named it the Ritz-Carleton. Oh, and look. Up there." Tile roofs gleamed in the city on the cliff beyond. "See that town? That's Constantine. Where I'm from. See that tower? Not the tall pointy one, that's the minaret. The next one down, the square one. That's where I went to school. My house is right next to it."

"That's, ah, pretty amazing." Joe kept watching her, knowing that she would eventually look back at him. She finally met his eyes, and he sat up next to her and took her hand. Silence hummed between them.

"You-hoo! Sana!" A nurse waved from one of the tents. "Is that the Ranger?"

Sana waved back and nodded. Another nurse wearing only underwear looked out, shrieked, and disappeared. Tent flaps tumbled closed. Joe looked away, pretending to be interested in the clotheslines until he realized that the drying clothes were brassieres and panties. He blinked, then turned back to Sana.

For a while he just held her hand, not knowing what to say. Being with her was like being safe at home again, like being with his aunt and uncle. Trees rustled above them, throwing slender patterns of sun and shade over the ground, and the clean flinty fragrance of sun-warmed pine drifted in the air. A straggling plant growing at the edge of the shade had bloomed with delicate lavender flowers, and Joe picked one for her. She tucked it behind her ear. He took her hands again and stroked her fingers, marveling at how slender they were compared to his. Her palms were rough. She was thinner than before. Her uniform was frayed from wear and her boots were stained and dirty.

She touched a half-healed scrape on the back of his hand, murmuring concern. He brought her fingers to his lips and kissed them.

She grinned at him, her old mischievous smile.

"I thought about you every day," he said.

"I thought about you too." Her fingers entwined in his. "I prayed for you," she added, a little hesitantly.

He smiled at that. A pine needle had tangled in her curls and he gently pulled it out and stroked her hair back into place. Silky strands caught on his calloused hands. Her eyes were beautiful and her nose was perfect. A delicious urgency welled up inside and he took a deep breath, getting ready to ask his question.

"What's this from?" she asked, fingering the old burn scar on his hand.

He let out the breath, deflated. "I got burned. When I was little."

She looked curiously at him. "What happened?"

It was a fair question, but he had to grope around for a moment before thinking of what to say. "My mom had this... friend, this boyfriend, one time..." That whole shameful part of his life seemed unreal now, like something that had happened to someone else, and he did not want to think about it now. He looked at Sana's clear eyes and smooth complexion. She must have been taken care of when she was little. She must grown up with her own parents, in a house, protected.

"My parents died when I was little." She was looking at him with the grave expression he remembered from their high school days, when she had always looked a little sad compared to the other girls. He looked down at her hands again and took courage from the scrapes and calluses on them. She was no sheltered girl anymore. She would understand.

"Well, my mom," he began, "had a bunch of jerk boyfriends." How was it that he couldn't remember those names anymore? But he could still recall their faces. "I used to steal stuff from them, cigarettes and things like that."

She waited for him to finish, and finally said, "They punished you?"

"You could call it that." His voice came out sounding more hurt than he had intended.

"My parents never beat me," she said, "but after they died my aunties did. My Algerian aunties, not Aunt Mary." Her eyes were clear and level, her expression composed. "I hated them."

He suddenly felt better. "Well, I sure hated those guys." Any child would have. "There was this one I remember, slapped the tar out of me because I came into the house at the wrong time, so I poured out all his hooch and ran away for a week." He felt a little hitch in his throat that was almost like a laugh.

Sana did laugh. "One time I got so mad I was going to put rat poison in their tea."

They both laughed. Joe put his arm around her shoulders and they just sat there together for a while, looking out across the camp and holding hands. A cool breeze passed over the pines and he pulled her closer to him, to keep her warm.

After a while the delicious sense of urgency returned. "Sana." He lingered over her name. "I never felt about anyone the way I feel about you."

She gazed steadily at him. "Me either."

"I know this is... maybe a little fast, and maybe we'll never get a chance to... I mean, we don't know if..." he ran out of words.

"Do you know what I'm trying to say?" he finally asked.

She nodded.

"I love you."

"I love you too."

He bowed his head. She pressed his hands and he looked back up. She was smiling. A tear ran down her cheek and stopped in her dimple.

The sight of the little glistening drop made him smile. She sniffed and smiled back.

"What would you think about... well, marrying me?"

"Yes!" She flung her arms around him. "Yes, yes, yes." She was laughing and he laughed too, for joy and sheer relief. He folded her in his arms and kissed her hair and rested his cheek on the top of her head, cradling her against his chest. Then he took her by the shoulders to see her face again.

"You mean it?"

She was smiling, all glowing eyes and dimples. "All my life."

He was practically her husband. That thought made him square his shoulders. He would take good care of her; he would protect her with tenderness and compassion; she would never regret his love. He put his hand up to her hair, running his fingers deeply through her curls, and her eyes opened wide at his touch. He took her face in his hands and wiped away the little tear, and as she closed her eyes and leaned toward him, he kissed her.

Later that afternoon, back in the canvas Ritz-Carleton, Margie and Checky pried the story out of Sana while they took their sponge baths. Obie had come for a visit and was looking through the perfume box.

"I figured he popped the question when I saw you kissing," Obie said. "You guys looked so cute."

"I knew he was going to ask you the minute you left," Margie bragged. "I knew it was in the bag."

"You guys." Sana smiled down at her helmetful of sudsy water, luxuriating in the rosy glow of love.

"Hey, if you and Joe live in Cedar Rapids then we can see each other all the time," Checky said. "We can go visit Mom and Dad and you can milk cows."

Sana smiled again, still wrapped in her romantic fog. "Sounds great."

"Do it two times a day for ten years," Obie commented, cautiously applying lipstick as she peered into the mirror. "I milked cows from the day I turned eight'til the day I left home."

"My parents want to adopt you," Checky said. "I think that shade's too pink for you. Try that coral-colored one."

"Are they drinking people?"

"Oh, no." Checky rinsed soap off Margie's back. "But I got a couple numbskull brothers I want to marry off."

"Good-looking?" Obie wiped pink lipstick onto the back of her sleeve and tried the new color.

"Six foot two, eyes of blue."

Obie sighed. "I dunno. When I get back I don't want to live in the sticks again." She tried out a tentative coral-colored smile. "I hope I meet a really great guy before I go back, like you guys."

"Big Red's always hanging around," Margie said.

"He's so sweet," Checky said.

"He's a goony puppy."

"He's a real hard worker," Obie said defensively. "I like him."

Margie held up her hands. "Whoa, I like him. I love him. Geez, guys, sorry."

Sana finished her face and arms and started washing her feet. A fine fuzz of silky hair covered her legs. "I haven't shaved since forever."

"Me either," Margie said. "We're just one big dirty happy

family here."

"At least we get along good," Obie said. "You guys oughta meet my folks. We got nooses in our family tree."

Adele joined Obie in front of the mirror and pushed back her curls, frowning at her reflection. "Doggone this hair."

"Adele," Sana said, "I don't think I've ever seen you look in a mirror before."

"Got your eye on somebody tonight?" Obie asked.

"Hmpf," was all Adele said.

The others exchanged looks and Sana started toweling dry. A woman's high-pitched scream shrieked out from somewhere. Another screech joined in. "Get it out! Get it out!"

"Holy cripes, what's going on?" a voice called from another direction.

"It's a scorpion," Adele said dismissively. "Girls!" she yelled in a voice pitched to carry through layers of canvas. "You are supposed to check for bugs every day!"

That silenced the commotion. Sana selected a bottle of nail polish from the lipstick box and started painting her nails. "So, there's cake and tea?" she asked after a moment. "What else?"

"Mike says they're making something out of Spam and biscuit dough," Margie said.

"Yuck." Sana blew on her nails and held her hand out to get the full effect. "I'm not eating anything pink. I just want to dance." *With Joe.* She smiled at the thought.

Obie frowned at her lips, blotted off most of the lipstick, and sat down on a cot. "I don't know how to dance."

"I can show you a few steps," Margie offered. "I taught these guys everything they know." She was rooting through her pack, strewing socks and panties across her cot. She pulled out something that twinkled in the late-afternoon sun. "Look, everybody."

It was a golden necklace with tear-shaped pendants dangling from the delicate links. "Mike gave it to me. Do you think it's real gold?"

"Let me see," Sana said, reaching for it. She turned the

necklace over, inspecting the work. "Yes, this is gold." The filigree patterns engraved on the necklace's pendants were as familiar as the lines on her own hand. It was the kind of jewelry she had seen in the Constantine markets when she was a girl. "Where'd he get this?"

"He went into town with a bunch of guys and there's a jewelry store there."

Sana held up the necklace to let the pendants swing and sparkle. The whole world was wonderful today. Not even the thought of her uncles could bother her anymore, because she was going to marry the love of her life. She handed back the golden necklace, smiling beatifically at nothing in particular.

"It's beautiful. I'm so happy for you, Brownie," she said in a burst of generosity. Love made it easy to be kind.

"Dang it." Adele was still in front of the mirror, dampening and combing her hair.

"Tie a ribbon around it," Sana suggested.

Adele frowned at her reflection. "Does anybody have a ribbon?"

"I have a scarf," Checky volunteered. The scarf turned out to be a square of silk with a pattern of pink and blue roses. They all clustered around Adele, tying the scarf into the narrowest possible band and fluffing out her curls around it.

"Now put on some pink lipstick. Perfect."

"That looks super sharp," Margie said when they were done. "Got a scarf for me?"

"I have a yellow one but I'm wearing it myself, Miss Gold Necklace."

Sana finished buttoning up her coveralls. "Please pass the perfume box." She browsed through the jumble of lipsticks and perfumes, trying out different shades of red on her wrist and sampling all the different scents. She had left her mother's gold jewelry back in the States with her high school teacher for safekeeping. But she did not feel the need for any jewelry tonight. Her soul was still sparkling from the kiss.

The nurses walked down the hill together and found a pack of soldiers waiting for them at the road. The men grinned and murmured hellos, looking at the women with hopeful, lonely faces. Soon each nurse was surrounded three-deep. Joe cut through Sana's group, his blue eyes and silver bars blazing, and took her elbow. Disappointed men walked alongside as they started toward the mess tent.

"How do you do, ma'am?" the closest soldier asked her.

"Why, fine, thank you." Sana said. "It's a lovely evening, isn't it?"

"Oh, yes. Yes ma'am. How you doing?"

"Ah, fine." She glanced sideways at Joe and felt his grip tighten on her arm. "You know, we nurses have heard such good things about what you're doing. We're all so proud of you."

Every soldier started talking about the raid or the camp or how good it was to see an American woman. Sana nodded and smiled. When they finally reached the mess tent they had to go in single file through a black-out curtain, and once inside the crowd thinned out as men headed for the tables loaded with cake and tea.

The tent was dimly lit, with a few hanging light bulbs gleaming on British and American flags hung along the walls. Within minutes, every nurse had been handed a mug of lukewarm tea and a plate of chocolate cake. Mike's pink Spam creation stood untouched. Sana and Joe lingered near the door, letting the crowd flow past them.

Adele was talking to the camp's commanding officer, with Checky and Obie at her side. Officers hovered around the three women, watching them with soulful eyes.

"Thank you." Checky accepted a cup of tea from a handy captain. "This is great. How'd they make chocolate cake out here in the middle of nowhere?"

The captain looked thrilled. "I think they used powdered cocoa, miss."

"Really great of the British to do this," Adele said to the colonel standing next to her.

He rocked back on his heels and folded his arms over his chest importantly. "Absolutely. The men really needed it."

Adele nodded. "Oh, yes." She balanced her plate on her mug and took a bite of cake.

The colonel frowned. "Ah, how's the cake?"

An awkward little silence followed as Adele chewed and swallowed before she could reply. Nine men waited to hear what she would say. Obie handed her empty plate to one of them and said to no one in particular, "I'm going to find Mike and Brownie," and walked off, trailing soldiers behind her.

Tennyson-Hayes and Dowling appeared. "Hello, dear," Dowling said to Sana. "Enjoying yourself, I hope?"

"Lovely of you to do this. Really wonderful." She heard Joe clear his throat. "May I introduce you to First Lieutenant Joseph Vesely?" she said grandly.

"Oh. Very nice to meet you, Lieutenant." He turned back to Sana. "I'm afraid we're having a bit of trouble with the gramophone. That last bit of transport over the Atlases must've jostled some wires loose, sorry to say."

"I'll take a look at it," Joe offered.

They all walked over to the dusty record player and Joe crouched down in front of it. Sana watched him as he took off the casing and studied the colored wires inside, intent as a little boy looking at a bug. He teased out a few strands of copper wire, completely absorbed, his eyebrows drawing together in concentration.

Sana browsed through a stack of albums. "You Brits think of everything," she said enviously. "You really know how to live out here."

"Well, we've been doing this for a while," Dowling said modestly. "Is there anything you nurses need? Can we perhaps procure a few of the finer things for you?"

"Socks and long underwear." Sana said promptly. She pulled out her pajama collar, dirty brown now instead of pink. "I've worn this every day since I left England."

Dowling and Tennyson-Hayes exchanged conspiratorial looks. "Socks..." said Tennyson-Hayes, nodding his head. "Women's underwear. Hmm..."

"And some Wangensteens, if you have any spares."

"Oh, we make those ourselves out of empty plasma bottles and old IV tubes." Tennyson-Hayes said. "We'll send some over."

"What about a sewing machine?" Sana asked, thinking about the big white cross.

They both laughed. "You're not the first to ask about that," Dowling said. "Not a chance. The tailor sleeps with it at night."

Joe finished reconnecting his wires and tucked everything back in order, then blew a ball of dust out of the needle's housing.

"Give it a try," he said. Sana flipped an album onto the turntable and delicately set the needle arm to play. A few preliminary skips and scratches sounded and then *In The Mood* rang out. Soldiers everywhere set down plates of cake and jumped to grab a partner. Joe shook hands with Dowling and Tennyson-Hayes, took Sana's hand, and led her out to dance.

He kept her close. She felt his hand at the small of her back, the hard muscle of his upper arm beneath her fingers. He was all hers now, his fine shoulders and the tender crinkles at the corner of his eyes. She moved her hand up along his arm and he tightened his grip as another couple blundered into their path. Obie's smiling face swung past them. A soldier was approaching, trying to cut in, but Joe swung Sana into a turn away from him and shouldered him off. She felt him lead her into a twirl, and as she swung out and then came back into his arms she laughed and he laughed with her. How had this marvelous thing happened, in a desert, in the middle of a war? She was going to marry Joe Vesely, and he danced like a dream.

Chapter Eleven

Kantara Pass

Joe drove down a street in the middle of Constantine, an MP armband on his sleeve, humming a Glenn Miller tune. Stately date palms lined both sides of the dirt road. Constantine sure was prettier than Arzew.

He checked the directions written on his patrol orders, pulled up to a little square house with three olive-drab jeeps parked in front, and abruptly stopped humming. Robichaux, who had been snoring away in the passenger seat beside him, woke up and yawned.

Even in the warm sunlight Joe felt something like a chill at the back of his neck. He looked around. A group of Arab men were drinking coffee on a shady terrace across the street, all staring right at him. Joe turned back to Robichaux, who was looking at the vehicles parked along the road and grinning his white-toothed smile. Joe glared and the grin faded.

"Come on." Joe got out and slammed the door. He strode up to house, knocked, and turned around to scowl at the men across the street. Robichaux strolled up, in no hurry to join him.

A gray-haired woman, shawled and barefoot, opened the door.

"Excuse me, ma'am," Joe said, and pushed past her into a darkened room that smelled like musty onions and stale tobacco. Soldiers lounged on the floor. They stared back and one of them blew out a long, alcoholic burp.

"Out. Now." The men focused on his armband and blinked in surprise. "Out... out... you're all gonna get the clap and go blind...

Out, soldier, right now..." He pulled up a protesting soldier by the collar, pointed him toward the door and kicked him in the rear.

The soldier plunged forward. "Aw, come on," another complained as he stumbled past. A third tripped over the woman's bare feet with his heavy boots. She shrieked in pain and slapped at Joe, protesting the raid in a stream of Arabic.

"Sorry, ma'am," Joe said over his shoulder. Robichaux seemed to be trying to herd the men outside without actually looking at them, implying that this business wasn't his idea. Joe grabbed his shoulder and redirected him toward a doorway on one side of the room, then pulled back the curtain of another. "MP!" he yelled at the dim forms on the pallet inside. "Out! Geez, Ratliff, what are you doing here?" His sharpshooter gaped around at him, lurched up and stumbled out, buttoning his pants and muttering.

Joe rousted five more men and Robichaux threw out three. Back outside, they ignored the growing neighborhood audience as they watched the soldiers reluctantly climb into their vehicles and drive away. A curse aimed at MPs everywhere floated behind on a cloud of dust.

They got back into their own jeep and Robichaux tapped a cigarette out of his pack. A swarm of children instantly surrounded them. Joe switched on the engine and gripped the steering wheel, still smelling the warm intimate scents of the women's bedrooms, seeing in his mind's eye the coupled huddlings of men and women in dark little rooms. A rush of desire shot through him, an electrifying urge that whipped into a hard physical fire. He revved the engine harshly to clear the crowd and forced the jeep through the line of outstretched hands, narrowly missing a boy waving oranges at him. Once clear of the crowd, Robichaux lit up and sucked in a lungful of smoke.

Joe looked at his watch. Nine and a half more hours of patrol, and then twelve more hours after that until he could see Sana again. He drove to the end of the street and looked at his watch. Three minutes had gone by.

He glared at his companion. "You sorry, spineless, limp-wrist piece of worm. You acted like an old woman back there."

Robichaux studied bits of trash along the road. "Yessir."

"You go in first next time."

"Yessir."

Joe looked at his watch again and sighed.

Sana, standing at the tail end of a long line for lunch, felt a colossal headache gathering right behind her eyes. A harsh breeze was blowing and her feet hurt. She was having a terrible morning and after lunch she and Joe were both scheduled go into Constantine on leave. Now that the moment was actually here, she wasn't sure she wanted to go anymore. What if she saw her uncles there? What if they saw her? What would they do? What would Joe think? Her stomach lurched at the thought. She wasn't even hungry. Why was she standing in line for lunch?

"Here you go, ma'am." Sana automatically held out her open mess kit for a helping of hash, two slices of fresh bread, and big spoonful of canned peaches. The teenage private serving out the peaches gave her a loopy gap-toothed grin and she forced herself to grimace back some sort of smile. Checky, a step ahead of her in line, stopped so suddenly that Sana bumped into her back and sloshed peach syrup everywhere. She choked off the cuss word that came to mind.

"Dang." That did not blow off nearly enough steam and she hissed through clenched teeth with pent-up frustration as they threaded through the noisy tables, looking for a place to sit. Sana headed for an empty table at the far end of the tent and sat down, sighing as she finally got off her feet. Checky lingered for a moment before sitting down, gazing at something outside the tent.

"Look at those poor kids," she said. "How'd they get clear out here?"

Sana followed her glance. It took her a moment to see what Checky was talking about, two dark-haired little girls sitting by the side of the camp road and blending into the colors of rock and sand as if they had grown out of the landscape. They stared solemnly at Checky and Sana, not moving except for their eyes.

Sana stared back. Their grave faces stirred a thread of recognition, a teasing flash of memory she could not quite pin down.

"Let's give them our food," Checky whispered. She crossed the road and Sana heaved herself back up on her feet and followed. The girls pulled bowls from their robes and held them out. Checky and Sana spooned over their hash and peaches, and then Checky firmly hugged and kissed each one. They made little courteous dips of their heads before disappearing into the shrubs.

"All these little kids are so skinny." Checky wiped her eyes. "It just breaks my heart to see them sitting there while we eat like kings and queens." The two women headed to the end of the lunch line again for refills. "They remind me of my little sisters," she went on. "I just hope my family never has to beg for food like that."

"They remind me of my cousins," Sana said. She could remember playing with her girl cousins, when she was little. The tantalizing memory of their faces floated nearer, right at the edge of clear recall.

"Are they still here?" Checky asked.

Sana looked at her blankly. "You mean those little girls?"

"No, silly. Your cousins. Do they still live here?"

Something painful gripped her heart. "I don't know."

The gap-toothed private served them more greasy hash and syrupy peaches. Sana followed Checky to a new table and sat down for a second time.

"Well, don't you want to find out? Maybe you'll see them today." Checky smiled sunnily. "I am so hungry. Hey, I got a letter from Mom and she says hello to you." She pulled a folded sheet of paper from her pocket. 'Dear Barbara, We are hearing lots of news about the wonderful job that our boys are doing over there. We are all fine except that your Dad is going crazy because of trying to find good help with the milking. We even hired the Aumann kids from down the road but they don't always get here on time in the morning and it just drives him nuts. At least we still have Orville with us and he has turned into a pretty good milker even though we had our doubts about him.'"

Hearing Checky read a letter from home usually cheered Sana up, but today it only made her irritable. "Mary's husband didn't sign up?" she asked, trying to hide her petulance.

"He tried to but they wouldn't take him." Checky took a bite of peaches. "He's got a gimpy leg," she explained. "Polio when he was little. Dad thought he was too feeble to be a good farm worker but I guess he's coming along okay." She took another bite and went back to the letter.

"Orville is still hoping for a boy but I bet him a dollar it's a girl. Mary says she is tired of being pregnant and she wants to have the baby and get it over with. We have everything ready and now we just need a good healthy delivery. I can't wait to have a baby in the house again. It's too quiet around here with you and your brothers all gone. Take care of yourself and remember to use your head and stay safe. We are very proud of you and everybody in town says to say hello and keep up the good work, we are all behind you. I hope that you and your nice friend aren't getting shot at or bombed or anything. You girls make sure you get proper rest and don't get run down with all your nursing work. Love, Mom.' Isn't that exciting? Little Mary's going to have a baby."

So much happiness made Sana even more depressed. "Uh-huh."

"What's the matter?"

"Nothing."

Checky looked up from her hash, concern playing across her open face. "Come on."

"I just have this terrible headache."

"Want some aspirin?"

"No."

The candid china-blue eyes widened at her snappish tone and Sana felt a sting of guilt.

"Sorry. I don't know why I'm so grouchy today."

Cheerful again, Checky beamed a smile. "Oh, that's okay. Just think of all the times *I've* been grouchy. Hah!"

Sana felt her headache ease. She took a bite of peaches. "I have never, ever, heard you say anything grouchy. Ever. To anyone."

"You just ain't been around, Frenchie girl. You know what? When we go back, I want you to come live with me. Mom would love it and you could just be with us and get a nice long rest."

Sana put down her fork. "Oh, Checkers." Now she was going to cry. "That's the nicest thing anyone's ever said to me."

Checky leaned over and hugged her, patting her back when Sana's hot tears overflowed onto her comforting shoulder. "I mean it. You just come home with me." When they finally gave a last hug and let go of each other she held Sana's shoulders and looked at her earnestly. "You will always, always have a home with me."

They both wiped tears after that. Finally Checky went back to her lunch and tucked enthusiastically into the rest of her hash. "So is Joe going with you this afternoon?"

The headache pierced right back "Yes," she answered, clipping out her words. "We both have leave to go into Constantine after lunch." *Although I don't even want to go now*, she almost added.

"Want to wear my scarf? The yellow one would look great on you."

"I don't think it's exactly uniform."

Checky rolled her eyes. "You're wearing pink pajamas, you've got blood all over your boots and you think people are going to say something about a scarf?"

Sana considered that. "He's pretty much a kind of, you know, by-the-rules kind of guy."

Checky waved her last spoonful of peach in the air. "Well, at least put some lipstick on. Even a barn looks better when it's painted."

After lunch Sana ran back to her tent for a quick wash. There was nothing she could do about her stained boots and coveralls, but she picked out a pretty shade of lipstick and rifled through Checky's bags to find the yellow scarf. She spent a fretful five minutes peering into the mirror tying and retying it, but the bow would not fluff up just right and the whole anxious business only made her headache worse, so in the end she pulled off the scarf, raked her hands through her curls, grabbed her helmet and headed out at a run to the entrance of the camp.

A little group of soldiers and nurses were loading up into jeeps. Even while she was still far away she saw Joe, recognizing him by the line of his shoulders and the way he stood so straight. He looked around just then and met her eyes. He looked so handsome in his clean new uniform that Sana took in a delighted breath as he walked out to meet her. She felt suddenly self-conscious in her dirty coveralls.

"Go on, give her a kiss!" someone shouted.

Sana looked down, embarrassed, but when she felt Joe's arm steal around her waist she looked back up into the eager warmth in his eyes. She loved that boyish look with all her heart. He put a finger under her chin, gently tipping up her face.

The kiss seemed to go on forever. The warmth of his lips on hers, the feel of his hand at the small of her back, tingled through her from head to toe. They finally broke apart and Joe tucked her hand into the crook of his arm and saluted the laughing crowd. She could feel his heart beating, thumping like a drum against her side.

This is what it must feel like to get married. They paraded up to a jeep and Joe handed her in as people clapped and cheered. He jumped in beside her and put his arm around her shoulders as the jeep lurched into gear and the little caravan started down the road. Sana floated along, wiping dust and tears out of her eyes.

Once she settled down to the pleasure of sitting so close to her official sweetheart, she began to look around. A few acacia trees dotted the rolling desert hills and silvery winter grass wound through the shallow *wadis*. It was a perfect day. The air smelled like sand and drying grass. It was the air of home.

The jeeps crept precariously through a steep ravine and then crested the hill beyond. On the other side a deep canyon dropped down in front of them, with a fragile-looking iron bridge crossing its airy expanse. Far below, a thin ribbon of water snaked along the bottom of the rocky gorge. Across the bridge stood the ancient stone-walled city, its spires and tiled roofs glinting in the sun.

"My God, we're not going to drive over that?" someone asked.

"That's Kantara Bridge and they say if a man's got a wife who plays around..."

Sana leaned over the side, staring. She had seen that bridge, had looked down into that deep rocky canyon before. A grove of pine trees stood on the other side, shading a little hollow in the side of the hill.

"...then he can bring her here and throw her over."

Laughter. "Where's the bridge for the men?"

The boys were allowed to play on the bridge, running back and forth above the rocky gullyt, but the girls had to stay with the grown-ups. The women spread patterned rugs in the shade and set out platters of kibbee and ruz. The men smoked and talked. We play beneath the pines, piling up mounds of prickly needles to make cradles for our dolls. I wear a pink dress with lace around the bottom and my cousin wears a dress with blue flowers. When we are called to eat, Daddy pulls me into his lap and feeds me bites of food. His scratchy moustache tickles my neck as he leans over to take another morsel from the platter, and when I giggle he laughs and nuzzles my cheek. Daddy is the king, I am the princess, and Mommy is the queen...

The jeep was driving forward. Everyone was going over the bridge. The piney hollow drew closer. *Mommy is the queen in her beautiful dress. My uncle with the hairy arms is sitting next to her.*

"Sana?"

The cruel uncle with the hairy arms. A blue-eyed man was talking to her but she looked past his shoulder at the pines. At first there were still people sitting there, dim shadows in the shade, but when she looked closely, she could not see them anymore. She put a hand on the side of the jeep, leaning forward and looking for those people again.

"Are you okay?" The remnants of the waking dream faded away. She was a nurse and she had come back to this bridge with the American army. How had this come to be, that she was driving over Kantara Bridge with a man her parents didn't know, an American man with blue eyes?

Think, yet not think; say nothing, show nothing, give nothing away...

"Sana." A hand felt warm on her shoulder. "What's the matter?"

"This is where I grew up." Her lips felt stiff. "My family had picnics there..." she pointed toward the shadowed ground. People around her were talking about how deep the canyon was, how much the bridge swayed, and the possibility it might collapse. "I remember all this. From when I was a little girl."

He said something. She felt a sudden strangeness knowing that she was a grown woman now, dressed in men's trousers and sitting next to an unmarried man who had his arm around her shoulders. She looked sideways at Joe. He caught her glance, smiled and took her hand.

He'll never want me if he knows what happened here. She took a deep breath as they drove past the empty stand of pines.

They took a narrow road that led into town through low earth-colored buildings, where savory aromas of fava beans and baking bread wafted from unseen kitchens. A rooster crowed. Children stopped playing at their approach and stared wide-eyed, and when the soldiers called hello and waved they either smiled back or ran in terror.

The road became a cobbled street. Date palms shaded larger houses now, with brick walls and wrought-iron fences facing the street. Wintery vines clung to the sun-bleached bricks and overhung the iron fences. Somewhere ahead she would see a convent school with a beautiful bell tower rising up against the sky, and then, down the street, a pink two-story house with roses in front. There would be a plate of dates and cookies on the little table under the acacia tree, and someone making tea.

The street took a sharp turn and became a narrow road again, winding in deep shadow between dusty buildings and then out into a market square. A few vendors had set up in the center, selling dates and nuts. Two donkeys dozed in the sun. A child playing with a stick called out, pointing at them.

The best dress shop had lace curtains in the window and a bell that tinkled every time someone opened the door. It smelled like cardamom and coffee. She sat on a little footstool, eating date cookies and sipping orange juice, while the shopkeeper held up dress after dress for her mother to look at. After Sana finished her cookies and juice, she could go up to the side of the grand glass display case and stare at the bracelets and necklaces inside. When her mother finished her shopping the shopkeeper would bring out the little girls' dresses, pretty confections of color trimmed in ribbon and lace, and she could pick one out.

Most of the stores bordering the square were closed, but one door was propped open. Brass platters and gold chains were on display in the window. Soldiers and nurses crowded inside, pulling money out of their pockets. Sana followed them in.

Coffee and cardamom... The crimson border painted high on the wall was still there, but faded to a wilted pink. The display case looked surprisingly small. The carpet on the floor was so dirty that she could not trace its pattern. A forlorn old footstool sat in a dusty corner.

Someone touched her arm and she was an Army nurse again.

"Do you want to get something?" Joe asked. He was jingling some coins in his pocket, eyeing the jewelry.

"I used to come here with my mother," she said.

"Really?" He looked around, taking in the dirty carpet, the dusty walls.

"You should have seen it before," she said. "Every store was open. You could buy anything. Bread, shoes. Olives. Men's suits. There were so many people you could hardly walk through the square. I would sit on that stool and drink orange juice while people held up dresses for my mother."

Joe nodded, his eyes roaming to the jewelry again. Sana impatiently walked back outside, across the square to the little group of vendors. By the time the Joe caught up with her she was deep in conversation with a pistachio vendor's wife.

"Sana? Sana." She turned around the second time he said her name.

"The convent's down that street," she said, pointing. *My*

mother said that if I ever got lost I should ask directions to the convent and then I'll find our pink house down the street. "Will you come with me, to see my house?" No one was allowed leave the group and go off alone.

He nodded. "Wait a minute." He strode back to the store.

They walked out of the square in the direction pointed out by the pistachio seller's wife, back into the neighborhood of gated houses. Poplars and junipers lined the narrow street, branching over walls and shading cobbled walkways. Three Constantine men were walking toward them. One of them spat at her as they passed. *A single woman should not go out in public with her hair uncovered, or wear men's clothes, or walk alone with a man who is not her family.* But up ahead, almost hidden behind the trees, she could see a square brick building.

It was so small! Hadn't the bell tower been higher? Surely it was not this short little square battlement? She slowed as she came nearer and saw the front door hanging open, swinging slightly in the breeze, creaking gently.

The windows were all broken. They were only black holes now, shards of broken glass rimming their sills, like a row of rectangular wounds pierced into the side of the building. Weeds grew over the little walk that led to the front step, and the step itself crumbling, the sharp edges fading away into the dusty ground like her the shadowy memories of giggling girls.

"You know where you are now?" She nodded, pushing away tears with the side of her hand. *The house is down the street. It's the only pink one. There was a wrought-iron fence and roses.* She walked as fast as she could, searching the road, but there was no pink house.

Wait.

The stucco was faded to a dim beige. There was a rusting iron fence. It did not look like her house. But it was.

She felt Joe's hand grip her arm. She walked forward through the little gate, oddly only waist high now. A gray wisp of thorny vine twisted along one corner of the house's front wall and she

189

could see pink paint underneath, where the sun had not yet leached the color away. There was her bedroom window, up there.

Dust and cobwebs covered the front door. She grabbed the heavy latch and her arm yanked against a solid lock. She pounded on the carved wood panels.

"Baby, wait," Joe was saying. "Let me go first." Her knuckles were bleeding and he took her hand and held it as he rapped briskly on the door. He looked up and down the street. "This is not a good idea."

No voices, no footsteps coming to the door. Sana tore her hand away from Joe's and ran to the back of the house. There was her little white wrought-iron table, tilting crazily under the acacia tree and covered with grime. There was the old garage, half fallen down, its roof only a gaping hole with sun-bleached wood beams stabbing out of it.

The back door was nailed shut. They were all gone. There was no one here anymore. She put her hands over her face and cried.

Joe had not liked walking down the street. It was too silent. He had glanced up and down as they walked, checking and cross-checking for potential trouble. There were too many dark archways and latticed walls, all perfect places for a sniper to hide, and it was not too great a stretch to suspect that someone loyal to the Reich could be watching them right now. Shooting two Americans would make a Nazi's day.

How long did Sana think they could be gone? He had asked the lead officer for twenty minutes. He had been given fifteen and they had already been gone for five. While he was in the store he had bought a gold necklace with a little cross, and now it was resting in his chest pocket, wrapped a little piece of paper, and he was on fire to give it to her. It would be their first present.

He had tried to explain to her about the fifteen minutes at the same time she started pounding on the front door. When they went around to the back he felt a little easier, partly because they were out of sight of the street, and partly because it looked so much like his own back yard at home. The old shack looked just like all the tumble-down sheds he had grown up with, half a world away. An ancient well with a hand pump stood near the faded traces of a garden and a rusty little wrought-iron table stood abandoned beneath a tree. It must have been her table. He could picture her there as a little girl, playing with dolls.

When she started crying at the back door, he took her in his arms and let her weep onto his shoulder, feeling manly and heroic for a moment as she sniffled into his uniform. But he could not help her, or make her safe, or protect her from the disaster that was overtaking them so fast. What on earth were he and Sana doing here? Why not just go home now? Why not enjoy some life in a little house like this someplace, just him and her, while they still could?

"Don't cry," he told her awkwardly. Behind her back, he checked his watch.

She quieted down a little. He could feel the flicker of her eyelashes through his damp shirt, her delicate bones and tender womanly curves, and he wanted to cherish her beauty and then crush her whole body into his own, all at the same time. "I love you," he said thickly. "I love you, Sana. I love you." He stroked the sweet curve of her back and a sharp hot rush of passion stabbed inside.

"You do?" She looked up, her long lashes wet with tears. "Do you really?"

He bent toward her a little. She closed her eyes. He kissed her, gently, then more urgently when he felt her face turn up and her lips respond to his. He took off her helmet and kissed her eyelids, her cheek, the point of her jaw and the silky warm skin of her neck, and then her lips again until they had to stop and gasp for breath. He stroked her hair and then he saw his watch. It was past the time when they were supposed to be back.

"We have to leave," he husked out, embarrassed to be trembling.

She shook her head. "I want to go inside."

He tried to master himself, for both their sakes. "No, we have to go now."

"It'll only take a minute."

"We'll come back when it's safer. Maybe tomorrow." He gave back her helmet. "You'll have more time then."

She looked frantically around and he knew she wanted some small thing to take back with her. The place was picked clean. What was left for her to take? A splinter from a board, a pebble from the ground? The little table had a pattern of roses in it, and the old metal was thin and

rusty... he stepped over to it and broke off one of the iron roses for her. Then he put his arm around her shoulders, very firmly, so she would know that it was time.

"Wait." Her voice sounded different. He looked down into her glistening eyes. "I love you."

"I love you too." He took her elbow and hustled her back toward the street. She was starting to cry again. Now that they were back where anyone could see them, this was no time for tears. He propelled her crisply along, positioning her on his left side to keep his gun hand free.

"You don't know about me. You don't know what happened to me," she was saying. She tripped over a cobblestone, probably because she couldn't see straight, and he steadied her back into stride.

"Honey, I love you and I'm going to marry you." Walking fast made him feel better. He thought of the necklace waiting in his pocket and gave her arm a little squeeze. "Remember?" He checked up and down the street again, not wanting any Arab men to see him drag a weeping dark-haired woman down the road.

Now she was telling him a story about when she was little, her head down, talking in a soft stream of words. He could just barely make out that after her parents died she had to go live with her uncle.

"You're kidding. That happened to me too," he said.

"You shouldn't marry someone like me. You should marry someone like you, someone who's... been... good..." She burst into another sob, wiping at her streaming nose and eyes.

"Sana, come on." He couldn't stop and hug her now, not in front of all these suspicious houses. "I love you. Let's just get back."

"I love you so much." She sent him a frantic glance as they hurried past the ruined convent. "I can't stand it if you don't want me now."

He smiled at her. Was that what this was all about? Her tumbledown house and her parents dying? "I won't. I mean, I still want to marry you. You know I don't care about the house."

He could barely hear her. "You have to know now or you won't want me if we get married and then you find out."

That stopped him. "What are you talking about?"

"Didn't you hear me?" The words took him by surprise. "Didn't you hear what I said? They used me that way, like a dirty, horrid whore! They made me! Like a dog! They slept with me! Do you understand now?"

They stared at each other. Joe felt his glow of happiness melt away. Sana paled under his gaze, unable to meet his eyes now that she had told her secret.

Half of him wanted to embrace her again and the other half wanted to go find her family and kill them. That would stop all this trouble. Tears spilled down her face again and his insides ached for her. He took her hand.

After a while she looked up, cheeks and lips still wet but her expression calmer now. She looked so beautiful, standing there in her helmet and dirty coveralls. "I don't care," he said. "I swear to God I love you. From right now til the day I die."

Her smile trembled up at him. He took her in his arms again and kissed her, not caring any more who might be watching. Then he tucked her hand into the crook of his arm, tenderly this time, and they walked down the street together.

The ride back to camp seemed a lot shorter than the trip into town. Late-afternoon sunshine glowed on the stony hills and cast blue shadows into the folds between them. Joe sat with his arm around Sana, her hand in his and her helmeted head on his

193

shoulder, the two of them in a world of their own. It would disappear, he knew, as soon as they got to camp, and then he'd be called back to the front and then it would be a long time before they saw each other again. *If we ever see each other again... When they saw each other again.*

She nestled closer and her softness rode against his chest. Love stirred him and he shifted on the seat. The camp was in view now, coming closer.

Sana sat up a little, raised her lips close to his ear.

"Meet me tonight."

His heart jumped up.

"Please." The words breathed warm against his neck.

He had to shut his eyes in the hot hard rush of wanting her more urgently than he had ever wanted anything in his life. And they were as good as married now...

"At the tent."

He tightened his arm around her.

The group unloaded slowly. Some headed off right away for their tents while others lingered in the cooling evening air, still talking, reluctant to go back to the daily routine. Sana stood close to Joe in the golden light, holding hands, locked into his gaze. His eyes were incredibly blue, his hands so warm... She shivered at the intimacy of his bare skin touching hers. The dull roar of the camp pounded around them and a gust of wind blew a strand of hair across her cheek. Joe stroked it back under her helmet, his fingers lingering.

A shadow crossed them just as the warning siren spiraled up in a piercing wail. A whistling noise was growing louder and Sana was trying to crawl under a truck to get away from it, but someone pulled her back and then the ground lurched and an explosion blasted her flat on the ground. Then she was dragged in a stumbling run through smoke and pushed into a trench just as another explosion ripped the air and a searing wall of fire shot up in front of her. She cowered to the ground, ears ringing, earth shaking around her. The acrid smoke of burning fuel scorched the inside of her nose and turned the air black.

The screaming whistles shrieked on. New explosions rocked the trench and debris rained down. More people tumbled in, squeezing her into a corner. She coughed, her lungs burning, and someone pressed a canteen into her hand. She took it automatically and held it, but the unseen hand grabbed it back, sloshed water over the front of her uniform, and jerked the wet cloth over her nose and mouth. She gasped for air through the wetness, closing her eyes as the world churned around her.

One lingering final ground-shaking blast. Then one more, farther away. Then, for a while, nothing. A roaring sound still filled the air. She opened her eyes. Three other soldiers crouched beside her.

"Holy Mackerel! A woman!" The soldier nearest to her, probably the one who had splashed water on her, stared dumbstruck at the damp patch on her uniform.

"I'm a nurse," Sana croaked, and tried to get up. The soldiers climbed out of the foxhole and pulled her after them. Dense swirls of smoke writhed in a nightmarish fog, turning everything gray, lit by red flames billowing from charred skeletons of trucks. Scraps of canvas and twisted metal littered the ground, luridly glowing orange and yellow from the fires. Someone was screaming and the agony in the voice made her shudder.

"Report... report... get going, soldier," a voice was saying behind her. "Sana!" She turned around, barely recognizing Joe, his face grim as death under a layer dirt and soot. Two steps and she was in his arms, crushed in a powerful hug.

"Oh, you're safe..." she said, just as he murmured "Thank God you're safe." They both smiled.

"I have to go report." He pulled a folded piece of paper out of his chest pocket and pressed it into her hand. "Look, our first present." He smiled and she saw a trace of the boyish expression she loved so much. "I bought it for you at that little store."

She fought down tears. "Please be careful."

He hugged her again. "Whatever happens, whatever you hear,

don't worry about me. Keep your head up." He gripped her arms tight, looking deeply into her eyes. "Keep on praying and everything's going to turn out okay." He tilted his head to get under the rim of her helmet and gave her a tender kiss. "I have to go now."

He let go of her, stepped back, and turned away. Sana took two steps toward the hospital and then glanced around. He was looking over his shoulder at her, too. The empty dividing them had widened, and now every step would make it wider still, turning into miles and then maybe hundreds of miles of desert, a whole world at war between them.

She ran for the hospital. Smoke drifted over the wreckage, stinging her eyes and burning her throat as she picked her way over the cratered ground. Men were already busy sorting out equipment, dousing flames, pulling scraps of canvas over dead bloody bodies on the ground.

The hospital had been hit. One ward tent was wrecked and another was on fire. Soldiers were chopping at the burning ropes and shoveling dirt on the flames. She could hear voices shouting in the triage tent and she hurried inside.

Adele and the company commander stood nose to nose. "You might as well paint a target on the ground!" Kelsey roared. "Just say 'Drop your bombs right here'! What in the world were you thinking?!"

"We were ordered to make that cross!" Adele shouted back. "How were we supposed to know it wasn't the right kind of cross?"

"You're wearing a Geneva armband for three months and you ask me that? Do I have to do everything myself around here, nurse?"

"I thought that our officers, our camp's commanding officers, would at least know what kind of cross..."

"You check with somebody else before doing any more dang-fool thinking! And I heard you asked the British for Wangensteens and underwear! You do not, repeat do not, ask them for one more thing. You need something, you ask your own army for it. Do I make myself clear?"

"I've been asking you for socks and long underwear and Wangensteens since we landed in Arzew..."

Red, watching the clash from a growing circle of nurses and medics, looked over at Sana in dismay. Something had to be done. Sana walked straight into the colonel, bumping him hard as if she hadn't seen him. Then she managed to trip over Adele, which finally stopped the fight.

"Lieutenant Toledo reporting for duty."

Kelsey glared at her. "Carry on." He turned on his heel and stalked away.

Adele was still breathing fire. "Don't you look at me like that," she snapped at Sana.

"What's all that about?"

"He said the raid was all on account of we made a plain white cross instead of a red one on a white background so it wasn't the Geneva cross and the Nazis took it for a military target instead of a hospital. After his own officer told us to make it! I cannot, I cannot believe the mismanagement and miscommunication and flat bad leadership I have to fight just to get things done around here. Have you seen Barbara?"

"No," Sana said. "Ma'am," she threw in for good measure.

"You're in OR, then. Margie's in here and Red's in shock ward. On the double."

The first case was prepped and waiting, the skinny gap-toothed teen who had served her peaches for lunch. A gouged-out hole in his chest bubbled bright red froth. Sana realized that Joe's piece of folded paper was still in her hand and she tucked it deep down inside her coverall before grabbing a tray and setting up for surgery. They worked by flashlight at first because the bombs had knocked out a generator, but the light bulbs flickered back on before they finished the first round of patients and a ragged cheer went around the tent.

Litter carriers kept up a steady stream of replacements: shrapnel wounds, shattered bones, legs blown off. Surgeons bent intently over each new wound, instruments clinking and machines humming in the background. The surgical teams rotated among the tables now instead of waiting for a new patient, stepping in as soon as a man was prepped and then over to the next as soon as the surgery was finished, letting medics close incisions and put in the final sutures.

Sana was assisting Schmidt as he picked splinters out of an abdomen when a woman's voice shrieked out in a piercing scream. It was so unexpected that everyone fell silent and glanced up for a moment, sending questioning glances around before turning back to work. Sana was still taking deep breaths to calm herself when Red appeared at her elbow.

"Lieutenant Ross says for you to come to triage right away, ma'am. She said for me to stand in for you. Sorry, sir," he added when Schmidt frowned.

Sana exchanged a glance with the doctor and stepped away. Seconds later she was in triage. A strange keening sound filled the tent and a cluster of people had gathered around one of the litters. Was it someone she knew? Joe, laying there, dead? She hurried over and stared down at the ravaged body for almost a minute before she realized that it was not Joe, but Mike, and the strange sound was Margie crying.

He was covered in blood from his neck to his knees, shreds of flesh showing through the tattered fabric of his trousers. Medics were setting intravenous tubing into both his arms. Adele was sprinkling sulfa into a huge red hole in his abdomen and a medic was trying to wind bandages around his middle as another held his hips off the ground. The white cloth instantly turned dark red.

Sana knelt beside them. *Not Mike. Not Mike. Oh, Margie...*

"Get the leg," Adele ordered. Sana pulled away fabric from a deep slicing gash that ran the length of one thigh, then sprinkled sulfa and tied the bandage. Someone pulled up a crate to use as an IV stand and connected plasma to one arm and an upside-down beer bottle to the other. Red blood ran down the tube. Sana looked at it in surprise, then over at Margie, who was wiping dirt and blood off Mike's graying face.

Adele checked the pulse again. "Put two IV's in each arm. I want plasma and blood on both sides. How's the blood supply?"

"We're down to five bottles, ma'am."

"Are you cleaning those empties?"

"Yes ma'am."

"Is that tent fire out?"

"Yes, ma'am."

"Go call in all the type O firemen right now and get them refilling those bottles with blood as fast as you can."

"Yes ma'am." The medics ran out.

Adele swung around to Sana. "I want you to special-care Mike all the way through surgery into post-op. I can't tie myself up that long, and Margie..." she shook her head. "Keep giving blood and plasma until the blood pressure comes up. Suction if you have to. Do whatever you need to do."

"Yes ma'am."

Adele put an arm around Margie. "You have to be strong for him. That's what he'd want you to do."

Margie dissolved into tears again. Adele looked at Sana. She nodded and moved closer to Margie. Adele hurried off.

Pulse, respiration, blood pressure... Margie was still keening softly, stroking Mike's blood-soaked hair and holding his hand. Sana patted her back and checked under the red-crusted bandages. His abdomen was deeply torn, intestines damaged. There was probably colon damage in back and she could see serious groin damage in front. The gash on his thigh would be the least of the problems. How could he lose so much blood and not be dead yet? Blood pressure dropping even farther... any lower and he would slip into irreversible shock.

Oh God don't let him die... someone arrived with another bottle of blood and can of plasma. Four lines were now flowing into his veins. Sana kept checking, rechecking. Blood pressure kept falling, falling... but then it held steady... and steady again...

Relieved, she hugged Margie. "How you doing?"

"He can't die now." Margie wiped her nose. "I just met him."

"If we can get him into surgery right away I think he's got a

199

chance," Sana said cautiously, wondering if she was right to offer hope.

"I'm going to save him." Margie defiantly pushed back her hair, smearing blood across her face. "He can't die. He can't die now."

Two litter carriers brushed past them, almost knocking over one of the crates. Margie jumped for it, yelling "Hey! You! Watch where you're going!" Men who had been lying quietly on their litters jumped and cried out.

This could not go on. "Marge." Margie stubbornly turned away. "Stop it. You're scaring the men. Cry later."

Margie looked around, eyes swollen.

"You can't quit on them." Sana held her gaze. "Now go get me another bottle of blood and a back-up plasma." Margie lowered her eyes and at first Sana thought she would not leave, but then she gently set down Mike's hand and went.

They took him in to surgery right after she replaced the plasma. Sana guided the transfer, calling for extra help to keep all the bottles and tubes in place as they moved him. When they laid him on the table and cut off the bandages Margie sobbed again at the sight of his mangled torso, and someone led her out.

Sana hooked up another bottle of blood. The two beer bottles dangling upside down looked ludicrously out of place in a surgery. O'Neal and Schmidt leaned over the table, assessing the appalling wounds.

"Repair this here first, then here, here and here. After that, resect the colon..."

"It'll take at least four hours and with blood pressure this low..."

O'Neal straightened up. "I need something to sit on. We'll be here all night if he lives that long."

They began the painstaking repairs. The surgeons worked standing up at first, then sitting down on stools as the night went on. Medics stacked up cans of plasma and saline where Sana could reach them. She called for blood so many times that a corpsman brought her a bucket full of filled bottles with dirt packed around them for insulation.

Five hours later they were working on the colon. Adele brought in coffee and the doctors stepped back for a moment, shaking out their hands and gulping down hot caffeine.

"Where's all these bottles of blood coming from?" O'Neal asked.

"We called in all the firemen and they gave blood, then we called the cooks and the quartermaster troops. We sterilize the used bottles and fill them up again."

"How do you fill up a bottle?"

"Oh..." Adele's voice was almost gone. Deep lines of exhaustion etched her face and her eyes were red with fatigue. "Put a needle in the vein, hook up a tube to a bottle. Drip blood 'til it's full." She rubbed her sleeve across her forehead and leaned back against an empty table. "We gave blood to all the shock patients tonight."

"This one wouldn't still be here without it," Schmidt said as he tied off a suture.

"How's he doing?" Adele peered to see over his hands.

Schmidt only grunted.

"Alive," someone said.

"What's the chances?"

No one spoke. "Doesn't look good," O'Neal finally said.

"Is he going to have to wear an ostomy bag?"

"Probably. If he lives."

"Poor guy."

"What about his love life?" someone else asked. Sana's heart pounded at the comment.

"Doesn't look good," O'Neal said again. He drained his coffee cup. "He's not going to be too happy when he wakes up."

"He's already got a love life," Sana said. Heads all around turned to look at her. "He's got one right now."

She stayed with Mike right into the post-op ward. Margie and Jo Ellen were waiting there and Sana told them about the surgery and how they had maintained blood pressure with a constant flow of blood and fluids. Her voice kept fading out as she talked and once she had to step away to cough.

She suctioned the abdomen as Margie replaced a bottle. "Remember to turn him every hour so he doesn't get..." her voice stopped working again. She made a huge effort to speak. "...pneumonia."

"Okay, hon, I got it. Go get some sleep," Jo Ellen told her. Sana walked out into the thin gray sunlight and stood there for a moment, blinking and trying to get her bearings. She wanted to sit down, and most of all she wanted to find her tent and go to sleep, but the camp looked different. All the fires were out, but smoke still rose from charred piles of debris and new tents had risen where none had been before. On the other side of the road soldiers were lined up for breakfast, getting hash and coffee from big cans on makeshift stoves.

She didn't feel right about leaving the hospital yet. Adele always double-checked the tents before she left a shift. Sana looked into the triage tent, then went back to the OR where medics were cleaning up from the night before. A man walked past her, carrying a bloody bucket toward the morgue. She followed him.

Inside all was dark and quiet. No muffled groans, no painful wounds. The men here had earned their right to lie peacefully. She turned to leave, respectful of their rest.

A shaft of light from the open tent flap shone on a lock of golden hair. She turned back. The contour of the figure laying there looked familiar. Sana slowly put out her hand, touched the fabric covering the face, and drew it down.

Blonde curls and a pink ribbon tied in a bow. Sana's skin went cold. It was Checky, cold and twisted in death.

Sana dropped to her knees, pressing her hands against her eyes, still seeing the lifeless face. *Oh, God, no.* It could not be. She would not let it. She shuddered and jammed her fist into her mouth to keep from screaming. *No. No! No!* It must be someone else. Sana opened her eyes to look again and the face was still there. Her stomach heaved up bile.

Tent flaps whispered open behind her and footsteps sounded. Sana took a deep breath and buried her face in her hands as two soldiers walked past her, carrying another litter. They set down their burden, then paused awkwardly beside her on their way back out.

"Ma'am? Are you all right?" one of them asked.

The anguish was coming at her now; she could feel it coming; she could not stop it and it was going to break her heart.

"Was she a friend of yours, ma'am?"

The anguish broke over her and flooded her soul. Sana bowed her head, defeated by it. Hands pulled gently at her, urging her to leave, but she shrugged them off.

Alone again, she could open her eyes. Checky's body was still there. Sana gently stroked the golden hair and chilly face, trying to smooth the harsh expression.

At last it looked more peaceful. "Hey, Checkers," Sana whispered. "I love you." She untied the pink ribbon and gently drew it out, thinking of the mother in the kitchen. "Bye-bye, Checky. Bye-bye now."

Outside the morgue tent someone was crying. Red sat there on the ground, weeping into a filthy towel as people rushed past him with litters and bandages. Sana sat down with him and he sobbed even harder at her touch, bawling out great heart-torn cries of grief. After a while she wept too.

When they could finally cry no more they sat, exhausted, gasping in shaky breaths. "She was so good," Red choked out when he could talk. "She was so good to me."

Sana's throat was hot and raw. She had no words anyway.

"Why would God have to take away someone like her?" Red asked. He gazed dully at the towel in his hands.

"I don't know," Sana said at last. "I just don't know."

Later on she walked and walked through the camp, but she could not find the nurses' section. Someone finally put her in a jeep and drove her to her tent. She rubbed a handful of water over her sticky face, slipped off her boots, and fell asleep without undressing.

Adele shook her awake after what seemed like only minutes. "Time to get up. You need to get up and eat something. Time to go back on shift." She helped Sana put her boots back on and walked her to the mess tent. Sana picked at a biscuit and Adele made her drink a second cup of coffee. By the time they left for the hospital, the night was fully dark and the camp was almost invisible under blackout. A cold flow of air steadily gusted from the hills, making a hundred unseen tent flaps whip and rustle. Ropes creaked gently all around. The world lay hard and frozen under a brilliant sweep of stars.

"Do you want to be in post-op with Margie?" Adele asked as they walked, chins tucked down against the wind. Sana nodded.

Inside the tent she looked around, dreading the sight of more misery. About half of last night's surgery cases were already awake, some sitting up in their cots and playing cards by the light of a dimmed tent lamp. Others lay silent, lost in ghostly layers of morphine. Margie was sitting next to the last cot of the row.

Mike's face looked like a death's-head mask, the eyes and cheeks sunken and his mouth gaping open. Only one IV was taped into his arm now, instead of four.

Sana helped Margie change his position, rolling him gently on his side and propping pillows to hold him in place, trying to work around the long black and red ridges of sutures that tracked around his middle and down his legs. Margie sponged his dry lips and replaced the plasma while Sana suctioned the stomach wound. Then they took his pulse again.

"What do you think?" Margie looked anxiously across at her.

Sana tried to sound more confident than she felt. "Let's try another bottle of blood." The kidneys could not possibly function with blood pressure so low. Margie bit her lip and Sana squeezed her hand. "We'll give him blood all night if we have to. At least there's plenty of donors."

They made rounds after that, checking Mike in between every other patient. A boy with a bandaged face and torso woke up as they tried to set a saline line into his arm.

"Stop... stop... it hurts..." he pleaded thickly, trying to shake free of the needle. "Stop, please..." Sana held him steady while Margie finished the job and gave him a shot of morphine. "There, honey, lie still. You'll feel better. I promise." Margie moistened the inside of his mouth and took his hand. "Just wait five minutes and all the pain will go away."

Sana longed to be the person in bed, the one sliding into dreamless sleep. As she worked she kept expecting Checky to look in, call hello, and make someone laugh before she left again. Dear Checky. Always saying something funny, even when she was changing bedpans. Especially when she was changing bedpans.

When they reached the end of the row Margie ran out for a quick trip to the latrine. Sana went next. When she undid her overalls something crackled next to her skin, and she remembered the little piece of folded paper Joe had pressed into her hand.

How many days ago had that been? She sat in there in the dark with her head in her hands, too tired to care about the smell, wondering how much time had passed since she had seen him. He had asked her to marry him? And she had said yes, hadn't she? They had danced all night together. It all seemed so far away.

She finally stepped back out into the moonlight and unfolded the paper, soiled now with sweat and dirt. A delicate chain sparkled in her hand, a gold necklace with a cross. He must have bought it for her at the shop in Constantine. How like him. *Oh, I love him so.* She thought of his tall straight body and the feel of his arms around her, the touch of his lips and the way his face lit up like a little boy's when something made him happy. The memory warmed her as she stood there under the frosty stars. She pressed his gift against her lips for a long time before she clasped it around her neck and headed back to the ward.

A man with a lacerated face and a bandaged chest peered anxiously at her. What would Checky say to him? "Well hello there, you big beautiful thing." Sana smiled as she took his pulse.

"Here, let me hold your hand. I always like to meet a good-looking guy."

The man managed half a trembling grin. "Hey, baby." His voice was weak. "When we get out of here..." he stopped for a breath, " ...can I talk you... into a date?"

"Sure." Sana finished counting and started marking his chart. "Let's see, one very romantic guy here. Us girls better watch out."

"You..." another shallow breath..."dance?"

"Uh-huh. I even sing."

"Lili Marlene?"

"Promise not to laugh?"

He nodded. The man on the next cot was watching them. Sana cleared her throat and hummed around a bit, trying to remember the tune.

"Underneath the lantern," the other man croaked out, "by the barrack gate..."

Sana found her voice. "Darling I remember the way you used to wait..."

A few more voices joined in. The man with the lacerated face smiled and closed his eyes. "'Twas there that you whispered tenderly, that you loved me... you'd always be my Lilli of the lamplight, my own Lilli Marlene..."

The night wore on. Sana and Margie suctioned wounds and checked vitals, bathed some of the dirtier patients and kept company with the ones who couldn't sleep. The sterilizer hummed and corpsmen splashed water in the laundry tent next door. A sleepy group of type-O soldiers shuffled in and lined up to donate blood, and Sana let them sleep on the ground as they waited their turns. At midnight someone brought mugs of coffee and sandwiches, and then more coffee a few hours later. The light outside changed from black to gray to golden. Finally the day shift nurses arrived, Sana helped Margie turn Mike onto his other side and check his vitals one more time, and then she dragged Margie back to the tent.

"I don't think I should've left him," Margie said when they

were halfway across camp. "What if he can tell I'm gone?" The clear morning light showed up the pallor of her face and dark purple circles under her eyes. Traces of dirty tears still lined her cheeks and neck.

What would Checky do? Sana tucked her hand through Margie's arm. "Listen to me, sister. You look like the bad end of a bar fight. Wash your face and get some sleep or you'll scare the poor guy when he does wake up."

Margie smiled. They trudged on, their heavy boots catching in the ruts. When they got to the tent Adele was already there, brushing her teeth and hanging up wet socks on the clothesline. Two big cans of water steamed on the little stove.

Sana flopped down on her cot, almost tipping it over, and closed her eyes. She could sleep. Oh, the sweet soft letting-go...

"Girls, wash your face and hands and take care of your feet before you go to sleep," Adele's voice said from somewhere far away. "You'll feel better when you wake up."

It was too much work to open her eyes. "No one cares. Everybody's dirty," Sana said.

"Both of you wash up tonight because I heard we're going to pack up and move tomorrow. Sana, sit up."

Sana dragged herself up to a sitting position again.

"Here." Adele handed her a helmetful of warm water and followed it with a scrap of towel and a sliver of soap. Sana gripped the helmet between her knees and dutifully washed. The warm water felt good on her face and she pressed the wet cloth over her eyes for a long time.

"Do your feet."

She slowly pulled off her boots and heavy socks. Her feet were grimed with dirt, even under all the layers. No one could keep clean in all this dust.

Washing her feet helped her feel better and she looked around the tent. Margie was listlessly wiping at her face. Checky's empty cot looked strangely tidy. There was no colorful jumble anymore, no more socks and scarves scattered underneath. The blanket was smooth and two neatly buckled canvas bags sat alongside.

Margie put her helmet down and started weeping again.

"Margie, please don't," Sana said. "I can't stand it. Please don't cry anymore."

"It's my fault." Margie suddenly pounded her fists on her knees, her voice edging up into a wail. "It's all my fault, because I took Checky out drinking all those times, I slept with all those guys..." She buried her face in her hands. "Oh, God. Now they're gone. Both of them gone. God took them away from me because I was bad and now it's too late for me to save them." Her voice cracked and she shuddered so convulsively that the cot beneath her trembled.

"Honey, dear, calm down." Adele hurried to sit beside her. "God's not getting back at anyone."

Sana rolled her eyes, heartache and fatigue pushing her over some inner line of good sense. "Come on, Margie, snap out of it. Mike's not dead yet."

Margie broke down into a new flood of tears and Adele glared at Sana over her head as she kept on talking. "Sana's right. Mike's still here. And it looks like he could make it. It'll take a while but he could pull through. You'll still be in love. That's not going to change."

"Why?" Margie sobbed. "Why did God do that to him? Why did he kill Checky? Why is he punishing me?"

"Listen to me now. God is not punishing you. It's this war, it's this horrid d—" Adele caught herself before she said the word. "It's this awful war. We're in a war, that's all. We're in a war."

"It's me. He's punishing me."

Adele rocked her, murmuring quietly. "Honey, he loves you, he's going to get you through this..."

Margie shook her head. "I messed up too much."

"I messed up too much too. We all messed up too much." Adele's eyes met Sana's. "That's not the point. The point is that we all mess up too much and the Lord saves us anyway."

"It's too late!" Margie said fiercely. "So what if I pray now? It won't bring her back. It won't make him like he was before. It's too late to pray."

"Honey, it is never too late to pray." Adele kept one arm around her shoulders and took her other hand. "I'll pray. He hears our every word."

Later on, after Margie had calmed down and finally fallen asleep, Sana lay wide awake and stared at the canvas above. There was no warm presence in the cot next to hers anymore, no more soft sound of Checky's breathing. Sana crossed her arms tight across her chest and clenched her jaw, determined not to speak. *If Adele tries to talk to me about the Bible now I'm going to scream.*

Adele sat with her face in her hands for a long time. Finally she got up and poked at the stove, banking the dying embers into a glowing pile.

"I have to go in now," she said, and gave Sana a thoughtful look. "Are you okay?"

"Yes."

"I hate war."

At least that was something she could agree with. "Me too."

Adele sighed and stood up. "Is there anything I can get for you?"

"Uh-uh." Sana blinked back tears.

"Well. All right. See you later." She patted Sana's shoulder and left.

The silence grew worse, pounding at her. Sana squirmed around onto her stomach, then onto her side. The blankets slid down and she tugged them back up. Her eyes felt scratchy. She turned onto her back again and stared at the dirty canvas above her.

The growling in her empty stomach finally forced her to sit up again. A little bit of warm water was left in the bottom of the can on the stove. She found a packet of cocoa, shook in the powder, sloshed it around and drank it straight from the can. She sat there with it in her hand, too depressed to set it down.

Checky was gone.

Why would God do that? Why would he ruin poor Mike's life, just when he had fallen in love? What about all the other soldiers

209

cut down in the prime of their manhood?

"I don't think you're so good," she said out loud. Margie stirred at the sound of her voice.

And God might do the same to Sana herself, or to Joe, at any time. She had practically invited Joe to sleep with her when they were riding back from Constantine. Surely God didn't do all this just to punish her? Or did he?

The idea sickened her. *You say you love us? I don't think you do. I wouldn't hurt anyone like this.* She stared at the little heap of glowing embers, seeing again all the amputated arms and legs, the cold dead bodies laid out in the morgue. *If this is what you do then I don't think you're good.*

The little leather Bible lay on Adele's bedside crate. She reached over and picked it up. *I work hard. I pray every day like I promised to. I think I'm better at keeping my word than you are. What do you have to say about that?*

The worn pages fell open and an underlined verse caught her eye. *'God is our refuge and our strength, a very present help in trouble...'*

Her soul trembled, wanting refuge. Where had God been when Checky needed help? Sana slapped the Bible shut and flung it across the tent. It thudded into the canvas wall and fell to the ground. That's what I think about you. She waited, fuming, for a cosmic reply.

Nothing broke the silence. There was no answer. After all their work, this was all. Nothing. *Well then, if you don't care about us then go be with the horrid Nazis. Go be on their side. I'm not going to pray to a God like you anymore.* She turned her face into her blanket and cried great wracking sobs until she fell asleep.

Chapter Twelve

Kasserine

Miles east of Constantine, high in the Eastern Dorsal mountains of Tunisia, a long convoy of Army trucks crested a hill, slipped and slid down the other slope, and pulled to a stop. Tired soldiers clambered out, yawning in the morning light. They had been jouncing up and down in the trucks for nineteen hours, and for the last six it had been raining.

"Whoever called this a road ought to be shot," Garcia said to Joe, for what seemed like the twentieth time, as they climbed out of a truck and looked around. Long folds of cactus-covered hills fell off into the valley below. The trace of road ran east, winding on between the hills. "This ain't nothing but a camel trail. Look at all that cactus. Just like El Paso." He yawned and rubbed his stubbly jaw.

Taffington unfolded his long legs and jumped off the truck. "Are we going to eat now?"

"There was this beautiful woman that passed out steaks while you were sleeping." Ratliff jumped down behind him and slapped him on the back. "I ate yours." Taffy smacked Rat on his helmet and the two of them shoved each other around for a while, happy just to be standing on the ground again.

"Get those dimwits in order," Joe told Garcia. "What a mess." They were traveling with a greenhorn infantry battalion just off the boat, and the long haul in the trucks had worn off whatever edge of order they might have had. Supplies were being handed down helter-skelter and the new G.I.s were already digging through them for rations.

Joe's company had been sent forward with the new infantry to scout ahead into the long mountain pass. The rest of the soldiers would follow with tanks and heavy artillery, and a brand-new U.S. Army tank brigade was on its way to join them and attack the enemy on the other side of the Dorsals. If everything went according to plan, they might even force the Germans clear back to the coast.

"Hey, those guys over there're eating K-rations!" Taffington yelled. "Geez, they got gum and everything."

Soldiers were opening crates and stuffing cans of rations into bags. Joe frowned. "Garcia, take Robichaux and go tell those guys to knock it off."

"I'll help," Taffy said. "Hey! Hey you!" Ten faces looked around, still chewing. "Those're supposed to be for everybody!"

"I ain't ate anything hot for two dang days," countered one of them through a mouthful of beans. "Go find yer own food."

"Get your hands out of those rations," Garcia rapped out. "Where's your NCO?"

The men kept on eating but they stopped opening new crates. Joe looked around and located an infantry sergeant struggling to sort through a stack of papers and supervise the unloading of a truck at the same time. He walked over. "Sergeant, those your men over there?"

The man glanced around and then back to Joe. "Forget it. I got real problems here." He waved a piece of paper. "I got to figure all this out." Instructions for assembling and firing bazookas were printed on the page.

"These're for bazookas," Joe said.

"I know that. I'm trying to find the parts."

Joe looked at him incredulously. Bazooka tubes, slings and supports were piled on the ground right in front of them. "These are the parts," he said. "Right here."

The sergeant turned red and fixed him with a bushy-eyebrowed glare. "Okay, well, you want to hear some more problems? Half these snot-nosed kids never held a rifle in their life and I gotta train 'em how to shoot." He leaned into Joe's face.

"Tomorrow. You gonna help me do that too? Lieutenant?"

Joe looked back at the hungry boys, now haggling over the little ration packs of cigarettes. No one man could possibly get this shambles to fight the enemy tomorrow, or even next week.

He gave up trying to solve the problem. "Garcia!" he yelled instead. "Go get some of those K's for us before the infantry eats 'em all."

Packs, rations, and tents were flung off the trucks. Mortars, machine guns and boxes of ammunition followed. Tanks of gasoline were handed down, barrels of water trundled out, and supplies piled up in random heaps. Joe made a list of items and sent his men foraging through the stacks of gear, and soon they had scavenged a stash for themselves. Every man carried his own water, rations, and weapons, plus as much ammunition as he could cram into his pack and cartridge belt. Robichaux had strapped on a pistol and two long knives with heavy curved blades that looked like they would be more useful for swamp hunting than mountain raids. Garcia carried an extra canteen.

Joe got the call to report for orders. Officers gathered at a table under a tarpaulin, listening to static radio chatter and poring over topographical maps.

The colonel switched off the radio. "Rommel's got tanks on the other side of these mountains and they're coming straight for us," he began. "And over here," he tapped the map, "Von Arnim's got a division of tanks and he's coming our way too."

"Yes sir," Joe murmured along with the rest. He had already been briefed about the German front, by Darby himself, at the base camp before they left.

"This will be our assembly area for the next few days. We are going to advance up this road tomorrow and stop 'em in their tracks. Where's the Rangers?"

"Here, sir," Joe called out.

"Look how the road loops, here." He pointed at the map and everyone crowded forward to see. "Your mission is to get straight over these hills tonight and dig in on the other side where you can control a good stretch of road. Take everything you can carry and do whatever you have to do to slow down the Germans until we get there. I want active defense. TNT. Mines. Mortars."

"Yes sir." Joe studied the map and narrowed his eyes. Darby's briefing yesterday had directed him to scout and raid along the road, not entrench against tanks with lightweight mortars and TNT. How long would they be there? What about water? He began mentally reviewing the gear he had just issued out, forming a new list of what they would need.

"One of our tank battalion's on the way but they can't get here for a week. There's a British division on the way and they can't get here any sooner. We have troops on the eastern side of the mountains between us and Rommel but the last report was not good. He's going through 'em like crap through a goose and he's on schedule get here before anybody else." He paused to let the news sink in.

"There's still a camp at Sbeitla." His finger stabbed again, at a place halfway through the mountains this time. "That'll slow 'em down. We are to hold these passes here, here and here. Army intelligence puts the Germans at about sixty tanks and we have fifty-four. I want tanks, artillery and antitank guns in position tomorrow, here and here." He wrote names along the road, assigning positions, and Joe hurriedly made notes on his own map. "The Germans'll be pushing hard, so watch out."

Watch out? Joe flicked a glance toward the officer. Was that all he had to say?

"And you Rangers, radio in when you see them."

"Yes sir."

"You know what," an officer pointed at the map, "the Rangers could take empty ration cans and fill 'em with rocks and string 'em on a wire across the road. Then they'd hear the cans rattle when the tanks come through."

"Uh, sir, you can hear tanks for miles away," Joe felt compelled to point out. The officer stared at him.

"Sbeitla's going to slow 'em down," someone else said. "Besides, everything points to a German advance through

Dernaia, not Kasserine."

The commander glared around the table. "My job here is to stop Germans, any way I can, for as long as I can, until that division gets here and kicks their tails, and that's what I'm going to do. We move out tomorrow."

"Yes sir," everyone murmured.

He straightened up from the maps. "We have some green troops here. I want it crystal clear that any soldier who leaves the line of fire without permission will be shot. I want a report from you," he looked at Joe, "as soon as you're in position. It is absolutely imperative that I get information about enemy activity as soon as possible in order to stop this advance."

"Yes sir."

"Everybody needs to understand what's at stake here. If the Germans get through us and get through these passes and get up this road, there's no troops left between them and the supply camps." His finger stabbed the map, pointing to the places they had just come through. "Thala, right here, and Tébessa, right here. Vehicles, fuel, weapons, hospitals, food. All laying right there like a birthday present, forty miles away. If they take those camps, they take back Africa. Get the picture?"

They would take the nurses to Berlin. "Yes sir!"

"If we slow 'em down now, then we'll stop 'em in the passes and eat roast kraut for breakfast!"

"Yes sir!"

As soon as they were dismissed Joe called Garcia and sent the men out again through the supply stacks, grabbing extra ammunition before the general rush began. Each squad could take one mortar, although it would be hard to haul a decent supply of shells over this terrain. They crammed as much ordnance as they could into their overloaded packs, shouldered their gear, and headed out. Each man carried only one canteen, but the map showed a little river winding through the valley, and they would get more water there. Joe set a blazing pace until sunset and then rested the men until the moon rose. They blackened their faces with spit and dirt, Garcia passed out masking tape to silence all their clinks and rattles, and then they moved out quietly through the dark.

The desert night was cold. They hiked in single file, gray shapes among the shadows, their breaths puffing out like silver mist as they climbed their way up rocky hills and picked through cactus down below. Stars blazed above, wheeling slowly around the sky. Once in a while some unseen animal rustled out of their path, or the eerie wail of a hyena made them jump and then grin at each other, embarrassed. When the slope steepened and became too treacherous to climb by moonlight, they stopped in the overhang of a cliff and napped.

The smell of morning woke Joe a few hours later. He sat up, muscles stiff from sleeping on cold rock, and looked around until he saw a sentry. He caught the man's glance and received a reassuring nod. All was well.

The pale gray dawn showed the valley stretching out below them. He yawned and pulled out his map. According to his notes they were almost in position and he looked out at the landscape again, mentally mapping their course. One more hour of fast marching should do it, and then they could set up the mortars. That was a welcome thought. If he wasn't all cold and achy, and if he just had a cup of hot coffee, and if he wasn't about to be attacked by tanks, then he'd feel pretty good about setting up the mortars, because they were such a pain in the butt to haul around.

He folded the map and tucked it into his field jacket. The gray dawn was turning pink now, stars fading into lighter blue along the eastern sky. Frost glittered on the rocks and the looming cliffs turned lavender and purple. They would have to start soon. Joe pulled out his latest letter, delivered just before he left Constantine. His uncle's plain strong handwriting showed clearly in the morning light.

Dear Joseph, We think about you every day... there followed some news about who was doing what in the neighborhood and how much snow had fallen since Christmas. *So many doctors and nurses left for the war that Dr. Smrha had to come out of retirement. Do you remember how he set your arm when you fell off the roof? You never did remember that day very well. Every time Doc sees me he asks about your arm. I sure hope you're taking care of it or he'll get after me.* Joe grinned. The old story was funny now.

Some of the women in the congregation are driving cabs now because the cabbies all signed up. I don't approve of women driving strangers around like that but they tell me they only work the day shifts and we all need to do our part. This war is really changing things around here. You should see Sears. It's practically empty because all the factories are making war equipment. It took an act of Congress to get plows for the farmers.

Your Aunt Kate and I read about the bombings and casualties over there and we pray every day for you. Our nation would be gone by now without men like you who are willing to fight for us. We do everything we can to help from our end but it's nothing to what you're doing. Joseph, I know you must be going through some hard times. When things don't go right people wonder where God went. Remember He's still there with you. The Lord hung on the cross and stayed there until he died for us. He won in the end, even over the power of the grave. Remember he's there and lean on him when you're tired. Ask for him to help you. He will always answer and he will deliver you from evil.

You'll pass through this hard time. There's a verse in Isaiah. "When thou passeth through the waters, I will be with thee; and through the rivers, they shall not overflow thee; when thou walkest through the fire, thou shalt not be burned." Here's another good one:. "Fear thou not, for I am with thee: be not dismayed, for I am thy God: I will strengthen thee; yea, I will help thee; yea, I will uphold thee."

Joe put down the letter, seeing again the flaming tanks with charred bodies hanging dead from their turrets. *"When thou walkest through the fire..."*

Garcia stirred and sat up. He gazed out over the hard-dirt plain, dotted with low scrubby clumps of brush. "Here I join the Army to see the world and I end up in a place that looks just like El Paso." He yawned and pulled out his canteen, shaking it to hear the water level. "At least I don't have to shave today." A low rumble rolled, like distant thunder, and he stopped with the canteen in mid-air.

217

Joe squinted to see the eastern horizon through the brilliant dawn. Was that just a hill way over there, or was it something else? He groped for his binoculars and heard rustles all around him as others sat up and did the same. The eastern end of the valley jumped into focus. Black shafts of smoke were rising straight up into the air. The distant rumble rolled again.

Burning tanks made straight black columns like that.

Men were already lacing up their boots and gathering their packs. Joe scanned back and forth through the folds of valley. "Taffington, get me a signal," he called. "On the double." Taffy scrambled for the radio.

The two of them had to carry it back around to the western side of their hill before they could make contact. When the battalion finally answered in a burst of static, the name of the commander had changed and so had their orders. "Do not lay mines. Repeat, do not lay mines because we got troops on the road coming your way," the new battalion commander shouted through the scratchy noise. "We're maybe five hours away. Set up your mortars close enough to hit the turrets at short range. Long-range fire won't do anything to stop 'em so hold your fire, repeat hold your fire, until they're close enough to do some damage."

"Affirmative. No mines. Hold fire until short range. Aim at turrets. What about trip wire explosives, sir?" Joe and Taffy stared at each other over the radio, waiting for the crackling reply.

A burst of unintelligible chatter broke out and faded away. The new commander's voice came through again.

"...radio as soon as you see the tanks. If you can't get through, fire four red flares and then four white ones to signal us."

Joe decided not to ask more questions. "We only have green flares, sir."

"Fire whatever doggone color you got! Continue your mission!" Crackle drowned out the voice again. Joe and Taffy looked at each other.

"Let's go," Joe said. They ran back around the hill.

When they had descended halfway down the slope a pair of German Stukas flew across the middle distance of the valley, so after that they spaced themselves out over the hills instead of traveling close together in line. Within the hour they were down the hill and moving faster. They stayed off the road, working their way through the *wadis* instead, in case anyone else was prowling this part of the valley. The rumbles kept growling in the east and the columns of smoke grew into a blackish haze.

When they reached their assigned position Joe didn't like it. It was too open. He finally opted for a rocky escarpment half a mile down the road, closer to the river and where they could set mortars back in the rocks for camouflage. They started digging in as fast as they could, scrabbling at the soil with helmets and entrenching tools, sweating in the cool air.

"Maybe that sound's our guys, clobbering them," Ratliff said, scooping dirt.

"Maybe it's your grandma." Taffy was arranging cactus branches for camouflage over the tell-tale black muzzle of his mortar.

"If my grandma was here we'd all be eating biscuits and gravy," Ratliff said. "Biscuits and gravy. Mm, mm, mm."

"If my grandma was here we'd be eating steak and eggs."

"If my grandma was here she'd scare you into getting that trench dug faster," Joe said. He thought of Josefina, frying onions at the stove.

They radioed battalion, refilled their canteens, and settled in to wait. The black haze in the east was thinning into gray now. Maybe the camp at Sbeitla had held out. Or maybe not.

A sudden tremor rocked the ground beneath them, raining gravel down the slopes. A clap of thunder cracked out of the clear blue sky. Someone shouted, pointing east. A tongue of flame was shooting up far above the edge of the eastern mountain ridge and black smoke boiled up underneath it.

Joe pulled out his binoculars again. Something really big had to have blown, to make that kind of bang. Something like Sbeitla's supply dump of gasoline and explosives, deliberately fired to keep it out of enemy hands.

He kept searching the valley, looking for anything that moved.

Finally he saw what he was looking for, a plume of dust rising along the road in the distance. When it came a little closer it turned into a group of loaded camels trotting along, heads bobbing and legs pumping every which way, followed by a slower line of donkeys pulling carts piled high with packs. People were hauling the donkeys along as fast as they would travel. He could see a woman carrying a basket and pulling a child by the hand.

Another cloud of dust rose up from behind the travelers and overtook them. A line of military vehicles careened around the group of Arabs and raced on down the road.

"Man your guns!" Joe shouted. They all drew down behind the rocks, tense and silent, shells at hand and eyes fixed on the coming targets.

"Those're ours," someone called. Everyone leaned forward, trying to see.

They were. Army trucks and jeeps packed full of soldiers tore past their hideout, not even noticing the tell-tale mortar barrels sticking out of the rocks. Joe finally jumped out and waved down a jeep. Seven filthy, red-eyed men were squeezed inside.

"What's going on?" Joe called.

"Rommel's coming. Pull out while you still can," a sergeant yelled back.

"What about Sbeitla?"

The sergeant shook his head. "Gone," he shouted.

Joe stepped closer and clamped his hands on the side of the jeep. "What happened to the hospital?"

The sergeant looked away. "Uh, they decided to stay."

Joe stared at the sergeant in disbelief. "You mean you left them behind?"

"We don't have enough trucks for five hundred wounded men, Lieutenant." "What happened to the hospital?"

"They decided to stay." The sergeant still couldn't meet his eyes. He shrugged. "Their decision." The driver beside him revved the engine and the jeep yanked away from Joe's hands.

"What about the nurses?" he shouted over the roar.

The sergeant waved his hand. "Better get your men out of here," he yelled back as they drove off.

Joe ran back to his little group. "He says Sbeitla's gone and tanks are coming this way." No one looked surprised. "He says Germans took the," his voice cracked in spite of himself, "the hospital."

Rat and Taffy stared at him.

"Don't worry, they don't shoot nurses," Garcia said. "They take 'em to Germany."

"Heck, she probably isn't even there," Ratliff told him.

"That's right," Taffy said. "She's probably not even there."

Joe clenched his jaw hard. *I'll go to Germany and get her back. I'll kill anyone who touches her.*

More trucks roared by, the faster vehicles pulling out around the slower ones, all of them fleeing westward through the haze. Halftracks and tank destroyers crammed full of men clanked doggedly along on their rolling metal tracks. A trail of ambulances brought up the rear. None of them seemed to notice the Rangers' mortars.

"Sir, radio..." the rest of Taffington's words were lost in a singing roar that burst right over their heads. Out of nowhere planes streaked down, firing into the retreating American convoy. Green fireballs flared and the rearmost halftracks burst into plumes of red and black, rolling helplessly off the road in fiery agony. The planes raked the column, turned around and came back again for another pass. Joe looked away from the sight of bodies tumbling out of vehicles through the flames. Taffington still had his ear pressed to the radio.

A voice came through. "Sbeitla is pulling out. You are to hold your position. Repeat, you are to hold your position." The voice faded into crackle.

"Hold your positions," Joe shouted, and heard the order echo down the line. He watched one of the rear-most ambulances stop and medics jump out, running towards the burning bodies.

The first camels were passing them now. The Arabs saw their mortars right away and stopped to offer eggs and oranges.

"I want more camouflage," Joe yelled as he waved them away. "Get some mud on those gun barrels!"

"Ask 'em what's going on," Garcia suggested.

"We already know what's going on," Joe said. He focused the binoculars down the road again. A dark mass of moving metal was forming there, covering the valley floor.

Back in Constantine, Sana helped her twenty-third soldier into clean pajamas, working around a leg amputation and a burn wound. She lifted the sheet back into place and smiled at him. Now the whole ward was fed, debrided, shaved, bathed, and resting in clean linens. Men were talking quietly. It had been a long hard day for the nurses and it wasn't even lunch time yet.

The boy's face was set in pain and his pulse was weak, but he was watching her. "I'll be telling the folks back home about you, ma'am. You sure are cute. Cutest thing I ever saw." He couldn't be more than eighteen years old. "I'll write you a letter." Brown eyes looked hopefully up at her.

"Why, thank you. When I get it I'll write you back," Sana said. "I don't get that many letters."

"Pretty nurse like you ought to get a lot of letters." The boy shifted on his cot, favoring his burned side.

"Does it hurt? Want a shot?"

"Uh..." he tried to look stoic, then gave up. "Okay."

Sana gave him a shot of morphine and a drink of water. The tight frown of pain faded away and his face relaxed. "Sweet dreams, soldier." He gave her a fuzzy smile before he closed his eyes, and she adjusted the sheet again so it wouldn't drag on his wounds.

"Ma'am, where do these go?" A greenhorn medic hovered at her elbow, holding a box of yellow tubing. Brand-new reinforcement troops had just arrived from the coast and they were handy for carrying things around, but not much good for anything else.

"Pack those in the trucks that are going to the mountains." Just outside her tranquil ward, the camp was swarming like an overturned anthill as soldiers tore down hospital tents and packed up all the supplies they had gathered during their time in Constantine. The hospital was on the move again. The wounded were being trucked off to the safety of a rear hospital, but the nurses and doctors would go with the soldiers and set up a new hospital closer to the front line. They were dividing all the supplies into two lines of trucks, one headed to the coast and one to the war in the mountains.

"Can I take these now, ma'am?" Red was clearing thermometers and swabs off the nurses' makeshift table before she even answered. Sana rescued her tin coffee cup just before he lifted away the battered crates. Two more soldiers barged into the tent and looked around.

"Okay, fellas." Sana pitched her voice strongly enough to let them know she was in charge and calmly enough to maintain her ward's tranquility. "You can take things out but don't wake up my sleeping beauties." Rebuked, the two men tiptoed through the cots and gingerly carried out supplies.

She held the tent flap open for them as they left and took the opportunity to look outside. The bright sunlight stung her eyes and started up the cough that had bothered her ever since the raid. She hawked hard to clear her throat, then looked around and spat, hoping nobody saw her. Lunch and the afternoon nurses should be arriving soon and then she could go pack her bags and put them on the trucks headed east.

She closed the flap and walked back to where Mike lay with an IV in each arm and Margie sitting on the floor beside him. His blood pressure was holding steady but too low to function normally. They still checked him every fifteen minutes, moistening his lips and tending his fluids, and they turned him every half hour. The doctors were amazed he was even alive.

"Doing fine," Margie answered her questioning look. She smoothed his blanket. "I just wish he'd wake up so I could talk to him before I have to leave." Adele had petitioned for Margie to go back with Mike, but the request had been denied. An experienced nurse was too valuable to let go now. "Did you see Adele?"

"No. I thought she was packing OR. Is there any coffee left?"

"Here." Margie poured her leftover coffee into Sana's mug.

Now that the crates were gone there was nothing left to sit on, so Sana glanced over the rows of patients one more time before settling down next to Margie. "This isn't too bad."

"The coffee?"

"The move. Are you nuts?" Sana yawned deeply.

"Hey, do you mind if I keep this for a while?" Margie sounded a little hesitant. Sana looked over. She was holding the little Bible.

"Oh, sure." She felt embarrassed. Margie must have found it on the tent floor. "I just have to give it back to Joe sometime."

"I was reading it to Mike. Listen to this part. *'Be careful for nothing; but in every thing by prayer and supplication with thanksgiving let your requests be made known unto God. And the peace of God, which passeth all understanding, shall keep your hearts and minds through Christ Jesus.'* Isn't that beautiful?"

"Uh-huh."

"I never read this stuff before. Isn't it great?"

"Uh-huh."

"I tell you, I just know that Mike can hear me. He moved a little while ago." Margie scanned his face and checked his pulse. "I really, really think he's getting better. It's time to roll him over."

"Let me see the bandages." They checked Mike in front and behind. The sight of his mangled groin made Sana shake her head.

"I think I'll change his saline now." Margie's voice sounded bright and strong. Sana glanced furtively at her, not wanting to start another crying jag.

"Don't worry." Margie's hands were steady as she replaced the can, and she looked calmly back at Sana. "That's not going to change anything. We found each other and he's getting better and that's what's important." She sat back on her knees, looking around the ward. "You know what?" She nodded at the cots. "I love it here. I wouldn't trade it for anything else in the whole world."

Sana looked at Margie's hollow eyes and stringy hair, then down at her own chapped hands. She smiled. "Yeah." Two men started singing *Lili Marlene* again. "I love it too."

It was almost dark before everything was finally loaded up. Margie pinned a note onto Mike's bag, promising to love him forever, and pressed a big red lipstick kiss on it. Everyone said their goodbyes. The nurses threw their bags into the trucks and clambered aboard, carrying extra blankets and rations for the ride. Adele stood with a clipboard, checking off names, but her face looked gray and her eyes were red. Margie finally took the clipboard out of her hands and told her to go get in a truck and sit down.

Sana lingered as long as possible before she boarded, clambering up into a truck just as its engines were cranking into forward gear. Margie passed her a blanket. "You look like you could use a nice hot cup of tea."

"Fat chance of that happening," Sana said. Another long road trip seemed too loathsome to bear. "I hate these trucks."

"Frenchie, you got to cheer up. Want a real drink?" Jo Ellen asked, pulling out a pint bottle.

Sana turned up her nose at the smell of the alcohol and grapefruit juice mixture that had been going around the Constantine camp. "No."

Adele was struggling with her blanket and pack, trying to find a comfortable position to sleep in. "What in the Sam Hill?" she rasped out. "That stuff'll kill you. Pour it out."

"Everybody's drinking it," Jo Ellen protested.

"Everybody's not a nurse. I wouldn't pour that stuff in a latrine."

"Let me smell of it," Obie said. "I could use a little something. I feel like I been drug through a knot hole backwards."

"Well, I grew up on homemade liquor," Jo Ellen said as she handed over the bottle. "My daddy used to carry a pint in his pocket all the time, in case of snake bite."

Obie chuckled. "My Daddy said that too. Then he'd say that he carried a snake in the other pocket, in case he needed a drink really bad." She sniffed at Jo Ellen's bottle. "I'll pass."

They all bedded down as best they could, snuggling close together against the icy drafts. The night was bitter cold, and the moon so bright that the hills gleamed silver against the starry sky. Obie and Jo Ellen traded stories about grits and okra for a while before drifting off to sleep. Sana stared out the back of the truck, lost in a maze of misery. Something about leaving Checky's body in a lonely desert was bothering her. It was so final, so sad. She wondered if she would ever see Constantine again, or the place where Checky was buried. She wondered if she would ever see Joe again. If she could just see him one more time, that would be enough. Just one more time again.

She drowsed in and out of a doze, always on the brink of falling sleep and never quite arriving. Someone snored in little snuffles and someone else kept hacking out a phlegmy cough. The trucks jolted along, climbing higher and higher into the mountains.

A dream was calling her when the truck stopped with a jerk. Sana groaned and opened her scratchy eyes. Were they taking a rest stop? She probably should go if she had the chance. A cold wind battered across the truck's canvas cover and she snuggled down deeper into her blanket. A plane droned overhead. *Theirs or ours?* A new chill prickled her skin. Surely it couldn't be theirs, not in the middle of the night like this. The snoring nurse kept snuffling along, unaware of any danger.

Tools clinked outside and voices murmured. Sana yawned and coughed. Margie sat up.

"Is it a bathroom stop?" she whispered.

"I don't know," Sana whispered back. "Do you want to go?"

"Yeah."

"Me too." They pulled out a blanket and scrambled over sleeping bodies into the gusting wind outside. Men were working on the lights of the truck just behind them. The soldiers waved and the nurses held up their blanket in a silent explanation. They picked their way over shadowy rocks and took turns holding the blanket for each other, struggling to keep the ends from flapping away in the wind.

Thunder rumbled and a flicker lit up the sky. An engine started up, then another, and Sana and Margie hurried back over the rocks. The trucks' lights were only narrow slits now, not round circles anymore.

"What's that for?" Margie asked.

"Blackout, ma'am. Didn't you hear that plane?"

"I did," Sana said. Thunder rumbled again and the sky lit up. "What's going on?"

"Bombs, ma'am. They're huntin' somebody."

"My God!"

"We'll be okay," the soldier said. Sana glanced up at the moon, creamy-bright in the sky, and looked hard at the soldier.

He looked back at her. "We'll be okay because the Lord's with us."

"Amen on that," Margie said. Sana did not reply. They scrambled back into their truck and burrowed down among the sleepers as it lurched forward again.

Sana pulled her blanket close against the cold. Any pilot could see the convoy clear as day in all this moonlight. They'd be sitting ducks for a plane. Shouldn't they stop and hide? But up ahead were wounded soldiers who would die if there was no hospital. Of course they had to go on. They would just have to take their chances. Probably no one would even notice a few trucks moving through the hills anyway. The rumble sounded again. *It doesn't matter if there's bombs. I am still mad at God and I'm not going to pray.* She pulled her blanket over her head and tried hard to go to sleep.

It seemed like they stopped again only seconds later. People started talking and gathering up the bags. Sana pulled her blanket tighter and clung to a dream, ignoring Adele's voice telling her to get up. The noises finally faded away and she slipped back into blissful sleep.

Someone shook her foot. "Ma'am. Ma'am, you have to get out now. We're leaving."

Her eyes were swollen and her throat hurt. Sana raised herself up on one elbow and focused on the helmeted face in front of her.

"Huh?"

"Sorry, ma'am, we're leaving. You have to get out now. Are you okay?"

She lay back down. He shook her foot again. "All right," she moaned. "Just stop it."

"There's coffee out here," he said helpfully.

Her head pounded in painful waves. "Would you please go get me some?"

"Sorry, ma'am. You have to get out right now. Here, I'll get these for you." He jumped aboard and tossed out her canvas bags. "Up'n at 'em. Rise and shine. Up... up..."

"Oh, geez." He pulled her up and helped her slide down the bumper, still wrapped in her blanket. The cold wind in her face jolted her awake. The air smelled like fresh snow.

"Over here," voices called. The soldier picked up her bags and propelled her over to the rest of the nurses and doctors, who were gathered around a barrel set over a fire. Margie gave her a cup of hot coffee and she sipped at it, holding the cup in one hand and her blanket with the other. People were grinning at her.

"I didn't sleep very well last night," Sana said, vaguely feeling a need to explain herself.

"The hospital here's not that bad," O'Neal was saying.

"Where are we?" Sana asked. People grinned at her again.

"Thala. It's this really great camp that the Germans built. You and Adele ought to go get some rest," Margie said. "You both look like you're coming down with something."

"I'm fine," Adele rasped.

"We can set up the wards without you," Red told her. "We got all these new guys to do the work."

"Adele, go lay down," O'Neal said. "You sound terrible."

"There's real beds in the nurses' barracks," Red added.

Everyone wanted to see the beds. Sana trailed along behind the rest as a corpsman led them to their quarters, which looked like a regular barracks building with its windows broken out, but inside there were beds with real mattresses and sheets and pillows on them. A shower room was painted glossy white and the brass

228

fixtures were so clean they twinkled. Two more soldiers were working inside, sweeping out glass and taping cardboard over the empty windows.

The nurses hustled all the men out of the building. Some of the women flopped right down onto the beds and closed their eyes while others started stripping off layers of clothing for a shower. A cold draft was still drifting through the room and one soldier tried to linger, claiming that he could tape cardboard onto their windows from the outside without looking in, but they sent him off for soap and towels instead.

Sana sat down on a bed, still clutching her blanket around her shoulders. Sleep, or shower? She heard water running, then a shriek about the cold. She lay back and closed her eyes.

A hand was shaking her again. She opened her eyes. Women were moving around, dressing and tying up their boots. "Get up," Margie said. "There's ambulances."

Sana sat up and shivered. She took a long swig from her canteen and went to the shower room. Nurses crowded the sinks, washing their hands and faces and brushing their teeth. Puffy-eyed, straggle-haired faces all looked into the long mirror and frowned at their reflections.

"The dang Germans would have mirrors," someone said. "Right when I don't want one."

Sana dashed water over her face and hair. No one cared how she looked anyway. From the other room she heard a voice start calling orders and then dissolve into heavy coughing. She hurried out and found Adele sitting on a bed, still coughing, with a group of nurses clustered around her. Sana reached out to feel her forehead. It was fever-hot.

"Oh, Adele, you're really sick. You can't go in like this."

"Want some aspirin?" someone asked.

"I think it sounds like pneumonia," said another nurse. "You better stay in bed."

"I'll come over later and see how everybody's doing," Adele said when she could talk again. "Here's the list for staffing. Sana, you're in charge until I get there. Margie, you're in OR this time. I want you to keep your skills up." She coughed again. "Now get going."

"Okay, chief." Margie gave her a quick hug. "I'll send over a doctor if I can."

"Don't you dare."

"I'll send that kid to finish taping the windows."

Adele smiled wanly. "Go on."

They grabbed cans of rations and ate as they walked. The camp sat high on a mountain and the wind was crisp and cold, blowing a few dry flakes of snow over the ground. Their pathway was a smooth paved road, winding gently among neatly kept buildings.

"Where are we?" Sana asked, wondering at the sight of cement after months of dirt.

"Thala," someone said.

The hospital turned out to be another clean little building, far too small for what they needed. Extra tents had been set up around it in the usual formation of triage, surgery and wards. Sana began to walk faster, thinking of all the things she would need to do now that Adele was sick and she was in charge. Surgery, bandages, plasma, blood... she could hear the low roar of many idling engines now. She started to run. When she came around the tents she gasped. The line of waiting ambulances stretched out of sight.

Joe studied the moving mass of metal at the other end of the valley while static crackled on the radio. Finally he sent Ratliff up the side of the escarpment to fire four green flares from its peak. Then he settled back down with his binoculars again to estimate the number of tanks rolling toward him.

A hundred? At least. The column spread across the narrow valley floor, with tank destroyers traveling on along their sides and a whole forest of black artillery tubes rising up behind them. Half-tracks followed the artillery, probably carrying infantry. And it looked like there might be even more tanks coming behind those. This was well over three times the size of their own force.

Joe lowered the glasses and kicked a rock in frustration. He should be out there right now — they should have been out there last night — they could have mined the road. He could have laid explosives. Why were they stuck in a bunch of useless holes by the side of the road? What good could they possibly do against those tanks, with their little mortars? He kicked the rock again, harder this time. Three faces looked around.

"Taffington."

"Sir?"

"Let's you and me take the radio up top." Maybe they could pick up the signal from the top of the escarpment and send back another report. The two of them started climbing, hauling the radio along, but when they were halfway up the slope two more Stukas droned across the sky and they flattened down among the boulders until the sound passed away.

A shower of falling gravel signaled Ratliff sliding down toward them, beaming from ear to ear. "Americans!" he shouted at them. "The battalion's coming! Right up the road!"

Joe grinned. The two columns would meet almost in front of them. And when they met, whoever was in charge of this mess probably wouldn't care anymore what the little company of Rangers did, as long as they did something.

"Triage as they come off," Sana directed. "Don't waste time cutting off uniforms. Immediate surgeries, over there." The receiving tents were full but trucks were still unloading, placing the wounded on the dirt anywhere they found room.

"Over here, please." Two grubby litter bearers paused and looked tiredly around at her. "Please put that one over here. In that row." Sana pointed again to the place where she wanted their man. "Thanks, guys. Thank you." She squinted her eyes against the wind, checking the action on the other side of the field, and backed right into five soldiers who were standing behind her. "What is it?" she asked.

"We're cooks, ma'am," one of them said. "We came to help."

"Great. You, go find more help right now. Chaplains, clerks, everybody. You two, get drinking water. Walk around and give out drinks. You two go get boxes of plasma from over there and put them out between the litters so we can get to them faster."

"Mom." She looked around. A soldier was stirring on the ground, his hand plucking at the bandage tied over his face. "Mom." Both his feet were gone and the bottoms of his legs were wrapped in reddened bandages. He moved again and pulled harder at his bandage. "Mom!" Only one empty curette was clipped to his uniform. Sana pulled a dose of morphine from her pocket and leaned over him. When she stroked his hair the boy quieted at the touch of her hand, then jumped at the little unexpected pain. She gently marked an "M" on the bandage covering his forehead and called a soldier to bring him water.

When she got the huge triage area finally moving along in its own routine, she went to the OR. Rows of men lay lined up on the ground along the tent, waiting their turn. Sana stepped inside and heard the quiet clink and hum of surgery, and she knew all was in order before she even saw the ten filled tables with teams clustered intently around each one. Busy medics flowed in a steady stream, precise as an assembly line.

She left to check the laundry and supplies. A stack of something along the outside of the tent looked like red and gray firewood, but it was a pile of amputated arms and legs. She turned her eyes away and hurried on.

Now people were running in from all over the camp to help. Chaplains and water carriers were moving through the rows of litters. She could start collecting blood now. Sana told three gawking mechanics to follow her back to the supply tent and loaded them up with needles and tubes. When she explained that they would need more bottles, the mechanics looked back and forth among themselves.

"I know someplace where there's lots of beer bottles, ma'am," one of them volunteered.

"Go out for fifteen minutes and bring back every bottle you

can find," she ordered. "Put them down over there and then go get the rest." They hurried off.

She pulled a cook to sterilize the bottles and sent a medic to set up a blood collection station by the side of the road. A group of truck drivers eating cold K-rations stepped forward first to give, still chewing as they held out dirty forearms for the needles.

The line of ambulances kept crawling forward. Triage needed more plasma, more morphine, more needles, more water, more sulfa. Injured men cried out as litters were moved and wounds oozed blood. When the sun set they would need flashlights. The small dry flakes of snow still whirled through the air and they needed more tents for the outdoor wounded. At the very least, they needed blankets.

She sent a chaplain for flashlights and a quartermaster for tents and blankets. The three mechanics came back with boxes full of empty bottles and she pointed them towards the sterilizer. More ambulances unloaded litters. Someone gave her a drink from his canteen.

When Sana went again to check on post-op, the red-gray stack of limbs outside the OR had tripled in size. She passed through the surgery tent on her way back.

Margie's team was between patients, eating crackers. Sana paused beside her. "What do you need?" she asked.

"Blood."

"It's coming. What else?"

"Just blood." Medics placed another casualty on the table. Margie scrutinized the new patient, who had a sucking chest wound. Mounds of dirty bandages had piled up between the tables.

"I'll get that laundry going," Sana said.

"Big Red's on it," Margie said. "He just went to post-op but he'll be right back." Her team's surgeon crammed a handful of crackers into his mouth and stepped over to the operating table, ready to start again. "We really need that blood."

"Okay." The number of donors was still outpacing the number of clean bottles available to fill. Where were those mechanics with more bottles? She headed back outside and collided with a tall shape in the dusk.

"*Vítáme vás! Promiňte*, darling!" Blue eyes and white teeth gleamed at her from a blood-smeared face.

"Wence!" He grabbed her in a hug that lifted her off the ground. "Oh, I'm so glad you're here! Have you seen Joe?"

"I dunno. They all look alike by the time I get 'em. You seen him?"

"Not since Constantine. Where've you been?"

"All over. *All* over." He straightened up and flashed a wacky grin. "They call me Mountain Man now. When they're not calling me Crazy Czech."

"No wonder. You look like Frankenstein."

"You look like Madame Dracula." Wence struck a pose like Bela Lugosi. "'*I come to drink your blood.*'" He pretended to bite her neck.

Sana glanced down at her bloodstained uniform and laughed. "What're you looking for?"

"Morphine."

"This way." She headed for the supply tent.

Wence hurried to catch up. "Where's Adele?" he asked as they sped along.

"Sick." Sana could see flashlights bobbing among the litters now, each little light surrounded by a nimbus of fine snow. A dark mass moving along the side of the field turned out to be men putting up tents.

"She must be dead if she's not working," Wence said.

"Pneumonia."

"Can I catch it if I try?"

"The way you look? Not even a germ would want to be around you." Sticky black blood was caked clear up into his hair. "Can you stay here for a while?"

"Naw. There's still guys out there."

They walked into the supply tent, and in the light Wence looked even more ghoulish than before. His face was covered with a matted tangle of dirty beard and his eyes were red. Wet blood gleamed up and down his coveralls.

"Criminently!" a fresh-faced soldier gasped. "Where'd he come from?"

"He's an ambulance medic and he needs supplies," Sana said. "Get him morphine, plasma, whatever he wants.

"Sir, do you want some sulfa?" another new corpsman stammered,

"I want a steak and a cold one." Wence sat down stiffly on a crate.

"You from Sidi?" the first soldier asked. "We heard Sidi got hit real bad."

"Ma'am?" One of the mechanics blundered through the tent flaps, carrying an armload of empty beer bottles. "You still want more of these?"

"How come nobody invites me to the parties?" Wence complained.

Sana inspected the bottles and sent the soldier out again. "How long does it take you to drive out to the men?" she asked Wence. "Can you take blood out to them?"

Wence shrugged. "You got enough?"

"Maybe. What else do you need?"

"Everything. Bandages." A corspman handed him two opened K-ration packs and Wence shoveled down hash and biscuits while people swarmed around him. Sana stepped outside to check the progress on the tents.

She came back just as he finished. The corpsman took away his empty cans and handed him a filled canteen. He drank it all, tipping it high to get the last swallow of water, and stood up to leave.

"I'll walk you over," Sana offered. "I'm going that way anyway."

They went back out into the dark. Flashlights bobbed on the field, but the shapes of tents were looming black against the sky now. Sana turned on her flashlight to keep from tripping over tent ropes. The snowflakes were getting bigger now, whirling like moths in the beam of her light.

"You didn't say how far you have to drive to get more wounded," she said.

"Not very far. Hey, I saw Rommel."

"You're kidding! What were you doing that far away?"

Wence was quiet for a moment. Finally he said, "He's not that far. I drove over a hill no more'n twenty miles from here and saw a whole bunch of German tanks coming right at me. I turned around so fast a litter almost fell out."

Sana stared at him. "Aren't there any troops between them and us?"

Wence was looking at the field packed with litters. "The hospital at Feriana pulled out and the one at Sbeitla got taken prisoner," he said. "That's why we brought everybody here."

Joe savagely jerked his trip wire and blasted another tank into smoke and flame, sending clouds of heavy brown dust rolling over his little hideout. He grabbed the canvas satchel of mines and charges and dashed to the next bit of shrub where he had set a wire for another charge. As long as smoke and dust filled the air, no one in the tanks could see him. He couldn't see them either but he knew where they were. He jerked the wire and the blast roared alive. Machinery screeched and crashed somewhere in the haze as tanks piled up in confusion.

While the smoke still boiled, Joe pulled out a flash-fuse mine and ran forward until he saw the massive steel tank treads looming out of the dust. He lobbed the mine carefully right onto a tank's rear deck and then ran for his life.

The blast shook the ground and he flung himself to the dirt and scrabbled for cover. He wriggled behind a clump of spiny cactus and looked back. Five tanks were stopped, but the rest clanked steadily onward. He hadn't even slowed them down.

Joe glanced over his shoulder at the escarpment, where Garcia would direct the mortar fire when the tanks got close enough, and then back down the road to where Robichaux's mines should be going off about now. He stared between the cactus spines at the lead tanks of the column, willing them to blow. A sudden burst of flame and smoke shot up, followed by a tremble in the ground and a thunderous roar. Dust surged in every direction. Robichaux must have planted them just right, to get such a good hit. He narrowed his eyes, watching the place where he knew Robichaux was hiding. He saw a dusty form race into the haze swirling around the tanks, and then heard the pound of a new explosion.

The smoke finally settled enough to see the damage. Four more tanks were pouring smoke but the huge moving convoy of steel fortresses rolled on. The leading tanks were almost at the escarpment now. A flash winked out of the rocks, followed by a puff of smoke and the sound of a mortar. One of the tanks faltered. Another flash, another puff. A different tank slowed, stopped, and turned its turret toward the rocks.

Joe flinched as boulders burst into the air. Garcia could not hold out very long against that kind of power. He needed to get back and help them. He flung a grenade between himself and the road and zig-zagged through clumps of cactus under the cover of its little explosion. Bullets popped somewhere around him. Right as the smoke thinned out he reached a shallow ridge and flung himself behind it, as flat as he could get against the sand. Something buzzed in the air over his head.

His throat was sandy and his nose hurt from the smoke. He coughed and spat a gob of dirt. The mortars were still firing, but they sounded shrill and tinny against the steady thunder of the tanks. Another blast rocked the ground. Was it Robichaux blowing up more tanks, or the Germans blowing up more rocks? He looked over his sheltering edge of sand. A thick black plume of tank smoke was rising from the road.

The cactus ahead of him looked dense enough to risk moving forward again. Joe crawled through the prickles, going helmet-first through the spiny branches and squinting his eyes against the dirt. He had to pull out his knife and hack through some of the thicker clumps, wincing at the wicked barbs of pain, until he reached the safety of a rocky outcrop. The mortars fired again and another tank stopped, aimed, and blasted rocks into the air.

How long could they hold out? Why hadn't the American

tanks arrived yet? He hitched a little farther forward to peer around the rocks. A helmeted head suddenly rose above him and Joe sprang up with knife in hand to attack what turned out to be Robichaux. They clung together for a moment, panting and gasping in relief that they had not killed each other.

The tanks were pounding away at the escarpment and now he was close enough to it that rocks from the blasts rained down on him. If he threw another grenade for cover, he and Robichaux could probably get over the last bit of open ground to join Garcia and the rest. Joe hefted his satchel of charges. And if he did reach his men? What then?

The mortars kept shooting their tinny little pops and the tanks kept booming back. If he could get to the escarpment he could go around the back of it, get up close to the tanks and shoot rifle grenades... if he hit a couple of them just right he could stop a few... and then if he could get in close enough he could pitch a Hawkins mine and do some real damage, smoke up the air so his men could get away... Joe pulled out a grenade, caught Robichaux's eye, and threw. It kicked up enough dust for cover and they raced to the escarpment just as a huge explosion rocked the air and the ground trembled beneath them. They were climbing up to see what had become of the Rangers on the other side when Taffington and Ratliff tumbled over the top and came sliding down, weapons and ammo right behind them. More Rangers followed. Joe grabbed Taffy as he slithered past.

"What're you doing?" Joe yelled.

"Garcia ordered us out, sir!" Taffington shouted into his ear. His face was streaked with dirt and blood. "We were out of shells anyway, sir!"

"Anyone get hit?"

Taffington looked away. "Yes sir."

"How many?"

"Everybody."

"What?" Joe grabbed the front of Taffy's uniform and pulled him around, a scream rising in his heart. "What'd you say?" Taffington stared bleakly at him and Joe dropped his grip. He looked around at the remaining men. Garcia was not there.

Rocks flew under his hands and feet as he bolted to the top of the cliff and stared down where the mortars had been. Not a single man remained. Shattered rubble stretched across the slope and smoke drifted across shreds of things he could not look at.

The cruel tanks rolled on below. He was too late. He had come too late to save them. He never thought that death would come like this, at least not this soon. He thought they would go home again. But he was too late, and they were dead.

Men were shouting behind him. Joe turned away and forced himself to focus down the hill. Ratliff was waving, his words lost in all the noise. He was pointing toward the western stretch of road. Another line of tanks had appeared, American tanks driving straight towards the Germans, with infantry following behind.

The men whooped and cheered from the slope below. Joe slid down the rocks to a ledge and pulled out his binoculars. The American column jumped into focus. He could see an officer standing up in the leading tank, looking determinedly down the road. They were still too far away to fire... it would take a while longer for them to get in
range...

The German tanks cranked up and blasted a new round across the sky. The American officer burst into flame. The column exploded into fire and smoke, some tanks with burning shapes scrambling from their turrets, most with no one getting out. A few shot back a scanty volley that fell to the ground halfway to the German line. Another German barrage boomed out and the whole American column shuddered to a halt, the leading tanks pouring out fire and the following tanks crashing into them. A third line of shells traced green fire high across the sky and fell behind the crippled tanks, ripping a slaughter-wave through the infantry. Shrieks drifted faintly through the air.

The German tanks kept on rolling forward, firing as they advanced, eating up the distance between the columns. The American tanks were now a mass of boiling fire and men were running into the desert, frantically trying to get away from the seething nightmare on the road. A truck at the end of the column turned around to drive away, then another.

When thou walkest through the fire I will be with thee... the words came back to mind, as clearly as if John Mark was standing there and saying them out loud. *Keep your head on straight...* Joe licked his lips, found his voice and called to his remaining men. Silent faces turned toward him and he gathered them together as death screamed on through the sky.

"We're going back. Pack up all the ammo you can carry," he told them. "Someone's got to hold this road."

They filled their canteens from the shallow river one last time before starting back across the hills. Joe set a course that was close enough to the road to keep it in view but far enough to camouflage them a little. They could not march at speed anymore, like they had on the way out. All the men were tired and banged up. One had a bad burn along the side of his neck and another one was walking with a broken collarbone tied up in a sling. The radio was gone. They walked on under the empty sky, skirting knots of cactus, climbing up hills and down ravines, always hearing the distant clank of tanks behind them.

The clanking finally stopped after sunset. When Joe crested the next hill he pulled out his binoculars and looked back in the fading light. He could see little white triangles, tents being set up in neat straight rows. The Germans would eat and rest tonight, and then continue their bloody march tomorrow.

Dang Germans'll probably get up extra early, too. Joe sucked on the pebble he had put in his mouth to take his mind off being thirsty. Where would they go next? Thala was not far away, and the big supply depot at Tébessa, with an airfield and huge piles of new ordnance, was only forty miles to the west. Rommel could head toward either camp and be there in a day. Did the camps even know how close he was? The officers back at the infantry base camp had not known.

The daylight was almost gone now and the pale track of road gleamed between the dark masses of the mountains, its dusty whiteness glowing briefly in the fading light. Something was moving on it and Joe pulled up his binoculars again, straining to see through the dusk. It was a group of men, walking slowly.

"Robichaux," he hissed, and Robichaux slipped noiselessly up next to him. Joe handed over the binoculars. "See that?" Robichaux looked and nodded. "Go find out who they are."

When Robichaux called back the all-clear signal, they clambered down to the road and jogged up to the other group. About twenty bandaged infantrymen were shuffling doggedly along, some supporting others as they walked. Joe moved into their view and called out the password calmly, careful to use a friendly tone of voice in order not to frighten them. The officer in charge turned out to be a chaplain and Joe fell in beside him.

"These your men?" he asked.

"No." The chaplain's face was invisible in the dark. "They were in the tanks."

"Where're you going?" Joe asked.

"I don't know. Back." He paused. "You guys got any water?"

Joe held out his canteen, keeping a hand on it as the other man took a drink. He pulled it back before it was emptied. "Sorry." There was a long way to go and there was no water except the river they had left behind.

"Okay," the chaplain gasped. "Thanks."

After a while Joe said, "We can't travel with you guys. We have to get farther down the road, in front of the Germans. We're going to set up explosives and see if we can slow them down."

A dry chuckle sounded. "Good for you, lieutenant. Watch out so you don't blow us up by mistake."

"There's a fork in the road up ahead of you," Joe told him. "You ought to bear north and head for Thala. It's closer. Get off the road if you hear anything. It'll probably be Germans."

The chaplain's voice sounded a little firmer. "That depends on how bad we get. If the Germans have water and we don't..." his voice trailed off. "Might be better for the men, if they take us prisoner. Better than just dying out here."

"You could divide into two groups," Joe said. "The fast guys go get help and the wounded ones go slow."

"We already did that. We're the slow ones." After a pause, he added, "I'm not leaving them."

A soldier slumped to the ground and everyone stopped walking.

"You guys go on," the chaplain said. "We better rest for a while."

Joe offered his canteen again.

The chaplain took another drink. "God bless you," he said.

Joe's group hustled forward in the moonlight, staying on the road and speeding across the level ground with the mile-eating stride they had learned so long ago. Joe chewed on half a ration bar and pondered over ammunition. The mortars were lost. They still had satchel charges with TNT, which could do some damage. They had some rifle grenades, hand grenades and Hawkins mines. A Hawkins could take out a tank. So could a grenade, if it was pitched precisely into an engine deck or a track. He could set up a first and then a second round of explosives. Maybe, if he found the right kind of terrain, he could bring down enough tanks to pile up into each other and jam up the road. If he planned out the hits just right, maybe he could do it again a little way farther down. They would seem like a much stronger defense force than they actually were.

He could picture it now. He could stop them, for a while anyway. He would not just lay random mines to blow up whatever hit them first. Every precious charge would have to be used strategically and there was no sense wasting good ammo on Americans by mistake. He laughed at the thought, then frowned at himself for thinking it.

The ration bar made him thirsty. Joe wet the inside of his mouth from the canteen and then replaced his pebble. After a while he started whistling a tune. Ratliff glanced back and Joe slapped him warmly on the side of his helmet to cheer him up. Rat jumped like a spooked rabbit.

They covered about five miles before he found what he wanted, a combination of rocky outcrops and thick cactus at a place where the hills closed in high around the road. He had just given the order to halt when they heard the sound of a motor.

"If it's a tank, shoot grenades at the tracks," Joe ordered. "If it's a truck, shoot the driver." He saw Robichaux's wolfish grin flash out before everyone vanished into the scrub. Clicks and rustles sounded as rifles were readied, and then all was silent under the desert stars.

Joe held his breath to hear better and stared hard down the road. The sound of the motor became more distinct, echoing off the rocks in the empty air. It was not a tank. It was a truck.

Something flickered from the west. A dark shape chugged into view, its headlights dimmed to slits for night driving.

"Hold your fire," Joe called hoarsely, and the order repeated on down the line. As the truck approached he recognized the pale circle with a dark cross painted on its front. He switched on his flashlight and stepped out, waving. The ambulance rattled to a halt.

"Watcha want first?" someone called through the dark. "The beautiful nurse or the steak dinner?"

"The password, idiot," Joe yelled back.

"You got no imagination."

Joe squinted. "Praz?"

"Ves?"

A tall form swung down from the truck and ran toward him. Joe grabbed it in a hug and felt a wet kiss smack onto his scruffy cheek.

"Yuck!"

Wence laughed and kept a brawny arm around Joe's shoulders, squeezing him tight in his iron grip. "Come on, baby, pucker up for me. How come you don't shave?"

"Nobody told me I'd get lucky today."

"What're you doing here?"

"What're *you* doing here?"

"Picking up wounded."

"There's a group about five miles that way." Joe's mouth cracked with dust. "You got water?"

"Yeah." The other men were gathered at the back of the ambulance, drinking from its water cans. "Here." Wence handed over his canteen and Joe tipped it up to get the blessed wetness, swallowing long sweet gulps of cool water down his dried-out throat. He lowered the canteen, took a deep breath, then raised it again and drank the rest before he gave it back.

"Hey, I just saw Sana," Wence said. "She's running the whole hospital now."

Joe stared at him. "You just saw her? Where?"

"Thala."

An alarm went off in the back of Joe's mind. "How come you're so far away?"

"I'm not. It's only a couple of miles from here."

"What?" Joe pushed away Wence's arm, gaping in surprise.

"Well, ten."

Joe felt his heart pound in rage clear up to his ears. "Doggone you!" he yelled. "What's the matter with everybody? Rommel will be there tomorrow! Doggone you all!" Wence took hold of his arm but Joe threw him off. "Move it! Go back and tell them to get out of here!"

"Whoa, now..."

"Shut up. I am not one of your patients. I am ordering you to go back right now and make that hospital clear out."

"Buddy, I already have my orders," Wence said mildly.

Joe stared at him. "You *have* to go back."

Wence held his stare. "There's more men out there."

Joe gritted his teeth. "Praz," he said, "You're going to run right into the Germans. You're going to get killed or taken prisoner. They'll blow you up before you even see them coming. Go back."

"I will." For once Wence was not smiling. "Right after I get my guys."

Joe clamped his jaw and fumed silently for a while. "Do you have a radio?" he finally asked.

"Just one of those British ones," Wence said. "They don't work with American radios so I can't send messages. But I'll get back before morning." He grinned again. "What're you girls going to do while I risk my life for freedom? Sit here and play cards?"

"I am going to stop the Germans," Joe said. "For as long as I can. Doggone you for a stupid Prazsky *dumkoff* just like your pig-headed father. You know you ought to go back right now and warn them."

Wence looked at him. "I kind of wish my dad was here."

Joe looked away. Karel Prazsky... the neighborhood giant with the bushy beard and massive shoulders, who could scare off a pack of thieving kids with one cold glare... oh, how good it would feel if old gray Karel was here with them right now.

"Sorry," he said. "I just wish you'd go back now."

"Don't worry, Ves." Wence did not seem upset. "I'll take care of her."

Chapter 13

Thala

Sana hurried along the paved walk to the nurses' quarters, keeping her head down against the wind and carrying a can of hot soup wrapped in a towel. Small dry snowflakes whirled through the air and drifted across the frozen ground. She was going to check on Adele, who had just been officially diagnosed with double pneumonia, and tell her that she would have to leave on the next available truck, because there was no penicillin at Thala to treat the pneumonia. She was not looking forward to what Adele would say.

She maneuvered her way through the barrack's heavy door and let a gust of air blast it shut behind her. All was quiet and warm inside. A few women lay sleeping in the beds at the far end of the row, tucked deeply into pillows and blankets. Margie was one of them, having just spent twenty hours on her feet in the OR.

Sana pulled a chair over to Adele's bed and put on a bright smile. "Adele? You awake?"

Adele opened her eyes, looked at her with a rheumy gaze, and broke into a heavy cough. Sana winced at the wetness in the sound.

"I brought you some soup." She ran a hand over Adele's hot forehead and took her pulse, then pulled out her stethoscope. "Take a breath for me.

Adele closed her eyes and took a breath, then burst into another clammy cough that shook her whole body and made Sana's own chest ache in sympathy. Finally the spasm ended, leaving Adele limp against her pillow and slick with sweat. Her breath came in little sobbing gasps as Sana gently dried her face and tucked another pillow under her head.

"I know that hurt," Sana whispered. Adele tried to clear her throat and gagged. Sana helped her sit up and handed her a cloth to spit in. The discharge was thick and bloody.

Sana tried to hide her alarm at the sight. "Look, I brought you aspirin and soup." Adele's pale face was already sweaty again. Sana piled pillows behind her back and made her swallow the aspirin. "Now drink this soup and I'll get you some more blankets. You'll feel better in a minute."

There were plenty of blankets because most of the women were at the hospital. Surgery was still going nonstop and only a few nurses could be sent back to sleep at any one time. Sana herself had napped for a few hours in the back of the laundry tent, stretched out on a pile of dirty towels, with strict orders for Red to wake her up if necessary.

Adele sipped at the soup while Sana bundled extra blankets around her. "What time is it?" she whispered.

"Afternoon," Sana said.

"You mean it's been a whole day?"

Sana smiled. "Two."

"I've been sick that long?"

"Uh-huh."

"And you've been working all this time?"

"Uh-huh. Now, don't strain yourself. You need to just rest and take it easy. Sit back."

"How many..." Adele stopped to take a shallow breath. "Men?"

Sana shook her head. "I think we're going to hit nine hundred today."

"Dear God." Adele closed her eyes, concentrating on holding back another cough. "Who's in surgery?" she murmured.

"Don't worry. We're rotating and everybody's getting a little sleep." Sana dabbed more beads of perspiration from Adele's face. Her cheeks were flushing now but she was shivering. "How's the headache?"

247

Adele looked wearily at her. Sana's heart sank. She tucked in the blankets a little more firmly. "Finish that soup, now."

Adele took another sip. Something like thunder rumbled in the distance and she looked at Sana again, a question in her eyes.

Sana nodded reluctantly. Adele sighed.

"You know you have to go," Sana said miserably. "You have to go someplace where there's penicillin."

Adele shook her head, more in sadness than in argument. "I hate to leave."

"I know." Sana took her hand and held it for a while. They heard the distant rumble again, and then the sound of shovels right outside the barracks, digging up dirt and gravel.

"They're digging foxholes," Sana said. "For when the Germans come."

"Why don't they get everybody out while they still can?" Adele shifted restlessly under the blankets. "They sent that other hospital back."

"We'll be leaving pretty soon. You're just going early." Sana forced another smile. "You're going to a real hospital and then you're going home."

Adele raised an eyebrow. "Don't be... so sure of that... young lady."

"Tough old turkey buzzard." She smiled again, a real one this time. "You just get better."

Adele put her hand on her chest and broke into a cough. She strained forward, hawking so hard that tears ran down her face, and Sana leaned her forward so she could spit out another gob of bloody mucus.

"Adele, hold on," Sana said, almost in tears herself. How far would she have to travel before getting penicillin? One day? Two? Could she make it that long? If she went downhill from the state she was in now... "Promise you'll just rest and drink soup and hold on. You'll get better right away when you get medicine. You'll be fine."

"When do... you leave?" Adele asked after a while.

"Pretty soon." The order to evacuate had not come yet, but

Adele didn't need to know that now.

Another rumble sounded and then a plane droned overhead. They both listened to hear if it was German or American. "Ours," Sana said. "See? We'll be okay."

A knock sounded and the door opened, letting in a blast of snowflakes. Two men brought in a litter. Sana let go of Adele's hand and started gathering her belongings into her musette bags.

"Wait outside a minute, you two," Adele said with a ghost of her old authority. The men stepped back out.

Adele reached out and took her hand. "Such a dear girl." She coughed and closed her eyes. "My wonderful heavenly father," she whispered, "please be with Sana now. Strengthen her, help her... watch over her and all my special girls. Protect them..." She paused and Sana could feel her holding back another cough. "We are helpless but... you are not. You are lord of heaven and earth and all of this is in your hands. I ask in... the name of Jesus Christ... for every one of them to stay safe..." Her hand tightened on Sana's. "Thank you for giving them to me."

Sana put her head down on the cot and sobbed. Checky was gone, Joe had not come back, he might never come back, and now Adele was leaving too. She was tired and hungry and there was no hope, no help coming. She cried her heart out into Adele's blankets, heaving sobs into the scratchy wool.

Adele stroked her hair and murmured reassurance. "You aren't alone. You have the Lord right beside you. He's right here. He'll carry you through. Don't cry, sweetie. It's going to be all right."

The wave of sadness finally ebbed away. Sana dried her eyes and raised her head.

Adele smiled. "You know what I'm thinking about?"

Sana shook her head.

"Psalm 73. *'My flesh and my heart may fail, but the Lord is the strength of my heart, and my portion forever.'* Remember that. The Lord will never, ever, let you down." Adele closed her eyes and paused for breath. "Be strong and do a good job, honey."

"I will." Sana took her hand again. "I'll be just like you."

249

"You're such a dear."

They hugged and then the two men came in again. "Sorry, ma'am, but we have to get you out right now," one of them said. Sana helped them transfer Adele to the litter and walked along beside it as they carried her across the field, trying to shield her from the wind.

"Well, I prayed for you," Adele said. "So don't worry. Don't take any guff... from those dang fool sergeants."

Sana laughed. "I promise."

"You'll do fine. Remember the Lord. I love you, dear."

"I love you too." They were at the truck now. The men handed up the litter and clanged the tailgate closed. Gears clashed and the truck jolted forward.

"Goodbye, Adele!" Sana called. "Get better!" The soldiers walked away and the truck drove off on its long trip over the western mountains. Sana stood there for a while, watching its trailing plume of dust dwindle further and further away. She had never felt so unequal to the task before her, or so alone.

She hurried back to the hospital, keeping her chin tucked into her collar and hugging her arms across her chest against the stinging snow. Low gray clouds covered the sky, except in the east, where a black haze was spreading across the horizon. A plane droned overhead and people looked up, searching, until the sound faded away.

The ward tents were packed with men laid alternating heads and feet so they wouldn't breathe in each other's faces. Sana rearranged the staffing, sent a few more nurses back to sleep, and went on to visit triage. She could hear the sound of motors and she braced herself to begin another round.

But there were no ambulances. Instead there was a line of trucks and halftracks traveling past the hospital, going away from the front now instead of towards it. Arab families were walking the same direction, towing camels and donkeys loaded with piles of baggage. Barking dogs and tired-looking children trailed behind the camels. An ambulance drove up but an MP waved it onward instead of signaling it to turn in.

"What's going on?" she asked the hollow-eyed corpsman on duty. His nose was dripping and his sleeves were rolled up, showing forearms with needle marks from giving blood.

He coughed and swiped his nose against his shoulder. "They're getting out before Rommel gets here."

"You mean the Army's leaving?"

"Well, yeah, ma'am. Look which way they're going." He coughed again. "Do you think we'll go pretty soon?"

"Probably." Sana looked around at the jumble of empty plasma cans and dirty bandages littered across the ground. The trash was knee-deep in some places. A distant rumble sounded.

"I don't want you giving any more blood," Sana said to the pale corpsman. "Get all the usable supplies together in one place. Next to the entrance, so we can leave in a hurry."

An icy gust of air blew the tent flaps open. Trucks and Arabs were still rushing down the road, dusty jeeps roaring past donkeys, everyone traveling at top speed. Sana picked up the cleanest blanket she could find and wrapped it around herself before hurrying off to the OR, where she found Schmidt and O'Neal standing outside drinking coffee. They looked silently at her, their eyes red-rimmed and gummy under stained surgical caps.

"Everyone's leaving," Sana said.

O'Neal nodded. "Rommel broke through the pass."

"Shouldn't we leave too?"

O'Neal rolled his eyes. "First we get an order from somebody, telling us to pack up because they're sending out trucks to get us. Then we get another order from somebody else, saying everybody hold positions, no withdrawal under any circumstances."

Sana looked from one to the other. "That's so ridiculous. Did you see the road?"

The doctors shrugged.

"So we're staying?"

Schmidt smiled at her, his tired eyes warm with affection, and patted her back. "No matter what happens, Toledo Ohio, at least we're in good company."

"We could get orders to leave anytime," O'Neal pointed out. "They say something different every hour. If trucks show up, we need to move out the men even if we don't go."

Sana thought about what would be needed for an evacuation. "I'll tell Red to start the packing."

Schmidt drained his coffee. "Honey, if I were you, I'd put a nurse on every truck that goes out of here with patients on it."

O'Neal nodded. "Somebody needs to decide who goes first and who goes later. The wounded, I mean."

Both doctors looked at Sana. "Okay," she said. "I'll sort the wards."

Back at triage, both the field and road were now clogged with honking vehicles. Cargo trucks were arriving from one direction and ambulances were trying to get around them from the other side. Arabs wove in and out of gridlocked vehicles, stopping once in a while to barter. Soldiers still stood in line at the blood collection station, sleeves rolled up, their faces pinched and red with cold. Her three mechanics were still sterilizing the bottles.

An ambulance lumbered off the road and rolled right up to the entrance of the triage tent. Two men on litters were lashed across its front. The driver leaned out the window.

"Can you take 'em?" he yelled.

"Yes," Sana shouted. The mechanics came over to help unload and Sana walked around to see how many wounded were in back. Tired faces looked out at her.

"Look at these beauties I brought you," the medic inside called over their heads. "Prime examples of manhood. Found 'em on the side of the road. Six burns, five shrapnels and a bunch of ambulatories. Fellas, lookie here. A beautiful woman. Just like home."

Someone whistled at her.

Sana recognized the medic's voice. "Hi, Wence."

"Hey! Sorry, everyone, hold your horses. This nurse's off limits. She's marrying a Ranger, God help her."

"You big lugs," Sana said, laughing in spite of herself. "Get out and go inside."

Men limped into the tent. Two of them were not even wounded. "There's not as many bad ones this time," Sana said to Wence.

"These are the ones who could walk out," he told her. "The bad ones are dead now. I saw Joe."

Dark swirls swam in front of her eyes and ate up the daylight. Someone was calling her name and Sana blinked herself back into focus. Wence was gripping her arms and talking to her. What had he meant, saying that he had seen Joe? Her mind skittered away from an answer.

She made her lips move. "Is he dead?"

"Naw, he's fine. Sit down. I thought you were going to pass out. Don't do it, babe, don't do that to me."

Sana sat down on a crate. She was sweating. She lifted off her helmet and ran her fingers through her matted curls, letting the cold air cool her down. "Where is he?"

"About ten miles up the road."

"So those explosions aren't from the Germans?" she said hopefully.

"It's a mix," he said. "There's some of ours trying to block the road. Bodies everywhere. How much longer you staying?"

"I don't know. We're packing now, in case we get orders."

"I promised a bunch of guys I'd go back for them." Wence looked around and pulled up another crate to sit on. It collapsed under his weight, sending him sprawling on the ground. "Oh, geez." He sighed and lay back on the dirt, right in the middle of the broken boards. "Oh, God help me."

Sana reached down and tugged on his hand. "Go in and find a cot. I'll wake you up in an hour."

"Naw, just leave me here."

"You're in the way."

"Somebody get me some supplies and a tank of gas. Red! Red! Where is that kid?"

"Get up. I'll find someone to do it for you."

Wence heaved himself off the ground and lumbered towards

the supply area. Two soldiers wandered up to her.

"Ma'am, we're supposed to start loading up the patients. Where do we start?"

Sana hitched her blanket a little tighter and looked around, thinking.

"How many can you fit in a truck?" she asked.

They looked at each other. "Maybe twenty-five or thirty, if we pack 'em tight," one said. The other nodded.

Thirty to a truck. Nine hundred men divided by thirty... but realistically, they might not be able to fit thirty patients onto every truck, especially if they needed room to lay flat and hang IVs. Each truck would need supplies for the long trip back over the mountains.

A flake of snow gently touched her cheek, then another. Sana felt a tremble begin deep in her middle, and all of a sudden her whole body shuddered with a spasm of despair. *Oh, God, don't let me start crying now.* A tear leaked out anyway and she wiped her cheek against the blanket, hoping the soldiers didn't see.

"How many trucks are there?" In spite of herself, her throat caught in a sob.

"Five." The soldier cleared his throat and looked away, embarrassed. "But there's more coming. Some of the trucks are flatbeds, ma'am, so maybe you better put the really bad-off guys in these covered ones."

Sana stared at the road. Men were still waiting for surgery, men in the pre-ops and post-ops still needed transfusions... there were so many wounded soldiers laying head to toe in the wards. The shudder seized her again. No matter how hard she tried, no matter how hard they all worked, she did not see how they could keep all these men alive.

White flakes whirled down and the far-off hills looked gray and misty through the falling snow. Another explosion sounded and a single ambulance drove off the field toward the murky east, probably Wence, heading back for another load. Then Margie showed up, took Sana by the arm, and firmly led her to an empty cot.

Joe was hunkered down behind a boulder, watching the first tanks loom into sight, when he felt a raindrop hit his helmet. Another tapped, and then another. The smell of rain breathed all around him and more drops pelted over the dusty ground.

Rain... he looked up and caught a drop right in his eye. Rain might actually help them, if mud bogged down the tanks. Unless it made his fuses wet and they didn't fire. He looked down the road again. No one in the tanks could see him yet, so he crawled out onto the road and checked the precious cache of dynamite that lay hidden under the gravel. The tanks were only about half a mile away now. His men were hidden close to the road, mines and grenades at hand. Everyone was ready.

He had rigged up half his dynamite at a place where the road narrowed to a pass that the tanks would have to go through by twos. If he timed the explosion just right, he could take out the lead pair and blow up enough rock at the same time to jam the road. Then, under the cover of smoke and confusion, the men could slip in close enough to the tanks to toss grenades right into the vulnerable tracks and turrets. The Germans would be stopped until they could clear the burning wreckage from the pass. Meanwhile the Rangers would run over to the next escarpment down the road, where Joe had already laid the other half of the dynamite, and do it all over again a second time.

A pair of enemy planes appeared out of the clouds and Joe involuntarily ducked as their shadows crossed over him. Those planes would come back to look for them after the explosion, but there wasn't much he could do about that now. They would just have to drop and hide if they heard planes coming.

Tanks clanked toward him in precise formation. Rows of moving metal stretched clear back to the horizon. As the huge mass loomed closer and closer, his plan that had seemed so brilliant last night began to look ridiculous, like a childish daydream taken too far.

It was impossible. He wiped his sweating hands and sucked hard on his mouth pebble. How could he have been so deluded? No one could stop this army with a few sticks of dynamite and a few dozen mines and grenades. What damage could he possibly do? Not much more than make a couple of dents in the armor. Probably the smartest thing would have been to get out while they still could.

The storm was blowing closer and long dark curving drifts of rain were sweeping toward him through the hills. Joe stared at them, thinking. No, he had done the right thing, no matter how he felt about it now. He was fighting as hard as he could with what he had, trying to hold back the Germans as long as possible, and if his plan didn't work then they would just keep on fighting until they stopped the tanks or died trying.

Maybe help was on the way right now. Maybe a whole division of U.S. troops would show up any minute.

The tanks were close enough for him to see their markings now. He studied them and glanced at the drifts of rain. What would reach him first?

Dear God, please don't let my fuses get wet. Please just hold back the rain for about one more minute and then let it rip and make lots of mud. Joe licked his lips. How long had it been since he had prayed? It seemed like forever. He had told Sana he was going to pray every day. Well, no use looking back now. *God, even if my plan doesn't work, please stop the tanks somehow and keep Sana safe. And Uncle John, and Aunt Kate, and Grandma and Johnny and Anton and Uncle Karel and Aunt Ruzina. And Rosie. And Stephen. Doggone that little troublemaker. If I ever get back home I swear I'll set him straight.*

The tanks were only fifty yards away. *Please, please God, let this work.* Sweat trickled down his neck and chest. *Whatever it costs, whatever it takes, that's fine, just make it
work...* thirty yards. The tanks were slowing down, pairing up to go through the pass. Joe put his hand by the igniter, his finger ready, waiting. The raindrops were coming down faster. *God, remember, the fuses. Just fifteen more seconds. That's all I'm asking.* The first tanks were almost in position. Ten seconds. Five. Four. Three. Two.

Fire and thunder exploded and Joe clung blindly to the rocks as a searing blast scorched past. Something knocked him over and rubble rained down. *They blew! They blew! Oh thank you God, they blew!* A flood of choking smoke came next and he kept his eyes closed tight and covered his nose, trying not to breathe the oily fumes.

His ears were ringing and he felt the next explosions more than he heard them. Were those bangs the Hawkins mines going off? His men should be throwing grenades by now. He shook his head and opened his eyes. Which way? Smoke was everywhere. He could just barely see the road so he crawled the other way, coughing and spitting sand as he went. More tanks were burning now. Someone said that it took twenty minutes for men to burn to death inside a tank. This would give them enough time to get to the second pass and get ready.

Two shapes ran out of the drifting smoke. "Come on!" Taffington yelled in his ear. "Come on, come on!" The other shape turned into Robichaux and they hustled him along, packs and rifles jostling as they ran. Rain was falling harder now and they slipped and slid across the muddy ground. Joe looked back at the blazing wall of fire behind them.

"We got twelve tanks," Taffington yelled. "All piled up on top of each other." They ran awkwardly, carrying the heavy satchels of grenades between them, and they had almost reached the second escarpment when Joe heard the sounds of planes. The air buzzed and dirt spurted up. Something hit him and he fell onto Taffington. They both tumbled to the ground. Robichaux jerked Joe's satchel from his grip and kept on running.

The sprinkle of rain turned into a downpour as Joe scrabbled to get back on his feet. One leg wouldn't work right. Taffington grabbed his arm and hauled him toward the rocks. They collapsed behind the nearest boulder, gasping for breath.

Robichaux crawled up, looking different than he usually did. Rain was bouncing off his curly hair and dripping through his eyelashes. Joe was still blinking at him, wondering what had changed, when he leaned close to Joe's ear and yelled, "I put my helmet over the fuse. Keep it dry."

Joe rested his head back against the rock. Rain drummed on

his helmet and danced in little puddles all around. Whether or not the fuse was covered by a helmet, the dynamite probably would not fire now. He should go check it, but he was so tired, and his leg was heavy and useless. Like dead wood. Dead wood that hurt. He gingerly pulled up his leg and ran his hand across the back of his thigh. He felt ripped fabric and ragged flesh, slick with blood. He closed his eyes, nauseated by the feel.

Taffington coughed, a strange wet sound. Joe opened his eyes and looked at him. Taffy's face was waxy-pale in the rain.

"You get hit?" Joe asked.

"Yeah," Taffy sighed, and coughed the soggy sound again. His right sleeve was red. "In the arm." He cradled it in his other hand. "It's not that bad. I'm left-handed." He sniffed and wiped at his nose, smearing blood across his face.

"You got a bloody nose?"

Taffington felt his nose. "I don't think so." He coughed again and blood splashed on his chin. Robichaux moved over to him and Joe started to get up, but when he moved his leg a burst of pain shot clear up through his spine, so intense the world turned dark for a moment and he wanted to throw up.

Robichaux gently leaned Taffington forward to check his back. A dark blotch stained the side of his battle jacket. Taffy held his hurt arm and shook his head.

"Don't mind me," he said. "I'll be okay."

"Just sit there for a minute." Joe took a breath, held it, and carefully moved his leg. If he concentrated, he could keep the pain down. "I want to go look at the road." With Robichaux's help he managed to crawl to a place where he could see what he had to work with.

The road was wider here, and the rocky slopes alongside were not as high. Rain puddled over the spot where he had laid the charges last night. He gnawed on his thumbnail. Without the dynamite, it would be much more difficult to block this pass. Even if they used every mine and grenade they had, and even if they hit every tank precisely right in order to blow it up – which probably wouldn't happen – it was very unlikely that they could do it again. All they could do now was lay some mines and hope for the best. When the tanks actually drove past, they could shoot rifle grenades at their tracks and try to cause some kind of foul-up.

Until they were caught, that was. The Germans would send out their own scouts now, looking for whoever was dogging them along the road. Even if the scouts didn't find them right away, that giant war machine would dig itself out and advance again. Maybe the combination of burning tanks and mud had delayed it for a while, but it would come eventually, and when it did neither he or Taffy would be able to run away this time.

At least the rain gave some cover for a while. They crawled back to Taffington and rigged a makeshift shelter for him with their field jackets, and Robichaux propped a canteen to catch a trickle of water that was running off a rock. The first aid packs were long gone, lost somewhere in the desert under a pile of rubble, but they bandaged their wounds with torn-up strips of uniform and shared a packet of aspirin that Taffington found in his pocket.

The rain stopped just as suddenly as it had started, and the sky began to clear. "I thought the other guys would be here by now," Taffy said. His lips and fingernails were blue. Joe looked over at Robichaux, who glanced away.

"How close are we to a camp?" Taffington asked. "Maybe somebody will come out and pick us up."

Joe thought of his map and slapped his chest pocket to see if it was still there. Paper crinkled and he pulled it out, wet and dirty but still readable, and tried to get his bearings. Robichaux leaned over to look and traced the line of the road with his finger, stopping at a point nearer to Thala than Joe thought was right.

"Naw, we're not that close," he said.

Robichaux shrugged and nodded toward the horizon, which was showing more distinctly now that the sun was coming out. Joe looked from the hills to the map, back up at the hills and then down at the map again. If Robichaux was right about their location, then Thala was only about five miles up the road.

But even if they were that close, there was no way to know if the hospital had moved yet, or if any help was on the way. They emptied their packs and sorted out the ammunition. A German plane flew through the remaining drifts of clouds overhead and they huddled down, faces flat against the muddy rock, sweating silently until the sound was gone. Robichaux used one of his giant knives to cut some branches off a cactus, and laid them over the top of their little shelter for extra camouflage.

A second plane droned nearby, flying low. They hunkered down again, holding their breath until it passed.

"They're looking for us," Joe said. "We need to set those mines right away." He raised his binoculars and stared down the road, looking for any sign of tanks, then glanced around at the sun, which was sinking into a spectacular sunset of orange and pink. "As soon as it gets a little darker."

A motor chattered in the distance, a small shrill sound, not the heavy clanking rumble of tanks. Joe and Robichaux grabbed for their rifles. The sound ripped out again, going up and down in tone, like a motorcycle shifting through its gears.

"You go down and get closer," Joe said. "One of us'll get it." Robichaux grinned and slipped away. Joe painfully hitched himself into a position where he could shoot, gasping and wincing as he moved, clenching his teeth to concentrate on keeping down the pain. He gingerly felt at the back of his leg again. Even with the bandage, blood was oozing out. Touching it made the pain flare up and he closed his eyes, forcing it back.

The motor sound grew louder. It was definitely a motorcycle. Joe sighted his rifle on the road.

The motorcycle zoomed around the cactus into view. Joe pulled the trigger and felt the recoil kick against his shoulder just as Robichaux's shot rang out. The motorcycle swerved and careened wildly along the road, finally skidding to a stop against a pile of rocks and cactus. Bodies flew off and the engine sputtered to a halt.

It was a German sidecar with a machine gun on the front, now lying tilted at a crazy angle with its front tire spinning in the air.

Robichaux looked out from his hiding place to see if Joe was covering him. He walked over to the scene and stalked around it like a suspicious dog before going close enough to poke at the flaccid bodies. When he was finally convinced that there was no danger, he shoved and heaved at the motorcycle until it rocked back down onto its three wheels. The whole thing was painted in tawny shades of brown, perfect camouflage for desert, and the sidecar was padded with leather upholstery. Robichaux glanced back at Joe again, grinned, then straddled the bike and kicked the motor on. It roared to life. He shifted into gear and rode it jerkily across the road.

"They must've been scouting out the road," Joe said, wondering at the sight. Robichaux proudly revved the engine. With his tangled hair, torn uniform and dark stubble of beard, he looked more like a pirate than a Ranger.

Joe leaned his weight back on his arms, trying to ease his leg, and thought about what to do now. Robichaux could place the mines into the road for him, then drive Taffington to Thala while he himself stayed here. If the first tanks hit the mines, then the other ones would at least have to slow down, and from where he was sitting he could fire the rifle grenades. If he got some good hits he might even be able to jam up the road again. Then the column would be held up a little longer, Taff would get help, and the hospital would be warned about the Germans in time to get out.

He looked at Robichaux. "I want you to set the mines and then drive Taffy into Thala," he said. "I'll stay here."

Robichaux placed the mines exactly as Joe ordered, covering them lightly with dirt and sweeping away his footprints behind him. He repositioned the shelter to give Joe more cover from the road and camouflaged it with extra mud and cactus. Then he piled the grenades where Joe could reach them, set the canteen close by his hand, and ripped up an empty satchel to make a new bandage for his leg.

The pain had changed. It was a constant, stabbing throb that sawed on his nerves and razored through his head whenever he moved. A kind of mental fog had come along with it, and he liked drifting in the fog because it dulled the sharp edge of the hurt, but when Robichaux put his rifle in his hand he blinked the fog away.

"You going now?" Joe asked. His mouth was dry already.

Robichaux nodded, and stared down the road for a long moment. Then he helped Taffington get into the sidecar, threw a last salute to Joe, and drove away.

The thin whine of motorcycle gears faded away and the silence of the desert fell around him. Joe rested his head against a rock and closed his eyes. The mental fog drifted back, and in its quiet he began to hear the wind. It whistled through the cactus and rustled over rocks, flowing sometimes near him and sometimes farther away, ebbing and returning like a breathing tide. He could not remember ever hearing the wind here before. There was always too much racket to simply sit and listen to it. When he was awake there was the constant noise of men and machines, and even when he was asleep there were certain sounds he had to pay attention to on some level, like airplane engines and footsteps and the soft deep breathing of the other men around him. He was so tired of all the noise.

The relentless dryness in his mouth and throat finally nudged him out of the fog. He picked up the canteen and gave it an experimental slosh. Half full. Joe took a sip of water, rinsed it around his mouth a couple of times to soak up the moisture before he swallowed, then carefully replaced the cap and set the canteen back down. The stabbing pain was gone now. His leg only felt numb and heavy on the ground.

Sana would be sad if he didn't come back. But she would know that he had done his best for her. He ached to see her one more time, to hold her and tell her how much he loved her. Loving her had made him happy, even in the middle of a war. It made him happy now.

His uncle said that God always found a way to bless people no matter what was going on. Joe smiled at the thought. Good old Uncle John. If he was here he'd come up with some kind of Bible verse. *Though I walk through the valley of the shadow of death, I will fear no evil: for thou art with me... thou preparest a table before me in the presence of mine enemies... surely goodness and mercy shall follow me all the days of my life, and I will dwell in the house of the Lord... forever...*

Dear God, I just want to go to sleep.

He closed his eyes, remembering scenes from another life. His mother in a pretty dress, sitting at a bar with a well-dressed man, and his grandma frying onions in the kitchen. Johnny and Stephen arguing about socks and his uncle preaching in their little church. Over at the back end of the Bible there was a part where the apostle John collapsed face down on the ground, dead tired, but the Lord Jesus Christ himself had appeared and said to him, "*It is I, do not be afraid.*"

Joe jerked out of a doze. Where was he? His mouth was so dry that his tongue was sticking to the roof of his mouth. He unscrewed the top of the canteen with shaky fingers and gulped the water, pouring it all straight down his throat until it was gone. After he finished drinking he looked around at the desert, at all the empty hills rolling off to the horizon, and then he remembered where he was.

Fear not, I am the first and the last: I am he that lives, and was dead; and behold I am alive, for evermore. And I am with you always, even unto the end.

Maybe this was the end. At least he was not alone. Joe sat up straighter so he could watch the road. When the tanks came, he would be ready.

Sana watched soldiers slam up the tailgate of a truck, latch it shut and wave at the driver. Gears clashed and the vehicle lurched forward over the rutted field. The next truck pulled up. It was a big flatbed, its bare platform wide open to all the bad weather coming at them.

She frowned as she glanced over her lists of patients, then at the rows of litters lying on the field, the blankets lightly covered with snow. "Okay, guys. Load up that row." Men started hauling patients up onto the back of the truck.

Sana looked next at her list of medics and selected a name. "Collins!"

A soldier packing boxes of supplies into the truck's cab turned around. "Yes ma'am?"

"You can go with this one. Do you have a flashlight?"

"Yes ma'am!" Collins boosted up one more box and went to fetch his bag. He came back carrying a pack over his shoulder, a bottle of liquor under one arm and a cook stove under the other. Sana eyed him wordlessly and then pointed at the truck's exposed rear bed, filling up now with litters packed side by side.

"You can't take the stove."

Collins opened his mouth to protest but she stared him down. He tossed the stove on a growing pile of other people's discarded belongings.

"Come on!" the driver shouted. "Let's go!"

Collins stuck the bottle into his jacket and tossed his pack into the cab. He climbed up onto the bed with the litters and the truck roared away.

Sana pulled up her collar. The clouds were blowing away, no longer leaden gray but cottony wisps of gold and orange, gleaming in the sunset. A few stars glittered in the crystal sky. The snow had stopped but the wind was colder now, and the moon would rise later on. The trucks were driving without lights. Orders had passed around to use flashlights as little as possible, but since some German planes had already flown right overhead and seen the camp, they were not working in the dark to hide from the enemy any more. They were only saving their batteries.

Hardly any trucks were coming back from the front now, but Arab families and footsore soldiers still walked along the road. All of the doctors and about two-thirds of the nurses had left already, packed by ones and twos into the trucks with the wounded. People were discarding whatever they could not take with them, and now jumbles of mirrors and alarm clocks, rugs and frying pans, lay strewn along the roadside. The local families glanced over the selection and occasionally picked up an item as they passed. Collins's stove did not last long. Two women tied a rocking chair on top of a donkey.

An ambulatory patient with a bandage over half his face was handing out cups of coffee from a tray. Sana remembered him, a good-looking boy with a messy shrapnel wound along his cheek and ear. Schmidt had sewn up his face a day ago.

"Here you go, ma'am," he said as he handed her a cup. "They say he's only five miles away now."

"Thank you." Sana warmed her hands around the scorching tin mug. There was no need to ask who the soldier was talking about. Rommel was the only topic of the day.

"How much longer?" he asked.

"Pretty soon." The hospital had received the official order to evacuate only an hour ago, but the trucks had arrived long before the order did and people had been shipping out all afternoon. Only a few more wards and a skeleton crew of staff were left to go.

The boy was still standing next to her. "Want some more coffee?" he asked helpfully.

"I have to let this one cool down before I drink it." He was so young that he still had downy fuzz along his jaw. "How's that cheek coming along?" Sana touched the edge of his bandage to check the swelling and he almost dropped the tray.

"Hey, I have a question for you," she said when he had everything safely balanced again. "When you were out there, did you see any Rangers?"

"I don't think so."

"Oh, well. I just wondered. I know some of them."

"Sorry to have to tell you, ma'am." The boy seemed to think that any soldiers not at the hospital must be dead. "I hope we leave pretty soon."

Sana smiled. "I'll put you on the next truck, if you want. I'll tell the medic that you're a helper."

The boy shook his head, carefully, in order not to aggravate his wound. "Naw, that's okay. If you're staying, I will too. Can't take off before the women do." He nodded confidently, inspired by his own bravado.

265

The next truck looked a lot better, a two-and-a-half ton with a covered bed and mattresses laid on the floor inside. Sana chose the most critically wounded to ride in it, nearly all of them still hooked up to blood and plasma. Then she looked for an experienced medic to travel with them.

There were not many of those left on her list. As soon as the last surgery was finished, Red and Obie had packed the OR and driven off with the precious surgical equipment. The doctors had gone with the first round of trucks, and Jo Ellen had gone with the second. Margie was managing post-op, sending out patients as fast as she could. Wence, whose big ambulance had been taken away from him, was sorting supplies and distributing them to the trucks according to the type of wounded they were carrying. The mess tent was long gone but a cook had stayed behind, to make coffee and Spam sandwiches until the end.

Soldiers were loading the truck in their own steady routine now, so Sana located an empty crate and sat down to finish her coffee. It tasted unbelievably bad. After finishing it she deep into her jacket and just stared down at her boots for a while. She should change her socks. There were socks in her pack, but her pack was buried somewhere in the pile of other people's bags by the triage tent. She would probably find it again when it was time to go.

Time to go... she propped her elbows on her knees and buried her face in her hands. Not one of all the incoming soldiers knew anything about Joe or any other Ranger, and now it was time for everyone to leave. Where was he? She had worn out her eyes looking for him. She had searched the face of every wounded soldier, every man walking down the road, hoping to see him tired but alive, his face lighting up with that boyish grin when she called his name and ran to meet him. But he had not come.

Someone turned on a flashlight and golden light shone out across the ground, glinting on the handles of the litters and the sweaty faces of the men. The light switched back off and everything was velvety night. Men's voices floated through the dark, along with grunts and shouts as they hauled the heavy litters. She heard a donkey bray somewhere, and children's high sweet voices calling to each other.

"Hey." Margie was standing beside her.

"Hi," Sana said, surprised. "How you doing?"

"We're done in post-op. How you doing?"

"There's still these guys on the ground plus two more wards."

Margie pulled up another crate. "I mean, how you holding up?"

"Oh..." The unexpected kindness pierced her heart. "Okay."

Margie put an arm around her shoulders and Sana leaned into the hug. Their helmets clanked and they both said "Ow!" at the same time. Margie laughed and Sana smiled.

Margie took her hand. "Listen. I prayed for Joe and I got this great feeling, this really strong feeling, that he's going to be okay."

Sana shook her head.

"Don't give up." Margie yawned and looked around. "Where's the coffee?"

"Inside triage. It's really bad." Sana heard a droning noise in the distance that was probably a plane, but it was too far off to tell for sure whose it was. "Here, take my cup."

Margie gave her another hug, took the cup and walked away into the night. A bright full moon had risen and its silvery light gleamed along the road, making it look like a pale gray river winding through murky hills. A single jeep chugged by, only a dark shape in the moonlight. A stray dog trotted silently behind it.

The big truck's tailgate clanged shut and Sana came back to the business of loading up wounded. She was out among the litters, choosing the next men to leave, when the distant motor suddenly roared down the road and through the field right behind her.

"American! American!" someone was yelling. "Don't shoot!" The motor sputtered to a stop. "American!" People were gathering on the other side of the truck and she walked over to see what was going on.

A soldier stepped in front of her, barring the way. "Stand back, ma'am. Let us handle this." Flashlights were flicking on now and she could see the bandage-faced boy among the onlookers, so she ignored the soldier and pressed on through the crowd.

A man was being helped toward triage, staggering between two soldiers. Another man was being searched. Everyone else stood in a circle around him, training their flashlights on something that looked like a double motorcycle.

"Look at that," someone said. "Never seen one of these before."

"Look at all that chrome."

Soldiers leaned forward, peering at the dashboard. "How fast do you think this baby goes?"

"Hunnert mile an hour."

The search of the driver had turned into a group discussion. "How far away do ya figure them?" someone asked.

"Five," the driver said. "Seven maybe. Whole bunch of 'em." Sana stepped closer. He was covered with mud and a scruffy beard, but he wore a black and red Ranger emblem on his tattered jacket.

She pushed the last man out of her way. The driver looked at her and his jaw dropped open in surprise.

"Have you seen Joe Vesely?" she demanded.

"Just hold your horses there, nurse," someone said.

The driver found his voice. "Yes ma'am," he said. "I know right where he is."

Sana flew across the field to the triage tent. Inside she grabbed Margie and hustled her out towards the supply station. "Joe's hurt," she panted, "and he's right up the road from here."

"Oh my gosh!"

Sana tugged Margie into a stumbling run. "This guy who just came in said he's still out there about ten miles up the road."

"Okay," Margie said, "but why —"

"He can't walk so he stayed out there to wait and blow up more tanks. And this guy knows right where he is and I asked if he was close enough to go get him before the Germans get there and he said yes." They were at the supply tent's entrance now and she paused, gasping and trembling, to catch her breath. "He said there were some others out there too, trying to walk in. So will you please go get me an ambulance while I find Wence?"

"Get you an ambulance?"

"Please, please, ask one of Mike's friends. Tell him I said to give it to you. Go right now." She pushed Margie towards the line of the waiting vehicles and ran into the tent. "Wence! Where's Wence?"

A tall shape straightened up. "Sana?"

She hurried over. "Joe's right up the road, he's got a bad leg wound and he lost a lot of blood. Let's go get him."

Wence stared at her. "You're kidding."

"One of his men just drove in on a motorcycle and told me. He says Rommel's not that close yet and there's still." She ran out of breath and paused for a deep lungful of air. "Margie's getting an ambulance." She grabbed an empty box and started throwing in bandages and sulfa packs. "And it's not just Joe. There's lots of other guys out there still trying to make it in."

Wence passed a hand over his face. "I'm not supposed to be driving anymore."

"Hah!" She piled plasma cans on top of the bandages, her hands trembling. "Nobody even knows you're still here. And nobody cares!" She flung in a final packet of surrettes. "Come on!"

"Look," Wence said in a soothing tone that made her blood boil. "Let me think this through before I drive you straight into the whole Reichland out there."

She turned around. "So stay here if you don't want to go. You have a family. I don't."

Wence gripped her arm. "I'm just saying—"

She flung off the hand. "I'm going to get him!"

Astonished faces were gawking all around her. Wence took her arm again and pulled her outside. "Look," he began. "I'll go but first let's..." he broke off as a battered half-ton truck chugged toward them in the starlight, clumping along over the frozen mud of the field. It rattled to a stop ten feet away from them. Margie looked out the open window.

"Ready when you are," she said.

In the end, no one challenged them about making one more run to pick up a few stray soldiers. Margie stayed behind to load up the remaining wounded and Sana, clutching a bucket containing the last precious bottles of blood, climbed up into the passenger side of the cab. Wence eased the truck out of the field and then worked the engine through its gears, picking up speed as they rolled away from camp. He drove without his headlights on, and the moonlight shone like silver water on the pale strand of road.

"If anybody says anything to me about this, I'm going to tell them that this crazy lieutenant nurse ordered me to do it." Wence said after a while.

"Okay." Sana's heart was pounding and her palms were sweaty. She wiped them on her pants.

"And I couldn't defend myself against you because I'm not allowed to carry weapons, so I had to go."

"Okay." The truck strained to climb a hill and she strained forward with it, gritting her teeth.

A big warm hand patted her back. "That was supposed to be funny."

Sana drew a shaky breath. "Thank you." She clenched her teeth to fight back a sob.

They drove in silence for a while. Sana stared out at the stars, taking deep breaths of the chilly night air, and after a while the breeze dried her tears and cooled the hot tight feeling in her throat.

"How far away did they say he was?" Wence asked.

"About five miles after we get down to where it's flat. He's halfway up a big cliff on the left."

They jounced along. "And he can't walk?" Wence asked as he downshifted, pushing the truck up a steep rise. "How bad is he?"

"All I know is it's a bad leg wound and he lost a lot of blood." Sana strained forward again, searching the shadowy landscape as the truck crested over the hill. "I don't see anything out here. I don't think Rommel's that close."

She took another long breath and settled back deeper into her jacket. The starry night, the engine's steady rhythm, and Wence's reassuring presence blended into a soothing sense of rest. It had been a long time since she had just sat still.

After a while she checked around the cab to see what kind of useful junk might have collected on its floor. She found a field jacket stuffed under the seat and pulled it on, relishing the extra warmth. Then she settled back again and took a long drink of water from a canteen.

She felt better than she had all day. "You know what?" she announced brightly. "I think everything's going to turn out fine."

Wence shot her a sidelong glance. "We're not even down the mountain yet." He hand-braked his way down an incline, tires slipping along the gravelly slope. Sana held her bucket of bottles filled with blood in one hand and braced herself against the dashboard with the other.

Halfway down they heard the distant drone of a plane. Moonlight flooded the hillside, outlining every rock and gleaming brightly on their truck. They didn't even have a Geneva cross painted on top for protection. Wence let up on the brake, the truck charged down the hill and they bounced hard onto level ground. He pulled up to a clump of cactus and cut off the engine. Sana shivered, listening to the sound of the plane coming closer.

Oh, God, please... She could not think of words. What did Germans do to people they saw on the road? Bomb them? Take them prisoner and shoot them later? Surely they wouldn't shoot a nurse. Would they make her go to Germany? What would they do to Wence? The droning faded away. Wence exchanged a glance with her and started up the truck again. The engine coughed and died a few times before it finally roared back to life.

Dear God. She gripped the bucket tight to keep her hands from shaking. *Oh, dear God, I'm sorry. I'm so sorry. Please forgive me for being mad at you.* She should have read Joe's Bible, she should have prayed, she should have listened to Adele and Margie. If

271

only... if only she had been a better person, then maybe the love of her life would have come back instead of getting shot and being stranded in the desert. Then none of this would be happening. If only... it was too late now. But Adele said it was never too late. *Oh, God, please keep Joe safe and help me get him back. Please don't let him die. This war wasn't our idea. We just ended up here somehow. Please, please, save him, please let us go back home together. Please, Lord, don't let him die. If he dies now I couldn't bear it.*

Wence nosed the truck up over a little rise, paused at the top and scanned the road ahead before rolling down the other side. Sana watched him drive. *Please don't let Wence die either. Oh, God. I am such a silly nincompoop. Please change me, make me stronger, help me do this.* She tightened her grip on the bucket and stared out into the dark, looking for a high cliff on the left side of the road.

The truck rattled to a stop and she opened her eyes. Had she been sleeping? Soldiers stood in front of her, waving.

They crowded around the truck, holding out helmets and cupped hands for a drink, too dry to say anything. Sana and Wence poured out water as fast as they could.

"I'm going to check around," Wence said when the rush was over. "You stay here." Sana nodded.

He came back right away and beckoned at her. "There's a couple guys we gotta take. You get in back and we'll load 'em up." Sana climbed down from the cab and into the rear, still holding her bucket of bottles. She wedged it safely into a corner and started pulling out supplies. How long would this take? What if there wasn't enough room for Joe?

She was ashamed of the thought. *Oh, God, I'm sorry.* How many times was she going to think that tonight? She pictured Joe laying somewhere out there in the dust, perhaps slipping into a coma by now, needing help. *I am really, really sorry. Please keep him alive for me.*

A cluster of soldiers handed up a wounded man. One arm was gone at the elbow, one pant leg was stiff with blood... the pulse was only a thin flutter under her fingers. Sana fumbled around in the dark for needles and tubing, and finally switched on her flashlight and held it between her neck and shoulder to see what she was doing.

"Here's another one," someone said, and a second man was helped inside. Wence looked in. "You set?" Sana nodded.

Seconds later she heard the slam of the driver's door and the sound of the engine being coaxed back to life. She grabbed for the bucket, keeping the blood safe as the truck jerked forward again.

The second man had a leg wound, a broken nose and a burn covering one side of his chest. Sana gave him morphine even before she helped him take a drink. "Here you go. Slow now... slow..." The man gasped and sputtered at the water, then settled down and slurped greedily from the cup. "That's it. You'll feel better in a minute." The nose must have bled a lot from the looks of his uniform, and his skin had the slack feeling of someone who had been without water for too long. She started plasma into one arm and blood into the other.

The truck's bumps and swerves came without warning now that she was in the darkness of the truck's interior. The thick damp air reeked of blood and urine. A queasy feeling began in her stomach, and then a dropping sideways lurch sent a surge of nausea clear through her. Sana doubled over and crawled on her hands and knees to the tailgate. Another dizzy lurch made her close her eyes and cling blindly for the cool metal edge.

Oh, help me. The thought struck her that the two men on the floor had suffered much worse than she was feeling. *Lord God, I'm a worm, I'm nobody, I don't deserve to ask for anything but please help me anyway. Please keep Joe safe, at least until we get there, because I just want to see him one more time. Just one more time. That's all.*

The tailgate bucked under her hands and made her raise her head again. She leaned out and gulped fresh air. A canteen was within reach and she took a mouthful of water.

He's worth it. I don't care how bad this gets if I bring him back. Was Joe thirsty right now, but with no water to drink like she had? Was he thinking of her? He was such a good person, the best man she had ever known. If he was alive he was probably praying. He was probably even praying for her. He was so much better than she was.

I'm not asking this for me anymore. Even if I die, or even if we don't get married, please save his life. Don't let him get killed. Oh, God...

The truck was slowing. Sana hastily took another drink and wiped her mouth. She heard voices and then soldiers were swarming at the tailgate, holding up helmets and canteens. She filled them as fast as she could while Wence helped another man inside, this one sweaty and limp with fever. Then they handed up one more soldier with an arm in a sling.

The man with the sling was lucid and she gave him a canteen to drink from while she went to work on the feverish one, feeding him sips of water before setting up the plasma. The one in the sling drained his canteen in a few greedy gulps and tried to help her with the tubing, but his one good hand was clumsy and only got in her way, so she handed him a blanket. In seconds he was asleep on the floor. The truck stopped again, but no men appeared this time. Surely they had gone five miles by now? Then she heard the drone, soft at first but growing louder and louder until it roared right overhead and rocked the truck with its blast. The feverish man cried out and Sana flung herself face down on the dirty floor, arms over her head. *No no no...*

The crescendo of sound faded away. The truck roared awake and chugged forward. Sana raised her head, tasting a rusty mix of blood and dirt in her mouth, and took a shaky breath. *Wence must have nerves of steel.* The feverish man was weeping, so she mopped his forehead with a wet cloth, then checked his pulse and gave him a dose of morphine. Her hands were still shaking from the scare, but she steadied them enough to give the shot.

They slowed, speeded up, and slowed again. The engine sputtered to a stop halfway up a hill and she held her breath and prayed until it revved back to life. What if they broke down out here? Then what? Then they would get shot or captured. What if Wence died because she had talked him into this? How could she face his wife? What if they reached Joe but he was already dead?

She bent over the soldier with the amputated arm and checked his blood pressure again. It was dropping.

If she kept giving out blood and plasma, there might be none left for Joe. She stared at the soldier sleeping trustfully on the floor.

How can I possibly decide these things? I'm not God. I can only do what I can do. This is killing me. Please let me get to Joe in time. I just want to see him again, just one more time, and tell him how much I love him. She closed her eyes and waited, listening for some gentle whisper, some sign that God was there.

Some things were right and some were wrong. She loved Joe Vesely, and she should do what was right, in honor of their love, even if he died or she died and they never saw each other again. It would be a way of truly loving him, even past the end of time.

She opened her eyes and gazed out at the stars. *I see it now. I see You. You are the Lord, the Holy and the Good. What You want, what You say, from now on, I will do it. My life, our love, is completely in your hands.* She replaced the soldier's empty bottle with a full one and watched the precious blood run down.

The truck stopped again. She heard a knock on the side of the truck.

"What?" she called over her shoulder.

"There's a cliff here."

Sana finished up her job in seconds and jumped out of the truck. There was indeed a kind of cliff on the left, more like a rocky hill really, but the closest thing to a cliff that they had seen so far.

"This guy said he was about halfway up?" Wence whispered, looking up at the rocks.

"Yeah," Sana whispered back. "So we just climb up there and look around?"

"Wait a minute." Wence went back to the cab and rummaged under the seat. He returned and held out a pistol. Sana looked at it in surprise.

"Can you shoot?"

"I guess so." This was not the time to learn. "You keep it."

Wence sighed. "I have one already. Look, here's the safety

catch." Sana watched impatiently as he tried to show her how to aim and fire.

"I really don't want it," she finally said.

Wence sighed again and stuck the gun under his belt. "If we find this numbskull I'm going to shoot him myself out of sheer aggravation. Okay, you go up that side and I'll go up this one."

Sana looked at the craggy rocks in front of her and sucked in a deep lungful of cold air. She wiped her sweaty palms on her jacket. "All right."

"If you run into somebody else up there, the password's 'snafu.'

She nodded, wiping her palms again. Now that she was going to climb it, the hill looked steeper than it had from the road.

Wence touched her arm. *"S Panem bohem."*

"What?"

"Go with God."

Sana got up on the first ledge and clambered to the next one, then the next, reaching out for handholds as she climbed. She heaved herself up over a shadowy rock and lurched straight into a stinging slap of cactus needles. Pain blazed along the side of her face. She yelped and tumbled forwards into a black crevice.

"You okay?" came a low call.

The side of her face throbbed where the cactus had hit, right beside her eye. Sana felt at the scratches. They burned, but weren't bleeding much. She straightened up, struggling to find invisible footholds in the dark.

"Sana?"

"I'm okay," she panted back across the cliff. "Some cactus."

After scrambling over two more boulders her heart was pounding and her arms were shaking. She rested for a moment, breathing hard and wincing from the pain of the scratches, not wanting to touch her face again and make it worse. *I'm climbing a hill in the middle of enemy territory because somebody said Joe was on a cliff somewhere? Am I nuts?*

She looked across the rocks to see how far Wence had climbed. She could just pick out a dim gray movement and hear the scrape of boots on gravel.

'Go with God,' he had said. Sana thought of how Joe had given her his Bible, of Adele reading it by the light of their little tent stove. *Fear not, for I am with thee: be not dismayed; for I am thy God; I will strengthen thee and help thee, I will uphold thee...* she grabbed for the next handhold and plunged upwards.

A few more rocks and she had to rest again. The truck on the road below her seemed small and far away. She wiped her throbbing eye with the back of her hand and looked up, then back down to the truck. This was, perhaps, halfway.

"Joe?" Her voice trembled in the darkness. "Joe?" she tried again, a little louder. "Snafu? Joe?" Hundreds of miles of desert in every direction, all of it dead quiet under the stars. "Joe! Are you here somewhere?"

She heard another scrape and clatter from Wence's side of the hill. Her arms and legs were trembling again, worse this time, and she patted over all the pockets of her borrowed jacket in hope of finding some leftover crackers or gum. She felt a lump deep on the right-hand side and dug up what turned out to be a scrap of ration bar wrapped in a clean sheet of toilet paper. She popped it in her mouth and tried an experimental bite. It was so dry that she would have to work on it for a while and soften it up before she could chew it, but just the feeling of food in her mouth made her feel better.

Another quiet rustle sounded in the night. Wence was calling softly, searching just like she was. Sana leaned against the rock, chewing.

"Hey," the soft call came again. "Hey. Sana."

"Yeah?" The bar was finally loosening up.

"Over here."

Joe had lain in a kind of darkness for a long, long time, fighting back the red claws of thirst that kept creeping up his throat.

He fought the red claws for a while by sucking on his pebble, but they kept edging in, growing over a little more of his throat, parching up a little more of his mouth, and soon they had completely taken over his whole body and the only way to elude them was to slip into the misty gray dreaming-place just beyond.

But he knew he was supposed to fight the red claws, so sometimes he came back from the misty gray and opened his eyes to see if the road was still there. Then the red claws came and tormented him with pictures of full canteens and cups of lemonade and tall wet glasses of cold iced tea, and he would finally have to slip back into the gray or else go crazy.

Except for when he fought red claws, he did not hurt. But he could not move, either, except to travel between the waking world and the gray-mist dream. The gray mist was much better, because the red claws were not allowed there and he was not alone, but still it was not really his place to be and so at times he made himself go back and open his eyes, look at the road and suffer the hateful claws.

It was during one of his in-between times that he heard her. He had been fighting the claws, but the world of the road seemed to be gone now, and he was fading away again into the blessed mist when someone called a name.

Was it his? Was someone calling? From the mist? No, it was from some other place, the canteen place, and then he felt a little brim of moisture, just a little rill of something wet, melt away one of the claws. A little more... a little more... oh. It felt so good. It was dissolving all the searing redness. Down... down... a little more again, and then the sweet gray mist reached out and tenderly bade him goodbye, because he did not need it anymore.

He was drinking in steady little sips now. His eyes were closed and he was drinking water. He rested, content to drink, feeling that same comfort that the mist had given. This was even better, in fact, because the claws were all gone.

Voices spoke and as he lay there he could feel life flow through him, just like water. He gently filled up with life again, and after a while he came back completely and knew where he was and who was with him.

Sana joyfully cradled Joe's head in her lap, feeding him sips of water while Wence worked on his leg. She stroked his hair and his face and told him how wonderful he was and how much she loved him. When he finally opened his eyes and looked at her, she was so delighted that she stopped talking and just grinned at him.

"First comes love, then comes marriage," Wence intoned as he cut off the blood-soaked rags. "Then comes Joe with a baby carriage." Joe blinked, not yet lucid enough to recognize a friendly dig when he heard it. Sana was too happy to care.

"That's right," she burbled. "I still can't believe we found him. Do you think we can move him now? How do we get him down from here?"

Wence tied off the bandage. "I kick him clear back to camp for pulling this jackass stunt, is how we get him down from here." He settled Joe's leg on the ground and checked his pulse again. "Let's get a little more water in him first." Joe's eyes were focusing better now and Wence slapped him on the arm. "Before I shoot you myself."

Sana gently smoothed Joe's collar. "We'll get you into the truck and then you'll feel a lot better." She held him closer, loving the feeling of his warm weight lying in her arms. "You know what, maybe we can drive straight to Tébessa. Or maybe we can unload the other guys at Thala and just go by ourselves. It'll be like a vacation." She took his hand and was thrilled to feel his fingers close around her own. "Hey, Wence, can the guy with the sling sit up front with you on the way back?"

"Shhh." Sana looked up, surprised. Wence's head was up and he was listening.

At first she couldn't hear anything but the soft sigh of wind rustling through the night. Then she heard another sound, something that did not ebb and flow like the wind, but pulsed low to the ground with a steady mechanical clank and rumble.

She looked quickly at Joe, to see if he had heard it too. His eyes were closed again. She tightened her grip around him.

Wence took off his helmet and scratched his head. "They sound pretty far off. Maybe we can still get out of here."

Joe stirred and licked his lips. "Get the ammo," he whispered.

"Get what?" Sana asked.

Wence searched among the rocks and found a bulky canvas bag. He slung it over his shoulders and stood up, listening for a long moment.

He turned back and crouched down to angle himself underneath Joe's arm. "Here, take his other side." They pulled Joe up to his feet and maneuvered down a ledge. After a few minutes of painful pulling and sliding they had to stop and rest.

The clanking sound was louder now. Sana craned forward, squinting down the road. Something glinted in the starlight.

Wence had seen it too. He eased Joe down to the ground and then pulled his helmet off and scratched his head. "Stay here," he said with a look that warned Sana not to argue. "I got to hide the truck before they get here. I'll be right back." He shrugged the heavy ammunition bag off his shoulder to the ground, then slid down the embankment and vanished in the darkness below. Sana heard the engine crank and falter... once... twice... three times. It finally fired up and chugged away.

She sat down behind Joe and wrapped her arms around him so he could lean against her. If the tanks would just pass by and leave them alone, then whatever happened after that was not her problem yet. He raised a hand to clasp hers, and she kissed the side of his neck.

"My brave girl." His voice was hoarse.

"I love you."

"I love you too." She could feel him smile. A chilly breeze swept across the rocks and they nestled closer together.

"I dreamed about you," he said after a while.

"You did?"

"Yeah. We were married and living in a house and you were fixing supper."

She kissed his cheek. "What was I cooking?"

"Mashed potatoes and gravy and a great big steak." She felt him take a little breath that sounded almost like a laugh. Sana rested her chin on his shoulder, listening to the clanking sound grow louder.

Wence reappeared out of the darkness with two loads of gear in his arms. He handed a filled canteen to Joe and a ration pack to Sana, then unshouldered a rifle.

"Can you shoot?"

Sana thought that the question was meant for her and said "yes" just as Joe held out his hand. Wence gave him the rifle and watched Joe as he took it, straining a little to balance the weight.

Wence pulled the pistol from his belt. "You want to take this now?" he asked Sana.

She nodded and he handed it to her. "Don't shoot unless you have to." A strobe-flash of green-white lightning whistled overhead and Sana, still holding the gun, clutched Joe tight around his middle.

"Hey!" both men exclaimed. Joe took the gun out of her hand and handed it back to Wence.

"Don't shoot me there," he said, grinning in the strange bright light. "You have to marry me." Sana buried her face against his shoulder, shivering with nerves and joy.

Wence stood up, studying the streaks of fire crossing the sky. Explosions crackled around them.

She cleared her throat. "I'll shoot," she said. "Just tell me what to do."

"Sana." Joe clumsily reached back and put his arm around her. "It's okay."

She shook her head. "I'll do it."

He hugged her tight, then tipped up her chin and kissed the tip of her nose. "Sweetheart, it's okay. See where they're shooting? Those aren't aiming at us."

Wence stuck the pistol in his belt and thrust his fists in celebration high into the air. Sana looked at Joe. He was grinning. She looked back and forth again. "What is going on?"

"That's our fire," Joe said. "Artillery. Someone came."

"Oh my God!"

"Yeah!" He squeezed her tight and kissed her again. "Can you believe it?"

"You mean it's from our side? We're safe?"

"Kind of."

"What do we do now?"

"Get out of here."

Later that night, as they sat together in the rear of the truck and watched the road fade off behind them, Sana told Joe about driving out and climbing up the cliff for him. They were sleepy and the little truck was cramped, but the engine's steady chug was comforting and they cuddled in the one remaining blanket, deep in a cozy fog of love. She was just drifting off, her head resting on Joe's shoulder, when she felt him stir a little and heard him ask a question.

"Did Robichaux warn you about the mines?"

She pulled herself back from the edge of sleep. "What mines?"

He sat up a little straighter. "You mean you guys just got out and walked around?"

"What are you talking about?"

He was quiet at first. Then she felt him laughing, a quiet chuckle deep in his chest. Sana raised her head so she could see his face.

"What's so funny?"

"Uncle John is going to love this."

"Love what?"

"The mines," he settled her head back down. "The ones in the road, that didn't go off."

Sana stared at the pale dawn lighting up the eastern sky. After a while she asked, "Did you think that I would come for you?"

He didn't answer for so long that she thought he had fallen asleep. "No," he finally said. "I really thought it was all over."

"The hardest part for me," she yawned, "was the climbing."

"Let's see that eye again." He turned her chin so he could see the cactus scrape. "You sure you're okay?"

She snuggled closer. "Really, I'm fine. It's nothing."

"Here." He carefully dabbed at it with a damp rag. "Better?"

"Um-hmm."

A little later on he asked, "Hey, did you ever get my, uh, present?"

"Oh, I forgot." She sat up and pulled out the gold necklace from under her jacket collar. "Do you like it?"

He peered at it in the growing light. "Yeah." He fingered the slender chain, then gently stroked a stray curl back from her eyes. "Poor baby, ran into a cactus." He drew her back into his arms and sighed. "I love you."

"I love you too," she murmured. They fell asleep together in the morning light, traveling the road back home.

Epilogue

Tabarka

The silky wash of surf surged forward, sweeping in over the beach and fading back again, murmuring the rhythm of the sea. The Mediterranean sparkled in sunny greens and blues. A trim little hospital stood just above the beach, and Joe and Adele were sitting on its back veranda, drinking coffee and soaking up the morning sun.

"I love the water," Adele said, gazing dreamily at the waves. "I never get tired of looking at it." She wore a faded-red burnoose draped over men's pajamas and a pair of Army socks. The two of them were still officially recovering, and they were waiting for Sana to join them for breakfast after her morning shift. The hospital had been abandoned a week before by retreating Germans, and the excellent coffee that had been abandoned along with it was delicious.

Joe wore only drawstring pajama bottoms in the mild morning air. "Me too." He carefully eased his bandaged leg out in front of him, wincing as he repositioned it.

Gulls circled above them, then darted off to dive into the sea. The first swimmers of the day were walking across the sand, their laughter ringing out over the wind and surf.

"How's the leg?" Adele asked.

"Better." Joe put down his mug and stretched his arms up

over his head. "I want to go swimming."

Quick light footsteps sounded and they both looked around. Sana came out, fresh and smiling in a crisp new uniform, carrying a tray loaded with toast and jam. She set it on the table and leaned over to give Joe a kiss. He pulled her down to sit beside him.

"Mmm, marmalade." Adele helped herself to toast. "My favorite."

"My mother did too," Sana said. "We always had it."

"We had grape jelly," Joe said. "Johnny ate it straight out of the jar and Aunt Kate had to hide it."

Sana laughed and took his hand. "How's the leg today?"

"Fine."

"He says he wants to go swimming," Adele said.

"You don't have a bathing suit," Sana pointed out.

"Those guys are in their underwear," Joe said. Both women looked over at the men on the beach. "Hey!" He tugged at Sana's hand.

"Maybe we could just walk along the shore and go wading," Sana said. "After the wedding."

"Is it today?" Joe asked, surprised.

"Uh-huh." Sana stroked his hair and ran a finger along his cheek. "You slept all day yesterday and now you're a day behind. You need to shave, honey."

"How'd they get their papers this fast?" Adele asked. "I thought it took three months."

"Oh, you know. Mike did it," Sana said. "Don't ask how." She leaned across Joe for another piece of toast. "You should see them. Acting like a couple of kids."

"Like someone else I know?" Adele asked dryly.

Sana and Joe shared an anticipatory look.

"What are you two kids up to, anyway?"

"Wading." Joe raised Sana's hand to his lips and kissed her fingers. "Since we don't have our wedding papers and we can't do anything else yet."

Sana giggled. A lone swimmer trotted across the sand toward them. It turned out to be Wence, tan and wet in the sunshine, holding a towel around his waist.

They poured him a cup of coffee and talked about Mike and Margie's wedding for a while. "So, Adele, when're you getting married?" Wence asked. "I thought you and Kelsey had something going on."

"Oh, no," Adele said. "Not me. I'm not marrying anyone. I put in for a transfer, for Sicily."

"Huh?" Wence said.

Joe put down his cup with a clink. "I thought you were going home."

"Adele," Sana said. "Come on. You've done your part."

"I'm not going home until it's finished," Adele said. "This is where I belong." She grinned. "Besides, I heard that Patton takes care of his nurses. Sicily'll be different."

"You ought to snag a man before it's over," Wence said. "You got the pick of the litter here. Marry some big dog and retire in Hollywood."

"Really, think about it," Sana said. "After all this, you deserve to have a good life."

Adele laughed. "I already do. The Lord is my portion." The Mediterranean gleamed beyond them, flashing in the sun.

LaVergne, TN USA
11 November 2009

163801LV00008B/1/P